Changing Lanes

A Roxy Adams Mystery

Claire Yezbak Fadden

ISBN: 979-8-9904739-1-1

Editors: Barb Wilson, Chris Hall
Book Cover: Liz Bank Design
Format: Enterprise Book Service, LLC
Publisher: Brightwood Books

Disclaimer

This story is a work of fiction. Names, characters, and incidents are
either products of the author's imagination or are used fictitiously.
Any resemblance to actual events, locales, organizations, or
persons, living or dead, is entirely coincidental.

For Windley, Grace, Maxwell and Miles.

Always for Nick.

Chapter One

Exhausted after working a double shift at the food truck, Roxy Adams trudged up the steps to the one-bedroom apartment she shared with her longtime boyfriend, Sam Reyes. Her feet ached for a soak in a hot bath, and her nacho cheese-crusted fingernails desperately needed a manicure. She shook her head, tousling her shoulder-length ebony curls to life. Now swirled with gray, the locks had been corralled under a hair net for most of the day.

Sixteen years ago, Roxy traded her life as chauffeur-to-the-stars to become a short-order cook at Sam's new business, Reyes of Sunshine Mobile Catering, in downtown Los Angeles. Before they met, she never went more than two weeks without a mani/pedi. Now she couldn't remember the last time she'd gone to the nail salon.

Recently, she'd been covering shifts for Sam. Sixty-hour weeks had become her norm, leaving no time to see her hairdresser and combat the salt-colored strands invading her pepper-colored ringlets.

Sam, who had better things to do than fry onion rings. Important things, like meeting with investors or sourcing supplies, leaving Roxy operating their business solo. Today he had left the food truck around noon, promising to see her at home for dinner.

The constant whirr of the nearby Pasadena Freeway buzzed in Roxy's ears as she unlocked their front door and stepped inside. When they had moved in, the landlord swore the freeway noise was minimal. Maybe true a long time ago, but today, the blaring symphony of motorcycles, cars, and trucks performed around the clock.

"Sam," she called out, kicking off her comfortable sneakers that added a half inch to her five-feet-seven frame.

No answer.

She closed the door, slid the deadbolt into place, snapped on a light, and moved to the kitchen. Roxy spotted Sam's *Go Ahead, Make My Day* coffee mug still on the center of their kitchen table, exactly where he'd left it that morning.

Her shoulders tightened.

Why can't he put the damn thing in the sink? Where is he, anyway?

Roxy dropped her purse onto a chair. When she snatched the mug to put it in its proper place, a note complete with a coffee ring stain on the upper corner caught her attention. Scribbled in Sam's barely legible handwriting, she read:

**Thought I could make this LA thing work, but I was wrong.
Heading to Tennessee to be with my grandkids. Sorry Rocks.**
Sam

What the hell…

Roxy's hands shook as she reread his words.

"I don't believe this!" she screamed, her gaze bouncing around the apartment.

The sneakers Sam usually left by the front door were gone. The change jar they kept on the counter was emptied out. Books from the corner shelf tossed on the ground, their flat-screen television—the one she paid for—was absent from its perch on the living room wall. Cables jutted out and dangled lifelessly, as though Sam yanked the set from the bracket.

"You took *MY TV*?" Roxy howled, launching his coffee cup against the spot where the flatscreen once *stood*. Ceramic shards confettied the top of the garage-sale credenza Roxy had refinished. Snakelike fingers of day-old-brown dregs dripped down the cream-colored walls and splattered onto the carpet.

"No. No. NO!" The guttural shriek erupted from somewhere deep inside Roxy's chest as she raced to their bedroom. Closet doors left open, drawers emptied, their home safe cleaned out. Only Roxy's passport and the pink slip to her beater car remained.

She yelled again, startled by fist pounding hard against her front door, interrupting her rant.

"Roxy! Rox-eee! Are you okay?"

Alma's panicked voice echoed, and Roxy immediately looked at her watch. Six-thirty. Her next-door neighbor's DJ shift started at seven in downtown LA.

Shouldn't she already be on her way to the station? I don't want her to see me like this.

The pounding continued.

"Roxy?" Alma shouted through the closed door, rattling the doorknob. "Is that you screaming? Are you all right?"

Roxy wished Alma would go away, but she knew better. That girl would persist until she figured out what was going on. There were worse things than having a true friend, one who deeply cared about her. Alma Sanchez was the opposite of Sam.

Selfish Sam had left her and the business they had built, without the common decency of a goodbye. Not a single conversation to prepare her for his abandonment.

A minute later the door opened, and Alma stepped inside.

"I used my key," she said, dangling it from her fingers. "Roxy, for God's sake, what happened? What's wrong?" Alma asked, assessing the chaotic state of the living room.

Roxy handed Alma the note before dropping to the floor like a bag of discarded laundry and surrendered to a downpour of tears.

Chapter Two

Roxy paced what might soon be her ex-living room, glad her last shift at the food truck was over. She'd never have to deal with Chuck again. That was the good news the bad news drowned out. With about five hundred dollars to her name, she needed a new job. And fast.

Three weeks had passed while she waited and hoped to hear from Sam. A frantic call begging for her forgiveness. Telling her everything was a big mistake, that he was sorry, and he was coming home.

But no call came.

Sam had vanished completely, taking with him any sliver of love she had felt for the man.

Taped to her front door that morning, Roxy found a handwritten note from Flora, the apartment manager, threatening a thirty-day eviction notice. She had crumpled the paper and thrown it near the empty television stand. Along with Sam, her sixty-five-inch wide-screen now lived somewhere in the Blue Ridge Mountains.

Next to the wadded notification rested a balled-up bank statement. The account where she and Sam had regularly deposited their pay held a hundred-dollar balance.

Once again, the reality invaded her. Sam was gone, cleaning out their bank account and leaving unpaid bills in his wake.

Roxy gulped back a tear and coiled onto her secondhand couch, stained and lumpy. She was on her own. Not that she couldn't survive. Roxy prided herself on being a strong, self-sufficient woman.

Still, she hadn't planned on moving into midlife alone and broke.

Practically in the dead of night, Sam had sold his business and left for Tennessee. Apparently, turning sixty lit a fire under him to move closer to the wife he had abandoned long before Roxy had met him.

Now that their children were grown and the responsibilities fewer, Sam had happily traded the hustle and chaos of Los Angeles for back-country fishing holes and lazy days with grandkids he'd never met.

At fifty-three, Roxy understood the draw of reevaluating your life, accomplishing goals before getting too old to remember what they were. She and Sam had chased those dreams together. After all, he encouraged her to abandon her career as one of the few female limo drivers in California, probably in the country. Instead, he persuaded her to join him slinging hash from his food truck on a side street near the corner of Vine and Fountain in downtown LA.

Roxy groaned at the thought. *Stupid. Stupid. Stupid.*

She'd given up pocketing hundreds of dollars in cash tips while meeting the area's famous, wealthy, and colorful. Sam supplied everything she had missed during her early years—a steady life, a reliable partner, a consistent income. Things she never had growing up in Downey. A solidness she'd never find in the capricious chauffeuring world.

It wasn't until the day after Sam's departure that she learned she had no business holdings, either. Sam's name was the only one on the food truck's ownership paperwork, and he had sold the entire thing to his long-time pal, Chuck Winston.

The thought of Creepy Chuck made her grind her teeth. Even now, weeks later, she still wanted to strangle the jerk.

"There's no mention of you in any paperwork," he had told her.

"But I'm half owner. He added my name when we moved in together," she argued, realizing she had never signed any documents. Heck, half of her measly pay was in cash, the other half dumped into their joint account, the account Sam drained when he left. Naïvely, she had trusted Sam with her heart and her finances.

"Well, that might be what Sam told you, but legally, I'm the owner," Chuck replied. "You still have a job here, though."

The truth covered her like a lead apron, the kind a dental hygienist draped over you before x-raying your teeth. Only this unbearable heaviness wasn't for her protection. Behind her back, Sam had been in business with Chuck, an LA money man with a questionable background and an even shadier investment record. Chuck, who always skulked around the food truck near closing time for as long as Roxy could remember.

She'd watch him in his three-piece tailored suit, sitting at a nearby picnic table. His expensively cut sandy brown hair and perfectly pressed attire contrasted sharply to the skateboarders, office workers, and construction guys milling around, all waiting for an order of buffalo wings.

Within minutes of his arrival, a "client" would show up and accept a small pouch in exchange for an envelope Chuck surreptitiously tucked inside his briefcase. If he spotted Roxy watching, he'd give her a grin and a nod before strolling to his Porsche parked down the street.

There was something sinister and dishonest about that guy, but she couldn't put her finger on what.

Sam got away from Chuck. He didn't give her the same chance.

To be fair, Chuck had offered Roxy a promotion to manager. But there were strings attached—an offer under the heading of *a little extra on the side.*

"Sort of the same deal you gave Sam," said Chuck, ten years her junior. "Ever since Nigel's mom flashed her boobs at me after a high-school football game, I've wanted to sleep with a cougar," he recalled, a demented grin on his face, apparently hoping this explanation made his offer acceptable. When Roxy pulled a face, he added, "Just a blow job now and then, an occasional romp in the back of the truck after the fry baskets are turned off. No big deal."

Bonking this guy, even once, would be the lowest point in her life.

Worse still, Creepy Chuck was a dad. He had a son and a daughter with his beautiful wife, Sonya. And even though Chuck and Sonya might be the worst two people on the planet, Roxy would never do anything that would hurt their kids.

Fortunately, his visits to the food truck had tapered off. A grateful Roxy wondered if Chuck had more pressing matters than emptying the cash drawer and harassing her.

No matter. Roxy, determined to turn her life around, would find a better job and shake off the grime Chuck spread over whatever he touched. She'd learn a new skill—or better yet, return to the one she'd mastered before she met Sam.

The familiar ring of her cell phone startled Roxy. It wasn't Sam's ring, but still, her heart seized, stumbling right back in love. She sat straighter on the couch and tidied her hair as if she were about to answer a video call.

Had God answered her prayers? Could Sam be calling?

Nope. Creepy Chuck, not divine intervention, spoke from the other end of the line.

She fell back against the couch cushions, disappointment receding as annoyance rose.

"I told you when I left today, I'm finished," she repeated evenly, calling in every last note of patience into her words. "What part of *I quit* don't you understand?" She held the phone a few inches from her ear, still easily able to hear the insults raging from the lunatic on the other end.

"Not my problem," Roxy bellowed back, fed up with the booming voice that persisted in telling her what she could and couldn't do. "Why don't you ask Sonya to help out?"

Chuck grunted, obviously ignoring her solution.

His wife wasn't the get-her-hands-dirty type. Roxy had learned this repeatedly during the many double dates Sam set up with the couple.

Dinner. A show at the Pantages Theatre. A night at a comedy club. Sonya arrived impeccably dressed, an air of superiority swirling around her shoulders. Clearly, she'd rather be anywhere else than with her husband's friends. Perhaps even with her husband.

Spending time with Sonya left Roxy exhausted. And any time spent with Chuck left Roxy longing for a shower as soon as she got home, her skin grimy after a night of deflecting Chuck's handsy manner, double-entendres, and off-color humor. What a mismatched couple.

"Please, Roxy, can you come back for a short time? You can't leave me in the lurch," Chuck continued, pleading his case.

"Like I said, those are your troubles. I have plenty of my own," Roxy replied, annoyed and exasperated.

She poked the disconnect button and tossed her cell onto the coffee table, where the phone immediately took an unlucky bounce and clattered to the floor. She rushed to retrieve it, stroking the screen as a precious lifeline before securing it inside the back pocket of her jeans.

Roxy wouldn't placate her former boss. His concerns weren't on her to-do list.

And now that Sam had disappeared, leaving her to forge her own future, she didn't have to pretend to like Chuck or Sonya anymore.

Maybe her life was improving after all.

Chapter Three

The next morning, Roxy looked around her kitchen. Her first impulse was to page through a printed phone book, but she had no idea where hers was. In fact, had she even seen one in years? Everything was online now. Folks surfed the internet to find a plumber or a florist. She wondered what people used nowadays for a toddler's booster seat or to press their daughter's prom corsage.

No matter. She plopped onto a chair, tucking her legs under the table. Giving into technology, she opened her laptop and searched for *limousine services*.

An irrational mix of fear and hope had kept Roxy from doing this weeks ago. Fear that she would no longer fit into the chauffeuring world and hope that Sam would return.

Over a decade had passed since Roxy had donned her chauffeur hat and tailored suit. Ride-sharing apps bulldozed the landscape she once ruled, stripping away the comfortable lifestyle she had previously enjoyed.

Unemployed with no money and no marketable skills, could she revert to the talents she'd perfected in the late 1990s and early 2000s? Could she bear to spend ten-hour days in four-inch red stilettos? In a world of Uber and Lyft, did people still use limos?

She found cached copies of old web pages of her former employer, Star-Struck Limousine, and spent the next several minutes combing through numerous hits spanning the last ten years.

She examined images of Stacy Newman, who Roxy knew previously as the dispatcher, with Bobby Schmidt, the owner. Apparently, the two had married and had kids. She grimaced, recalling that Bobby didn't seem Stacy's type.

Worse, Star-Struck Limousine ceased operations some five years ago, and apparently, the Schmidts called it quits, too.

Too bad—it might have been easy to ring up Bobby and ask for my old job back.

She continued surfing for limos in LA county. Numerous web pages appeared on her screen, populated with dozens of listings, infusing her with hope.

This was still a business.

Roxy felt lighter as she took in the variety of names. Fanciful Limos, Jewel's Limousine Service, Lux-R-ee Limo, Stacy's Sleek Limousine Service…

Still paging down, she stopped at Ride-in-Style before scrolling back a few entries.

"Well, I'll be damned. She started her own company."

Roxy clicked the Stacy's Sleek Limousine link. The webpage opened, revealing a sparkling panorama of downtown Los Angeles at night. Overlaying the image, shiny black limousines, luxury sedans, party limos and buses fanned out, awaiting revelers.

She pointed her mouse to the dropdown menu and clicked the *About Us* tab. A photo of Stacy appeared, years older than the last time Roxy saw her, but the golden-haired bombshell's personality shone through.

Roxy scanned the promotional copy and stopped when a group photo of six beautiful women caught her eye. The ladies, attired in form-fitting black suits, smiled coyly at the camera. The caption read:

Owner Stacy Newman, far right, with her staff of chauffeuses.

Chauffeuses? What did that mean?

Roxy had been called a *chaufferette*, a *chauffeuress*, and her least favorite, *go-ffeur*. She quickly looked up the term.

Chauffeuse: the feminine version of the French word chauffeur.

All the women sported shoulder-length hair or longer. She examined the five blondes, including Stacy, and one woman whose hair color landed somewhere between copper and auburn. With her black curly tresses—now more wavy than curly—and her not-as-perky 36Cs, Roxy wondered if she would be at home in that lineup.

What could be more perfect? Only lady drivers.

Taking a deep breath, Roxy dialed the 1-800 number on the screen. Her call went to voicemail.

You've reached Stacy's Sleek Limousine Service, where our cars aren't the only things sleek and beautiful. Please leave your name, number, and date of your event, and we'll get right back to you. Beep!

"Uh… this message is for Stacy Newman. Stace, it's Roxy. Roxanne Adams. Hope you remember me. I drove for Bobby in what seems like eons ago. I'm hoping we could catch up a little."

Roxy took a deep breath, realizing how nervous looking for work made her.

It had been a long time since she applied for a job, and the thought of being out in the world again turned her legs into jelly.

"Anyway, hoping all is well with you. Please give me a call soon." She rattled off her number, repeating the digits a second time more slowly. "It's Roxy," she stammered. "Bye."

Chapter Four

Roxy spent the rest of the morning at the kitchen table searching and submitting resumes to online employment sites. A humbling experience when she realized she had few skills that matched today's job market.

Frustrated and dejected at her prospects, Roxy listened when Chuck phoned later that day, begging for her return for one week.

The combination of a hundred-dollar bonus for training the new girl, combined with the reality of Flora expecting her full rent in a few days, aided her decision to show up in an hour.

Roxy agreed to work one more week at the food truck and train the new girl, Angela. Of course, in Chuck's underhanded negotiations, he threatened to keep her final paycheck if she didn't do him this favor. She knew he couldn't legally do that, but Roxy didn't have the time or energy to fight him—she needed the money.

And hopefully, by next week, she'd have found a better-paying job.

A week later, she watched Angela, the new hire, hand an avocado and sprouts sandwich with a side of sweet potato tots to an androgynous-looking millennial.

Thirty minutes until closing. Thirty minutes until I'm done with Chuck.

A half hour later, Roxy released the latches holding the pass-through window frame in place, lowered the awning, and secured the lock from the inside for the last time.

She thought back to the first time she had closed the truck by herself. Sam hadn't wanted to leave her in downtown LA alone, but he had business across town that he wouldn't return from until well after nine. What kind of business, he never said. She had never asked.

Chuck waited outside in the parking lot. He waved goodbye to Angela as she walked to her car. Roxy took in the way his eyes had lingered on her twenty-something-year-old butt. Working in the catering business would help her keep those buns toned, but eventually, they'd show the same saggy, wear-and-tear all middle-aged women fought.

"She's not your type," Roxy snarled, forcing Chuck to shift his eyes from Angela's derriere to Roxy's glare.

"Maybe not," Chuck agreed, "but she don't know that yet."

"For Christ's sake, Chuck. Sonya deserves much better than you."

"Probably, but we have this don't-ask-don't-tell arrangement. I don't ask how much she puts on the AmEx, and she don't tell me what to do in my free time." Chuck's grin caused Roxy's stomach to curdle.

You sick, dumb asshole. Men never realized the gems they possessed, always looking for a younger diamond, only to find out that the world was full of cubic zirconia.

Sighing, she extended her hand. "You have my money?"

"You sure you won't change your mind? I can pay you more than old Sammy did." He paused. "And I won't pester you for any extras. Promise." He pushed his palms together pleadingly.

"I'll pass, thanks anyway."

"Rocks, please, you've been here since the beginning."

"Yeah. I'm chasing sixty, Chuck. I need to plan for my future. Working for you, well, as lovely as it's been, won't afford me the lifestyle I'd like to grow accustomed to."

He smirked. "Yeah, I get you. Maybe there's another way."

"*Jeee-susss.* Just get off it. I'm not—"

"No, no. You don't understand. I have a career opportunity for you that won't have you slinging burgers. Or me, for that matter."

"Maybe in my next life. Right now, I'm putting the Chuck Wagon in the rearview mirror." *Like Sam did.* Roxy scowled and held her hand out farther. "Pay me."

He slid her final check, along with a small wad of twenties, into her hand. "Here's a few extra bucks to hold you over until you find something else."

She nodded a half-hearted thanks and unfolded the bills. *Two hundred won't cover my rent until another job pops up, you cheap son-of-a-bitch*, she wanted to yell.

Instead, she bit back her words and walked away, shoving the cash along with her check into her crossbody bag. She reached for her cell phone.

A missed call from an unknown 213 area code flipped her heart. *Sam? Or could Stacy be calling me back with the answer to my problems?* Roxy knew the only person with solutions was Roxy herself.

Still, she wouldn't mind if a white knight—male or female— would come along and rescue her. She dialed the number.

Sure enough, Stacy answered, and they chatted briefly. Roxy offered to take her to dinner. Stacy's suggestion to meet at Brentwood's, one of the area's pricier restaurants, made Roxy gulp. How could she afford a fancy dinner? She would have to figure it out if she wanted any chance of restarting her career.

That's what credit cards are for, she thought of her nearly maxed-out account. *I'll pay off the tab, eventually.*

Chapter Five

After talking to Stacy the previous day, Roxy instigated a search for the perfect power outfit to wear to dinner, one that screamed professionalism, charm, class. She had immediately phoned Alma, explained her run in with Chuck and why she desperately needed her advice on how to pull an outfit together.

The thirty-something woman responded quickly and now both Roxy and Alma stared at a closet full of what Roxy playfully called her "clothes of the past."

"My mamma has these." Alma pointed at a pair of brown chiffon palazzo pants hanging to the side. Roxy recalled they had been chic in the dance clubs some twenty years ago.

When Alma was thirteen.

"Mom's are a rust color. She wears them with—"

"I get it. I get it. I'm old."

"Not old, just older." Alma smirked and rolled her brown eyes, as if to remind Roxy not to take life so seriously.

"Disappointment, heartbreak, and setbacks are life's potholes," Alma often said. "Fall into them or step over them. Either way, the choice is yours."

Truth was, Alma spent little time on people not interested in moving forward, learning ways to improve their lives. And she walked the talk. Roxy recalled a long-ago happy hour, clouded by too many margaritas, when Alma opened up about how she became a radio personality.

"Less luck and more work, if you want to know the truth," she had opined, pouring an oversized serving of añejo tequila in the blender.

"I navigated some ugly human potholes, but things turned out okay for me," she said after describing when, at eighteen, her mother's drunk boyfriend came on to her. He was the third dude to pull that crap in as many years.

"So I moved out, spent a few weeks on my girlfriend's couch until I could afford a studio apartment," she told Roxy. "I got a clerical job at a Bakersfield radio station answering phones, doing the billing. You know, the usual stuff, like keeping the coffee fresh. I watched and learned how the disc jockeys amassed an audience."

"You were a secretary?" Roxy asked in disbelief. She couldn't imagine Alma in any job where she wasn't bulldozing her way through.

"You make it sound like a bad thing," Alma replied, somewhat annoyed. "Anyway, one night a DJ phoned in sick, and the general manager let me fill in a late-night slot. You know the rest of the story."

Roxy delighted in listening, happy at the good fortune of Alma's friendship. Alma was *happening*, and after cornering the market on *happened*, Roxy needed all the *happening* she could get in her life.

Despite their age difference, Alma grounded Roxy in ways that made her trust in second acts. A second chance to capture the life she wanted, the one she thought she had secured until Sam dumped her.

"I can't believe that asshole had the balls to come on to you," Alma said, removing the palazzo pants from their hanger. "Or maybe I can. He just waited until Sam was out of the picture to make his move. You never had anything nice to say about Chuck."

"Sam always did, though," Roxy defended. "At least in the beginning, when Chuck came through with the bucks to replace the roof."

"Well, Chuck with the bucks is nothing more than a big, fat fu—"

"Don't say it. Even though you're right," Roxy laughed, holding up a halter dress and discarding it in the same motion. "Chuck is my past. Right now, I'm looking to the future."

"Good riddance to that jerk. And maybe to these, too." Alma waved the roomy trousers.

"Joke all you want. Those pants are back in style." Roxy's teeth clenched so tight that a crowbar couldn't pry them apart.

"Heh. I'll bet. I was in diapers when they were trendy."

"You're here to offer fashion sense, remember?" Roxy huffed, grabbing the chiffon pants from Alma, and tossing them in the *NO* pile. "How about these?" she asked, holding up a pair of faux black leather skinny jeans. "I bought these in this century. Probably not as old as you, but close."

"Early 2000?" Alma asked. "I was in sixth or seventh grade."

"Stop. I need your help, not a history lesson."

"Okay. Okay. Let me see how they look on you."

Roxy slithered into the pants, thrilled that the tapered cut lifted her butt and flattened her tummy. "What do you think?"

Alma paced around Roxy, arms folded, nodding. "Are you holding your breath?"

"No," Roxy replied, insulted.

"Well then, in that case, not bad. Not bad at all. Let's find a top that shows off your big boobs and somewhat flat stomach."

Alma rifled through Roxy's closet, rejecting most every option. "Let me loan you something," she offered, obviously convinced the current selection wouldn't do.

"Naw. You're already doing enough by taking me seriously. You do take me seriously, right? I mean, you don't believe I'm too old to—"

"Don't even say it. Roxy, you are the most amazing, giving, talented woman I know. You were my first friend in LA. When I questioned my abilities, you kicked me in the butt. So guess what? I'm returning the favor. And in those jeans, your ass looks pretty hot for an old lady." She shoved a set of blouses still on their hangers into Roxy's hands. "You pick a top. Won't matter, anyway. I'm going to work on your shoes. Shoes are the most important part of the look."

Roxy ignored the comment and busied herself choosing a blouse, dismissing several clingy tops that clung to the wrong curves.

She had thrown the few clothes Sam left behind in black trash bags and claimed his side of the closet for her blouses and jackets. Yesterday, Roxy had shoved Sam's stuff in her trunk, planning to drop off the bags at a nearby homeless shelter the next time she was in the area.

She slid blouse after blouse along the wardrobe pole, enjoying the luxury of having the entire space to herself. Finally, she settled on a cream-colored top with a simple jewel neckline and a finished edge that fell just above her hips. She turned to where Alma sat crossed-legged inside the closet, eager to show off. "Hey, what do you think?"

Alma glanced over her shoulder. "Looks good." She wedged herself up to stand, holding up papaya-colored, open-toed mules with wicked heels as long as a fountain pen and about as slim. She blew away the gathered dust. "You haven't worn these in a while."

"Not comfortable when you're handing out hot dogs," Roxy defended, pointing to her collection of stilettos and slingbacks tossed haphazardly in a pile.

Alma swung the pair around suggestively before handing them to Roxy. "Try these on. Bet they got you in lots of trouble." She flashed a leer. "The good kind."

Roxy fingered the silver buckles and the tapered heels, memories flooding back. "I might have worn these the night that rock star invited me to his penthouse."

Alma inched closer. "Tell me more."

"It was after one of those music awards shows. I was driving him home. He was drunk… and well… what *was* his name?"

"You're kidding. You don't remember his name? Or you just don't want to tell me." Alma frowned. "Spill the beans, girl."

"Nothing to spill. He invited me up. I said no. Drunk or strung out, I couldn't tell. And I… well, I was falling for Sam." Roxy placed the shoes on a nearby dresser. "Maybe I should have given the dude a chance."

"A little late for that." Alma dug farther into the closet. "How about these stilettos?"

"Nope. They hurt my feet."

"When did you wear them last? When Dubya was president?"

"Probably." Roxy's eyes widened as the truth hit her hard. *Years before she'd met Sam.*

Before she had fallen for him. Before she put everything into a relationship that burst as easily as sticking a pin in a balloon. *Pop!* Pieces of her heart scattered randomly into the air.

Alma shoved the shoes at Roxy. "Put on the mules. Let's see what we've got."

Roxy strapped them on and modeled the outfit with a spin and a flourish. "I'd forgotten how much I love these pants."

"The look suits you," Alma agreed, satisfied. "Now, what will we do with your hair? And God, your makeup. Do you even wear makeup?"

"Alma, my friend, you're not fixing me up for a date. I'm interviewing for a job, remember?"

"Yes, of course I do. I always keep my eye on the prize. But you know, your look gets you through the door. And you have the look. We just have to unearth it, clean off the sediment, polish you up a bit. Then, the rest is up to you."

"You sound like I'm a fossil in an archaeological dig," Roxy retorted, realizing Alma spoke the truth.

A person had to tunnel deep for what they wanted in this life. In the end, what happened was ultimately up to them.

Their decisions. Their passion. Their choices.

Right now, Roxy's choices: crazy high heels, pants that hugged her bum, and a growing belief in herself.

Not a bad start.

Chapter Six

Roxy's legs bent like limp spaghetti, but they still managed to hold her upright as she walked into Brentwood's Steakhouse on the outskirts of Hollywood. The scent of sizzling porterhouse drifted through the air as though on a mission to find her. She soaked in the aroma.

Pure heaven.

Roxy allowed her eyes to adjust to the darkness, regaining the poise of the statuesque goddess she hoped to exude. She ran her fingers through her ebony tresses, sending her waves bouncing in every direction.

Her newly cut layered bob complemented her oval-shaped face. Well, that's what her stylist claimed when she presented Roxy with the $110-plus-tip total. She was in better shape than most women half her age, even though her tall slender frame toted a few extra pounds around the middle.

Roxy still turned heads.

Slowing, she scanned the room for the person who could give her a good job doing the one thing she had once been great at— driving a limo.

All morning, Roxy had fretted about what she should say. She couldn't remember the last time she'd interviewed for work. How could she showcase her now-rusty talents? Would Stacy dismiss the idea, viewing Roxy as an aged used-to-be?

Roxy shook the thought loose and gathered herself up to her full height, teetering atop the four-inch-heels Alma had unearthed.

The f*ck-me shoes resurrected from the early 2000s weren't helping Roxy project the vision of a woman who had it all together. If anything, she looked more like a bag lady about to drop it all, and it would take hours to pick up the pieces scattered along the way.

Gulping a deep breath, she wobbled forward, battling the panic mounting in her head and put her focus onto the uneven terracotta tile leading to where Stacy sat in a far corner of the restaurant.

Sexy woman walking…

Her bold-colored shoes made a statement. They radiated the inner confidence Roxy was attempting to regain.

Yeah, that's right. I'm wearing orange, and it looks good on me!

Today, however, that message was broadcast warningly in wavering gulps. *This is a bad decision. Go back to your slip-on sneakers with the Velcro straps.*

Roxy's vibe radiated anything but sexy. Hell, she'd be lucky if she didn't kill herself on the way to the table. What was she trying to do? Be someone she used to be but wasn't anymore?

Her mind spun.

Stacy would see right through this ruse. Her company couldn't afford the workman's comp to insure a rickety, nearly sixty-year-old on the verge of osteoporosis. Instead of hiring her as a chauffeur with the chance to pull down some big bucks, she might offer Roxy a desk job where she couldn't hurt herself unless an uncooperative copy machine launched a surprise attack. Safe, sure, but no one gave out big tips for shuffling papers.

Roxy proffered a wave in Stacy's direction as a waiter passed by, catching her off-guard. At the last minute, she spotted the tray packed with club sandwiches and salads heading straight for her. She swung wide to avoid a collision and ducked, evading a crash.

Roxy spun on her heels, nearly doing the splits. Once she regained her balance and a shred of composure, Roxy realized the entire room had been watching as though she was a circus act, teetering on the high wire.

A breath of air released from deep inside her chest, simple gratitude for not landing on her ass. A full second later, applause broke out. Shaking off her embarrassment, Roxy put her hands together in prayer pose and bowed, grateful for the flexibility her weekly hatha yoga classes provided.

She looked up to see Stacy standing, leading the ovation. "Man, Roxy, you haven't lost a step," she declared, pointing to the chair across from hers.

Roxy grabbed the ice water sitting nearby and took a swallow. "Thanks," she said after downing another mouthful.

They made small talk during the appetizers. Roxy had stared at the jumbo shrimp—five dollars apiece—and sighed. She apologized for her awkward arrival. "Not exactly the entrance I aimed for, but…"

"Well, obviously you've kept yourself in shape," Stacy observed as the waiter placed their Louie salads on the table. She forked the tiniest piece of crab. "Not easy to do after forty, much less fifty. I know." Stacy slid the tines between her lips, bestowed a closed-mouth smile, and chewed. "You look the part of a top-notch *chauffeuse,* and after watching your acrobatic entrance, I've no doubt that Foxy Roxy can still perform the way you used to."

Chapter Seven

Foxy Roxy.

She couldn't remember the last time someone called her that.

Roxy observed Stacy across the linen-covered table, a candle flickering between them from inside a glass orb.

"They say it's not what you know, it's who you know. To that I'd add, it's how good you look. And girlfriend, you're still rockin'."

Stacy nodded for Roxy to pick up her nearly full wine glass before giving a little tap. "To you and getting older and looking better."

"Everything you're saying is sweet, and I appreciate having a cheerleader on my side." Roxy hunched, slumping in her chair. "But the fact is… well, the reason I called… Stacy, I need a job, and I needed it yesterday."

"I was surprised to hear from you," Stacy said, still swirling the wine in her glass. "Thought you and that Sammy guy rode off into *happily ever after.*"

Roxy blinked to keep the tears at bay. "Yeah, life is funny like that. You see, the thing is… Sam left. All I have now is a half-empty fridge, overdue rent, and his horny business partner. I gotta get out of that apartment and move as far away as I can from the food truck and Chuck Winston."

"Chuck Winston?"

"Yeah, Sam's former business partner." *And current snake in the grass.* "Even though I want nothing to do with him, he keeps turning up. I can block him on my phone, but I don't want him to know where I live."

"Are you afraid of him?" Stacy asked, true concern in her voice.

"No. Not in a physical way. It's just that"—Roxy leaned in—"once Sam became involved with him, things started changing, and not in a good way. The fact is, Chuck has no place in my life, now that Sam is gone."

Stacy tapped her ombre-painted fingertips on the table. "Why does that name sound familiar? *Chuck Winston*." She rolled the name around in her mouth as though it was a marble. "Maybe we've driven him to some event or something. Anyway, dearie, you don't need to worry about Chuck or finding work. What I have in mind—"

Before Stacy could finish, a tall, willowy woman with flawless ebony skin and an equally radiant smile approached their table. Stacy stood to hug the woman. "Roxy, this is Cecile. Honey, this is the infamous Roxy I've told you about."

The woman extended her hand. "Cecile Jordan. I'm pleased to meet you." She released her grip and scooted to her place on the right side of Stacy. Roxy hadn't realized until that moment the table had been set for three. "I hear you got shit done in the early days. You paved the way for the rest of us."

"Paved the way?" Roxy was confused, not just by the conversation, but by the obvious affection Stacy and Cecile shared. Were they involved? Far as she knew, Stacy was straight, but things change.

She examined Cecile for clues. Where had she seen that face before? It took a few seconds to recall the staff photo on the website.

Yes. Of course. The gorgeous redhead in the back row.

"Now I remember," Roxy blurted. "You drive for Stacy's company."

Cecile giggled a response. "Sort of. And I'm part owner."

"Wow, that's great. You two started the business together. I'm impressed." Roxy wished she had as much to show for her years on earth.

"Stacy is the founder. She did most of the heavy lifting," Cecile said. "I was smart enough to marry her. Now it's our business. And if you ask me"—she leaned closer and cupped her hand against her face—"it's a whole lot easier than raising six kids."

"Six!" Roxy swallowed, her eyebrows going up.

"Did you know Bobby and I had three?" Stacy asked.

"Naw. You weren't even dating when I left," Roxy said.

Stacy pointed to teenage faces on the lock screen of her phone.

"They're gorgeous," Roxy commented, noting the bright green eyes and blondish-brown hair. "Good thing they took after your side."

"Cecile has three children as well," Stacy said.

Roxy swallowed, taking in the depth of the two women. They shared a commitment, a business, and kids. Three things Roxy wanted and likely would never have.

"The boys play on the same club soccer team. That's how we met." Cecile supplied the details before shifting her gaze to Stacy. "We're a colorful version of the Brady Bunch."

"I loved Bobby," Stacy added, filling in the quiet. "But we weren't a good match. Took a few years to figure that out. Luckily, Cecile was there for me on some long, lonely nights." Stacy waved her hand. "Enough about ancient history. We want to talk to you about a job."

***

After another round of Brentwood's signature Old Fashioneds, Cecile peppered Roxy with questions: why had Roxy left a lucrative career to work in a roach coach?

The answer: Love, misguided love.

As the moments passed, Roxy felt more at ease. She had a lot to offer Stacy's company. Her people skills just needed to be updated.

The chance to return to the career she loved and to do it working for Stacy ignited Roxy and tied her up in knots of anticipation. She barely ate her meal but did manage to down a second bourbon. A dizzy feeling invaded her brain, part alcohol, part dream-come-true.

Could the worst be behind her? Could she let go of the mistakes, the misjudgments? The out-and-out terrible choices she had made over the years? Could she bury the image of Sam being the love of her life?

Stacy's strong, slightly slurred voice interrupted before Roxy could answer any of her mental questions.

"When I heard your message, I said to Cecile that you were one of Star-Struck's top earners. Our most requested operator," Stacy added.

Roxy bounced her gaze between the two, their rapid-fire accolades flying at her continuously. "You want me to work for you? As what, a dispatcher like you were?"

Stacy laughed. "Hardly. We're not wasting you behind-the-scenes the way I was. Bobby was a shortsighted SOB. Not totally his fault, but times have changed."

"Listen, Roxy, we want you out in front, directly meeting the clients and maybe mentoring our staff. Definitely not pushing papers," Cecile added.

Roxy couldn't believe her ears. She quickly accepted before Stacy or Cecile could change their minds—or the bourbon wore off.

She exhaled in celebration of the freedom a paycheck would bring. But the bigger relief came with the work itself. She wouldn't be an office manager or file clerk. Stacy and Cecile wanted her chauffeuring skills.

"You had quite the following," Stacy continued. "After you quit, imagine the nightmare I had explaining to clients that you were no longer with Star-Struck. People thought you'd changed companies and insisted I tell them the name of the new place. I finally found out where you had gone and passed along the information, but no one bought the story that you left us to work at a food truck."

Stacy spoke the truth. The first time a former client ordered lunch at *Reyes of Sunshine* might have been a coincidence. But after more customers from her past happened by, she knew they hadn't made the drive for barbecued wings. They had come to see for themselves that Foxy Roxy had traded luxury limos for a career in food service.

A couple of her older, dearer clients—the ones she drove off-the-books to a doctor's appointment or some other activity—worried that she'd been taken against her will.

"Honestly, honey, who in their right mind would give up glitz and glamour for this?" Miriam Hooper waved her arm at the food truck. "That's just stupid." Her sister Agnes stood next to her, nodding in agreement. "Love does make you do stupid things."

Was loving Sam stupid? Seemed that way now.

"I'm sure you'll gather the same loyal following with us as you did at Star-Struck," Cecile said, pulling Roxy out of her cocktail-induced reminiscence. "It's a real bonus to cash in on your expertise, your style and glamour. Well, your…YOU!"

"My You? What do you mean?" Roxy had been more bewildered by Cecile's exuberance than her words.

Stacy shook her head. "You left a mark on the industry, Rocks. A real trailblazer. How do you not know that? You're the reason I started my business. The reason I only employ women. You beat the odds and left a road map for the rest of us to follow."

Trailblazer! Stacy's proclamation stunned Roxy.

"I… I was just earning a living. Lucky for me, I loved the work, and I was good at it."

"Exactly. In an industry that didn't welcome women. That's what makes you a class act." Stacy slammed her palm on the table. "You were always about the job. Personalities never got in the way."

"Really Stacy, I wasn't trying to make a statement. I was in it for the paycheck," Roxy defended.

"Understood. Still, you never let the mean tricks discourage you."

"Mean tricks?"

Stacy licked her lips and drew back in her chair. "You don't know, do you? The male chauffeurs hated you. You were one of the very few women chauffeuring at the time. You took the plum jobs. The high-profile clients requested you, and the guys hated that."

Roxy answered with a shrug. "I guess I was too busy working to pay attention. Didn't have time for office gossip and politics."

Suddenly she remembered some mean shenanigans. Shaving cream smeared across the seats of her limo twenty minutes before she was to pick up a client. Or mysterious bird turds splattered on the windshield where there were no trees or telephone wires around. At the time, she simply wrote them off as harmless pranks.

Now she knew they were more. They were warnings to a young woman to stay in her lane.

Could those same warnings apply now that I'm ready to change lanes?

Chapter Eight

Two days later, Roxy pulled into the lot of her new employer's building—not much more than an enlarged corner in an industrial park—and took a deep breath.

How could it be that Stacy had transformed the despair Roxy had endured for weeks into a new beginning?

Well, partially new. In many ways, Roxy's life had boomeranged back to the beginning since Sam had left nearly a month ago.

Roxy hoped returning to the job of her thirties with the sensibilities of a woman in her fifties would be a good thing. A positive step forward.

A small sign attached to the wall—*Stacy's Sleek Limo Service*—confirmed she was in the right place. That and a fleet of onyx-black vehicles parked precisely in a row behind a chain-link fence.

She checked her makeup in the rearview mirror before leaving her car, painfully aware of the beads of sweat dripping from her armpits. She tugged her blouse away from her body, hoping the material hadn't stained.

I haven't been this nervous since I gave a speech in front of my eighth-grade civics class.

Roxy rang the buzzer and turned around to take in the space.

A harsh whir of wheels on metal came from an adjacent building. Roxy watched as carts heaped with dirty linen were being pushed up a ramp into a commercial laundry. Sandwiched in between the laundry and the limo service, a third unit had its roll-up doors wide open. Roxy peeked to see what appeared to be an artisan pottery maker expertly loading various pieces onto a drying rack. What an eclectic selection of businesses.

She sucked in a gulp of air, quickly realizing clay dust and lint had mixed with her oxygen, causing her to cough. She inhaled again, but not as deeply. The first day on a new job was anxiety-riddled for everyone, but to Roxy, today blossomed like the luckiest day ever. A few random particles in the air wouldn't bring her down.

Roxy pinched herself at how easy slipping back into her old life could be, now that she knew Stacy believed in her. Was it naïve to imagine regaining what she'd lost being blinded by her love for Sam? Love sure could mess up your vision, but she was seeing clearly now. It would take patience, commitment, and persistence—qualities Roxy had in abundance.

Well, once she rebooted them from the dark corner of her soul.

"Hey."

Roxy swung around to face a smiling Stacy. "You're right on time." She unlocked the door and ushered Roxy inside. "First things first, let's get you outfitted."

"Outfitted?" Roxy asked as she was guided into a small changing room.

"We don't like the term uniform. Sounds too much like a costume. We prefer outfit," Stacy said, dismissing any further discussion. "Decker will be here soon."

Before Roxy could question Stacy, a stout man, maybe ten years her junior, tapped on the door and approached without waiting for approval.

"Meet Decker Klein, the man who makes us look wonderful."

Holding a fabric tape measure in his hand, the tailor bowed slightly. "A true pleasure," he said, before regaining his stance.

Roxy detected an Eastern European accent, maybe Swiss or German, but hesitated to ask.

"Come back to my office once Decker is finished with you." Stacy turned and disappeared down the hall.

Roxy eyed the man, the yellow tape measure still dangling from his hand. Attached to his wrist sat a red pincushion that reminded her of the tomato-shaped one her mother had used. His was missing the tiny strawberry dangle.

He wasted no time taking her basic measurements. "Relax," he said as she squirmed. "Stand as you normally would. I'll get the best fit that way."

Roxy immediately sucked in her stomach. *I need to lose twelve pounds and quick.*

"And breathe," he said, smiling. "This isn't the first time you've been fitted for clothes, am I right?" he asked. "Surely a wedding dress or other special occasions."

"No wedding dresses. Actually, nothing in, say, the last thirty or forty years." Roxy pulled a face remembering being measured for her parochial school uniform. Forest green-and-black-plaid pleated skirts that no one looked good in, coupled with snowy white blouses sporting a Peter Pan collar. Her hem had to touch the floor when she knelt, or one of the sisters would send her home.

After school, Roxy and most of her seventh-grade girlfriends rolled up the waistband to improvise mini-skirts. Where had that thirteen-year-old's maverick spirit escaped to? Was that the last time she'd gone against authority?

"Most of what I wore for my last job I picked off the rack. Does it show?" she asked as he measured her bustline.

"You seem nervous, that's all. But this is an uncomfortable situation, total stranger sizing you up, so to speak."

"You did catch me by surprise, but I'm excited to have my *outfit* fit properly," she said, meaning every word. "Do you typically make house calls? Or is this a special favor for Stacy?"

He grinned, revealing a gold-capped incisor. "Stacy is the only one I offer on-site services to. She's been a good friend. Thanks to her, I now own a tailor shop in Westwood. So, I stop by any time she requests. A small way to show my appreciation."

Decker continued measuring and writing down her statistics until Roxy thought there wasn't any part of her left to assess.

He handed her a black suit and a crisp white blouse. "I'll step out of the room while you change."

In the mirror, Roxy examined the poly-wool blend. The suit was breathable, easy to move in and held its shape. Every employee donned the same midnight black; however, the effect was anything but cookie-cutter. From the website photos, Roxy appreciated how each driver had accessorized the outfit, with jewelry, ties, or scarves, highlighting individual flair while still presenting a uniform company appearance.

Minutes later, radiant at the fit of her new threads, she called for Decker to reenter. He pointed to a small riser for her to once again stand on.

"You have remarkable posture," he said after helping her step up. "I usually have to remind my clients to stand tall, shoulders back and all that. Your natural carriage is a wonderful asset."

Roxy had never been complimented on her posture and took pride in the comment.

Decker adjusted the hemline and fussed with the bust darts. After a few nips here and tucks there, her appearance improved.

Too bad he couldn't work his magic on the pooch that had been hiding under her cook shirt for over a decade. She feared, even with expert tailoring, these pants would accentuate her sagging butt and thickening waistline. A skirt might be more forgiving. Maybe she'd ask Stacy about that, with the promise to not roll up the waistband.

"I'm told you're going on a ride along tonight. I don't have time to fully prep your suit, but this will do for today." Decker gently turned Roxy around to get a better view in the full-length mirror.

She suppressed a gasp, amazed at his technique. With these pants, there was no saggy booty. "This is unbelievable," she said. "Decker, I don't know—"

"The fit will get better. I'll have something ready for you tomorrow. I'll leave a new outfit on a hanger near your locker."

Roxy gave him a quizzical look. "Locker?"

"There's a much larger changing room, complete with lockers, vanities. Everything you professionals need to look, well, professional. Stacy will show the room to you on your tour." He leaned in as though about to divulge a confidence. "You're in wonderful shape," Dexter murmured, leaving off *for a woman of your age*. "If you don't mind my saying so, a few Pilates moves a couple of times a week will work wonders on your abs."

Roxy's hackles went up. *The nerve…*

But when she sent him a hateful stare, compassion looked back. His advice was sound, his motivation sincere. No doubt Stacy had shared her backstory.

Roxy's first stop on the path to a new life would be learning to recognize constructive comments as support, not as a call to arms. Decker offered genuine help. Was she secure enough to accept it?

Roxy assessed her silhouette in the mirror before stepping off the platform. She hugged Decker and pulled back. "Thank you," she murmured, gratitude in her voice. "Thank you so much."

Chapter Nine

After changing back into her own clothes, Roxy retraced her steps to Stacy's office, eager to get started.

There was a lot to learn. Lane assist, automatic parking, and keyless entry—all were automotive advances that had occurred since she last chauffeured. Improvements her 2004 Camry definitely didn't possess.

As she neared the office, she overheard Stacy and Cecile chatting. Not wanting to interrupt, Roxy waited until there was a break in their conversation before she poked her head in. "Hey!"

"There she is. All finished with Dex?" Stacy asked.

"He's amazing. Wait till you see what he pulled together for me to wear tonight. First time in years my butt doesn't sag." Roxy didn't bother to mask her excitement. "I've never felt so good about an outfit. And he said my tailored clothes would fit even better."

"He's God's gift to garments, that is for sure," Cecile said. "Ready to get familiar with the fleet and learn the 'Sleek way' of doing things?" she finished using air quotes to emphasize.

"Absolutely," she enthused. Next Monday, Roxy would be a commercial driving academy student, but today, she'd immerse herself in learning what was expected at headquarters.

"Let's take a tour, get you acquainted with the fleet." Cecile moved toward the hallway leading to the gated yard where Roxy had seen vehicles parked when she first arrived.

Roxy followed, strolling through the lot, mouth agape at the variety of vehicles available for rental. Executive sedans, stretch limos, convertibles, even classic cars, and a smattering of party buses. Roxy climbed behind the wheel of several, trying them on for size. Except for the touch screens, nothing seemed all that foreign.

She took in the sweet, earthy scent. A refined mixture of pebbled bull leather, the tickle of imagined champagne bubbles, and luxury enticed her. An excited sparkle grew bigger, as the familiarity of the job she once adored flooded her insides.

I can do this. I can still do this.

"Well, what do you think?" Stacy asked, joining them some thirty minutes later.

Seated behind the wheel of a stretch SUV, Roxy checked out the console. "This will be a cinch compared to the old days," she said, fingering the sound system controls. "Everything is right here within reach."

Stacy grinned. "Technology has streamlined the logistics. I'll agree with you there."

"Simplified," Roxy retorted.

"What do you mean?"

Roxy climbed out of the SUV and closed the door softly. "Well, for example, years ago I drove this middle-aged cardiologist and his young wife to lots of events," Roxy said, recalling an especially stressful evening. "This one night, he was on edge, jumpy and anxious. For a heart surgeon, he could have benefited from the same stress-reducing advice he gave his patients. His laid-back wife, on the other hand, acted just the opposite. Dr. O'Neill, his name was.

"Anyway, his pager beeped a few minutes into our ride. We were ten minutes from their destination, but he insisted I find a payphone. Like right now. So, there I was, holding the wheel with one hand and thumbing through a Thomas Guide, trying to locate the nearest phone. Finally, I pulled over in front of a hotel. He ran inside and used theirs.

"A minute or two later, he reappeared. I rushed him to the hospital for an emergency and then took her to the gala. Today, he would have used his cell phone and skipped all the drama. Or my GPS system would have guided me."

"True." Stacy nodded. "Was it Bill O'Neill? His ex, Maggie, is still a client."

"Sounds right," Roxy recalled. "Boy, she was a firecracker. Bubbly personality, nice as could be. Aglow in a flaming red ball gown, her boobs pushed up so high, I worried she'd suffocate on her cleavage." Roxy's eyes widened. "She wanted me to go to the gala with her. Said she didn't want to go in alone. I declined but told her I'd wait in the parking lot. If the event was a drag, I'd be right there."

"This has to be fifteen years ago or more," Stacy guessed.

"Probably longer," Roxy affirmed. "I had only driven them a couple of times before I quit to work with Sam. Didn't take long to figure out Maggie liked herself a good time. Anyhow, she came out of the ballroom about an hour later. I figured she had stayed the requisite time to save face and was ready to leave. Instead, she told me she found a ride home."

Both women smiled, shaking their heads.

"Here's the skinny on tonight's run," Stacy continued. "We are shuttling about a hundred players and staff from a visiting football team to their midweek team dinner and back to their hotel. We'll split them up into two buses. You'll ride with Jade on the way there. She should be here in a couple of hours, and you can meet her. I want you to come back on Cecile's bus. Pay attention to both of their styles. Watch how they prep their vehicle, how they interact with the clients, how they handle themselves."

"I'm familiar with the routine," Roxy said, suddenly defensive. It had been awhile, sure, but some things she didn't forget, like how to treat a paying client. "Have things changed that much?" she softened.

"We're dealing with quantity when a party bus is involved. Totally different from driving a couple to the symphony," Stacy explained, no tinge of judgment in her voice. "Everything is amplified. This is a traveling happy hour. Gotta pay attention to the same problems as a bartender would, only *you're* moving."

"Understood." Roxy lowered her eyes, realizing Stacy was coaching her, not dissing her.

"The drive home is always the toughest," Stacy continued. "The guys get rowdy, handsy, and sometimes sick. Watch how Cecile diffuses potential hassles. She has an amazing talent for bypassing trouble before the problems bubble up."

"We've had some of these guys before. For the most part, they're good fellas, just letting off steam before their big game," Cecile said. "Keep your eye out for the few who can't handle their liquor—usually the younger, immature dudes. Those few will be the majority of your problems. I assess them on the way to the hotel, which gives me a leg up on how to play things on the ride back."

Roxy thought about this. Typically in the past, she made judgments about her passengers depending on how they interacted with her. Some were friendly, some were snooty. And some… well, their mammas didn't teach them how to act in public. "Playing the psychologist is a larger part of the job."

"We wear many hats," Stacy said. "Therapist, guide, caterer, seamstress."

"Seamstress?"

"Yeah, you remember. Inevitably the mother of the bride's zipper gets stuck, or the best man will split his pants. No one-trick ponies here," Cecile reminded.

"Never had to sew up someone's britches, but I do remember making emergency stops. Once for *lady products*, once for pantyhose, although no one wears those anymore," Roxy recalled. "And oh yes, trailing back to retrieve a forgotten corsage. We're more than drivers. We're problem solvers."

Being able to do many things at the same time and do them well—that summarized Roxy's life with Sam: cook, bottle washer, purchasing agent, confidant, lover. She chuckled, realizing the actions of her past qualified her for her new role in ways she hadn't imagined.

"Absolutely," Stacy said, looking at her watch. "We leave at six to pick up our passengers. It's around two. Go home and put your feet up for a few. Be back here by five. I'll show you the rest of the facility, introduce you to our team, and we'll get you squared away then. And Roxy, bring those orange shoes you wore the other night. They'll look awesome with your outfit."

***

Roxy watched as Stacy and Cecile headed toward the offices. She lagged for a moment, scanning the collection of vehicles that comprised Stacy's Sleek Limousine Service. In their short time together, the pair had acquired a wide selection, ensuring they could meet the needs of most any client.

She puffed a relieved sigh, feeling grateful the new gizmos and gadgets hadn't been as intimidating as she anticipated. Based on her experience, she knew she could awaken the skill to expertly captain any of them, even the extended SUVs. All the bells and whistles didn't change a thing. Driving was still driving. The most important element of the job remained true: show her clients a safe, worry-free, good time.

I've got this.

She turned to leave, letting her gaze land on the party buses neatly lined up on the far side of the lot. *Maybe I don't.* She allowed a sliver of doubt to creep inside. *How do you maneuver such a machine and keep an eye on thirty-some folks at the same time?*

She didn't know how long she had been standing there, cemented to the asphalt when she spotted Cecile approaching. She shook off the fear and met her halfway.

"Can't take your eyes off them?"

"Oh, what? The party buses." Roxy licked her lips, knowing anxiety colored her words. "They are enormous, aren't they?"

"But together, we'll always have more power," Cecile said. "Stacy will never leave you alone operating one. Many businesses use a single chauffeur. But, for groups this size, we travel in pairs. One for driving. One for crowd control."

"That's a relief," Roxy said, her apprehension dissipating.

Cecile nodded and placed a thick envelope in Roxy's hand. "Here's your enrollment packet. You'll love the folks at Friendly Roads," she said, with too much enthusiasm about the driving academy.

Roxy couldn't tell if she was serious or being facetious. Going back to school, albeit driving school, could be viewed as a step backward, but she refused to think that way. Any chance to learn, to further her education and refresh her skills, should be coveted.

"I'm excited for the training," Roxy said with a nod.

"Stacy and I know you're an investment that will reap great returns."

"Thanks for the vote of confidence," Roxy said, not wanting to question the wisdom of her career change.

Cecile pointed to the manila envelope Roxy held. "Trust me, you'll pick up this stuff in a snap."

As they walked, Cecile filled her in on what to expect during the six-week course. "You'll attend classes Monday through Thursday.

You need 140 hours of training with fifteen hours behind the wheel before you can test."

"This sounds thorough," Roxy said.

"Oh, they are very thorough and professional. These guys offer more than the state minimum requirements. That's why we use their services."

Roxy nodded. Prepared was always better.

"The other part Stacy didn't mention is that, while you attend class during the week, we'll need you on call for weekends, possibly Fridays, too. Are you up to that?"

"Of course. The sooner I get back into action, the better," Roxy said, enthusiasm lacing her words.

"Great. Back to the schooling. You'll spend most of your time prepping to pass the written exam, but there's other stuff we need to address, too," Cecile continued.

Roxy's insides tumbled. "Like what?" *Agility tests, strength requirements, physicals.* Tasks she would never be able to achieve.

Cecile waved her hand dismissively. "Proof that you can work in the country legally, pass a drug test, and be fingerprinted. Don't worry. You've got this nailed. You're much better prepared to ace this test than I was—or any of our other drivers, for that matter."

Grateful for Cecile's pep talk, a barely perceptible sigh escaped from Roxy's chest. Scale-a-wall or bench-press-your-own-weight wasn't on the list.

Sure there would be challenges, but how hard could operating a party bus be?

Sounds like fun on wheels.

Chapter Ten

Thirty minutes later, Roxy flopped onto her sagging couch, joyous to be home. She kicked off her loafers and collapsed against the worn cushions. A thirty-minute nap would be a welcome respite, but because of LA's infamous traffic, her three-hour break had shrunk to two hours and fifteen minutes.

Minus the time it would take to get back to Stacy's before five. She allowed her eyes to close for a moment, risking slumber in exchange for a chance to clear her mind.

Months ago while waiting for her dermatology appointment, Roxy had read an article about the six most stressful life changes. She thought the concept interesting but gave it little regard. Now that she'd collided with three of the six during the past few weeks—career shift, relationship ending, financial instability—she wished she had paid better attention. Sadly, while she focused on loving Sam, she'd never thought about the future. About being prepared.

Had she lived with her head up her... well, in the sand?

Roxy sighed. And she was about to undertake a fourth. The landlord had given her an extra fifteen days to get last month's rent together. If she didn't start raking in some big tips soon, moving in with Alma might become a reality.

Though reconnecting with Stacy made some of the stress easier to shoulder, Roxy realized she still needed time to absorb, reflect, and adjust. It was a struggle to accept that she had to begin again.

At thirty, she was willing to be the rookie, the novice, the new kid. But at fifty-something, reinventing herself was tough to imagine, much less accomplish. Unwittingly, her trust in Sam had landed her in a terrible game of Chutes and Ladders, with every spin sliding her back to Start.

Stacy and Cecile had been encouraging, insisting Roxy was valuable, her past chauffeuring knowledge beneficial and needed. She felt a mixture of gratitude to them for the second chance—and resentment at herself that she needed one. The nagging insult of starting over wouldn't relent, leaving her with an anxious, busy mind refusing to relax, even for a few minutes.

Roxy reached for the packet Cecile had given her earlier, unhooked the clasp and slid out a sheaf of paper. Clipped to the top was a note and a check for three-thousand dollars.

Cecile and I want you to be successful and not worry about trivial things like food and rent.

She had punctuated the end of the sentence with a hand-drawn smiley face.

Hoping this will be enough to get you through the next few weeks until you're our newest commercially licensed driver, and on the schedule where you can stabilize your income!
Glad to have you on our team,
Your pal (and boss), Stace

Tears swelled in Roxy's eyes. Other than to confess that she needed a job, Roxy hadn't mentioned the financial hole Sam had left her in.

Somehow Stacy knew. Instead of worrying about how to pay the rent, Roxy could concentrate on acing the CDL test. *Driving party buses must be big business.*

She glanced at her watch, feeling lighter than she had in weeks. *Gotta leave in fifteen minutes. Better find my orange-colored-stilts-that-passed-for-shoes and put them by my purse.* She shuttled to her closet and rummaged around before remembering Alma had borrowed them for an awards show she hosted the night before.

Was Alma still at home, or had she already left for the radio station?

Roxy grabbed her phone and spotted a missed call from Sam. Her heart skipped and then stopped. His name hadn't appeared on her screen for weeks. She thought she had gotten used to never hearing from him again, unless it was to ask her to ship the junk he'd left in their apartment to his new digs.

She shook off the mixture of hope and uneasiness.

He must have called while I was inventorying the vehicles at Stacy's. What does he want?

For the first time since he'd left, Roxy considered that Sam might be in trouble. Maybe he needed her. She shook her head as though erasing the possibility.

You left me, dude. Whatever you need will have to wait.

She scrolled to Alma's number, tapped the screen, and paced. "Hey, Alma. You still home?"

"For about five more minutes. You okay?"

"Yeah, I'm great. Just need my orange shoes for work tonight."

"Well, well, well. Hoping those shoes work some magic on a client?"

Roxy imagined Alma's satisfied grin, framed by layers of long chestnut brown hair. "No! Girl, get your mind out of the gutter. It's a long story."

"I have time."

"I don't. Can I pop over to grab them?" Roxy asked.

"Of course," Alma answered. She didn't disconnect, and Roxy realized her friend was waiting for additional details.

"All right, I'll tell you everything over lunch tomorrow. My treat."

***

Perched atop her T-straps, Roxy pushed open Sleek's front door and hustled toward the offices. The orange stilt-like shoes prevented her from dashing, much less running, and made her regret putting them on in the car. She wasn't late, but she wasn't as early as she had hoped to be. A four-car pile-up on the 110 absorbed the twenty-minute cushion she had allowed herself.

Beads of sweat gathered above her brows, and she hoped Stacy wouldn't detect her perspiring at the simple task of showing up. But where she expected to find her boss, instead she found a note taped to Stacy's door.

Head down the hall. Changing room on your right.

Ah, the changing room Dexter had told her about. She ambled the thirty or so steps to find *Ladies Only Changing Chamber* stenciled on the frosted-glass door.

She turned the knob, and her jaw dropped as she took in the expansive space. A canopy-style skylight infused the room with an airy feel. Walls covered in pastels of blue, yellow, and lavender added to the magic. This was nothing like the locker room in her old high school gym.

For one thing, the space smelled heavenly—a mixture of linen, balsam, and maybe lavender. She spotted a diffuser in the corner and inhaled deeply. That's when she read *R O X Y*, spelled out in a mixture of large and small rhinestones affixed to the front of a full-length locker. On a nearby garment rack, a beautifully tailored suit hung. The one Dexter had promised.

"Nice, huh?"

Roxy turned to see a woman about her height leveling an impish grin in her direction. She had one high-heeled foot perched on a wooden bench that extended between the rows of lockers. The twinkle in her piercing green eyes reinforced the playfulness in her voice. Roxy recognized those eyes from the website photos and guessed Jade to be in her late twenties or early thirties.

"Jade?" she asked.

"Yes. And based on you staring at this locker, I'm guessing you're Roxy."

Roxy nodded. The pair turned to face the bank of lockers and admired the handiwork on each. "Very pretty," Jade finally said.

"I didn't realize I'd get all this fanfare," Roxy said. "What an exceptional welcome."

"You have no idea. Everything about working here is exceptional." Jade's eyes crinkled with a smile. "Best place I've ever pulled down a paycheck."

"I'll bet."

"Stacy and Cecile take pride in their business. And they show us appreciation in hundreds of ways. Decorating the changing room is one of many, but I think it's their favorite. Those two spend so much time coming up with individualized themes for the lockers. My locker's over there." She pointed across the room.

Roxy took in the glimmering letters outlined in pieces of jade-colored stone. "Very stunning," she said, meaning every word.

"I made things easy with a name like mine. So did you. They had a heck of a time figuring out something for Margo," Jade said.

Roxy glanced around and finally asked, "Daisies?"

"Weird, huh? Cecile found out that Margo was named after her grandmother, Marguerite. She switched to Margo in grade school because it was easier for her friends to pronounce."

"I still don't understand," Roxy confessed.

"We didn't either until Cecile explained that marguerite is a type of daisy. And of course, Margo always loved daisies. She just didn't know why."

Roxy grinned. "And for Simona? Why carousel horses?"

"Long story. I'll let her tell you, but the quick version is she loves merry-go-rounds. Her ambition is to ride one in every state. She's up to thirty-seven or so," Jade volunteered.

"That's an unusual goal."

"More of a hobby. Apparently, as a kid, she watched a movie where stationary carousel horses detached from the roundabout and rode off with the characters on board. She's been a fan ever since."

"You and Jade are hitting it off, just like I knew you would," Stacy said, her voice booming behind them.

Both women whirled around, startled by the comment.

"Hey, Stacy." Roxy stepped closer. "I couldn't find you or Cecile when I got back, just a note taped to your door sending me here. This room is nicer than my apartment, and bigger. And my locker... wow, I've never had anything bedazzled in my name before."

"You like?"

"Are you kidding? I keep pinching myself to make sure I'm not dreaming. Jade shared a little history about the décor," Roxy said. "And the other *chauffeuses* I haven't met yet, Margo and Simona."

Cecile joined them. "Margo won't be in today, but you'll meet her soon enough," she said, heading to her locker, covered with photos of what Roxy suspected were her kids.

She apparently sensed Roxy staring. "Mine was *glitterized* too, way back when. Stacy went all out with stars that blinked off and on." She pointed to a couple of spots that glimmered from the top corner. "Over time, I switched the stars out to these precious faces. Of course, you can change your locker front any time you like."

"No way. I love the gems. Makes me feel cherished. Like I've found buried treasure. Maybe I have."

Stacy and Cecile beamed.

"Oh, before I forget," Stacy said. "Mark your calendar for next Thursday night. You're going to Simona's bachelorette party. I'm closing shop, and we're going to celebrate. You should be done with class by five. Gives you plenty of time to get here before we leave at eight."

"Stacy hired a competitor known for their hunky drivers," Jade said. "It will be a fun night. A lot more laughs than what's in store tonight with the football players."

"But this gig definitely pays better."

Roxy turned to where a strawberry-blonde woman walked toward the carousel locker and opened the door.

"There's our bride-to-be now. And she's right. Everyone should do okay this evening, just keep your eye on the prize. No penalties, no fouls. Players shuttled to and from safely and sanely," Stacy emphasized.

"Simona, you're riding with me on the way out," Cecile said. "Roxy, our new hire, is with Jade."

"Pleased to meet you." Roxy extended her hand. "And congratulations on your upcoming wedding."

Simona gave her a strong shake. "Wedding. That sounds stuffy and staid. I'm all about the party afterward." A twinkle of light danced from her blue eyes.

"You two can catch up later," Stacy directed. "Start getting ready. We can't be late picking up those running backs and tight ends," she joked. "And Roxy…"

"Yes?"

"Those fellas are gonna love your shoes."

Roxy looked down at her feet realizing the orange high heels didn't pinch her toes the way they had an hour earlier.

Could the shoes be magical like ruby red slippers and transport her to an enchanted land of tailored clothing, spa-like surroundings, and people who genuinely cared?

So far, her new job seemed less like work and more like going on vacation with great friends.

Sam's leaving may have been the best thing that had happened to her in years.

Chapter Eleven

Later that night, Roxy leaned across the rolled-down privacy partition at the front of the VIP bus, peppering Jade with questions as she drove through the busy city streets. She had many concerns about procedures, protocols, and rules of conduct. What insider information could Jade impart that would get Roxy through the next four to five hours unscathed?

Jade maneuvered the bus with ease around bicyclists, pedestrians, and old men who wouldn't survive the day if their mini coupe couldn't cut off a bus and beat Jade to the red light. Roxy only hoped to someday imitate Jade's skill, patience, and grace.

You can't teach this skill in any driving school. This was innate.

"Basically, we're shuttling a bunch of guys to a frat party," Roxy said. "I've never worked a large group, much less thirty guys with testosterone off the charts. I had a rowdy bunch of ladies celebrating a fortieth birthday once. They threw their bras out the window while we cruised down the 405. Guessing this will be something like that but magnified."

"Kinda, sorta, but hey, it's not all bad." Jade sounded confident. "Sure, they'll be blowing off steam. You'll hear some, shall I say, inappropriate language and witness some crazy stuff. All harmless, for the most part. The important thing is to set the tone. Yes, you're driving a party bus. Yes, this is a fun way to travel, but we're not running a bacchanal."

That's an odd comparison: drunken revelry, sexual experimentation, and wild music.

"I'm worried I'll blow the whole deal. That I'm not up to the task, at least not until I get more training," Roxy confessed.

"You are up to this. Hell, Roxy, from what Stacy says, you broke barriers no other woman could," Jade said over her shoulder, keeping her focus on the road.

"Stacy's memory of me might be exaggerated. The way I used to be. The way she'd still like for me to be. A lot of years have passed since then," Roxy admitted.

"Well, I don't know you from Eve, but I see those same bad-ass-woman-in-charge qualities already. The way you take command of a situation. You have a calming effect without the stuffy Debbie Downer fingerprint." Jade pulled into the semicircular hotel driveway and parked behind Cecile's bus.

"That's nice of you to say, but—"

Jade unbuckled her seat belt and turned to face Roxy. "You got this, girl. Otherwise, Stacy wouldn't have hired you, and she wouldn't have sent you on this high-profile run."

"I suppose."

"Here's my mantra: Breathe in. Knockers out. Smiles on."

Roxy snickered.

"Let's do this." Jade pushed the button to open the passenger entrance door before climbing out of the driver's side.

Roxy waited for her to circle around the vehicle. The pair walked toward Cecile and Simona, already standing on the curb, deep in conversation with a man holding a clipboard. Moments later, the four women stationed themselves by the bus seconds before a brawny army of young men poured through the hotel's revolving door and herded toward them.

"Well, if it isn't my beautiful Jade," said a wiry player, his head covered in dreadlocks, lifting her hand to kiss. "Gem of my heart. Jade, girl, you know I'm riding with you, lovely." He adjusted his crotch in a way that made Roxy wonder if his personals were too large to fit his *chonies*.

"Good to see you, Leonard. I expect you to be the gentleman tonight." Jade licked her lips as though to soften the warning. "Show these rookies how to behave."

"Ab. So. Lutely," Leonard replied. "You be the lady. I be the gentleman."

"Come on, man, get your ass on the bus." Another player shoved him in the back. "I have a date with a plate of lasagna, and you're in my way."

Roxy craned her neck to see the speaker, but instead of seeing another football player, she saw Sam, looking disheveled and frantic, standing off to the side. She blinked, and he was gone.

Startled, Roxy rose on her tiptoes for a better view but whoever had been there had disappeared.

Sam? It couldn't be. Sam was in Tennessee, not Hollywood.

Convinced she was imagining things, Roxy shuffled forward toward the bus with the crowd, sweeping Leonard along with them.

Minutes later, Jade stood at the head of the vehicle. "Welcome, Portland Pythons!" Jade shouted, her enthusiasm a little over the top for Roxy's taste.

Is she really jazzed to be driving these fellas? Will they each tip separately? She doubted it. Most looked like this might be their first trip away from home.

Jade continued, "This is Roxy Adams. She'll be assisting in the coach, while I'm driving."

Roxy waved.

"Hey, mama," a deep voice boomed from the back. "Didn't I see you on season three of *MILF Manor*?"

Roxy blushed and slunk behind Jade. *Oh God, here we go. Age jokes.*

"Knock that stuff off, Drayton," Jade scolded.

"I was giving the babe a compliment," he continued, punching the guy sitting next to him. Laughter filled the space.

"Oh, so funny." Jade returned to her spiel. "At this time of day, the ride over to Mama Luigi's will be around thirty minutes. I'm counting on you fellas to be on your best—"

That was when a cone-shaped boob attached to a life-sized inflatable woman smacked Jade on the side of the face. The blonde blow-up doll, arms akimbo, had been launched from the back of the bus.

"For Christ's sake!" Jade bellowed.

An assistant coach, the same guy Roxy had seen with the clipboard earlier, untangled the plastic lady from where Jade stood and grabbed her microphone. He turned to face the crew. "Okay, guys, let's give Jade a round of applause."

An apathetic ovation rose, as the sound of beer cans popping and beverages pouring flowed in the background. "And she has Miss…" He held his hand over the mic. "What's your name again?" he whispered.

"Roxy."

"Miss Roxy to keep you comfortable and coherent. It's a short drive to pasta and Peronis. I know you all can behave yourselves for that long." He handed the mic to Roxy, as though turning control over to her.

Jade smiled, then mouthed *you got this* before making her escape to the driver's seat, where she'd be safely ensconced behind the now rolled-up privacy screen.

Roxy clutched the microphone like a lifeline, combing her brain for something to say.

A few men gathered at the wet bar near the rear of the bus, the strobe lights adding to their festive mood. Apparently, a teammate had linked his phone to the sound system and a crash of cymbals, alternating with synthesized bass and snare drums, blared from every speaker.

"Hey, Miss Foxy, can you toss Jolene my way?" a bald player shouted from the back.

"Can I do what?" she asked, barely able to hear him over the noise.

"Jolene. You know—the blowup doll."

She has a name?

"Oh, of course," Roxy said. She couldn't let these bozos get to her. Not on her first run. Roxy had faced rude and rowdy customers, both as a chauffeur and while serving at the food truck. She could handle this.

None of them had ever launched a naked, vinyl life-size woman in her direction, though.

"Can you pass her to that young man?" she asked the nearest player, pointing at him with Jolene's head.

"Guess so," he replied. "But not before I get a dance."

"Man, Jones. Gotta show off all the damn time. Give me the doll," Baldy demanded.

"Can't you see we're in love?" Jones insisted, swirling in place, Jolene tightly in his arms.

"Put some clothes on that broad," another player shouted.

"Wish my girlfriend's tits looked that good."

"Get a better girlfriend," Jones said, still gyrating with the doll.

"When I do, I'll give you my ex's number, since you like teacup-size titties."

A Portland Pythons jersey came flying through the air, and Roxy ducked.

Leonard picked up the shirt from the ground. "Here, put this on her. Cover her ass, at least. Maybe later she'll dance on the stripper pole in the back."

"Remember the time we snuck that exotic dancer onto the bus?" Jones asked no one in particular.

"Remember!? That was one of the best birthday parties y'all ever threw for me!" Leonard proclaimed.

"Until Lolita smacked you in the head with a vodka bottle," Baldy said. "Told you three times to keep your hands to yourself, but you didn't listen. Now we're stuck with plastic instead of the real thing."

"It's important that everyone understand the safety—" Roxy yelled above the music as Jade slammed on the brakes, lurching the bus to a sudden stop, and pitching Roxy forward, nearly knocking her off her feet.

"Oh, God!" she screeched.

Jade lowered the privacy screen. "Everyone OK?"

"We're cool," Leonard answered.

Baldy peered out the front windshield. "What the f… Jones… Jonesy, isn't that your old lady?"

"You mean Sheila? Nah. She's back in Oregon," Jones answered.

"Sure looks like her, down to those fake Goldilocks curls and leopard-skin tights," the bald player said, Jolene still in his grip. "Hand me a beer, Leonard. Things are about to get interesting."

Through the tinted windows on the back of the bus, Roxy took in the line of cars piling up behind them. In a few seconds, horns would begin a loud, angry serenade. Roxy struggled to remain calm. She lowered the see-through partition enough to hear Jade arguing with the woman Baldy had described, asking her to move out of the way.

Sadly, the leopard-skin clad woman wasn't convinced.

Finally, Jade asked, "Uh, Jonesy, can you pop your head through the partition? Seems there's a young lady interested in seeing you."

"Ah, shit," Jones said, realizing Sheila was causing the delay. "Girl, move your ass out of the way!"

"She wants to have a word with you," Roxy managed. "Perhaps you can convince her to step out of the street and onto the sidewalk where we can straighten things out."

"You hear that, Sheila? Get out of the street. We'll pull the bus over," Jones directed. "You crazy bitch." That part he said under his breath, but loud enough for Roxy to hear.

"What did you do to get her riled up?" Roxy asked.

"You women take everything serious. I mean, hey, a little flirting, and the next thing I know, she's getting fitted for a wedding gown," Jones explained. "I'm not ready to walk down no aisle and definitely not with that space case."

Roxy *tsked* him. "You jilted her?"

"Not really. But she's gonna tell a different story."

"Jones, get this settled and fast," the assistant team manager said, panic seeping out in every direction. Roxy heard the guys call him Alvin and since he resembled a chipmunk, she wondered if Alvin was his real name or a moniker the team had bestowed upon him.

Jones shifted toward the bifold doors, but before he could exit, his ex girlfriend stormed up the steps. A moment later, she whacked him with an uppercut to his chin.

Someone taught that girl self-defense. That was a clean hit.

Jones pulled his arms up to shield his face as Sheila continued punching, landing a good one here and there. Finally, two players subdued her. "What are you doing?" Baldy asked. "You need to calm down, girl. Just calm down."

"He's a son-of-a-bitch!" Sheila shouted. "All love and romance until he has to stand up and be a man."

Jones licked the blood trickling from the corner of his mouth. "I told you last week and last night on the phone, I ain't marrying you. I like you fine, but that's as far as it goes."

Sheila hauled off with a roundhouse punch, but Jones ducked in time, causing the woman to tumble, falling onto a nearby bench seat.

"Sweetie," Roxy said, infusing a serene tone. "I know how it feels to think you're in a committed relationship and then find out you're not. It sucks—big time. But beating the crap out of the dude isn't going to make him want to be with you."

Roxy scooted next to her, draping an arm around the woman whose fury and rage was deflating. Sheila slumped, now a puddle of sorrow and embarrassment.

"How do *you* know?" Sheila barked, reaching for anger that dissipated into the air.

"I'm a little older than you. I've seen a few things."

"Yeah? Like what?" Sheila grunted.

Roxy inhaled, debating whether she should meet this girl where she just landed—on the intersection of hurt and despair. Roxy had resided on that corner for the past several weeks and wouldn't have listened to anyone telling her anything. Still, she had to try.

"Look, Sheila, I lived with and loved this guy for fifteen years. About a month ago, he up and moved in with his not-quite-ex-wife. Cleaned out our bank account and left me to fend for myself."

"Damn," Sheila said, swiping at her running mascara.

"And you know what? He did me the biggest favor of my life. Everything is better without that asshole. And—trust me when I say this—you will be much better without Jones. There's the perfect person out there for you. And if you're spending all your time worrying about this chump"—she hooked a thumb in Jones's direction—"you'll never find the right guy."

Sheila gulped and hiccupped at the same time.

"Someday, you'll feel joy in your heart, and you'll know." Roxy looked up to see Jade standing in the door well. "Go with our driver, Jade. She'll call you a cab and make sure you get home safe."

The woman nodded, blonde curls bouncing with every shake. "I know you're right. I-I couldn't let him drop me like I was... I don't know. Like I wasn't worthy."

Roxy slowed her delivery. "Sheila, you *are* worthy. And gorgeous. And strong and smart. Too smart for this fool. You already know that, though."

Sheila shook her head and accepted a tissue from Alvin. Roxy stood, waiting to guide Sheila toward Jade and, hopefully, on to a better future.

Before leaving the coach, Sheila turned, raised her hand, and flipped Jones the bird. She exited to the cheers of every player on the bus.

Roxy sighed inwardly. *Some days you're a driver, some days a therapist.* If she could handle this group and their insanity, she could handle anything.

She would keep telling herself that until it was true.

Chapter Twelve

With stomachs full of carbs and chianti, an artificial calm took over the inside of the bus. Roxy took in the sleepy football team. Even with Cecile having to circle back and pick up a missing team member, making the return trip back to the hotel take nearly twice as long, the ride resonated with a mellow and relaxed vibe.

Once underway, for the second time, a brief skirmish broke out over the music selection. Roxy hooked her playlist to the vehicle's sound system and Motown tunes filled the air.

No one complains when listening to rhythm and blues.

This bus's Jolene, christened Flora, garnered little attention. With a full head of painted-on dark brown curls, she slumped discarded against the side of a bench seat, while a few players tossed Velcro darts at a target with their Sunday opponent's logo in the bull's-eye. Minus a complaint about stocking the wrong brand of vodka and a drink crashing to the floor, the journey was uneventful.

Roxy and Cecile returned the party bus to the yard, and Roxy drove home, reaching her front door well after midnight. She could hardly wait to collapse in her bed. The evening had been exhaustingly long and mentally challenging. Her feet ached as though clamped in matching vise grips for the past six hours. What few gray cells she had functioning earlier were rapidly draining of power.

In the interest of getting home quickly, she and Cecile hadn't changed out of their uniforms. She unfastened her shoes and took great care to hang her expertly tailored suit on the wardrobe pole in her closet before stripping off her underwear and shimmying into a nightgown.

Not bothering to wash her face or remove her makeup, Roxy fell forward, landing face-first in the middle of her bed and quickly fell asleep without getting under the covers. The jolting image of Sam, his hands in his pockets, shirt collar up, eyes peering at her, faded. Had she truly seen him, or was her mind showing her what she wanted to see?

In what felt like minutes later, a *chirp, chirp, chirp* from her phone startled Roxy awake. She rooted about to see the clock. *It couldn't be morning already.* But it was. *Ten-thirty.* She wiped sleep from her eyes and answered.

Alma wanted to try a new place for early brunch.

"Can you be ready in thirty?" Alma asked.

Roxy yawned and weighed her options. *Go back to sleep and waste a day off or get back into the world, starting with brunch.*

"They have killer Bloody Marys," Alma wheedled. "But in full disclosure, the restaurant is a new advertiser. My boss wants me to try their cuisine. Great PR, he said. Will you go?"

Roxy walked to her bathroom sink, now fully awake. "Of course. I can't fall back to sleep now, anyway. But can you give me forty-five minutes?"

A little over an hour later, the two curled into a booth in the back of the Americana-style restaurant, sipping the best Bloody Mary Roxy had ever tasted, with candied bacon and a rim coated with *tajín*. The perfect mixture of sweet and spicy.

"It won't be hard for you to talk up this place on air," Roxy teased, hoisting her nearly empty glass. "I'm ready for a second."

"You go ahead, girl. I'm driving. Not often a chauffeur gets chauffeured," Alma added, laughing at her own joke.

"On Monday I start those commercial driving classes." Roxy traced the rim of the glass with her tongue, coaxing a bit more zing to accompany the final few watered-down sips waiting in the bottom of the glass. "Not sure if I'm up to this gig at this point in my life."

"Are you kidding?" Alma argued. "From what you said, you handled those jocks with minimal effort. Got everyone to where they needed to be safe, sound, and entertained. Roxy, you are the goddess of control. And you don't even know it."

"Last night seemed more like babysitting. I couldn't let the kids overtake the playground. And when I witnessed the grief of that poor woman, Sheila... Well, I knew I had to help her, and you know what? Talking to her helped me, too.

"I deserve better than how Sam treated me. He ended things in such a mean, matter-of-fact way. Looking back, he started changing maybe six, eight months ago. I didn't recognize the signs. You know, relationships go through stages. I thought whatever was wrong, we could ride out. How naïve I was."

Roxy's phone buzzed. Without wanting to interrupt their conversation, she unzipped her purse and tilted the phone to read the screen. "Well, what do you know."

"What?" Alma asked, signaling the waitress to replenish Roxy's drink.

"Another call from Sam."

"Has he been calling you? What does he want?"

"I have no idea," Roxy said, pushing down the anxiety creeping along her throat. "I thought I saw him last night standing near the pickup spot for the football team."

"You thought you saw Sam?" Alma asked, incredulous.

"Crazy, right? The man is two thousand miles away. And anyway, how would he know where I would be?" Once again, she wondered if Sam might be in some kind of trouble. "Maybe this is the next stage of breakup grief—seeing things," Roxy dismissed.

Alma agreed. "Probably just someone who looks like Sam. He doesn't stand out in a crowd, you know."

Roxy closed the zipper and moved her purse behind her. "Maybe not. Either way, I don't want to talk to him. And he never leaves a message. Whatever he wants won't be good for me. I've got to make a clean break, move my life forward. I'm questioning, though, if driving again is the right move. At least driving these bigger vehicles."

"Can't you talk to what's-her-name?"

"Stacy?"

"Yeah, Stacy," Alma continued. "Tell her how you feel. Maybe you can drive the smaller parties and help out on these larger groups instead of driving."

Roxy pondered this for a moment. Earning her commercial license would stretch her talents and provide her skills she didn't currently have. Was Stacy challenging her to leave her comfort zone? Or did she and Cecile really need another commercially licensed driver?

"They've done so much for me already. I don't want to let them down and maybe let myself down." Roxy sat a little straighter against the padded booth. "I need to do this or find out that I can't. Come tomorrow morning, this old gal is going back to school."

Alma raised her hand for a high five.

Roxy slapped Alma's palm as the waitress set another Bloody Mary in front of her.

Alma lifted her half-full glass to clink against Roxy's. "To higher education."

Roxy took a sip. "To brighter days."

Chapter Thirteen

Not wanting to be late to her first day of school, Roxy left home thirty minutes early. No way would she fall victim to LA traffic, lane closures, and freeway snarls again.

She pulled into the lot and gazed at the endless string of industrial buildings populating this side of town. Since she wasn't expected to check in at the registration desk for fifteen minutes, Roxy scrambled out of the car and took in the loading docks to her left, buzzing with warehouse employees and forklifts. She spun around to look behind her at the rows of diesel trucks lining the backside of the lot.

Will I be driving one of those behemoths?

To her right, a commercial garage spread out across four oversized bays, all full. She gaped at a semi balanced on a hydraulic lift as a technician replaced a missing front tire. Next to the building was a graveyard littered with truck parts and engines in what appeared to be various states of repair dotting the land.

This is where old Peterbilts go to die.

"Pretty amazing," a male voice interrupted her thoughts. "How do they get thirty-five thousand pounds of metal off the ground? I wouldn't want to be under one of them checking the oil."

"Me neither. Not even sure I want to learn how to drive one," Roxy quipped.

The young man inhaled. "I know what you mean, but they're paying truckers a ton these days, and if I want to move out of my parents' house as much as they want me to, I'll be pushing one of those guys around the streets soon. I'm Jason," he said, extending his hand.

"Roxy Adams."

"Are you enrolled here, too?" he asked.

"Uh. Yes." She looked at her watch, realizing that being early could now make her late. Reaching inside her car, she grabbed her purse and closed the door. "We better get moving," she said over her shoulder, hurrying toward the *Friendly Roads Driving Academy* sign. "You coming?"

"Right behind you."

Roxy guessed most of the students would be like Jason, intending to become licensed long-haul truckers or construction vehicle drivers. She had no desire to operate either. She was strictly interested in the consumer side, the fun side of the transportation business. Sadly for Roxy, because of their size and larger occupancy, operating a party bus required a commercial driver's license.

To keep this job, Roxy needed the training to step into Cecile's shoes if needed and be able to drive a bus full of halfbacks and defensive linemen to the stadium and not take any guff. Simply speaking, being the best limo driver wasn't enough. She needed to operate a party bus as capably as chauffeur a bride to her wedding, with equal skill, class, and efficiency.

Checking in at the front desk, she asked for directions to the CDL class. Roxy ignored the shocked expression—no, the pity and disbelief—that painted the young girl's face. Her long red fingernail, as red as the girl's hair, pointed her toward the hall. A *tsk-tsk* followed Roxy as she headed in that direction, as if to say *What's an old woman like you want with being a trucker?* The same question bounced around Roxy's mind.

"Don't pay her no mind," Jason said, jutting his chin in the direction of the teenybopper receptionist. "Look, I'm going to hit the head, I mean, the bathroom. See you inside."

"Okay." Roxy watched his back as he trotted in the opposite direction.

She entered the cavernous classroom and gasped.

God, I'm back in high school Driver's Ed.

To her amazement, before her stood individual driving modules—two to a row, three rows deep. Each station, outfitted to appear like the inside of a truck cab, seemed like a video game one might find inside an arcade. Her eyes widened.

Whoa, state-of-the-art simulators.

She cautiously walked around the room, searching for a classmate or an instructor, but there wasn't a soul anywhere.

Where were the other students?

With all the glee of a teenager who scored her mother's keys to the family sedan for the first time, Roxy slid behind the steering column of the simulator in the far corner. She examined the three HD displays surrounding her; the screens appeared to create real-world conditions. Roxy reached for the gear shift and pushed down on the clutch. The video monitor sprang to life, and she nearly leaped off the seat.

"Hey there, little lady. Don't jump the gun. Class don't start for another fifteen minutes."

A tall-drink-of-water of a man with graying temples approached her. He was wearing a green plaid flannel shirt tucked into his stone-washed jeans that clung to all the right spots. He pressed a toothpick between his teeth the same way she held straight pins while she sewed.

Roxy didn't want to stare, but she did anyway. This man was gorgeous, spelled with a capital G. She half expected to be the only female in the class, but she knew she'd be the oldest until she saw this guy. Career choices for women had expanded during the past two decades. She was no longer the exception, the lodestar she once was. And now she wondered if she'd still be the most mature pupil.

Her classmates would be young bucks, fresh out of high school with something to prove.

Or worse, guys who had flunked out of college, after realizing the only thing they were good at was beer pong. Maybe a thirty-something making a career change might round out the student body. This heavenly hunk of a man was easily in his fifties, and he wore his age well. He had nothing to prove, no parents yelling at him to get a job. He must be the teacher, she decided.

"Oh." She clambered out of the seat, catching the toe of her sneaker on the raised platform and nearly toppled.

He reached his arms out, caught her by the waist, and lifted her slightly before setting her feet on the floor. "You okay?"

"Yes. Of course." Roxy dusted off her jeans and regained her composure, although she wasn't sure if the near fall, or being caught by an angel, made her legs rubbery. "The front of my sole got caught on the side. Guess I'm a little eager to get started."

"I understand. Alex Montgomery, pleased to meet you." He extended his hand forward, his gold wedding ring glinting.

"Roxy Adams," she responded, surprised at how easily she had kept the disappointment out of her voice. "Looking forward to taking your course."

"My course?" he questioned.

Before answering, Roxy turned to see a handful of folks enter the room. Her long-awaited classmates.

The high school grad. *Check.*

The college burnout. Oops, there were two. *Double-check.*

Her friend, the Gen Zer in search of meaning, returning from the restroom. *Check.*

A youngish woman with short red hair and a tattoo sleeve of roses and sunshine entered last, wearing a brilliant smile to match. *Didn't have her on my bingo card.*

Finished with sizing up her classmates, Roxy turned to where Alex stood, waiting for him to address the class and direct them to the simulators.

"Welcome to Friendly Roads Driving Academy. Such a corny name."

Roxy spun around as the tattooed woman spoke.

"I'm Rita Penn, your instructor. From what I've seen in my paperwork, everyone except..." She thumbed through the sheets on her clipboard. "Roxy Adams is here for their Class A Commercial license. Roxy, you're the rowdy one... only needing a P endorsement to add to your Class C for you to drive party buses, am I right?"

"I'm a limo driver," Roxy quickly added, embarrassed at being spotlighted and doubly embarrassed at assuming Alex was the teacher. She slid her gaze at him in apology. He leveled a smirk, acknowledging her mistake.

"The rest of you fools want to drive tractor-trailers and flatbeds," Rita verified.

"Well, not anymore," Jason said. "I want to be rowdy with Roxy."

"Me, too," Alex seconded. Her classmates tittered their agreement.

"All right, everyone can be rowdy with Roxy later," Rita admonished. "For now, let's get to work."

As the small group moved toward their modules, Alex whispered, "Looks like you've formed a fan club. Roxy's Rowdies."

Roxy turned to see his bright smile, and her legs went weak. *A fan club.*

Maybe these next few weeks wouldn't be as dull as she had thought.

Chapter Fourteen

The first week of instruction went smoothly, due to Roxy's ease at book learning. The modules made understanding the safety and operating procedures seamless. Stacy had checked in with her on Tuesday to hear about the class, and Roxy happily reported that, with each hour of instruction, her confidence grew.

The part she didn't say out loud was her self-assurance lasted as long as the big rigs remained stationary.

Stacy reminded Roxy of Simona's party in two days and then reviewed the weekend schedule. Friday night, she'd be on prom duty—always exciting, but usually stressful shuttling a car full of unchaperoned teens. The following Saturday, she'd be driving a young boy and his family to a Hollywood movie premiere as part of a charity event.

Years ago, Star-Struck Limo had donated services to worthy causes like this wish-granting charity. Apparently, Stacy continued the tradition she and Bobby generously originated. Roxy had enjoyed those assignments, bringing joy into the lives of people struggling with critical illnesses or other life-altering catastrophes.

By Thursday, things switched quickly from theory to the real world. Roxy and her five classmates, now known as the Rowdies, were up to their elbows in engine grease as Rita instructed them on vehicle maintenance.

"We have a few slightly used jumpsuits, but stains sometimes seep through," Rita mentioned earlier in the week. "I've ruined too many of my best jeans by relying on coveralls. My advice is don't make my mistake. Wear clothes you don't care about. And ladies, save that manicure appointment for later."

Roxy found herself excited to learn the inner workings of buses and trucks. During her years of driving limos, she had done little more than gas up the vehicle and tell the maintenance staff if something was awry.

She took pride in the aesthetics, the stuff that would awe her clients. On the outside, her car gleamed in the sunshine. On the inside, unique decorations to celebrate a Tuscan-themed sixtieth birthday or a bachelorette party. What happened under the hood had remained a mystery she had happily left unsolved.

Today, though, as Rita explained each engine part, Roxy took on a new appreciation for the wonder of machinery, the innovators who created the mechanisms, and the folks who kept the pistons churning.

The class split into two groups and huddled on each side of the semi, leaning in over the popped hood. Roxy peered at the nest of wires and metal as Rita droned on, comparing a diesel truck engine to a gasoline-powered one. "They both have pistons, a cylinder block and head, a crankshaft," Rita continued.

Roxy's thoughts drifted away. Science had always interested her and, at the same time, confused her. *Pistons move up and down, valves open and close.*

"This goes over my head," Alex whispered, bending over her shoulder.

Roxy jumped, nearly falling off the stepstool Rita had supplied her. With one hand around her waist and the other on her arm, Alex steadied her. "If I wanted to be an auto mechanic, I would have signed up for that class," he continued.

Roxy turned, immediately frozen by Alex's deep green eyes, brought out by the emerald-colored polo shirt he wore. *Wearing our throw-away clothes, are we?*

"I've never seen a limo engine either," Roxy said, regaining her composure. "Still, it's a good idea to be familiar with the vehicle's components, don't you think?"

"You're right, of course," Alex said. "It's just that I'm more interested in driving the trucks, not learning what drives them. Know what I mean?"

"I do." The answer came from Rita, not Roxy. "Y'all will have time to discuss what we learned today. Right now, I need ears on, mouths off."

Roxy widened her eyes, feeling like a five-year-old scolded by the kindergarten teacher. She turned back to the exposed engine without a word. A half hour later, Rita called for a break. Roxy hurried toward the restrooms, not needing the facilities, but needing to separate from the group.

Alex caught her just as she reached to push open the swinging door. "Sorry I got us in trouble with Ms. Penn there. I thought we might get sent to the principal's office," Alex said, adding a chuckle.

"Things did feel like elementary school. Notes being sent home to Mom and all that," Roxy admitted, feeling lighter than she had in months. She didn't need to be stone-face-serious all the time. Levity, perhaps an infusion of reality, balanced the demanding scales. Yin and Yang.

Could Alex be a handsome ballast to her swaying boat?

"Hey, I know you're wanting to..." Alex jutted his head as if pointing at the *WOMEN* sign on the door. "Wondered if maybe you'd be available for a cup of coffee or drinks, if you drink. Or, well, dinner?"

"Tonight?" Roxy said.

"Yes," Alex said. "Do you have to work?"

"No, it's not that."

"Oh, sure. I understand. Just thought I'd ask." Alex tilted his head to the side as though looking for a dignified escape.

"I don't mean to be nosy, but you're wearing a wedding ring. I'm guessing Mrs. Alex wouldn't like you inviting female students to coffee."

Alex looked down at his hand and immediately twisted his wedding band. "You're right there. Becky wouldn't like that even a little bit."

"Well, then." Roxy turned on her heel and pushed open the restroom door. "I'll see you back in class."

"Before you go... well, I don't mean *go*. You know what I mean. Anyway, I don't want you to get the wrong idea. I've been alone for nearly two years. I've worn this for thirty-seven years." He raised his hand to display the ring. "Thirty-five of them were with Becky. The ring is a part of me. I'd feel incomplete without it on my finger."

Releasing the door, Roxy turned back and stepped toward Alex but remained silent.

"Been trying to change my life, ya know. Do some new things, meet new people. My kids say I can't sit home forever," Alex said.

Roxy nodded, wondering if she misread this man, or if he was spinning a line as long as the Nile. She couldn't tell if he was sincere or feeding her a line of crap.

"You lost your wife?"

"It's a long story. One I'd be willing to share over coffee if you're interested."

"How's Monday?" she blurted before putting her hand over her mouth, attempting to recall the words.

Roxy sensed that Alex left a lot unsaid—and what he wasn't saying made her uneasy.

Chapter Fifteen

"Roxy!" Stacy shouted from the door well of the bus. "Get in here! We're about to leave."

Roxy scurried to Stacy, surprised at the deep excitement in the woman's voice. *You would think this was her bachelorette party, not Simona's.*

"Let me introduce you to Herb," Stacy said, standing alongside two men, both taller than her. "He'll ride with us in the coach. He's crowd control, like you were for Cecile and Jade."

"Pleased to meet you." Roxy took in a handsome young man. Herb's six-foot frame was clad in a green, gold, and black plaid kilt. Under an open waistcoat, a black T-shirt clung to his muscled chest. From a leather strap cinched around his waist, a fur pouch hung near his crotch. Completing the look, knee-high socks held up by matching garters. Herb apparently took his role seriously.

A second man, attired in a kilt as well, stepped forward extending his hand. "Hank," he said. "I'll be driving you ladies tonight. Stacy told me a lot about you."

"She has, has she?" Roxy turned to Stacy and smirked. Hank appeared older than Herb and perhaps two inches taller. His kilt was paired with a tuxedo jacket, sans shirt. Roxy wondered what Stacy's connection was to these two fellows.

This couldn't be the standard set-up for a bachelorette party. Could it?

Cecile joined the group. "Hey, Roxy, glad you're here. This will be fun, especially since Hank and Herb are testing their new idea.

Stace and I said we'd be willing guinea pigs, even though, well you know…"

"It's not our thing," Stacy supplied, "but we're always ready to help a fellow chauffeur out. These guys are introducing a Scottish theme to their regular bachelorette package. This might be big," she said, more to Hank and Herb than to Roxy.

"Well, that explains the kilts," Roxy said. "They provide the entertainment as well as the transportation?"

"Sort of," Hank replied. "We want to streamline planning an extraordinary evening."

"And make it easier to expand your bank balance," Cecile joked.

"That, too. None of us do this for free. Sincerely, we want your opinion later tonight after you've experienced the concept. The good, the bad, any suggestions to improve the product."

"I'll be happy to share my thoughts," Roxy agreed. She wondered what the price point for this party would be. The bill for most bachelor and bachelorette parties were footed by the best man or the maid of honor, usually not by people with money to burn. Still, she'd keep an open mind. If what they were selling was a one-stop shop, they might have a winner.

"Come inside," Herb said as Roxy stepped onto the party bus. The leather wraparound seating and the song "Oh, I Wanna Dance with Somebody" blared from the surround sound speakers, welcoming her. LED and laser lights flashed along the seats, leading Roxy's gaze to where ladies gathered near two stocked bars. She couldn't get close enough to tell exactly what the bars were stocked with, but she did spy a tray of sandwiches and scones nearby.

Clearly, Hank and Herb were preplanning to soak up too much alcohol from the partiers.

The interior had been transformed into an enchanted land. Rustic wood slices dotted the surfaces, a set of bagpipes occupied one corner, and what Roxy guessed to be an overstuffed Scottish sheep—complete with a thick, shaggy coat, coiled horns, and extra-long lashes—filled the other corner. The animal was so realistic, Roxy thought she heard it bleat.

Near a hanging tartan plaid tapestry, giving the impression of a Scottish castle, a Scottish lass braided hair into Celtic knots. A few women had already lined up for the experience.

Roxy had anticipated a small affair with Stacy, Cecile, Jade, and Margo rounding out Simona's guest list. She mistakenly believed this evening doubled as a team-building opportunity with a chance to enjoy a party bus as a client, maybe even spy on the competition.

Instead, she was involved in market-testing and now meeting several women probably two decades her junior.

She studied the interior. The space allowed for the twelve or so ladies to fit easily and act as if they hadn't been let out in years. The twenty-to-thirty-somethings wore dresses so tight Roxy immediately thought of sausage casings, their cleavage overflowing and booties cupped with barely enough fabric to keep them covered.

What surprised her most was the life-sized blow-up dude doll reclining in the back near the bar. She later learned Simona had christened him *Scottie*. Wearing only a tam o'shanter, Scottie was the target for the ladies to fling oversized wedding rings at his inflated erection, while holding a cocktail in the other hand. *What was it with party buses and blow-up dolls?*

The first stop was wine tasting and appetizers, with a local winemaker pouring the selections, including one imported for the evening from the Fife region north of Edinburgh.

Dinner was a fifteen-minute ride away, just enough time for Herb to pass through the bus, refill drinks, and check on the guests. By then, bored with toying with the inflatable, the women took turns at flipping the hem worn by a real Scotsman. Herb played along, admonishing the ladies that the rumors were true; Scottish men didn't wear anything underneath their kilts.

But he certainly did.

After dinner, the bride led the revelers singing oldies at the restaurant's dueling piano bar before reboarding the bus to drop in at a country-western saloon for line dancing. The whole event ran five hours, start to finish. Herb and Hank had done their homework, partnering with nearby establishments that provided a good time, on time.

By midnight, the guests were home safely, each promising a detailed review posted on their social media accounts for H and H within the week. All except for Roxy, who didn't "do" social media.

Before falling asleep, she jotted down her impressions to pass along to the guys, grateful for this fun night of distraction. *There is life after Sam, and it's pretty darn good.*

Chapter Sixteen

Roxy slept in the next morning, a welcome break from having to be at the driving school by eight a.m. all week. When her alarm buzzed at ten, she felt rested and ready to tackle that night's run.

At Stacy's request, she arrived early to decorate the inside of the limo. Cecile provided an ocean of fake diamonds and battery-powered red candles swirled to resemble a blaze, all to match the prom theme, Fire and Ice. She was learning that Cecile and Stacy didn't miss an opportunity to amaze and delight.

Roxy arranged the silver-and-ruby colored goblets and snapped a few photos before heading to Van Nuys to collect eight twelfth graders and play chauffeur/chaperone for the evening.

Some thirty-five years had passed since her own prom at the now-defunct Bateman Gardens where Louise Weldrip discarded her undies in one of the gondolas. For a second, Roxy imagined the flowing teal chiffon dress she wore that night and Les... was that his name?... in a gun-metal gray tuxedo. A slight grin snuck across her lips, recalling him asking her mom for help to pin the orchid corsage onto the bodice of her dress.

These rites-of-passage had definitely evolved since Roxy had been a senior. Still formal, with the fellas providing their dates with a corsage, but the cluster of flowers was attached to the young lady's wrist, not pinned to her non-existent bodice strap. From what Roxy could tell, there was nowhere else to attach the smallest of posies on the wide, bandage-sized dresses of satin and silk. The girls wore strapless tubes that barely covered their bums, complete with heels so high they made Roxy feel as though she were in Mary Janes.

The four couples, with accompanying parents posed for a variety of photos: the girls, the boys, the couples, individually, and as a group. The last picture taken featured the parents and younger siblings gathered around the limo parked on the street. Neighborhood looky-loos peeked out of their front doors to witness the pageantry.

Coolers filled with sodas, waters, flat and sparkling as well as juice, provided by Stacy, emphasized the no-alcohol-allowed agreement all parents had signed. Roxy wondered why the kids weren't asked to add their signatures. In a few hours, Roxy would return these teens to this same driveway, safe, sound, and hopefully sober. She prayed the parents' gratitude would translate into generous tips.

That morning, her landlord had left a kind, yet firm message on Roxy's voicemail. *Rent was late. Again.* And because Roxy had paid last month with a post-dated check, Flora now required a cashier's check within the next two days. Otherwise, she'd begin the eviction process.

The chattering group piled into the car, the ladies having a rough time covering their asses, literally, as they climbed aboard First stop was dinner before transporting them approximately fifteen miles to the dance site, a renovated barn on the outskirts of Santa Monica.

Things were calm at the steakhouse, but somehow after dessert and before the dancing started, a bottle of Southern Comfort had made the rounds. The beverages provided by the company became merely mixers to the youngsters. Roxy hadn't frisked anyone before getting into the limo.

Wearing such skimpy dresses, the girls couldn't have smuggled in a tube of lip balm, much less a flask of whiskey, so it had to be the guys. She watched them through her rearview mirror, each gulping down their drinks and gyrating to the music.

Dread seeped along the seams of the evening. Roxy knew she'd be cleaning up puke before the night ended.

Chapter Seventeen

Roxy maneuvered the limo up the winding drive leading to Hasting Ranch. The vista reminded her of a scene from a late-fifties western where the land baron lived behind enormous gates seared with the ranch's cattle brand. As she arrived at the top of the hill, she wasn't disappointed. A large **H** with a stylized **R** were emblazoned into each side of the ornamental ironwork.

A guard opened the gates and waved her through, pointing toward a hillside where an imposing structure, backlit with the sunset, promised enchantment. "After you drop off your guests, park on the mesa adjacent to the barn."

Roxy pulled forward, passing under a metal arch emblazoned with *Welcome to Hasting Ranch*. She finessed the vehicle's long, onyx body alongside other limos jockeying for position in front of the barn. Climbing out of the car, she straightened her jacket and proceeded to open the door. She lifted the handle and yanked, spilling a young fellow to the ground.

"Thank you, ma'am," the freckled face said, as Roxy extended her hand to pull him to his feet. He swayed back and forth.

"Sorry," he apologized. "I was lifting from the inside," he explained, dusting off his suit with both hands. "Guess I don't know my own strength." He extended his elbow to who Roxy presumed was his date. She linked hers with his, and the pair traipsed off toward the lights and the music, giggling along the way. Two by two, the rest of the crew followed behind, none of them any steadier on their feet.

"I'll be right here when your dance is over," Roxy shouted to their backs. One guy waved without turning around. "Maybe I am too old for this work," she muttered to herself. Still, she knew tonight would help cover the rent—that is, if the parents tipped well for returning their babies safely.

She drove the limo to the mesa and parked before turning her attention to resetting the inside of the limo, including clearing out trash. That's when she discovered not one, but three bottles of alcohol. How did they smuggle them in? No way could those skinny guys have hidden that under a tuxedo jacket.

Holding a garbage bag, she tossed plastic cups of partially consumed beverages. So nice of Stacy to provide mixers for these neophyte drinkers. She quickly removed what little was left of the booze and replaced it with an ample supply of soft drinks and bottled water. Pleased, Roxy stuffed the trash bag into the trunk and looked at her watch. Barely five minutes had passed.

She gazed around, taking in the open expanse of the venue. Now she understood why people were drawn to this barn. Hard to believe this unblemished acreage existed near the congestion and tumult that was Los Angeles. A haven of beauty, nature, and serenity that those teenage kids were currently shattering as the night progressed.

A formal dance in a real barn. Roxy grumbled, walking closer to the entrance where she stole a peek inside the rustic building. The barn doors were thrown open offering an inviting view of weathered wood planks lining the walls. Her eyes tracked up to the apex of the ceiling's high slanted roof where a magnificent crystal chandelier hung from the midpoint. The entire space roared to life, ablaze with what appeared to be thousands of candles of varying heights.

"People get married or host all sorts of formal events in barn settings these days," Stacy had told her during her briefing of the assignment. "This country look is in style right now. Very trendy."

Roxy had frowned at her boss. "Chic turns into trouble real quick," she responded, "if the ranch hands lose track of a cow or two. What happens if old Bossie wanders back home before she's supposed to, leaving a trail of patties behind?"

Stacy shrugged her reply and dropped a set of keys in Roxy's hand, perhaps giving up on the lesson. Roxy had been under the impression that this was a working farm. But as she stood on what could double as a wraparound front porch, she realized that, with the possible exception of a field mouse, no livestock had ever set foot inside this *barn*. At least not in this century.

"Hey. There you are."

Startled, Roxy spun around, suddenly eye to eye with Sam. Her legs seemed to disappear as a rock the size of a semi took up residence inside her stomach.

"What are you doing here?" Roxy hissed, hurrying away from the clump of guests, chaperones, and other drivers. Every fiber of her being wanted to scream, to tell him what an asshole he was, and what misery he had put her through. Shout the vilest insults. Pound his chest with her fists for the horror her life had become.

How could he have left her virtually destitute and then show up here like nothing had happened?

Sam followed closely, speaking in an exaggerated whisper. "Doll, you didn't answer my calls. I need to talk to you."

Roxy stopped near a tree, searching for cover from inquisitive eyes. "Not here. Not now. Not ever." Her voice rose with every word. "Go back to Tennessee and volunteer or something. Just get the hell away from me. And don't call me *doll*."

"*Muñeca*, you don't understand," his voice softened. "There's a problem I—"

"I understand all I need to," she said, her hiss now dripping with venom. Until this moment, she hadn't registered how much she despised this man. What he had done to her—leaving with no thought of how she'd make ends meet—could never be forgiven. He could take his problems and shove them somewhere unnatural for all she cared.

She continued walking, noticing faces glaring curiously in their direction.

"Roxy," he pleaded.

She turned on her heel, for the first time truly seeing him. Stubble dotted his face, adding context to his bloodshot eyes and disheveled hair. "How did you know I was here?"

He wiggled the phone in his hand. "Find Friends."

Oh, crap. Was that app still activated?

"Sam, this is my place of work. Work I need to dig out from the black hole you dropped me in. So, before I say what I really think, just leave. You're good at that." Her heart threatened to escape her chest, but she knew she couldn't fall for any of his BS. She was getting her act together. Sam would only derail her.

He grabbed her arm and pulled her to him. "You've got to listen. I'm in real trouble, and I need you to do something."

An insincere laugh bubbled up. "Do something *for you?*" Roxy squirmed away, hardly believing Sam's nerve. She put her hands on her hips. "Tell you what. How about you do something for me, like give back half the money you swiped out of our joint account?"

"I don't have time to discuss that now," Sam hurried on. "What I need—"

"And you think I give a flying flip about what you need? Far as I'm concerned, you can crawl back to wherever you were and drop dead," she shouted, louder than she intended.

"Hey. Hey. Everything okay, Roxy?" A protective hand reached around her waist and pulled her back. It was Hank, this time wearing pants instead of a kilt.

"Everything is fine. Sam was just leaving," Roxy snapped.

"Not until I get a minute with you," Sam protested. "I need your—"

"Look, *Sam.* This woman is on the job. This is a magical night for these kids, and we don't need you bothering people while they're enjoying themselves. We'll have enough trouble once all the whiskey and vodka kicks in. So, my advice. Take your troubles elsewhere. Talk to Roxy another time."

As Sam stalled, other drivers gathered behind Hank and Roxy. "Only going to say this one more time. Dude, hit the bricks," Hank emphasized.

Sam's shoulders slouched. "Roxy, please. You don't understand. I didn't *want* to leave you."

Roxy cast her eyes to the ground. "Do me a favor and just go away, Sam. Go far away."

He finally walked to a parked car, climbed in, and sat for several minutes before starting the engine and driving off.

"Who's that?" Hank asked.

"My ex who thinks he can waltz back and forth and have me bail his ass out of whatever mess he's gotten into."

"Did he threaten you?"

Roxy shrugged.

"Are you afraid of him? I mean, is he the kind of guy who is dangerous? Did he ever hurt you?"

75

"He broke my heart, but I'm getting over that."

"He seemed desperate. Are you protecting yourself?"

Stunned, Roxy stared at Hank. She had never needed protection from Sam. "He'd never hurt me."

Hank shook his head. "These things can escalate. I've seen worse happen. Do you own a gun?"

"No!" Roxy snapped. "I wouldn't know the first thing about having a gun. And I can't conceive that Sam would physically hurt me. But…"

"But what?" Hank prodded.

"He's not acting himself." Roxy recalled the note Sam had left: *Thought I could make this LA thing work, but I was wrong.*

At the time, she trusted their relationship. But they weren't "an LA thing."

What had made Sam act out of character, markedly different from the man she thought she knew?

"You need to defend yourself. If not with a gun, get a baseball bat and keep it nearby. Or a steak knife, although you have to get pretty close to use it," Hank said.

"What are you talking about?"

"Have something ready if this guy comes back. I don't know the dude, but he reeked of desperation."

"You have no idea. Everything about that man is desperation and despair. The kindest thing he ever did was to leave. Now I need him to stay gone. Permanently," Roxy said, puffing herself up with a forced certainty.

"That sounds ominous," Hank said.

Roxy glared. "Take it any way you like. All I know is if Sam shows up again, jerking me around, he won't like my reaction."

"Be smart," Hank finally said. "Notify the cops if he continues to stalk you and let them handle the matter."

Roxy considered this. Could a few phone calls and Sam showing up at her job constitute stalking?

"I hadn't thought about that," she said. "Thank you for being my savior. I don't know how far Sam would have pushed things if you and your friends hadn't appeared."

"Sometimes I wear a cape, other times a kilt," Hank teased. "We *chauffs* have to stick together." He grinned before walking into the darkness where the other male chauffeurs had congregated out of sight, waiting for the prom to end.

As she watched his back disappear into the night, she considered what Hank had said.

Was Sam harassing her? Or was he in trouble like he claimed? She would call Alma tomorrow and get her take.

In the meantime, she needed to prepare for the plastered teenagers who would be pouring out of the barn in the next hour or so. She prayed they were happy drunks, not the belligerent kind when she returned them to their parents.

Chapter Eighteen

By the time Roxy sat across the table from Alex at the Orange Blossom Café on Monday night, the last thing she wanted to talk about was engine maintenance schedules. The six hours in class had dragged on, with more information about pistons and crankshafts than Roxy ever cared to know.

She had insisted they drive separately, even though the school was less than a half-mile away. If things went south, she wouldn't depend on Alex for a lift back to her car.

After about thirty minutes of casual conversation, a slice of pie and a pot of hot tea, Roxy relaxed, sharing the antics of prom night. The same misadventures she had told Alma about, only she didn't mention Sam's surprise visit.

As the minutes ticked by, a long-forgotten twinge she recognized as chemistry spread through her. Could she be romantically attracted to this man? So much in his life mirrored her own.

His wife, Becky, had died. And like Roxy, he was mending his heartbreak by changing careers, altering his life, pretending not to look back—every strategy Roxy found herself implementing.

Reinvention, the new midlife crisis.

A beep from her phone once again interrupted their first date— if sharing a cup of tea together could be called a date. Six missed calls and four messages had come through in the short time she and Alex were together. All were from Sam, except one from Chuck.

Sometime close to nine, Alex walked Roxy to her car and made certain the engine started before he headed to his vehicle. If he wasn't a five-star gentleman, he sure pretended to be. With the motor running, she left the gearshift in park, deciding to listen to her messages. The first one from Sam seemed civil.

"Roxy, I know you don't want to talk to me, and I don't blame you. I'm sorry for hurting you. I have something important—urgent, actually—to tell you. Call me."

The second message, recorded minutes later, reeked of mounting angst.

"Roxy, believe me. This is a matter of life and death. Mine. Call me back, PLEASE."

The third and final message dripped of torment. "I need your help, Roxy. Please. I left a key in the pocket of my blue baseball jacket. It's hanging in our closet. Well, I guess it's your closet now. Please call me when you hear this message. I *need* that key."

Sam's plea echoed despair and resignation, as though he was giving up on a battle he hadn't waged. "Please, please call me. I promise to never bother you again once I get that key."

Roxy turned off the engine and fell against the seatback. The pang in her heart spread through her chest. Could Sam really be in trouble? And why should she help him, especially after the way he had hurt her? Discarding their years together as though tossing a used tissue in the garbage.

She hated the growing worry gnawing at her. Hurt and humiliation aside, the Sam she had loved—still loved—wouldn't have flaked like a teenager with a short attention span. Sam was an in-it-for-the-long-haul type of guy. Predictable, steady. He had never been tempted to try all thirty-one flavors, satisfied with rocky road. He wouldn't have traded her in for another life so easily.

Roxy shook her head. *Nope. Nope. I'm not going backward.* The man clearly needed help, but she'd be damned if she'd be the one to save his ass. Fool me once and all that. Whatever crap he left behind, too bad. He should have taken all his stuff with him when he absconded with her TV, her money, and her heart.

Had she even seen his blue jacket? If she did, it was in her trunk stuffed in a trash bag along with the rest of his faded polos and out-of-style golf shorts. She'd meant to drop those bags off this week but never got around to doing that. Frankly, she'd forgotten the clothes were there at all.

She deleted Sam's messages and listened to Chuck's, barely making sense of his ramblings. From what she could piece together, the new girl wasn't working out. Perhaps she wasn't proficient in after-hour hummers.

"Could you find it in your heart to come back for a shift or two?" Chuck begged, in his ask-don't-ask tone that made Roxy's teeth ache. "I'll pay double your usual rate." Almost as an afterthought, he added, "By the way, have you heard from Sam?"

The nerve of that guy. Roxy swiped across the screen, deleting that message, too, before tossing her phone in her purse and pulling out of the parking lot.

She drove home, imagining the trouble Sam might be in. Life or death? What key could possibly help him with that? Why was he still in LA instead of Tennessee? Was he ever in Tennessee? Why was Chuck interested?

Roxy yawned, both bored and tired with the entire drama. Class began at eight the next morning, giving her barely enough time to start a load of laundry and catch some sleep. Although she would gladly spend time with Alex again. And the bonus: coconut cream pie for dinner.

As she climbed the steps to her apartment and approached her front door, an odd sensation swept over her. She shook off the theatrics, put her key in the lock and turned the knob, instantly realizing it was already unlocked. Pushing the door open, she took one step inside.

Most of her belongings had been rifled through and left strewn across the floor. Nothing appeared broken, but someone had ransacked her house, searching for... what? The key Sam had rambled on about?

Roxy fished her phone out of her purse. She checked her watch and dialed Alma instead of the police. Her DJ friend should be finished with her slot at the radio station by now.

"Are you on your way home?" she said when Alma finally picked up after several rings.

"Well, not exactly," Alma replied, a tint of exasperation in her voice.

"Someone ransacked my apartment."

"What? What are you talking about?" Alma asked, suddenly interested.

"Are you alone?" Roxy asked, hearing a voice in the background.

"I'm... a... I'm on a date, but I can get home in, like, a half hour. Are you okay?"

Roxy hung her head, so wrapped up in her issues, she'd forgotten people have their own lives. "Oh, my God. Alma, I am sorry. It's just that this Sam thing gives me the heebie-jeebies."

"Heebie-jeebies," Alma scoffed. "You old folks sure have colorful language."

"Don't start."

"Are you okay?"

"I'm all right."

"How did they get in? Did they take anything?" Alma asked, panic mounting in her voice.

"The lock on the front door looked jimmied. I can't tell if anything is missing. Most of my stuff is on the floor. God. Damn. Sam."

"You think Sam broke in? Doesn't he have a key?"

"I changed the locks, remember?"

"Oh, yeah. Forgot. Sorry. So Sam tossed your place?" Alma asked.

"Pretty sure."

"Why would he do that?"

"Because it's the only thing he hasn't done to ruin my life," Roxy said. "Like I told you, he's pissed I haven't answered his calls and Friday night when he ambushed me at work, one of the drivers sent him on his way."

"What does he want?"

Roxy considered the baseball jacket, the one with a key.

"I have no idea," she replied, but maybe she did.

"Call the cops. I'll be there in thirty minutes," Alma said.

"You will *not*." Roxy cleared her throat. "I'm perfectly fine. I've figured out what happened here. There will be hell to pay when I get hold of Sam. Apologize to your date for me."

"Are you sure?" Alma asked, her tone unconvinced.

"Absolutely," Roxy reassured. "I'll see you in the morning."

"You might. And then again," Alma singsonged, "you might not. If things go well, I won't be home much before lunchtime." She hung up.

Despite her current situation, Roxy delighted in the thought of Alma's romantic exploits. She flicked on her apartment's overhead lights and surveyed the mess. "God. Damn. Sam," she repeated. "You didn't need to trash the place. I'll give you the stupid jacket."

She dialed his number, ready to unload on him, but he didn't give her the satisfaction. The call rang and rang before connecting to his familiar voicemail message.

"You've reached Sam, the man who can. Leave a message."

And she did.

Chapter Nineteen

Friday couldn't arrive quick enough for Roxy. Rita Penn's lectures and hands-on class work were overkill. Practical guidance on how to prevent clients from getting blitzed or how to repair a deflating party doll would have been more useful. She was ready for a day off. Time to loaf around and let her brain rest.

The next day, she prepared to chauffeur nine-year-old Elliott Stone and his family to a glitzy Hollywood movie premiere. She arrived early at the limo yard and, after a quick check-in with Cecile, changed into her perfectly fitted uniform. Decker worked miracles, just like Stacy promised. No muffin-top or buttons pulling oddly across her chest, leaving gaps in her blouse. Her jacket cuffs hit the perfect point above her wrists, and her pants skimmed the top of her instep. Finally, she understood the importance of buying well-made clothes.

In truth, she knew quality clothing hung better on her frame. However, when her checkbook balance aligned with bargain basement pricing, she learned to cultivate a discount persona. Someday, when she had a few bucks in the bank, she'd plead with Decker to overhaul her entire wardrobe.

As she readied the car for the evening, melodic tones echoed from the front seat where she had tossed her handbag. The ringtone wasn't personalized; rather, it was the factory default setting. *Unknown Caller* imprinted across the screen.

Roxy climbed in the driver's seat, hesitating to answer what could be a telemarketing pitch. Had Stacy given her number to tonight's clients? Was there a complication?

By the time she answered, the caller had disconnected. A few seconds later, a ding sounded, signaling a voicemail. Concerned she had missed important client information, Roxy hurriedly pressed *Play*.

Sam's broken voice met her ears, his tone dropped so low that Roxy had difficulty understanding what he said.

"Ah, Roxy. Um, thanks for calling back." His words poured out slowly as though having to be coaxed from a deep, dark place. "You're an angel. I deserve every angry thing you said."

Was Sam crying?

"I have to explain. There's so much I should have told you. To apologize for."

Roxy gulped down air as goosebumps spread across her skin.

Sam sounded petrified. And right now, his terrified voice cracked in a pain-filled way. That guy never backed down from anyone or anything.

What had happened? What or who was frightening him? A pocket of love… no, this was simple human compassion… rose in her chest.

"I never left for Tennessee," he continued, as though beginning a confession. "Haven't talked to Lola in five years, and the kids want nothing to do with me. You're my life and you always were. I had to leave. Make everything look real. That's why I took the TV," he said in a sheepish tone. "Sorry, doll. I know you loved watching your shows on the big screen. And I'll return the set as soon as I can."

Roxy blinked back tears, aware Sam was in serious trouble. Her Sam, the one she'd been in love with for so many years, hadn't deserted her. She hadn't been wrong about him. She knew the man; at least, the parts Sam wanted her to know. And now he was in danger.

"I should have trusted you when all this started, but, well, I didn't want you to think less of me. I'll explain later. Right now, I *need* the key from inside the jacket pocket. You hate when I show up at your job and now that you disconnected me from your Find Friends app…

"Well, I don't know where you are anymore. So, can you put the key under the trash can near our bench by the food truck? You know the one."

Suddenly Sam sounded rushed, as though looking over his shoulder, anxious to get off the call before he was caught. But who was chasing him?

"Text me on this number when you've dropped off the key. You're probably working tonight, but seriously, the sooner the better. Not sure how far these guys are willing to go."

These guys? The tiny knot inside Roxy's gut expanded to the size of a billiard ball.

What was he asking her to do? Drive across town and sneak a key under a metal garbage can? No chance of making that happen tonight.

Roxy looked out the side window. Cecile stood near the limo, arms crossed. "Hey, you'd better get moving if you're going to get to Sherman Oaks."

"Oh, my gosh, I lost track of time," Roxy apologized, jumping out of the car, nearly knocking into Cecile. She glanced at her watch, disbelieving the hour. The Stones lived thirty minutes from here. "I'm on my way."

She gave the vehicle one last visual assessment. *That will have to do.*

By five o'clock, Roxy had ushered the Stone family—mother, father, and three children, Elliott being the youngest—into the limo. First, she'd ferry them to a hosted dinner before the sci-fi film screening, followed by an after-hours cast party where Elliott would meet the stars. Stacy told her that young Elliott and his family would walk the red carpet, as part of this special night, paparazzi on hand, snapping photos along the way.

Roxy kept the privacy screen up but could still hear muffled chirps of excitement as the family settled in, *ooh*ing and *aah*ing at the features and conveniences of the luxury automobile. Stacy hadn't briefed her on the child's condition, but from being around him for these few minutes, Roxy recognized Elliott as a special kid.

That evening she played fairy godmother, granting Elliott's every wish. Even the night sky contributed to the magic, with stars twinkling as though every dream he had ever held in his short nine years would come true tonight.

"Mommy, I'm meeting my favorite movie star, from my most favorite movie series. And..." Roxy overheard him say as the family walked toward the restaurant, "...we get to ride in this big fancy car with the prettiest lady, except for you, Mom."

Roxy blinked back tears. More than one person was realizing their dream tonight. Making a difference, being seen and appreciated.

After dinner, the family reloaded into the car for the short drive to the theater. Several limos were already lined up to deliver leggy ladies and tuxedo-clad gentlemen.

Roxy checked her makeup and ensured that her uniform was pristine, no wrinkles or cockeyed seams before she hurried to open the door. She extended her hand to Elliott. Under his mop of brown hair, she watched his blue eyes expand at the number of people waiting for him, including what appeared to be the entire cast, applauding. Camera flashes popped and electrified laughter filled the night air.

Roxy circled back to the driver's side of the car, ready to move before the family entered the theater. She managed to glance at Elliott and the movie's leading man as they posed against a backdrop with the film's name. The boy beamed; his smile outshone even the most polished actors. As she parked, she regretted not witnessing every second of this wondrous evening.

That was the good thing about driving a limo. Roxy had a front-row seat at special occasions. She created magic, sprinkling her own brand of fairy dust along the way.

Not a bad gig, especially tonight.

She followed the white-gloved parking attendant's directions and settled her car some four hundred yards from the entrance alongside other limos, Bentleys, and a Rolls Royce.

Then she waited.

Juxtaposed against the vibrant excitement of a few minutes ago, were the empty hours drivers spent waiting for their clients. Some filled the time by taking a nap or eating a meal. Others caught up on their leisure reading or scrolled social media. One fellow who Roxy knew used his down time to learn Spanish.

Some even drove home and spent the waiting hours there; that was a practice totally against company policy. "These folks aren't paying you to have dinner with your family!" Bobby had shouted at a new hire dozens of years earlier before firing him. Roxy had never forgotten.

Stay on site and in sight of your patron.

From where she parked, she had a straight shot at the neon marquee flashing the theater's name, beckoning moviegoers since the golden age of Hollywood. Roxy had always wanted to watch a film in this historic theater but never made the time. Sam always had other plans, more important plans than any Roxy could devise.

Sam. Interesting how his name rhymed with damn. All those wasted years...

Why didn't she see the time slipping away? It was never the right time to divorce Lola.

Never the right time to marry her and start a family.

Now, it was too late to have children of her own. But it wasn't too late to start her life over. Do the things she wanted to do. Go places, like a fancy movie theater or a trip to Paris.

Damn Sam. He stripped so much away, and he still had a hold on her.

Nearly nine-thirty on Saturday night, and what was she thinking about? How life could have been different if Sam had wanted the same things she wanted.

Her thoughts strayed to Alex. Could she be falling for another man with the same M.O.? Crap, she couldn't let that happen again.

Sam had left an indelible mark on her. Early tomorrow, she'd do what he'd asked—paw through the bags in her trunk, find his jacket, and dig out the key. Then she'd spend the better part of her Sunday driving to downtown LA and back home.

Of course, she'd text Sam once she'd hidden the key, hoping Chuck wouldn't be skulking about when she made the drop. That man had a knack for showing up where he wasn't wanted.

Nearby cars revved their engines, snapping Roxy out of mapping her future. She turned toward the theatergoers gathering under the marquee, some chattering, some waiting for their cars to approach the curb.

She pulled in line behind the others. The Stones were headed to a Hollywood after-party.

Now *that* was something to put on her bucket list. Not driving folks to one, but actually being an invited guest.

Chapter Twenty

With the Stone family securely inside, Roxy joined the stream of town cars and stretch limos snaking their way through downtown Los Angeles toward Tamarind, the site of the cast party. Alma had mentioned the trendy Italian-Thai Fusion restaurant, but Roxy never had the urge to dine there.

What was Italian-Thai fusion anyway? Spaghetti stir fry? She shuddered at the image, praying the two cuisines would never meet up in a bowl of Pad Thai.

She stopped the limo near the eatery's entrance behind a misty gray sports car with a price that could easily finance her retirement. Roxy had spotted many luxury cars that evening, most sporting sleek designs and high-performance engines. Tooling around in one of these racetrack-ready vehicles trumpeted fortune and success.

A valet opened the passenger door and assisted a young woman, maybe five feet four inches at the most, to effortlessly exit the car. Her date—or boyfriend or husband—took longer to escape.

Roxy giggled, watching him painstakingly pivot his large body to the left and unfold his legs before extending them toward the ground. Obviously, he'd performed this feat several times before. From the length of him, she guessed the man easily topped six feet. Holding her breath in anticipation, she expected him to bump his head on the door jamb.

A puff of relief escaped her lips after he had masterfully extracted his basketball-player-sized self from behind the steering wheel. He stretched to his full size, demonstrating that Roxy had underestimated his height. After handing the keys and a tip to the valet, the man gathered his lady on his arm, and they entered the restaurant.

Roxy moved into place and parked. By the time she circled the limo, Elliott and his family had piled out, excitedly heading toward the entrance.

Roxy pulled the dad aside and pointed to where she'd be parked across the street. He confirmed her number and that he would text when they were ready to leave, sometime close to midnight. He thanked her before scurrying off to catch up with his family.

Several horns honked, encouraging Roxy to hustle her buns. She quickly climbed back in and drove to the lot reserved for larger vehicles. With two hours of dead time ahead of her, Roxy rustled around the front seat in search of the brown paper bag lunch she brought.

As she unwrapped her turkey and avocado sandwich and readied herself to take a bite, a tapping sound jolted her.

Roxy rolled down her window. "Yes?"

"Hey, I'm Will. I work for Lux-R-ee Limo. Don't know if you were told, but the studio arranged a buffet for the drivers in a room adjacent to the party. Want to join us and grab a bite?"

"We can get food and freshen up," a female chauffeur standing behind Will added.

He gestured with a jerk of his head. "That's Deb. You're the new girl with Stacy, right?"

Roxy nodded.

"So, what do you say—wanna come?" Will asked.

Roxy glanced at her day-old turkey on wheat and shoved the sandwich back inside the plastic bag before tossing the entire lunch onto the floor. She grabbed her purse and locked the car. "I need to get some things out of the trunk. Refill the drinks and stock the snacks first," she said.

"We all have to prepare for the ride home," the woman said, sweeping her arm around indicating everyone nearby. "We'll head back in plenty of time for that."

Grateful for the invitation, Roxy scurried out of the automobile, closed the door, and pushed the lock on the key fob, waiting for the beep to signal security.

The three caught up with a group of some fifteen colleagues, hungry and in need of bathroom facilities. In addition to meeting new people, before the night ended, Roxy would experience Italian-Thai fusion.

Won't Alma be impressed.

Chapter Twenty-One

Roxy sipped sparkling water with a slice of lime and gazed around the dimly lit side room where the chauffeurs tasted most everything the colorful buffet offered. She lifted a forkful of the restaurant's specialty, surprised at how delicious the stuff tasted. Alma's birthday was coming up shortly. Maybe they'd come here.

Or… she could invite Alex to dinner.

After finding out how expensive the menu was, of course.

She listened to the spirited chatter of her new tribe, her fellow drivers deeply engaged in conversations. She missed being around people who shared common interests, goals, experiences. Living and working with Sam for so many years had stripped her of connections, along with her self-esteem.

Piece by piece, she vowed to inch her life forward and regain the old Roxy, now years wiser.

Tomorrow morning, she'd leave the key where Sam designated and text him not to contact her again. With a little luck, they'd never cross paths. If Sam decided to make things difficult, next week she'd look into filing a restraining order.

A couple of guys swapped war stories about drunk celebrities, each with an anecdote crafted to top the other fellow's hilarious tale. Across the table, Will and another man she didn't recognize shared their recommendations for the best fly-fishing spots in Colorado.

Roxy glanced at her watch. A quarter to twelve. Mr. Stone had said he wanted to be on the road by midnight. Roxy stood, excusing herself from the group. She thanked Will and Deb for including her and dropped a few bucks in the tip jar for the waitstaff before trekking toward the parking lot. She had just enough time to tidy up the limo and restock the drinks before the Stones joined her.

The crunch of gravel against her soles accompanied Roxy as she approached the lot. The cool night air dusted her skin, energizing her hopes. *New day, new beginning.* Satisfaction spread across her face, like the giddy promise young lovers knew when embarking on their future. Potential, challenge, reward—all hers for the taking.

She glanced across the rows of parked cars and realized one of the trunks was left open. That was odd, but maybe the driver was already there doing what she was preparing to do.

As she got closer, she recognized the limo with the open trunk—hers.

But how could that be? She had locked the car—she was sure of that. Another few steps revealed her cooler with the drinks now stood on the outside of the vehicle.

Was someone robbing her?

"What's going on?" she yelled, not realizing several of the drivers had begun streaming out of the restaurant.

"You okay?" She recognized Will's voice hurrying toward her from behind.

"I don't know. Looks like someone is taking stuff from the limo." Roxy hurried her pace, emboldened by other people nearby.

She looked around but didn't see any movement. No one was lurking or running away.

That's when she screamed.

A scream that vibrated from somewhere deep inside her chest, a direct response to the horror smacking her senses. A banshee cry as though a bucket of ice-cold water doused her, sending shock and disbelief pulsating through every nerve.

"What?" Will said, now flanked by several drivers. "You okay?"

Roxy, frozen to the spot, pointed.

Inside the trunk lay Sam, his body crooked in an unnatural coil, blood pooling from several wounds. His face tilted toward her, his cold eyes staring as though offering a final apology.

Other drivers formed a semicircle, gasping at the sight. The whirl of a siren blared as an arm grasped her by the waist, but the hold wasn't strong enough.

With the edges of darkness closing in, Roxy fell to the ground. *Sam was dead.*

Local Food Truck Vendor Found Fatally Stabbed

Early Sunday morning, the body of 60-year-old Samuel Reyes was discovered inside a limousine's trunk by chauffeur, Roxanne Adams. Reyes, the owner of Reyes of Sunshine Mobile Catering, had sustained numerous stab wounds and was pronounced dead at the scene, according to a police spokesperson.

Officers arrived outside Tamarind Restaurant where Adams had parked the vehicle while her passengers attended a Hollywood movie premiere after-party at the Los Angeles restaurant.

Reyes was recognized by Adams, his girlfriend. The county medical examiner later confirmed the victim's identity. No arrests have been made in connection with the stabbing as of Wednesday morning.

The incident remains under investigation. Police encourage anyone with information to call their tip line at 1-800-JUSTICE.

Chapter Twenty-Two

Seated on a cedar bench, a fluffy white towel wrapped around her midsection, Roxy sweated, willing toxins to be flushed from her system. Barely two feet away, Alma, clad in the same too-short towel, rested against the bench, eyes closed.

When her friend suggested escaping to a health spa, it seemed like a good idea. Both women, desperate for solace, prayed the spa karma would wash away the horror of the past several days.

So far it hadn't.

The Monday after discovering Sam's dead body, Roxy had been summoned to a Hollywood police station to answer a few questions.

With their good-cop/bad-cop behavior on full display, two detectives took turns, mostly asking the same things in different ways, as if trying to catch her in a lie.

What was she doing prior to discovering the body?

Why had she left her limo unattended?

How long had she known the deceased?

A knife had been found at the scene. Was she missing one?

Where had she been earlier that Saturday?

Had their relationship been troubled?

The two men had relentlessly interrogated her, questioning her every movement, motive, and reaction. She left drained of spirit and questioning her culpability for Sam's death.

Could she have prevented the murder?

She stretched her neck and waited for a pop, stress releasing in small increments. A facial, a salt scrub, and a fifty-minute hot stone massage had done little to relax Roxy or dim the memory of Sam's dead-eyed stare. Not much of a chance that twenty minutes in a sauna would have better results.

Roxy had planned to treat Alma to a birthday celebration. Instead, her best friend had persuaded Roxy to join her in a spa day.

"If ever there was a woman who needed a day of pampering, Roxy Adams, it is you. Let's call this my birthday getaway," Alma added, even though she wouldn't turn thirty-four for several weeks. Her friend had lovingly arranged to skip work on Monday, a valiant attempt to get Roxy's mind off the tragedy of a week ago.

The newspaper article left Roxy even more upset. "I'm not his girlfriend," she hissed, the fire in her words matching the dry heat permeating her body.

"I know. Lame-ass reporters get half the story right, half the time." Alma's critique, more in support of Roxy than in condemnation of the fourth estate, rang hollow.

"You read the article. Makes things sound like we were still a couple. Like maybe I had something to do with his death," Roxy said defensively.

"No one thinks that. Seriously, the cops will investigate," Alma said. "They'll find out you had been separated for several weeks. You were over him."

"Two months," Roxy emphasized.

"What?"

"We were separated for two months and a couple of days. Two months of me scraping by to make rent. Finally, when I start moving forward, building a little security, this happens. My life is ruined."

"Nothing is ruined. Well, nothing more than what you've already gone through. Things might be easier, in fact. You said you wanted Sam out of your life, that he was dead to you," Alma added.

Roxy widened her eyes and shuddered. "Well, yes, but not dead as in doornail."

If Alma thought this, would other people, like the police, think I wanted him killed?

"In any event, everything will be sorted out. Enjoy the time off to collect yourself."

"Wish I could." Roxy stood, tilted against the wood-planked wall, and placed her bare feet on the bench slats while remembering the interrogation at the police station. As soon as she got home, Roxy had combed through her kitchen drawers only to realize a carving knife missing from her matching set.

"I'm afraid I'm being framed for Sam's murder," she confessed, telling Alma about the missing cutlery. "After all that had happened, I didn't want Sam in my life anymore, but I didn't want him dead either."

Alma pivoted to face her friend. "You're imagining the worst, and you have to stop. You'll end up with a nervous breakdown if you don't let up."

"You're right. I'm a mess." Roxy rubbed her hands together, mulling over how life had gone to hell after Sam left. She didn't guess her circumstances could get any worse than the possibility of being homeless.

Ha! Since Sam's death, she'd been forced to take leave from work, delay her training at the commercial trucking school, and borrow money from Stacy to make that month's rent. And today, Alma insisted on paying for her own birthday party.

"Thanks for picking up the tab. When this is all over, I promise—"

"Shhhh! You stop. There's no one else I'd rather celebrate with," Alma said. "Except for my new dude, but he was busy today."

"Alma," Roxy chided.

"Just kidding. I didn't even ask." She winked.

The two sat in silence for a few beats, eyes closed, absorbing the healing sensation the dry heat offered.

"How did Sam's killer know where I was?" Roxy finally said into the cloudy air, unable to keep from returning to the topic.

A new fear clawed through her. *Sam hadn't broken into her apartment. His murderer had. Would he come after her now, looking for Sam's key?*

"Huh?" Alma responded, her mind obviously on pause.

"How could they have timed the murder?" Roxy continued. "We were in the restaurant about an hour."

"Beats me. Maybe they killed him earlier and waited to dump him in your limo," Alma said, sitting up to adjust her towel. "Look, I'm good for another two minutes, then I have to get out of here. If I stay any longer, I won't live to see my next birthday."

Roxy wiped sweat from her brow. "Sorry. I've been preoccupied with everything. Sam. The murder. His dead body stuffed inside Stacy's limo. How will I ever be able to make that up to her? Waking her up after midnight to drive the Stone family home. Cleaning blood out of carpet is impossible. And the negative press," Roxy huffed. "I won't be surprised if she lets me go."

"You're back at it. Spiraling downward instead of soaking in the rejuvenating vibes."

"I can't stop my mind from rolling the facts over and over. They play like a television news headline scrolling across my brain on repeat. Nothing adds up."

Alma ran her palms down the sides of her face. "I hope they're right about saunas reducing wrinkles. I saw so many tiny lines around my mouth in the mirror this morning. I swear none of them were there yesterday."

"You're purposely trying to make me laugh," Roxy squealed. "And it's working. I *will* find a way to make this up to you."

"There's nothing to make up. You'd do the same if the tables were turned, only you'd be getting the senior discount."

Roxy rolled her eyes.

"Seriously, Rocks, it's not your job to make the pieces fit." Alma moved in closer. "You're not the one who will solve Sam's murder. There are professionals for that. I'm sorry he ended up like this. I liked him in spite of the times we'd butt heads. He was a little quirky, but an okay guy in an odd sort of way."

Roxy smirked at Alma's description of Sam. He was no altar boy, but while they were a couple, Roxy thought Sam was trustworthy.

"Look," Alma said, reaching for Roxy's hand, "you'll go wacky if you keep dissecting every detail. And you're going to make me wacky, too. I'm too young for the funny farm."

Roxy let go of a breath she didn't realize she'd been holding and straightened. "I'll let the detectives do their thing. In the meantime, we're here to celebrate you, my favorite newbie! Hell, you're still not old enough to run for President."

"True. But at least I'm not checking out my Medicare benefits like—"

"Okay. Okay. Boy, that's a cold shot," Roxy said with a laugh. She stood, adjusting her towel, making sure the hem covered her cheeks. "Let's go. We have lunch and peach bellinis waiting for us in the garden café."

Alma popped up from the bench. "Now you're talking," she said, securing her own towel.

After sliding into their spa slippers, the pair made their way from the steam room toward the outdoors. The bright sunshine nearly blinded Roxy, much like her blindsided interrogation days ago.

Of course Alma would challenge Roxy's impatience, painting a rosy picture that everything would turn out fine.

Just wait for the professionals to do their job. That's easy for Alma to say. Roxy had a harder time believing.

The day before she had watched two men poke around her apartment building near the dumpster. The same two detectives who had interrogated her days earlier. What were they looking for? What if they had already done their job and were simply waiting to arrest Sam's murderer?

Simply waiting to arrest her?

Chapter Twenty-Three

By the following Wednesday afternoon, Roxy could barely stand the boredom of being cooped up at home. She had methodically wiped down the insides of her kitchen cupboards and cleaned out the fridge. Even both of her junk drawers received attention, although at the end of the process, she still possessed more twist ties, decks of cards, and matchbooks than she needed.

For the second time in two months, Roxy reorganized her closets, removing blouses from the last century, a pair of too-tight pants, and sandals she deemed worthy of donation. With all that had happened, she had wanted to avoid this task, avoid Sam's baseball jacket, for fear of a flood of guilt-riddled memories overwhelming her.

She steeled herself before gathering the culled items and toted everything to the carport and unlocked her trunk. Three black garbage bags filled with Sam's stuff occupied most of the space where Roxy had left them over a week ago. Tugging open the plastic drawstrings of one partially filled bag, she shoved her few items inside.

With Sam's death, it seemed heartless to dump his few possessions, so she had paused her plan to take them to the local donation center.

What was the appropriate amount of time to let pass before discarding your now-deceased ex's castoff clothes anyway?

For the next few minutes, she sorted through the bags, unloading T-shirts, sweaters, and ripped blue jeans before she found the jacket, the one she had bought Sam for his forty-fifth birthday.

Roxy carried the jacket and the memory back to her apartment where she hung the cobalt blue coat onto the pole in what had been Sam's side of the closet. She stared at the sole remaining piece of his wardrobe dangling from a hanger, lost in emotion.

A tear trickled down her cheek, recalling how she could hardly wait for him to open the gift. He had modeled the jacket for her. "A perfect fit," Sam declared, before hugging and kissing her.

A month later, he had asked her to move in. Even though he'd said his divorce from Lola would take another five months to be final, Sam convinced her that they didn't need to wait. Somehow the divorce never came through.

How wrong she had been to trust him. With the palms of her hands, she pushed the tears away and straightened her spine. *Stupid, stupid girl in love.*

From where the jacket hung on the closet rod, Roxy dug through the pockets, searching for the key Sam had been desperate to recover. Once she located the tiny silver prize that had cost Sam his life, she held it gingerly between her fingers.

From the small size, she guessed the key would fit a gym locker or maybe a safe deposit box. Where had she seen this before? The Zoo's coin-operated lockers where families stored their lunches?

She turned the key over in her hand. What resembled a boot, or maybe an impression of a sleigh, was embossed on one side of the hard plastic yellow stub. On the other, in bold lettering FSR-444 stared back at her, offering no indication of what it might open.

She had forgotten about the key when the police detectives questioned her. Was it too late to tell them now? They would know how to match it to a lock. She carefully slid the key inside her jeans pocket and rummaged through her purse to find the card the detective handed her in what seemed like an eternity ago. She dialed the number and waited, only to be told the detective wasn't in. She was forced to leave a message with the desk sergeant.

Roxy tucked the phone in her back pocket and paced the tiny apartment. The once-perfect home for her and Sam, complete with a window box planter and a back patio, now seemed like a cage she had to escape.

Stacy had promised to call in a few days to check in. *How many days are a few anyway? Two, six, nine?* Roxy knew she should be patient. The trouble with being patient was it required having patience; a virtue she struggled with daily.

What difference does it make if Stacy calls tomorrow, or I call her today, Roxy rationalized before digging out her phone again and dialing. Stacy picked up on the second ring.

"Roxy. I've been thinking of you but didn't want to intrude," Stacy said.

"You could never intrude. You've done everything to make this easier."

"How are you doing? I mean, with all that's gone on?"

Roxy licked her dry lips. *You have no idea.* "I'm okay. Well, actually, I'm bored to tears. Sitting around the house is driving me batty. This is worse than the COVID lockdown. I'm the only one isolated."

"Do you have to stay home? Did the cops tell you to do that?" Stacy questioned. "I mean, are you in any danger?"

Roxy considered this for a minute. "There's no reason for whoever killed Sam to come after me," she said, her tone dropping. *The key.*

"Good. Good. Wanted to make sure you're safe and all right."

"I am," Roxy replied, a bit too quickly. "The thing is… I was wondering if there's any way you'd okay me going back to class tomorrow. I've already missed a lot of time. I don't want to delay getting my license longer than I have to."

Stacy waited a few beats before answering. "You've gone through a traumatic event. Cecile and I want to be sure you've had enough time to process what's happened."

"I'm going to process the horror of Sam's death easier if I'm busy. I'd gotten used to him not being around, but not permanently. Not this way. It's blowing my mind that someone killed him. But the truth is, it's not helping anything for me to sit in this apartment and dwell on… well, you know."

Roxy took a deep inhale. "I'm going crazy. My friend Alma said I need to let the police do their job. And while they are, I'd like to do mine, too. What do you say?" Roxy pleaded. "Can I go back to driving school?"

Stacy didn't answer, so Roxy filled the conversational gap.

"I understand why you don't want me on the schedule for a while until they arrest who did this at least. I have a friend… really, a classmate named Alex. He'll keep an eye out for me, if that's what you're worried about."

"A classmate, huh?" Stacy finally replied. "Sounds like there's more to this story."

Glee spread across Roxy's face, and she puffed a deep exhale through her teeth. "A friend and fellow student."

"Sure," Stacy drew out the word. "You'll have to fill me in later. In any event, you didn't withdraw from classes, so I'm guessing you can show up tomorrow at the regular time. I'll give them a call to make sure."

After a few more pleasantries confirming Roxy's state of mind, Stacy disconnected.

Roxy held her cell phone as though she possessed the golden ticket. Going back to class was her way out of this eerie, unsettling zone she found herself moping through.

Sam was gone, really gone, and that reality crushed her. The past ten weeks had helped Roxy to understand that what once was true love had devolved into convenience. Their relationship had become comfortable and steady when what they shared should have been passionate, spontaneous, and exciting. She loved Sam and the history they shared. But at some point during the recent forced retooling of her life, she recognized she wasn't in love with Sam Reyes.

And, had she lifted her head up from the fryer occasionally, she would have known she hadn't been in love with him for a long while.

The past year or two had been particularly erratic and stressful for her and for what she thought was their business.

At a moment's notice, Sam would take off with Chuck on junkets, sometimes for days, leaving her to run the food truck alone from opening to closing. There were many nights he came home late, his clothes disheveled and disbelief in his eyes, as though he had been on a bender. If his phone rang late at night, Sam jumped as though he'd stepped on a hot coal, then scurried to their bedroom or the patio to answer, out of Roxy's earshot.

Yes, things with Sam had been strained at best, and she had denied behaviors she didn't want to see, in case they led to problems she didn't want to deal with. What was that saying about sticking her head in the sand? She'd left her ass in the air.

Roxy plopped onto her couch, immediately thinking of Alex and his jade green eyes. A tingle swept across her like a chorus of butterflies fluttering their wings against her skin. The thrill she missed for many years. The sensation she had traded for stability.

Alex.

What would he think? I'm sure by now everyone at the driving school knows about the murder. And that I found the body. How do I explain this? Maybe Alma is right. I should stay home until everything is sorted out. That would be the safer, smarter thing to do.

She ran her palm against a small bump in her jeans pocket where the key was nestled. That magical fluttery feeling of new love quickly replaced with a cold fear.

What if the killer knows I have what they're looking for?

Chapter Twenty-Four

The California sun glowed brighter for Roxy on Wednesday morning as she wended her way through freeway traffic, eager to rejoin her class. The shadow of Sam's death still hovered inches above her head, never venturing far from her thoughts. But for the next several hours, she would focus on her future instead of who murdered Sam and if the killer was a threat to her.

What did that stupid key open, anyway.

While she was at work, Roxy had used Alma's extra house key to get into her apartment. For safekeeping—and until she could come up with a better idea—Roxy snuck onto the patio and buried the worrisome key under Alma's geraniums. Now that Sam was gone, the odds were strong someone new would be searching for it.

Stacy had called last night with the happy news. Rita welcomed Roxy's return but cautioned that Roxy wouldn't qualify to take the commercial driver test with her classmates. During the several days she was absent, she had missed nearly half of the required behind-the-wheel training hours.

"Rita also mentioned everyone is worried sick about you. They want to see you," Stacy had said.

That last bit of news lifted a heaviness nesting in Roxy's chest. She had been concerned that Roxy's Rowdies, as Alex had dubbed them, would believe the newspaper accounts, misinterpret what had happened, and distance themselves from her and her drama.

She should have known better. God placed good people into your life without their awareness, or even their consent, knowing they will be needed. He'd been working overtime in Roxy's case since Sam's desertion.

Her unlikely friendship with a radio deejay had blossomed. Stacy, Cecile, and the *chauffeuses* had embraced her quickly and accepted her into their inner circle. Even Decker, the tailor, was on her team. And now this mismatched group of students, united with the goal of improving their lives, had become her peeps. Roxy needed to see them as much as they wanted to see her.

She pulled into what had become her usual spot and parked. As she exited the car, she heard, "Roxy!"

She turned to see Alex approach, his arms opened wide. "I've missed you," he said, enveloping her in a hug.

"We all have," Jason, her Gen Z friend added, jogging from where he parked to join them. "Things aren't as much fun around here without you."

"I'll bet," Roxy said, giving him a smile. "You're disappointed because I haven't been here to divert Rita's attention from you goofing off."

"Could be, could be," Jason agreed. The trio walked toward the truck yard. Within a few steps, Jason hurried his speed, separating from them.

Did he sense they needed to be alone?

"I wanted to call and check on you," Alex said after Jason was out of earshot, "but we never exchanged numbers. I didn't know how you'd feel about me asking Rita for your personal information, so I waited, hoping to hear from you."

Roxy took in his sincere expression, his green eyes glinting in the sunshine.

"We didn't think about exchanging digits, as Jason would say," Roxy said, amused at the conversation.

He shook his head. "Thought I'd see you the next Monday. And now it's Thursday, nearly two weeks later."

"The time passed quickly and slowly if that makes any sense," Roxy reflected. "I couldn't stay at home waiting for them to arrest the killer. I was going stir-crazy. Rita is an angel for letting me come back after so many absences."

Alex stopped and put his hands on Roxy's shoulders. "You'll get back in the groove," he insisted. "And I'd be happy to help you catch up."

"Like study partners?"

"You could say that. I'd benefit from spending more time on this stuff, too."

Roxy gazed past Alex toward the school entrance. What looked like a small flock of sparrows flew by and landed on the branches of a nearby tree. Chirping in concert as though celebrating the spring day, they rejoiced for new beginnings, just like Roxy.

"I'm glad you took some time, though." Alex's words interrupted her thoughts.

"I'm sorry. What did you say?" Roxy asked.

"Only that I'm glad you had time to... well, get over this. From what I read, that had to be a traumatic night. Finding a dead body in your car. I can only imagine. The paper said he was your boyfriend."

"*Ex*-boyfriend," Roxy emphasized. Was Alex's interest more than courteous curiosity? "Papers always get something wrong."

"Still, discovering a corpse is bad enough, but then to realize the body belonged to someone you love—"

"Used to love. We broke up. He left me, remember?" Roxy groaned at the curt angst in her voice and attempted to soften her tone. "It's been nearly three months since he walked out. The man left me with nothing. That's why I'm here, learning how to drive an eighteen-wheeler. I'm picking up the pieces, as the song goes."

Alex nodded. "Sounds like a rough breakup."

Roxy averted his gaze. "I didn't want to get into all the details of my wayward love life when we were having coffee a few weeks ago," she said, slowly turning to look at him. "I was working through a lot of changes."

"Wow, I'll say." He glanced toward the school. "We'd better get inside."

They strolled in silence until Alex asked, "Do you have time for coffee after class? We can swap phone numbers then, and you can give me the whole story, if you want to."

Roxy thought about this for a moment. She liked him but his probing questions left her uneasy. Was he only curious about her relationship with Sam? They'd gone out once, certainly not an invitation for an ongoing interrogation.

And she couldn't shake the odd notion that he knew more about the murder than he was saying. Almost as though he was weighing her story and deciding if her truth matched his.

"Well?" Alex prodded.

"How about dinner instead?" she replied, thinking she might have a few inquiries of her own to pose. "There's a lot to tell."

Chapter Twenty-Five

Roxy and Alex walked toward the parking spot where they met that morning. Studying how to react to road hazards and reviewing the finer points of tire safety had made the day drag. Still, her studies took her mind off her recent worries.

Regaining her big-truck mojo—the tiny bit she had managed to absorb before Sam's tragic death—challenged her brain. There was so much she had forgotten during the days she missed, replaced with thoughts of criminals, murder, and a tiny mystifying key.

For what might be the twentieth time, Roxy questioned the wisdom of pursuing this goal. She admired female long-distance truckers who spent their careers driving all over the country. Luckily, Roxy only needed the "P" for passenger endorsement on her driver's license, but Stacy insisted on the additional training.

Roxy glanced at Alex and smiled inwardly. In spite of her frustrations, she knew there was a reason for everything. *I wouldn't have met him, if not for this class.* The realization sent a mixture of apprehension and desire through her veins.

"Do you want to drive separately?" Alex asked, apparently noticing her staring at him.

She didn't answer right away.

"Roxy, you okay?"

"Oh sorry, Alex. My mind has been traveling on its own these days. It's like answers are forming in there, and I have to let them percolate. What did you ask?"

"Do you want to ride with me or take separate cars?" he repeated.

"Separate cars, I think. That way I won't bother you to bring me back here. Where do you want to go? Burgers, Chinese, sushi?" Roxy infused excitement into her voice, hoping Alex wouldn't catch the uneasiness pulsing through her.

"You like sushi?" Alex asked, apparently surprised at the choice.

"Well, no. Thought you might, though, and I can always find something on a menu." Roxy paused. "What's around here, anyway? Or should we pick a place closer to home?"

"My home or yours?" Alex said, adding a wink.

Roxy blushed. "Oh. Where do you live anyway?"

"About fifteen minutes south," he answered. "And you?"

"West Hollywood."

"How do you stand the traffic?"

"I don't. Once I get a few paychecks under my belt, I'll search for a new place, with cheaper rent," Roxy said, knowing that leaving Alma and finding a bargain apartment were impossible targets to hit.

"Are you thinking of something closer to your work? Where are they located, anyway?"

"Universal City. Probably not going to find a more reasonable rent if I move there. Maybe I'll stay where I am. I'm centrally located for most of LA."

"You don't need to make any decisions right now," Alex said. "Except what to order for dinner."

She chuckled. "You're right. I'm barely keeping up with the basics."

"Let's do burgers," Alex suggested, changing the subject. "I know a place not too far from here. Two blocks down and on the left. Follow me." He turned toward his vehicle.

"Aye, aye, captain," Roxy joked, scurrying to her car a few feet from his. "Oh, my God!" she shouted, causing Alex to return to her side.

"Roxy, are you okay?"

She caught his gaze and redirected it. "Looks like I'm not following you anywhere," she said, pointing to her flat tires.

Alex crouched down to inspect the damage. "Did you drive through a construction site?" he asked, an incredulous tone to his voice.

"What? No," she answered, insulted he'd consider the idea.

"These back two tires have sinker nails in them. See the checkered head? That's how you can tell."

She nodded, taking in the gold-colored circles flush against her tread.

"They're used for framing on construction sites. Lucky you didn't have a blowout on the freeway." He stood and walked to the front of the car. "That's weird. Your front two seem okay. No nails."

A few moments later, Jason and Rita joined them.

"What the heck?" Rita said after viewing the damage. "Didn't know you'd be applying today's tire safety lesson so quickly."

"Looks like she ran over a box of nails," Jason said, coming to the same conclusion.

"I did not!" Roxy declared, fully annoyed at the prospect.

Who'd purposefully drive through a building site?

"Seems like someone helped her along," Alex added, back to examining the destruction.

"What do you mean?" Roxy asked.

Alex motioned her to kneel near him. Jason and Rita huddled behind. "I checked out her front tires. They are fine. But look at the back two. Someone hammered these bad boys in there," he said, pointing to where the nail heads were visible. "I'm guessing they were just deep enough that, by the time Roxy drove here, they would puncture the rubber. They've had all day to do a slow leak."

Roxy stared at her destroyed tires and then at Alex. "Someone did this on purpose? Maybe kids in the neighborhood," she said, not wanting to believe the damage was anything more than juvenile antics, even though her roiling gut signaled otherwise.

Alex stood. "This wasn't a teenager's stunt," he said, reaching his hand out to help Roxy regain her footing.

"Where do you park your car? In a locked garage or on the street?" Rita asked.

"I have a carport, but it's not locked. Anyone in the building—actually, anyone—can go in there." Roxy shook her head in disbelief. "This must be a prank." She reached for her phone. "I'm calling Alma to check if anyone else in the complex had a similar problem."

A few minutes later, Roxy hung up. "Alma walked up and down the parking stalls and didn't see any nails. She said everyone's tires are perfectly fine. Seems I was targeted."

"Could this have anything to do with the murder?" Jason asked, vocalizing the obvious. "I mean, we all know what happened, at least what the papers said happened. Sounded gnarly. Maybe the killer wants to send *you* a message."

"Seriously, Jason." Rita scowled. "You watch too much *CSI*. Can't you see you're scaring Roxy?"

Roxy appreciated Rita wanting to protect her, but she knew Jason was right. Whoever killed Sam wanted her scared.

But why? She was already frightened. She didn't know anything that could point the police in their direction. Except for her call to the detectives about the key.

They couldn't know about that, could they? No one had returned her call, anyway.

"Look," Alex said. "These can't be patched. You'll have to get replacements. It's nearly six, and the tire stores are closed or closing soon. Your car's not going anywhere. Let me take you to dinner, and we'll deal with this tomorrow."

"Should we call the cops?" Jason asked. "I know, I know. I watch too many crime dramas, but if someone sabotaged Roxy's car, maybe there are fingerprints on the nails, or… I don't know. Seems like we can't leave things like this."

"You have a healthy sense of danger, Jason, no matter what TV shows you watch," Alex said. "He's right. I'll call. At the very least, we'll get the police to file a report."

Alex stepped away from the group and got out his phone. "They're on the way," he announced minutes later.

Roxy buried her face in her hands.

How had her life gone so far off the rails? What else could go wrong?

Chapter Twenty-Six

Over an hour later, Roxy bit into a juicy cheeseburger—just what she needed to calm her nerves. The cops had arrived quickly, more quickly than Roxy expected, to take the report. After answering a few questions, she and Alex left with a case number and little hope of discovering who had vandalized her tires.

They drove to Chubby's, a hole-in-the-wall that locals, along with a few lucky tourists, discovered and kept secret. Nestled in a strip mall between a postal store and a nail salon, Roxy would have overlooked the tiny restaurant if Alex hadn't driven her there. The waitstaff, dressed in blue jeans and paisley-patterned red shirts, served burgers on sheets of parchment covering tray-like tin pans. Fries were casually presented like a torch in a paper cone.

Roxy complemented her meal with a chocolate milkshake, forgoing anything stronger.

"Nothing makes you feel better the way chocolate can," she said to Alex, after slurping a huge gulp.

He took a swig of his craft beer. "Oh, I can think of a few things."

"You handled everything with the police like you've done that a time or two before," Roxy said. "Seemed like you were talking to old friends."

"Only one way to talk to law enforcement—friendly." Alex ran a fry through a puddle of catsup. "The officer said he'd file his report tonight, and we could request a copy sometime after nine tomorrow morning."

Roxy was skeptical. "What will I do with a police report?"

"Hopefully nothing but having a paper trail is worth the precaution in case this turns out to be more than an unfortunate coincidence. Not sure if you can use one to get your insurance to reimburse you for the price of two tires," Alex added.

Roxy arched her eyebrows. Another unexpected and unaffordable expense. "Oh, yeah. I have the minimum coverage on my car. I'm sure it doesn't cover getting pummeled with a nail gun."

"I hadn't thought of that, but you might be on to something. That makes more sense than pounding in the nails one by one with a hammer. A nail gun could have done this quickly if they didn't have the dial on full power."

"Don't you have to plug those in?"

"Not if the guy had a cordless model. He could have popped all those nails into your tires and been gone before anyone noticed."

"Tools do that?" Roxy asked, resting her hand on the suddenly tighter waistband of her slacks.

"Oddly enough, you can frame a house with a cordless nail gun these days and use different pressures to determine how deep the nail goes. Power nailers, they call them."

"You certainly know a lot about a lot of different things, Alex… What is your last name?" she asked. "I've forgotten."

"Montgomery. Like Montgomery Clift but better looking." He beamed wider as if to sell her on the idea.

"The actor? My mom thought he was dreamy. He died before I was born and maybe before you were born, too," Roxy teased.

"I think I'm older than you. But of course, a gentleman never asks." He bowed his head and looked up at her under a fringe of straight eyelashes.

"And a lady never answers." Roxy smirked. "Without listing numbers, I'm gonna guess you and I share a great deal of pop culture. Music, television shows, a love of Guns N' Roses and *The Simpsons*."

Roxy continued fishing for his age. "Do you remember where you were when Reagan made his Berlin Wall speech? I graduated high school right around that time."

"Finishing my junior year," Alex said.

"I'm older?"

"Junior year in college. Makes me the elder. So, you wondered how I knew about Montgomery Clift. He might have died before I was born, but you know, all the great actors live on in the late-night movies," Alex said.

Roxy took another bite of her cheeseburger and chewed, using the time to consider the many facets of Alex. "What kind of films do you enjoy?" she asked before taking a sip of milkshake to wash down the burger remnants.

"Oh, westerns, I guess. Anything with action, race cars, gunfights."

"No love stories?"

"I'll sit through them, but I'm happier if a bank heist or prison breakout gets mixed in."

"You're an action-film kind of guy with a dab of romance," Roxy summarized.

"You got me." Alex nodded. "And for you? Sci-fi? Thrillers? Dystopian horror?"

"Ah, not quite." Roxy frowned at the thought. "Comedy. I'm a sucker for a good rom-com."

"Isn't that an oxymoron?"

Roxy took offense before noticing the grin sliding across Alex's face.

He held up both hands in surrender. "Just kidding. I'm a fan of a good rom-com, too."

"Are you asking me out to the movies, or…"

"Yes, I guess I am. Your schedule has loosened up, right? You're not chauffeuring until this Sam thing gets sorted out."

She shuddered at the words *Sam thing*. Alex sounded too cavalier about his death, like she was replacing an appliance instead of mourning a long-time friend and lover.

"You okay? Did I say something wrong?"

"No. No," she repeated, wondering if she had been overly sensitive at his poor choice of words.

"What do you say about tomorrow night? Or Saturday? I could pick you up at your place. That is if you don't think I'm being too forward."

"Saturday night would be perfect." Roxy reached for her bag, pulled out a pen and wrote her address on the corner of the grease-stained parchment paper, along with her phone number.

"You know I could put your information into my phone," Alex said.

"Technology has eliminated many niceties, like a girl writing down her number and giving it to a guy." She tore off a strip of paper, folded it, and handed the note to Alex. "We probably should get going," Roxy added, satisfied with herself. "Tomorrow comes earlier and earlier these days, and I still have to figure out what to do with my car."

Alex signaled for the check. "Let me drop you off," he said, digging in his back pocket for his wallet. "And I'll pick you up in the morning around eight. Plenty of time to call a tow truck and get to class before Rita gets annoyed." He waved her note in the air. "Now that I know where you live."

"Alma is on her way to pick me up. I just texted her that we're done." Roxy reached for her handbag. "But I'll take your offer for a ride in the morning. I don't want to bother her twice."

"I'll wait until your ride arrives," Alex said. "I'd love to meet the woman behind the soulful voice of Los Angeles."

Roxy pushed down the fluttery tickle in her chest. *Too soon. Too soon,* her conscience repeated. But was it? Could Alex be the man she needed now? Her heart could hope.

But her brain kept sending *beware* signals. For now, though, she'd ignore them.

Still, later that night, she wondered how he could know her friend Alma was Soul Sanchez, the radio DJ.

She'd never told him.

Chapter-Twenty-Seven

Minutes later, Roxy's phone dinged, and she read: *Out in front.*

"Well, guess I'm going. My ride is here." She held up her screen to Alex as evidence.

Alex, already paying the bill, stood, waiting for Roxy to gather her purse. "I had a nice time," she said as he walked her toward the door. "Despite the earlier calamity."

"Not the best way to start off our first real date," he said to her surprise.

So this was a date.

As promised, Alma parked in front of the restaurant, barely two steps away. She popped out of the driver's side, hurrying to extend her hand toward Alex, much like Roxy's father had done when meeting her prom date decades ago.

"Alma Sanchez," she greeted. "Roxy's neighbor and best friend."

"Nice to meet you," he said, giving her hand a gentle shake.

Alma shot Roxy an approving glimpse.

"Alex will pick me up in the morning," Roxy rushed the words, "and help get this tire stuff straightened out before class."

"Awesome," Alma said. "Well, let's go, girl. I've got a shift in about an hour." She scurried around the car and climbed inside, leaving Roxy alone with Alex.

He pulled her nearer to him and pecked her cheek. "I had a wonderful time, too, despite the earlier problems. But we'll get all that taken care of. Sleep well, my lovely."

Roxy nodded.

"And now that I have your number, I'll text in the morning when I'm on my way."

"Thank you." Roxy climbed into the passenger seat, her heart pounding. Alex pushed the door closed and waved.

As soon as traffic allowed, Alma pulled away from the curb. "Spill the beans," she demanded before Roxy had fastened her seatbelt. "Every. Single. One. Start with the tires and finish with hot facts about that gorgeous man. Girl, your toast always lands jelly-side up, don't it?"

"What are you talking about?"

"You know. Two months ago, Sam dropped you like smelly socks. And today, you're out to dinner with that hunk." Alma motioned her fist with a thumb up in the direction of the restaurant. "Are you Irish or something? Rabbit's foot in your pocket?"

Not feeling particularly lucky, Roxy offered a nervous giggle. "He is a bit too perfect, isn't he?" she agreed. "Did good fortune land him in my lap? I like him and all, but there's something odd I can't put my finger on. Like meeting Alex was preplanned, not as organic as I want to believe."

"Don't go looking for trouble. Lord knows trouble's been tracking your butt down all on its own."

"Still, he knew stuff that I didn't tell him. Either he's a stalker or…"

"Or what?" Alma asked.

"I have no idea. My head is jumbled in so many directions. I can't see straight. Anyway, I don't want to find another man. Sam just died. Well, actually, murdered. I'm focused on getting back on my feet. Paying off bills, and maybe, just maybe putting aside something for my future. I literally have nothing to my name. No business, no assets, no family. On every level, I'm starting at the bottom. Below bottom. I can't begin a relationship."

Alma stayed silent.

"What?" Roxy finally asked. "You think I'm looking for problems."

Alma nodded her head so strongly, Roxy worried she might hurt herself. "Yes! You are a magnet for attracting nonexistent trouble. You know, Roxy, sometimes God opens a window. Don't be in a hurry to close it. At least not yet."

"We're going to the movies Saturday night." Roxy slid her gaze away from Alma, not wanting to measure her reaction. A second later, instinctively she looked back.

"Well, good for you. Glad to see you're not moping around the building." Alma stared at Roxy as though measuring if she should continue. "Facts are facts. Sam left you. He got into some bad stuff, Lord knows what, that got his ass killed. None of that is because of you. I know it's hard. Still, you deserve to get your life back. With this dude, or some other, don't matter. All I'm saying is enjoy a night out with a good-looking guy. Who knows where this might go. For your sake, I hope, into a bedroom. You need some serious—"

Roxy interrupted. "You don't think it's too soon?"

"Too soon for who? Do you like the guy?" Alma sounded irritated at the question.

"Well, yes. What I know of him. But, in my day, we took things slow."

"If you took things any slower, Rocks, you'd be in reverse."

"By your standards, maybe. This gal needs to pump the brakes a bit."

"You need to pump something, and it ain't Alex's brakes. How long has it been since… well, you know?"

Roxy pulled a quizzical face.

"Don't play dumb with me. Since you had sex. When was the last time you and Sam did it?"

"Did it?"

"Hide the salami. Make love, whatever."

Roxy let out a burst of laughter. "We used to call it having dessert."

"Sweet, indulgent, and wicked. All that whipped cream."

"*Let's have dessert* was our secret message. I hadn't thought about my sex life in a long, long time. But now that you ask, we made love a couple of days before Sam left. We had the best sex we'd had in years. Almost like he needed to drink me in and still couldn't quench his thirst. Afterward we spooned, all sweaty and spent, lying on the bed like two teenagers."

"Had the sex gotten stale?" Alma asked.

"Boy, you don't have any qualms getting personal, do you?"

"Well, was it?"

Roxy sucked in air. "I wouldn't describe our sex life as stale. More like routine, reliable. The way everything in our lives ran on schedule, from ordering food truck supplies on Tuesdays to Wednesday and Saturday hump days.

"So when Sam came home early that Sunday night with a nice bottle of wine, I should have suspected something was wrong. We had a wonderful evening, joking and recalling stories. He wanted to reminisce about the early years. Sort of a walk down memory lane on how good the good old days were, you know. When we finally fell into bed, Sam devoured me as if he needed to remember every detail. Like he was loving me for the last time."

"As things turned out, he was." Alma stared straight ahead, her features turning cold. "That jerk had one last screw with you before he went back to his wife. What a douche."

Roxy blinked rapidly considering the possibility, but it didn't add up. The way Sam acted that night exuded a temporary farewell, not a final goodbye, like a soldier leaving for war and tucking his girl's photo in his pocket to get him through the rough times ahead.

But what rough times did Sam face? And how could she have been naïve about the depth of misfortune he had landed in?

"I've known and loved Sam for a long time," Roxy said after a minute. "You might be right about him just wanting a piece. Could have been split-up sex. But I have to say, it didn't feel that way. Everything seemed deeper, more intense, sort of... remorseful in a sense. That night, our connection was solid—not something that shouted, *We had some good times, didn't we, babe.*"

"Sorry if I sounded harsh. No reflection on you. I can't stand men who take advantage of women," Alma said.

"Are we still talking about me?"

"Yes, of course."

"What happened to that guy you started seeing a few weeks ago? You never told me his name."

Alma licked her lips. "Rudy."

"And?"

"Not sure. Could be I got played." Alma slid a quick glance in Roxy's direction before turning her attention back to the road. "Or could be I'm in love. Gotta wait and see how things shake out. Guess I'm right where you're at with Alex."

Roxy exhaled. "Just two gals on an adventure. Tune in tomorrow for the next episode."

Alma scrunched her face. "No other way." She pulled up to the curb in front of their building. "Sorry I have to drop you off and run."

Roxy accepted a brief hug. "You told Alex that you're my best friend, and you were not exaggerating. Thank you, Alma, in more ways than you know, for helping me through this. I have a hunch that good things are waiting for us in the days ahead."

Roxy retrieved her keys, climbed out of the car, and watched Alma pull away.

Would her premonition come through? Happier times for the two of them.

She prayed this was true, but a niggling dread that had been her constant companion since Sam's death portended a different ending to their adventures.

Chapter Twenty-Eight

Boom. Boom. Boom.

"What the heck is that?" Roxy shouted into the emptiness of her bedroom, groggy from being awakened from a deep sleep. She rolled over to check the clock on her nightstand. **7:30** stared back in red LED digits. Her phone listed three missed calls from Alex.

"Crap, I overslept."

She threw her robe on and rushed toward the source of loud banging.

"Alex," she said, reaching the living room, unlocking the front door, and turning the knob. "I slept in, but I can be ready to go in… Chuck?" Roxy wiped sleep from the corner of her eye in disbelief. "What are you doing here?"

"Good morning, beautiful. I brought coffee." Chuck pushed past her, holding a carrying tray and a paper bag. "Scones, too."

"Why are you here?" Roxy demanded. "And please leave. I've got to get ready."

"For what? That stupid class you're taking?" Chuck pulled out a kitchen chair and sat. "Driving a truck isn't your style. Besides, I have a better offer for you."

He knew how she'd been filling her days. Still, why would he have an opinion? Once she quit the food truck, he had no time or interest in her, unless she would give him a handy.

She shook her head, eager to erase that image. *Yuck.*

Chuck gestured for her to join him, but Roxy remained glued to where she stood, robe pulled tight, arms across her chest. "Just leave. We don't have anything to talk about."

"Not even Sam's death?" he asked, unpacking scones and setting one on a napkin for her. He licked the sugar glaze from his fingertips. "Sit down, Roxy. We have a whole lot of catching up to do."

"Excuse me?" Alex stood in the open doorway. "Hope I'm not interrupting. Uh, Roxy, did you find another ride to class?" he asked, obviously confused—and Roxy hoped, disappointed—to see another man in her kitchen.

"No. No, I haven't," she responded quickly. "Chuck was leaving, weren't you?"

"Well, when you put it like that." He got to his feet. "Chuck Winston." He extended his hand to Alex. "Roxy and I used to work together. I stopped by to offer my condolences. Roxy and Sam were a pair for a long, long time."

Alex remained quiet, as though assessing Chuck.

"Wanted to see how she is doing. Both my wife and I are concerned about her," Chuck added.

Asshole never checked on me after Sam left town. She released an inward sigh of relief for that small mercy.

Roxy slid her gaze from Chuck to Alex and cringed.

What is he thinking?

Quicker than necessary, she took a few steps toward Chuck and patted his arm. "That's kind of you and Sonya, but as you can see, I'm fine. And I'm in a rush." She guided him past Alex in the direction of the door. "If I need anything, Alex will gladly take care of it for me."

Chuck nodded. "Nice to meet you," he said to Alex. "Rocks, I'll give you a call later today. Perhaps we can pick a better time to catch up."

"There's nothing to catch up about," Roxy said.

"Well, okay. Enjoy the scones." Chuck flashed his snowy-white teeth that had cost him thousands, offered Alex a hasty salute, and left.

"Well, that was weird," she said by way of explanation.

"Surprising for certain," Alex agreed. "Mind if I take one of these?" he asked, pointing to an untouched scone.

"Help yourself," she said. "Give me fifteen minutes, and I'll be ready. I know we'll be late for class. Maybe we can take care of my tires during our break," Roxy pleaded.

"Yum, cranberry, my favorite," Alex said between chews. He shooed Roxy toward her bedroom. "Rita understands we need some time this morning."

"You've talked to Rita?"

"Look, go get dressed. We'll figure things out on the drive."

***

Thirty minutes later, Roxy buckled up before eyeing Alex as he pushed a button to start his car. "I've got to get used to that," she said, hoping to break the icy vibe settling around them.

Was he jealous of Chuck?

"Used to what?" Alex asked, looking over his shoulder before putting the car in gear and pulling out into the flow of traffic.

She pointed to his dashboard. "That keyless ignition thing. I still insert an actual key into an actual keyhole and turn the whole enchilada until the engine engages. Firing up the car with a button seems unreal to me."

"It's real, all right. Something like eighty percent of autos have keyless ignitions now. Standard equipment," Alex said, suddenly sounding like a new car salesman. In spite of the balmy morning, he wore a cigar-brown blazer over his T-shirt and jeans. In fact, he always wore some sort of jacket or coat, no matter the weather.

"Yeah. No more keys and, nowadays, no more AM radio. We gain in one arena and lose in another."

"A few car companies still have AM radio. For the most part, I—and the rest of the world—use satellite," Alex said. "Don't you?"

"Oh, yeah. I'm digging the sounds of the '70s on satellite radio when I'm driving my uses-a-real-key automobile."

"When you get a newer car—one that was manufactured in this century—you'll understand what I mean," Alex teased. "And who says *digging* anymore?"

"I can dig it. You can dig it. He can dig it." Roxy grinned, making a vague reference to the Friends of Distinction's monster hit. "Anyway, I don't want a newer model. All your car does is beep or chime or buzz at you for every little thing. That would drive me nuts," she confessed.

Alex chuckled. "You get used to modern conveniences. Assuming you ever trade in that classic you're tooling around in."

"Tooling around. Mr. Montgomery, you *are* showing your age. Who says tooling around anymore?"

"Oh, plenty of people say toolin'," he declared, merging into the fast lane before glancing at her. "'Tooling around' is a perfectly good phrase."

"When we were in high school, maybe," Roxy chided, entranced by the playful look in his eyes, his iciness now defrosting. Alex enjoyed teasing and being teased. She liked that. "You're more old-fashioned than I am, except for you adopting so easily to the new auto technology."

"I've always been an early adopter. Cell phones, streaming services, meal prep kits. You name it, I'm the first on my block to try it. Makes me a trendsetter, I suppose."

"That fits. You seem like a risk-taker to me. Someone who leads, not follows. A trailblazer."

"Guess that's true. Never liked being told what to do," Alex agreed. "Especially when my way is always the right way."

"Really?" Roxy asked, drawing the word out to several syllables.

Alex turned and winked at her before returning his focus to the road. "Just seeing how far I can pull your leg before you punch back."

Roxy remained quiet, her not-so-secret way of punishing him. Finally, she asked, "Today will be in the high eighties. Won't you be hot wearing that coat?"

Alex ran a hand down his lapel. "I threw this on this morning. The weather was chilly at my place. Don't worry, I'll stash the coat in my locker before class."

She wrinkled her nose.

"Well?" Alex continued.

"Well what?" Roxy replied.

"Are you going to tell me about Chuck, or do I have to guess?"

"Tell you what? That he's a certified asshole who never gave a crap about me or Sam in all the years I've known him?"

"How long have you known him?"

"Since Sam bought the food truck," Roxy replied, reflecting on the coincidence she'd never considered until now. Chuck had been there from the beginning.

"And?" Alex pressed.

"And what? He came by occasionally to talk to Sam. Every once in a while, he'd bring his wife, Sonya, along. Now that lady was something else. She had her nose stuck up so far in the air, I wondered if the tip was frozen."

Alex pushed on. "Why was Chuck at your place at the butt crack of dawn?"

Roxy belly laughed. "Butt crack. I like that."

"Well?"

"I guess he's after something. Something that has nothing to do with me being okay. I'll bet Sonya doesn't even know he came over. She's more the send-flowers-and-scrawl-a-meaningful-sentence-on-a-card type to show her insincerity."

"Huh?"

"Sonya and I were never close, even though Sam and I often double-dated with them, if you can call four adults going out to dinner a double date. Sonya was into high-society kinds of things. Theater, galas, the kinds of events that get your picture in the paper. Her European accent added to her allure. She mentioned once that she was born in a small town near Vienna."

"She's Austrian?" Alex questioned.

"Could be. She sounds exotic. Her elocution, so to speak, sets her apart."

"I heard what you did there, so to speak."

Roxy smirked.

"What's she doing with old Chuckles, then?" Alex asked. "They don't seem like a match."

"Oh, Lord, they aren't. Chuck is beer and pretzels, Sonya caviar and Veuve all day."

"They say opposites attract," Alex said.

"Doubtful in this case," Roxy said. "Anyway, I remember one night the four of us went ice-skating. Sonya practically exploded in fury at the idea and spent most of the night picking herself up off the cold, icy rink. That was the last time we went out together."

"How long ago was that?" Alex asked.

"Maybe a couple of months before Sam left." Roxy paused, thinking about how mad Sonya was at Chuck that night. She had torn her expensive ski pants and was livid. "I got the feeling she wanted out of her marriage, but they had two kids. And when you get used to diamonds, trips to Europe, and a new sports car every other year, leaving gets to be tougher and tougher."

"I see," Alex said. *But did he?*

"Look," Roxy continued, "if it's all right with you, let's talk about something else. Like maybe you."

"Me?" With one palm, Alex clutched his chest in an exaggerated fashion. "What could possibly be of interest about little old me?"

"For starters, what job did you have before deciding to become a trucker? You never told me."

"You mean how did I earn a living before my renaissance?"

"Well, yes."

Alex grinned. "Now that is a long and complicated story. One that will require more time than we have now." He took the freeway off-ramp, the school a minute away. "Maybe after our movie date tomorrow."

"You look like a corporate guy," Roxy pushed. "Did you work in finance? Accounting? Government?"

"You assuming I'm a white-collar guy turning blue?"

"Well, yes. Has there been any dirt under your nails since fifth grade?"

Alex smirked. "I garden."

Roxy dismissed his reply. "Another clue, that's an expensive jacket, all laundered and pressed. Sam basically hung his coat up on the floor. His jeans had permanent wrinkles."

"You're saying I dress nice." He pulled into the driving school lot. "Why, thank you."

With little time left to drag any details out of Alex, Roxy dropped the questioning. She could wait until Saturday night. After a movie and popcorn, she'd reopen the interrogation.

Once Alex turned off the engine, she grabbed her purse and headed toward Jason and Rita.

"Give me your key," Rita shouted, her hand outstretched.

Roxy quickly detached the car key from the ring. "Here you go," she said, tossing her house keys back inside her purse. Along with Rita, she and Jason watched as the operator attached chains to the front bumper's tow hooks and hauled Roxy's vehicle onto his flatbed.

"We thought we'd get things going," Rita said once Alex joined them. "George is a former student," she said by way of introducing the tow truck operator. "He'll have you fixed up by lunchtime."

We? "That was nice of you, Rita. But—"

"Rita told him to hold on to the damaged tires in case the police need them for evidence," Jason said.

"Good thinking," Alex said. "George can always recycle them later."

"Evidence for what?" Roxy straightened as though an electrical shock vibrated through her. "This was on purpose," she croaked, no longer able to hold on to the fantasy. Someone wanted to intentionally harm her.

"I don't know. Better to find out what's going on first and toss the tires later," Alex grumbled, and stepped away to answer his ringing phone.

Roxy scowled and turned to Rita. "I appreciate you helping me. Thing is… um, well, how much will all this cost?" she asked, afraid of the answer.

"Don't worry. George did the tow as a favor. I told him that you're a girl on a tight budget. He'll give you his best price for the tires." Rita waved as George pulled away, Roxy's car bouncing as he turned the corner. "He'll call with an estimate. In the meantime, everyone, let's get to class."

Roxy ambled alongside Alex, his phone an inch away from his ear, but she couldn't hear the conversation. Alex disconnected his call.

"Shouldn't you hang up your fancy blazer first?" she directed. "You'll get grease or dirt or something on the sleeves if you don't."

"You're sure worried about my wardrobe," he sniped. "Just for that, I'm keeping my coat on. Let's see how dirty I can get today." He strode toward the school entrance. Roxy allowed him the space.

Is he acting strange? Or is my imagination operating at hyper-speed? I've missed some sleep. Maybe that's why my brain is slaphappy.

As Roxy approached the rest of the students, she knew her angst wasn't from overreacting.

Someone *had* dumped a dead body—Sam's dead body—in her limo, along with her kitchen knife. They had thrown her possessions around, leaving her feeling unsafe and violated in her own home. And, as much as she didn't want to admit that Alex was right, her tires were confettied with nails on purpose. Chuck showing up this morning clinched the reality. Chuck had something to do with all this, although Roxy couldn't be sure how.

She was in danger.

Imagination or not, something screwy was going on.

And with Alex, too. He asked a lot of questions that seemed outside the boundaries of a getting-to-know-you courtship. And his apparent coziness with law enforcement left her uneasy, too, although she couldn't pinpoint why.

She suspected Alex had reached out to Rita to get her tires replaced, probably at his expense. All his help and consideration could be explained under the umbrella of friendship, perhaps the hope of a deeper relationship, if they had known each other longer.

Still, that didn't explain his attachment to wearing a dress coat while working on greasy, messy trucks.

At that moment, as though he sensed her watching him, Alex turned. He grinned and waved before entering the garage.

That's when she recognized a bulge under his right armpit.

Suddenly she thought of the gun holster Sam started wearing under his jacket some six months ago. She scrunched her eyes closed as if when she reopened them, things would be better.

Nope. Everything was still crappy.

But perhaps some pieces of the puzzle were finally falling into place.

Chapter Twenty-Nine

Thursday had flown by in whirlwind fashion, with Roxy cramming more automotive wisdom into her brain than any soul would ever need. After class, Alex drove them to George's garage to retrieve her car. Mysteriously, but maybe not surprisingly, four tires, not two, had been replaced.

"There's some mistake," Roxy protested. "Only the back two got nailed."

"True," George said. "But the front two hardly had enough tread for a nail to puncture."

She couldn't argue with that. When was the last time she had replaced those tires? Roxy's chest tightened at the imbalance of her checking account in relation to the price of four new tires.

She swallowed hard, preparing herself to absorb the large number. "Can I have the bill?"

George shook his head. "Nope. You have a guardian angel. Everything is paid for, including an oil change. You're a lucky lady."

Not feeling especially fortunate, and too frustrated to argue, Roxy thanked him before turning to Alex. "You're the angel?"

"Nothing angelic about me. Just want you safe," he said. "Totally selfish motives."

"I will pay you back, just as soon as—"

"Roxy, I know you will. No rush. Do you want me to follow you home?" Alex asked, effectively changing the subject.

"No need," Roxy answered too quickly. "I am a little worried about parking in my carport, though. Whoever did this isn't done."

"Someone is messing with you. Don't let them."

Roxy nodded, as though infusing resolve into her DNA.

"I doubt they'll pull this same stunt again," Alex continued. "Call me when you're safely inside your place and then get a good night's sleep."

"I'll soak in a hot bubble bath first." Roxy imagined the warm water covering her, wiping away the stress, delighted at the twinkle in Alex's eyes.

Too soon for that, but maybe one day…

He grinned as though reading her mind. "Add in a glass of wine and you have the makings of a relaxing night." He walked her to the car and opened the door. "I'll phone in the morning, and we can decide what movie to go see."

"Perfect. Hope there's a comedy playing. I need a few laughs."

"Don't we all," Alex agreed, stepping aside to make way for her to pass.

"I'll let you know when I'm home." She plunked down behind the steering wheel wondering what she had done to attract this savior. Fortunately, her brain was too scrambled to overthink her good fortune, so she went with the princess-like aura.

She sent a quick wave at both George and Alex standing together near the service bay, baffled at what they could be talking about.

The bill, probably.

She pointed the car in the direction of home. Several minutes later, Roxy locked the door behind her, then texted Alex of her safe arrival.

She gladly gave in to the appeal of a steaming bubble bath and a glass of cabernet. She willed her mind to rest from the day's events, to quiet the avalanche of fears relentlessly bombarding her brain. Warm water blanketed her.

Roxy closed her eyes and imagined every negative thought blowing away. That meditation trick worked for a while. But questions continued to rise like puffs of smoke from a chimney.

Why was Sam murdered? Am I still in danger?
Who is Alex Montgomery?

Chapter Thirty

Midmorning on Saturday, Roxy leaned against her kitchen counter and fidgeted with her phone, delaying a call to Alex. She hated canceling their date, but she had no choice.

Minutes earlier, Stacy had phoned in a panic. Something about one of her kids, and she needed Roxy to take her exhibitor spot at a local bridal fair. As she listened to Stacy, Roxy staggered to the kitchen and turned on the coffee brewer, waiting for the magic elixir to percolate.

"This is one of the big three," Stacy had told her. "We get a large part of our bookings from those brides and wedding planners every year. They make up a significant slice of our revenue. I have to have someone there to showcase our business, or the organizers will give our spot away to another limo company."

"A bridal fair?" Roxy questioned groggily, barely two gulps of caffeine now fueling her focus. "Like a trade show? For weddings?"

"Exactly. You probably attended stuff like that when you managed the food truck," Stacy said, a hopeful glimmer in her voice. "There's no one else to ask. Cecile and the other drivers have clients today. Please, please," she pleaded. "I know you're working through your own stuff, and I wouldn't put this on you, except—"

"Stacy, you've done so much for me. I'm happy to repay a tiny bit of your kindness. And this sounds like fun. Everyone there will be planning a joyous occasion. Just the diversion I need."

"That's the spirit. Thank you. Thank you," Stacy said, an air of relief wafting through the line. Stacy briefed her on what to expect. "I'll have everything you need to set up inside of Twenty-Four." Twenty-Four was the company's newest vehicle, not the one where Sam's body had been found.

"Sorry to dump this on you in such a rush," Stacy continued. "The event is sponsored by Shady Glen Golf Course. I'll text you the address and the fair's website so you can familiarize yourself with the layout. Someone will be there to tell you where to park. It's usually in front of the entrance."

"No problem. I'll figure things out," Roxy said, hopefully not promising more than she could deliver.

"The trouble is that they open at noon, and the show doesn't close until seven. Except for potty breaks, you'll have a long day on your feet, all by yourself. I can't guarantee someone can stop by to spell you. If you have to go to the restroom, lock the limo."

Roxy glanced at her watch. She barely had time to shower, dress, pick up the limo and drive across town to the show site. "Don't worry. I'll get ready now. I'll be mingling with those brides before you know it."

"I owe you one," Stacy said.

"Hardly," Roxy replied. "Hope everything turns out okay with the kids."

"Yeah, well, it's Bobby up to his same old BS. Everything will be fine. I need to be there in person to make sure. Anyway, check later in the day and let me know how things are going or if you have any questions."

"Will do." Roxy ended the call and stood in the same spot, staring at Alex Montgomery's contact, sandwiched between Aileen, her cousin, and Andrea, her hairstylist.

She wanted to know Alex better, not just on the personal front, although she had to admit a few sparks definitely flew. She harbored a deep curiosity about the man, especially since she didn't believe he had upended his life to become a trucker. Something else was at the root of the hidden persona he kept tucked away, and she wanted to find out what.

Besides, she hadn't been to the movies in years. Roxy missed the big screen, the smell of freshly popped popcorn, the way her shoes sort of stuck to the cement from spilled sodas.

And she wanted to thank Alex for everything he'd done to keep her life on an even keel—or at least the appearance of an even keel.

And now she'd have to break their date.

Because he was a gentleman, he'd say he understood. But truly, it was Roxy who was disappointed.

She jumped at the vibrating phone in her hand. *Alex Montgomery* appeared on the screen.

Gotta tell him. "Hello."

"Hi, Roxy. Sorry to call so early, but something's come up, and I won't have my phone with me most of the day. Can we nail down a film you'd like to see and figure out the timing?"

Roxy puffed air through her lips. "Funny thing, Alex, I was just about to call you."

"Don't tell me you've changed your mind," he said.

"Not exactly, but I can't make the movies tonight. Stacy needs me to fill in today."

"What?" Alex sounded exasperated. "You just found a dead body in your limo. She can't let you drive people around. Doesn't she know that?"

"She does. I won't be a chauffeur today. I just need to dress like one," she said, pleased with her teasing reply. The sound of a chair being dragged across the floor screeched in her ear.

"I have a few minutes before I have to leave," Alex said, interest creeping into his tone. "I'm sitting. Explain this one to me."

As Roxy relayed the main parts of her conversation with Stacy, the anxiety in Alex's voice lifted.

"You'll be spending all day talking to bridezillas?" he summarized.

"Well, I hope not. I can do without all the wedding drama."

"Okay. I understand you have to help Stacy out. Maybe brunch and a movie tomorrow?"

"I'd love that."

"Great, I'll pick you up at noon."

"See you then." Roxy clicked off and ran toward her bathroom to take a quick shower.

As promised, she was parked in the appointed spot, wearing her Decker-designed outfit and a smile on her face when the hordes of brides descended.

She prayed most of the bridezillas stayed home.

Chapter Thirty-One

Roxy stood tall in front of Twenty-Four, Stacy's custom-built limousine, eager to greet the future wives and their entourages of moms, sisters, mothers-in-law, bridesmaids, and champagne-sipping cousins.

While most of the bridal expo was set up inside the golf course ballroom, a few exhibitors like Roxy were stationed outside the entrance under an ornate cupola. Arriving on-site with fifteen minutes to spare, she sized up her fellow exhibitors. On her right, a thirty-something disc jockey with a flair for theater played a variety of tunes, in what must be his attempt to showcase the range of music literally at his fingertips.

To his left, purple and silver balloons in the shape of a large arch stretched to the sky, swaying in the mild breeze. She watched two young—by Roxy's standards—women erect the semi-circle and secure it into two decorative pillars, making a festive backdrop. Those ladies now stood underneath their balloon canopy with a banquet table in front of them displaying the array of balloon colors and arch sizes the brides could choose from.

Next to the balloon gals, as Roxy dubbed them, a photo booth popped up, complete with a photographer who encouraged her to sneak over for a snapshot. Since things hadn't gotten underway yet, Roxy took advantage of the invitation, trying a variety of hats, signs, and poses. She tucked the strips of silly pictures into her pocket as a souvenir.

Even though she was disappointed to miss her date with Alex, today would be fun. She tingled with anticipation of meeting new people, of having new experiences. A blue sky, sunshine, and the promise of fresh beginnings—exactly the vibe Roxy sorely needed. For the first time in a while, streamers of hope and possibility flowed into her thoughts, replacing the dread and anxiety that had taken up residence in her mind for weeks.

The first few hours slid by with Roxy fielding questions and sharing the magical luxury of a limousine. She loved hearing each potential client's fairy-tale story. Every bride-to-be seemed set on outdoing the next in excitement, expectation, and expense.

Do you offer a fifty-percent discount to seniors?

Can you waive the four-hour minimum? We only need a ride to the church and back.

My dress is a size six. Can I lose thirty-five pounds by the summer?

As Roxy finished explaining what a young woman and her fiancé could expect from Sleek Limo on their wedding day and what those services would cost, she spotted a familiar face. Hank, of Hank and Herb fame, approached her.

"Remember me?" he asked as the couple walked away, heading toward the balloon arch.

"Hi, Hank," Roxy answered. "Oh, I remember you very well." *You stepped in the night Sam harassed me at the prom site.* "But you look different in street clothes."

"Yeah, I get that a lot." He snorted. "No one remembers me, just the kilt."

He pointed to the stack of *Scottish Enchantment* brochures Stacy had directed Roxy to display, along with Sleek's promotional material.

"So smart to market to the bachelorettes. I've had several inquiries. It was easy to recommend your services after the amazing job you did for Simona."

Hank searched the space. "I don't see Stacy."

"She had a last-minute conflict and asked me to fill in."

"Oh. And everything is going okay?" Hank questioned, apparently perplexed at Roxy's presence.

"Yes. Just busy, which is a good thing. It's clever of her to cross-promote with you," she said, making conversation but keeping her focus on a woman filling out a raffle form and placing the slip of paper in the upside-down chauffeur's cap doubling as an entry box.

"Clever for both of us," he agreed with a nod. "They only allow one limo company to exhibit, so we share the cost of the space. Works out for everyone." Hank looked around and jutted his chin in the direction of the balloon arch. "Those two are at every event. Where do they get the energy or the bankroll to afford that many trade shows and fairs?"

"This does seem to be big business," Roxy said. "Excuse me for a minute." She made her way to the woman still at the table filling out an entry. "Do you have any questions?" Roxy asked, "or would you like to look inside the car?"

The woman clicked the pen closed and put it in her purse. "Oh, no. I'm fine," she said, dropping an entry form into the cap. "Thanks, anyway." She scurried off, and Roxy lifted the entry out of the hat.

"Hmmm," she huffed, realizing the woman had filled out several. She held up the duplicate forms. "This probably happens all the time."

Hank joined her and shuffled through the slips of paper. "She was sly, though. Look, different names, with the same phone number. Like nobody would catch on to that."

"Should I toss them out?"

"Leave them. Makes it look like lots of folks are interested. Anyway, Stacy will cull through them at the office."

Roxy nodded.

"Hey," Hank said, "if you want to get a bite to eat or use the facilities, I can man the car for about thirty minutes, then I have to take off."

"Well?" Roxy answered, unsure if she should leave everything to his watchful eye.

"Herb or I usually stop by to give Stacy or Cecile a break. She didn't mention that?"

"She said she couldn't guarantee that anyone would be able to relieve me. But then again, her day had gone sideways, and she was in a super hurry when she called."

Hank looked at his watch. "It's nearly two. I need to hit the road by two-thirty, two-forty-five at the latest," he said.

"Maybe a quick potty run," Roxy said.

"Take your time. I hear you've gone through some, shall we say... challenges recently. Man, a dead body in the limo. I've chauffeured for maybe fifteen years. Never had that happen before."

Roxy swallowed. "And here you are again, coming to my rescue." She hoped the comment would dissipate the growing anxiety mounting in her chest.

Hank had seen her fight with Sam. He must know the dead body in her limo was Sam's. Two separate facts that didn't add up to anything, but still she struggled to shake off the shades of guilt that seemed to be painting her.

"Sorry to hear about him, but I'm glad you're okay. You *are* okay, right?"

Roxy turned toward the balloon ladies and the young couple. She listened as they suggested songs to the DJ. "Play something from the eighties," the one who appeared slightly older requested.

The other woman pulled a face. "Nah. No oldies but goodies."

"The eighties aren't oldies," the first woman complained.

"Well," the DJ interjected, "by today's standards they are. But hey, I still get a lot of requests for hair metal and glam bands."

"Roxy?" Hank touched her arm. "Are you all right?"

She turned to face him. "Absolutely. I was eavesdropping on the great debate they're having." Roxy shifted her gaze back to the DJ before pivoting to Hank. "Does eighties music qualify as oldies?"

"Never thought about that. I guess so. That's last century," Hank said. "Look, sorry if I asked too many questions. I didn't know I'd run into you today, but I'm glad I did. I've wondered how you've been since that night at the prom. But seems like you're doing well."

"I am," Roxy stuttered. "This is the first opportunity Stacy has given me since... well, since Sam's death. I'm glad to be where everything is upbeat and raucous. Weddings are a fairy tale come true, and I need some happily ever after in my life these days."

Hank nodded. "Well, go use the restroom and get a bite to eat. I'll wait until you get back—that is unless you don't want to miss the greatest debate since Lincoln-Douglas. Their next topic: peanut butter, smooth or chunky."

Roxy grinned. "I won't be gone ten minutes." She retrieved her purse from the front seat and paused to face Hank as three women approached the booth, one wearing a *Here Comes the Bride* white satin sash.

"Thank you again for helping me when you did. I don't know what I would have done, especially now with how everything turned out."

"No problem. Under my Highland shirt, I wear a blue tee with a large red S on the front for occasions such as that one." Hank reached for his wallet. "Do you mind bringing me a bottled water when you come back?"

"I got it," she said, waving off his cash. "The least I can do for a superhero."

Chapter Thirty-Two

Roxy nibbled shrimp and brie samples as she walked around the exhibit area, taking longer than the ten minutes she had promised Hank. She had already wolfed down two beef sliders and three tiny cupcakes, while watching willing soon-to-be brides and not-so-willing grooms follow along during a dance lesson. The festive atmosphere in the grand hall made Roxy wish she was planning a wedding, if not her own, then maybe Alma's.

The expo showcased florists, makeup artists, hair stylists, and honeymoon travel planners. There was even a dedicated section for ceremony officiants and furniture rental. If she had the time, Roxy would have stayed to watch the fashion show starting in thirty minutes. This truly was "the one-stop shop for all your bridal needs," as the banner hanging above her head proclaimed.

Several booths offered cold bottled water with their contact information printed on the wrap-around label. Roxy requested a couple and headed to the limousine, hoping she hadn't taken advantage of Hank's kindness.

She walked out of the main hall and into a knot of people gathered near the photo booth. She followed their gaze to where Hank stood near the limo, one hand in his pocket, the other whirling in the air for emphasis. He gestured as though confused by what the two men in suits asked.

The suits, one who boasted a horseshoe-shaped mustache and the other a more senior fellow, appeared equally unhappy with Hank's response. Just beyond them, two female security guards—

or were they police officers—seemed to be scanning the area looking for someone.

Roxy wondered what could have happened in the short time she had been gone.

Had someone been robbed? With her free hand, she reached for her purse tucked under her arm, reassuring herself that she wasn't the victim. In any event, she needed to let Hank leave.

She moved carefully down the steps, holding out the water bottles.

"Here you go." She handed him one before turning to the suited gentlemen. "Is everything okay?"

"Roxy—" Hank began but was interrupted.

"Are you Roxanne Adams?" the man with the mustache asked.

"Why, yes," she answered, searching Hank for a clue as to what was going on. "Is everything okay?" she repeated, facing the three men. "Has something happened to Stacy? Or Alma? Or…?" She couldn't finish the sentence. The names of people she loved and cared about were too numerous.

"I'm Lt. Reynolds with the LAPD. You've already met Detective Scavino."

"I have?" Roxy knitted her brow. *Was he one of the detectives who had questioned me? Why didn't you return my call?* she started to ask, but the first man broke in.

"Ms. Adams, you are under arrest for the murder of Samuel Miguel Reyes. You have the right to remain silent."

"I'm what?"

He continued reciting the Miranda warning.

Roxy froze, thoughts bombarding her with the realization.

She was being arrested for Sam's murder. Hank's sorrowful, apologetic face emphasized her fate.

The DJ had stopped his music. The engaged couple, the balloon girls, and the photo booth operator stood nearby, as though viewing a circus act. She was the bearded lady.

"Do you understand your rights as I've explained them to you?" Lt. Reynolds questioned.

"What? No! You've got to be kidding." A panicked screech escaped her mouth. "I didn't kill Sam! There's some mistake. You've got the wrong person."

Detective Scavino approached and turned Roxy away from him. He grabbed her right wrist behind her back and clapped a handcuff on. "Yes, ma'am, you will have your chance to tell your side." He reached for her other hand.

"What chance?" Roxy yelled, turning to face him. "I phoned you *weeks* ago with information about Sam's death, and you never called back. And now you're arresting me? In a public place with all these people watching?"

Scavino yanked her elbow hard enough to jerk Roxy toward him. He secured the second handcuff before answering her. "Never got a message from you, ma'am. But if you have something to share, you can put it in your statement. Come with us now."

His overly calm, stoic demeanor made Roxy's palms sweat. Scavino wasn't listening to her. He couldn't care less about her innocence. He was a "just the facts, ma'am" cop. The kind her grandmother had loved to watch on TV in the 1950s.

Roxy wanted to shriek the words, but a desire to avoid a bigger scene than the one exploding before her eyes won out. "Why are you arresting me? I haven't done anything."

"Maybe not," Scavino said. "But new evidence has been uncovered that paints a different picture."

"New evidence. What are you talking about?"

"Blood spatter found at your apartment building confirms the murder scene."

"Sam was murdered at our apartment?" Roxy asked, barely able to believe what the detective was saying.

"Yes, and the time of death has now been established to be Saturday afternoon, not late that night," Reynolds added. "In your earlier statement, you told us you were home all day Saturday. That you didn't leave for your run until around four."

Roxy gulped. They had found Sam's blood behind the trash bin, and she had no alibi for the time of death. "Where are you taking me?" she finally managed to choke out.

"You'll be booked at the station," Scavino answered nonchalantly. "Then photographed and fingerprinted. You should watch TV crime dramas," he said, displaying a piece of his insulting personality.

"It didn't occur to me to make mental notes after each episode of *Blue Bloods*," she snapped, no longer worried about making a good impression.

"That's enough, Ed." Lt. Reynolds stepped forward to face Roxy. "Ms. Adams, we'll follow the usual protocols. After you're booked, you can make a phone call. Request to see your defense attorney or wait for the public defender's office to appoint one. You'll then be arraigned, and the judge will decide on bail."

Defense attorney. Bail.

Roxy had no money to afford either.

A dark veil of doom enveloped her, the opposite sensation of the beautiful white, lacy veils she had watched delighted women try on minutes ago. Veils of happiness, promise, joy; counterpoint to the coal-black netting shrouding her.

Any prospects she had entertained about climbing out of debt, of maybe starting her own business, of having something to show for her life, flickered like a lighter out of butane. Small sparks of promise, but in the end, nothing.

How could this be happening?

"Hank, will you call Stacy and stay with the limo until she gets here?" Roxy said, both arms now secured behind her. "Someone will have to drive the limousine back to the company. Tell her what happened and apologize for me."

"I will," Hank said. "I'm sure this is all a mistake. They'll straighten everything out," he continued, but Roxy could barely make out his words. The two women she had mistaken for security were police officers escorting her to their patrol car.

"I'm being framed!" she shouted at the officers as though she was trapped in a scene from a B-rated film noir.

But her crime drama was real. Sam was murdered, and whoever killed him wanted Roxy to get the blame. Or be tangled up in court until they could locate what they'd been after.

On the short ride to the precinct, Roxy stared out the backseat window, once again pondering the small key she had found in Sam's jacket.

A stronger urgency infused her.

That key will lead me to what happened to Sam.

And answer why I'm now in the crosshairs of people who are so desperate, they kill to get what they want.

Chapter Thirty-Three

Roxy squinted as she was led to the booking area, avoiding inquisitive gazes, and denying the dire wretchedness of her circumstance. The station's artichoke-green walls, combined with a severe lack of windows, intensified the sorrowful backdrop.

Roxy was under arrest for murder.

Sam's murder.

She grimaced as an officer held her hand steady, inking each finger and then rolling the pad side to side, leaving a black image of whorls, loops, and arches on a large white index card.

In a better world, Roxy could be fulfilling a requirement prior to visiting an exotic destination like Japan or Argentina before boarding her plane. Or perhaps completing the final step of a background check as part of landing a desirable government job.

As the pads of her fingers were pushed inside of each designated box, (*r. thumb; l. middle; right four fingers taken simultaneously*) Roxy knew there was nothing desirable or exotic about what was happening. The dingy jail, coated with the smell of desperation and perspiration, confirmed that fact.

Roxy had already posed for her mug shots. *Look straight ahead and don't blink. Turn right. Okay, now turn left.* Except for holding a placard in front of her chest with her name, booking number, date of birth and weight prominently displayed, the process wasn't much different from the DMV. Guaranteed the photo would be terrible, but then again, who wanted a glamour mug shot?

Now Roxy sat in a molded, hard plastic chair, one of a dozen lined in a row against the wall on the far side of the booking room. She shifted her bottom weight from one cheek to the other, searching for a comfortable position while waiting for the next step. When her efforts proved fruitless, she decided to practice her yoga breathing to tamp down her anxiety.

Officer Green, the younger of the two, had brought her here, to this humiliating reminder that she wasn't in charge of her life. Frankly, despite her determined spirit, Roxy hadn't been able to control anything since Sam had left.

She had endured this level of nerve-racking dread some five years earlier while waiting for the results from a mammogram. Her doctor had ordered the additional test because she had seen something in the first one.

For days, Roxy could barely breathe, awaiting the unknown. Sam had consoled her, reminding her that everything would be fine. And after three days, the second mammogram came back clear. Sam had been there for her, pulling her through a dark time.

But there was no Sam to console her today. No one who cared whether she went to prison or not.

Roxy's gaze strayed to where the two uniformed officers chatted, one propped against a counter, finishing up paperwork, the other sipping from a water bottle. Their stoic demeanor added another layer to the worry mushrooming inside.

Curious about their discussion, Roxy angled toward them, hoping to overhear a word or two. When they turned in her direction, she quickly shifted her attention disinterestedly to the floor. She forced herself to keep breathing deeply. Inhaling air would replenish her soul. But the stale oxygen in the small room struggled against entering her lungs.

Drained and helpless, Roxy deflated like a volleyball after absorbing too many spikes. How many more knocks could she take before being knocked out?

Mentally, she made light of the police procedures, as though she was on the set of a sitcom. A feeble attempt to keep the stress-induced acid that roiled in her stomach from lurching up her throat and onto the floor. Roxy could barely maintain composure, her heart rate easily climbing upward of one hundred beats; pounding as though her pulse jumped by five beats every few seconds. If she allowed herself to sink into the seriousness of the moment, she would never regain sanity.

Roxy had to remain calm and think clearly. She had to figure out what that key from Sam's jacket opened.

From where she sat, she saw an officer retrieve the photo booth pictures that had fallen out of Roxy's pants pocket and onto the faded linoleum floor.

Had those pictures been taken only three hours ago?

The officer placed the strips on top of Roxy's folded clothing before shoving the pile into an oversized plastic zippered bag, along with her cell phone, purse, and shoes.

"All your personal items will be available to you once you post bail," the senior officer said, offering a compassionate smile.

When asked later, Roxy recalled that both women had been kind and sympathetic, guiding her through the procedures, as though they had been play-acting. Like booking Roxy wasn't for real, just a staged event.

And for Roxy, everything had seemed like a fantasy, a fictional nightmare happening to someone else. She convinced herself of that up until a matron led her to a jail cell, and the heavy door clanked closed behind her.

Roxy inclined forward, resting her face against the cold steel, and peered through the bars. This was reality, not make-believe.

She turned around in the six-by-eight-foot space, claustrophobia encroaching. Finally, she plopped onto her wafer-thin mattress and stared at the ceiling, counting the minutes until she would be arraigned and hopefully released on bail.

She had made two of her three authorized calls—one to Alma and the other to Stacy. She quickly dismissed notifying Alex.

As soon as they learned when the arraignment was scheduled, both Alma and Stacy had promised to be there, assuring Roxy that this was nothing but a big mistake. The worst kind of mix-up.

But, unlike Alma and Stacy, Roxy wasn't convinced today's events were random.

Sam's dead body crammed into the limo's trunk wasn't accidental. Someone had deliberately searched her apartment, leaving tables knocked over. They stole her carving knife, murdered Sam with it, and conveniently left the bloody weapon with her fingerprints to be found at the murder scene.

The police detectives arresting her in a public place? Definitely planned.

What had Sam gotten himself into?

Gotten her ensnared in?

She had to find out, but she couldn't unravel anything or prove her innocence from a jail cell.

Roxy had to get out of there—and fast.

Chapter Thirty-Four

It wasn't until Monday morning that Roxy's arraignment was scheduled. She spent Sunday locked inside a cell, reflecting on how she got to this nadir in her life.

That, and how prison oatmeal could perhaps double as mortar.

By midmorning, she entered the courtroom, still clad in prison garb, and immediately searched for a familiar face. Alma's or Stacy's in particular. Any acknowledgement from those gathered in the gallery would have lifted her spirits, but she didn't recognize a soul.

Before she had the chance to feel sorry for herself, an LA public defender approached.

"Roxanne Donna Adams?" He used her middle name; her grandmother's name. She knew Grammy Donna wouldn't be proud to have her namesake dragged through this mud.

"Yes, that's me," Roxy hurried to reply before the stout, gray-haired man moved along, a stack of manila file folders in his grasp.

"Great, great," he said, somewhat relieved. "I'm Malcolm Jump." His tone was devoid of emotion.

"Like jump rope but without the rope?" The words tumbled out of Roxy's mouth before she could stop them.

"It is," he said, not amused and obviously overwhelmed by the number of clients he was appointed to represent. From his looks and weathered appearance, Malcolm Jump had seen everything. To him, Roxy was maybe the sixth of dozens of clients he'd represent today. Just another faceless criminal in a long line of "I-didn't-do-it" scumbags looking for an easy way out of a bad situation.

"Ms. Adams... May I call you Roxanne?"

"Roxy, please," she said, hoping to regain whatever points she might have lost with her earlier crack about his odd last name.

"I've done this for a lot of years. Our best play here is for you to keep quiet. I know Judge Bilks. She's got a soft spot for women, especially ones who have been victims of domestic violence."

"But I'm not a victim," Roxy protested. "Sam never hit me or anyone for that matter. Ever." *He was a good man,* she thought, *even if he dumped me without any warning.* "He wasn't violent, and I didn't kill him. I never would want Sam dead."

"Yes, yes, of course," Attorney Jump agreed, barely acknowledging her words. "No matter. When the judge asks you how you plead, you stand up and say not guilty."

"No kidding," Roxy blurted, then covered her mouth.

"Look," Jump continued, steamrolling over Roxy's obvious concerns. "You have no priors, and you're not a flight risk. You'll be out on bail by early afternoon. That is, if you keep your mouth shut. Say yes, ma'am and no, ma'am. Can you do that?" he asked, the snark in his voice palpable.

She nodded, tears welling in her eyes, threatening to spill at any moment.

"You do have someone who'd put up bail for you, right? Could be as much as two-hundred thousand," he asked, realizing he should have addressed this earlier. "They'd need to come up with ten percent of the amount."

Not really sure, Roxy nodded yes, anyway.

Some thirty minutes later, a middle-aged judge, a woman who could have been in Roxy's high school algebra class, set bail at half a million dollars.

"You are accused of first-degree murder," the judge said. "I'm sympathetic to the plight of abused women. Still, murder is a heinous crime, and the bail amount must reflect that."

Roxy's chest hardened, and she buried her face in her hands.

Five hundred thousand dollars. A fifty-thousand-dollar bail bond.

She would be stuck in jail until her case came to trial and possibly forever. Even as good a friend as Stacy had been throughout the past couple of months, Roxy couldn't ask her to post $50,000 to get her out of this ninth treacherous ring of hell.

A gavel slammed against a wooden surface, as though the judge placed the final exclamation point on a sentence. A bailiff assisted Roxy from the defendant's desk and escorted her toward the exit where a matron met her. Roxy turned back to see Jump smile as though things went exactly the way he had hoped.

Ramon Dawson. The bailiff called the next case.

Roxy had glanced again over her shoulder, only to watch Jump shift her file to the bottom of the stack. He opened another, redirecting his attention to the next case, leaving Roxy, a naïve criminal, alone to wait and wonder.

Chapter Thirty-Five

Hours later, the clanking of metal against her jail cell snapped Roxy awake. She propped herself onto her elbows and looked in the direction of the clatter.

Through sleepy eyes, she deciphered the silhouette of a stout guard holding a stack of haphazardly folded clothes against her chest; the same clothes Roxy wore when she got arrested three days earlier. With her free hand, the woman jangled a large key ring, wiggling one inside the lock until the tumblers released, and the door creaked open.

The guard dropped the pile of garments onto the foot of Roxy's cot. "Up and at 'em," she chirped. "Lucky girl. You pulled the Get Out of Jail Free card. Well, not free. Someone coughed up some big bucks."

Roxy rubbed her eyes as though hoping to see a happy ending to this nightmare. "I've been bailed out?"

"Didn't I just say that?" The guard's tone switched from chipper to clipped before Roxy got both feet on the floor. "Get dressed. You'll get your shoes when you sign out. I'll be back in five minutes to escort you." She glared at Roxy and left, slamming the metal door hard and turning the key with such force that the bolt sharply banged into place. She jerked one of the cell bars back and forth as though verifying an animal was safely contained in its cage. "Five minutes," she repeated.

Roxy got the message, although she didn't need encouragement to move quickly. The faster she got out of this hellhole, the better.

She gathered the rumpled remains of her beautifully tailored suit and cradled the bundle to her bosom. The suit that represented the first sign of her gaining control of her life; of normalcy. Tears welled in her eyes. She blinked them back; she hadn't allowed herself to cry since this fiasco began.

Roxy let her tears flow but only for a few seconds before swiping them from her cheeks. She stripped off the drab prison uniform, dropping each piece onto the cement floor as though every fiber was infested with lice. Pulling on her dress pants, she slid into her long-sleeved white shirt, both irreparably wrinkled from spending hours shoved inside a zippered pouch. Roxy tucked her shirttails into her waistband and turned in search of a nonexistent mirror to see how she looked, much like Cinderella might have done before the ball. Surely a fairy godmother had something to do with her posting bail.

She straightened her back in anticipation of the guard returning.

That's when she realized her suit coat was missing. Before she had time to wonder what had happened to it, the guard reappeared.

Was she early? Was she trying to catch Roxy unprepared? *Fat chance.*

"All right, Miss Lucky. You ready?"

"Yes, ma'am," Roxy said, running her fingers through her somewhat flat curls. Having a chance to brush her teeth would have been nice, but she knew what they said about beggars. Or murder suspects.

"This way." The guard gestured toward a motorized security gate. Within seconds, the door groaned open, and Roxy walked to where another officer waited at the reception desk, her stout escort no longer needed.

"Roxanne Adams?" he asked.

"Yes, sir," Roxy replied, stepping toward the counter he stood behind.

He placed a short stack of forms in front of her and handed her a pen. "I need you to sign here and here."

"What am I signing?"

"The first document is an Appearance Notice. The second is your property receipt."

"But I'm missing a few things," Roxy protested.

"Your possessions are in that box." He pointed to a cardboard carton at the foot of his station.

Purse, phone, shoes, suit jacket. "Everything seems to be here," Roxy replied, shuffling through the box.

"Leave your state-issued shoes over there," he said, jutting his chin toward a wire mesh container. "Once you're ready, I'll notify your ride."

Roxy dragged the box with her possessions to a nearby bench. She yanked off the orange canvas clogs and tossed them in the collection bin before slipping on her slingbacks and retrieving her handbag from the carton.

Thank goodness. She released a grateful sigh after checking that the two twenties Stacy had given her for incidentals were still in her wallet.

However, her license, credit cards, and even her library card weren't in the same slots where she had left them. The pockets of her suit coat were turned out. Someone had pawed through her things.

Was this standard practice? Or were the police looking for something?

"Ready?" the desk sergeant boomed.

Roxy jumped. "Oh. Sorry. Yes I am." She tucked her belongings into her handbag, before standing to pull on her coat, tucking the pockets into place. She secured the strap of her purse on her shoulder and stared at the officer, waiting for her next instruction.

"Hey."

She spun around. Alex. Handsome, level-headed Alex.

I don't want him to see me here, like this.

"Seems you got yourself into a bit of a scrape," he said, with a tiny curl of his lips.

"Alex." She fell into his open arms. He held her as her heart pounded against her chest. "How did you know? Did you put up my bail?"

"Let's get out of here," he murmured into her ear, "and then we can talk. Do you have your things?"

Roxy nodded. He took her by the hand and guided her toward the exit.

They stepped onto the sidewalk, and Roxy blinked repeatedly. The bright sunshine in stark contrast to the dim, gloomy jail cell pressed her to take a full minute to acclimate her eyes.

She fished sunglasses out of her purse. "Which way to your car?"

Alex extended his arm to the right, and Roxy walked in that direction. The silence between them expanded, neither saying a word until they were inside his sedan. "Do you want to go first, or should I?" Alex asked.

"I don't know," she stuttered. "Where do I start? What questions do I ask? I don't understand what is happening to me." To her embarrassment, tears welled in her eyes.

"All right. I'll go first." Alex started the car and headed toward the freeway. "I wasn't the one who secured the bond for your release. Stacy and Alma did. They asked me to pick you up. Thought you'd be happier to see me."

Roxy huffed. "Damsel-in-distress, knight-in-shining-armor sort of thing?"

"I was thinking more along the lines of Prince Charming." Alex took his gaze off the road. His glistening eyes and cockeyed smile forced a grin.

"If you're trying to make me feel better, it's working—a little."

"Good. I'm taking you to Sleek so you can get your car. And talk to Stacy."

Roxy gulped, her body already nauseous, churning at the idea of facing her boss. "How could she ever want to talk to me again?"

"Obviously because she's a great friend. Coming up with half the money for your bond should be proof enough," Alex said.

Roxy considered the truth in his words. "It's bad enough that I embarrassed myself, but those detectives arrested me right in front of the *Sleek Limousine* sign. I was representing her company. She doesn't deserve this headache, the bad press, and whatever else."

"Nobody deserves what's been happening to you, Roxy. We all get it. You didn't kill anyone. And you're certainly not dumb enough to hide a dead body in the trunk of a vehicle you're responsible for. Something else is going on. Your friends are determined to help you," he said. "And I am, too."

Roxy glanced at Alex, his profile strong and firm. "You barely know me."

"I know enough," he said.

Roxy closed her eyes and tilted back, letting her body go limp. She longed for her roiling stomach to calm and for this nightmare to end.

Stacy, Alma, and Alex believe me. How will I ever repay them?

Chapter Thirty-Six

Roxy and Alex walked toward Stacy's office, Roxy deliberately slowing her gait.

"I'm nervous about seeing Stacy... um, well, everybody," she confessed. "After dragging the company into my abyss, I don't know what to expect."

"Don't expect anything," Alex said. "That's my motto. That way you're never disappointed."

Roxy scrunched her face in displeasure. "That's a defeatist way to live."

"Maybe. But you'll be disappointed less often and occasionally delighted by an unexpected outcome."

Alex opened the office door, and immediately Stacy barreled toward them, aiming for Roxy, her arms flung open.

"Are you okay?" Stacy grabbed her in a momma-bear hug. "We've been worried sick. Hank called as soon as the police took you away. How is any of this happening? How stupid are these people? You'd never kill Sam."

Cecile stepped up, offering a hug of her own. "We tried to get you out that night, but we couldn't do anything until they set the bail amount. And they wouldn't release you until today," she added. "Some lame excuse about the stupid computers being down, but really, they don't process anyone on a Sunday or after seven. Interferes with their beauty sleep, I guess."

Roxy untangled herself from their hugs and attempted to perk up an errant curl with her fingers. "Being locked up definitely interferes with any sleep, beauty or otherwise. I haven't had a good snooze for the past two nights. My cot creaked like a wooden raft, covered with the thinnest, cheapest padding."

She pinched her thumb and forefinger together, leaving a paper-thin space in between. "The kind that comes free with new carpet and the salesman pressures you to upgrade. And look what they did to Decker's beautiful suit," she lamented, running her hands down the front of her wrinkled uniform.

"Not to worry. A good dry cleaning and everything will be like new," Stacy said, stepping aside to make room for Jade and Margo.

"Girl, this is messed up," Jade said. "But everything will get straightened out."

"And we are here for you," Margo added, giving Roxy's upper arm a squeeze and then hugging her.

"Simona would say the same, but she's in the Bahamas on her honeymoon, so she's a little, shall we say, preoccupied right now."

"Yeah, with that hunky hubby she snagged. And speaking of hunky…" Jade slid her eyes toward Alex standing near the doorway. "Who do we have here?"

"Ladies, this is Alex Montgomery, my driving school classmate. Alex, meet the ladies." He smiled and waved but stayed by the door.

"Nice to meet you in person, Alex. And thank you for bringing her here to get her car," Stacy turned toward Roxy. "We've been in a panic since Hank called us with the news. All things considered, you look okay."

"I suppose. I don't understand how the police investigation results in me being the prime suspect," Roxy said. But recent facts told a different story. *Sam had been killed where I live, with my knife; his body dumped in a car I was driving.*

"Me neither," Cecile said, her eyes wide. "I'm no professional detective, but even to an outsider, none of this adds up to Roxanne Adams is a killer."

"Let's go into the dispatch room and have some coffee," Stacy suggested, gesturing for the group to head down the hall. "We have a few things to tell you. Not sure what they'll mean or how they tie into what's happened, but Cecile and I think you'll find them interesting."

Roxy stopped. "Interesting? Like…"

"Like how Sam knew where you were on the night he was found dead."

"What? How could he have known?"

Cecile put her arm around Roxy and gently moved them toward the door. "That's what I want to confess. I should have told you sooner. I screwed up big-time."

"Alex, join us?" Stacy asked.

Roxy broke away from Cecile and shifted toward Alex. "I've already taken up enough of your time. You must have better things to do."

"On a Monday afternoon?"

"What about trucking school?" Jade asked, wedging her way in between the couple.

"I'm missing class, too," Roxy snarked, slightly annoyed at Jade's question, a blatant excuse to talk with Alex.

"Well, of course you are," Jade said. "But you've been in the *hoosegow*. I'm guessing you'll be excused for your absence."

"Hoosegow?" Roxy bit.

"Sorry. I didn't want to say jail." Jade lowered her eyes.

"Glad to see you back," Margo said, embracing Roxy once again.

"I'm glad to be here," Roxy said, meaning every word.

Margo tugged Jade's sleeve. "Let's go. We have runs this afternoon," she said by way of explanation.

After the two women exited, Stacy turned to Roxy. "Well, let's walk over to dispatch. Alex, as I said, you're welcome to join us. But if you need to get back, we understand."

Alex glanced at his watch. "I've already missed most of the day. And Rita knows where I'm at, so I wouldn't mind hearing the news you have to share."

Roxy opted for a bottle of water instead of coffee and stood across from Cecile and Stacy. Alex distanced himself by sitting on the far side of the room.

Roxy sensed the anxiety level had risen several degrees during the few minutes it took to walk to the dispatch room. She couldn't imagine what the women had done to make them visibly tense.

Unless they left dead Sam in her trunk, there wasn't much for them to feel guilty about.

"You want to start?" Stacy asked Cecile.

Cecile licked her lips and hesitated. "It's hard for me to say this, so I'm just going to spill it out. Right after you left to pick up the Stone family for the movie premiere, Sam stopped by. He insisted I tell him where you were. Said it was crucial. That you had something he needed." Cecile gulped in a large inhale before continuing.

"At first, I was shocked to see him here. Really caught me off guard. Then I got irritated. He had put you through so much, I didn't care what he wanted. I told him to get the hell out, or I'd call the police. He pleaded with me to contact you. Said you weren't answering his calls. Well, when he said you didn't want to talk to him, I dialed 911. Before I tapped the connect button, he left. I thought he was gone, and I got busy with some paperwork and other stuff. I don't remember exactly what."

"And?" Roxy said, encouraging her.

"When I looked up from my desk a few minutes later, he was coming out of here."

Roxy gave Cecile a puzzled look.

Cecile pointed to a large white board near Roxy. Each driver's name listed vertically; adjacent were that day's assignments.

Cecile swallowed, remorse coating her. "This is how Sam knew where you'd be. And that's how whoever killed him knew how to frame you." Cecile exhaled. "I am sorry. I should have walked him out of the building and made sure he drove away. Roxy, I-I... I had no idea."

Roxy absorbed Cecile's words.

"Whoever killed Sam knew where you'd be because of our assignment board," Stacy continued. "After they killed him, we think they followed you to the movie premiere and then to the after-party waiting for the chance to—excuse me—dump the body," Stacy stammered.

"That's a solid guess," Alex said from his corner of the room. "Makes sense."

Roxy shifted her eyes from Alex to Cecile, apologetic, repentant, and guarded. "This isn't your fault. If anyone is to blame, it's Sam. And maybe me for not answering his calls, for not listening," Roxy said, stepping toward the woman to touch her hand.

"Why should you?" Stacy defended. "He had burned every bridge. You wanted to get as far away from him as you could. Start fresh."

Roxy released Cecile's hand and glanced at Alex, surprised to see him pitched forward, a look of deep attention now painted across his face. She thought he had stayed out of a sense of loyalty more than genuine interest. But now she wasn't sure. He appeared to hang on each word Cecile said, as though he would recount everything in detail later.

Roxy turned her attention back to Stacy and Cecile. "I agree. The last person I wanted to talk to, or see, was Sam. But I returned his call the day before and left a message when he didn't answer. The morning of the Stone family run, he called back. He must have used a burner phone with no caller ID, so I didn't answer. When I listened to my voicemail just before heading out to Sherman Oaks, he had left a confusing message. Something about never leaving for Tennessee." Roxy blinked back tears. "He and Lola didn't have any type of relationship. He still loved me, and that's why he left. To protect me. He said he had gotten himself into something deeper than he could handle, and he needed me to return this key he left in his baseball jacket."

"Key?" Alex interrupted. "A key to what?"

"That's just it. I don't know. It's a tiny key. Fits some type of locker or maybe a safe deposit box. I had planned to do what he asked and put the key under the garbage can near the food truck, the next day. Then I could be through with him."

Roxy dropped her head in her hands, trying to hide her tears. "I didn't realize how right I would be. That night, he turned up dead. In my limo. I never got the chance to—"

Alex stood. "Do you still have the key?" he asked, seemingly ignoring Roxy's emotional breakdown.

Roxy barely lifted her head in a short nod. Alex had suddenly become engaged in asking probing questions. "Why?"

"Because that key might be what they've been looking for."

"Who?" Stacy asked.

Roxy stared up at Alex. She couldn't decide if she was perplexed or annoyed by his pointed inquiries. Certainly she was stunned by his interest now that she thought about the past several weeks. A few things nibbled around the edges of her brain. Alex asking an innocent question here, giving a pointed opinion there, or offering insight she hadn't requested.

"Practically everyone," Roxy answered, uncertainty at the core of her response. "Whoever broke into my house. The cop who pawed through my wallet. The jerk who nailed my tires."

"That key must be important. And you have no idea what it opens?" Cecile asked.

"Not yet," Roxy answered. "I've been thinking about it. Where Sam might have gone to secure evidence or something to protect him. Illegal drugs. Cash. Could be anything, anywhere."

"Do you still have the key?" Alex repeated, sounding bothered that she didn't respond earlier.

"Well, sort of," she slowly confessed.

"Roxy, either you have the key, or you don't. Cecile is right. We need to find it and figure out what it unlocks." He flashed his winning smile apologetically, apparently aware he'd come on too strong.

"Well?" Cecile asked, obviously as invested in the key's whereabouts as Alex.

Roxy huffed. "I hid it at Alma's. And right now, that seems like the only smart thing I've done. For a while I hauled the key around in my purse. Lucky for me, I moved it because, if the police were looking, they definitely would have found it when they riffled through my possessions." She sighed. "This is surreal. I didn't realize the police could go through your personal stuff without something like a warrant."

"That's true for the average person. But in your case, they can perform a full search of everything: your car, your pockets, your purse, once you've been arrested," Alex said, reclaiming his seat. "But they would have had to do that at the time of the arrest, not after you were booked."

Roxy furrowed her brow. Her uneasy nibbling sensation had turned into chomping.

How does Alex know details about police procedure?

"Nothing was searched when they arrested me. Not my pockets, my purse, nothing. They just hauled me off, with barely enough time to ask Hank to call Stacy."

Alex looked perplexed as though he was sifting through the facts before he spoke again.

"You know a lot about how the police operate," Roxy said, her statement more of a question.

"Well," Alex cleared his throat. "Someday when you're not under arrest for murder, we can swap stories. Right now, you need to retrieve the key and figure out what it opens."

Both Stacy and Cecile voiced their agreement.

Alex was right. Still, something about his paternal handling of the situation bothered her. She had hoped there was a love affair in their future, but an uneasiness washing through her and settling in her stomach left her skeptical and scared.

Alex didn't know her well and the truth of the matter—she didn't know him at all.

Chapter Thirty-Seven

Roxy dialed Alma on her drive home. The meeting with Alex, Stacy, and Cecile had left her anxious and unsettled.

Was she imagining things about Alex or was her intuition doing what it did best, questioning everything? Alma could talk her down when her chaotic brain took control. But today, her friend's phone rang unanswered.

"Alma. Are you home? I'm out on bail, and I need to talk to you. Can we get a coffee or something stronger tonight?" Roxy looked at her watch. *Too early for Alma to be on air.* "Hope you're out doing something fun with that new fellow. Call me later when you have a minute. I need you."

Roxy disconnected and tossed her phone on top of her purse. She tuned her radio to KODO and sang along to a vintage R&B song. After the next song ended, she heard:

"This is Soul Sanchez, spinning the tunes that make you move. Coming up at the half hour, all the news to keep you on cruise."

"There you are my friend, hard at work," Roxy shouted into the emptiness of her car. "Call me!"

From the apartment parking lot, Roxy spied Alma's planter box, a trail of ivy draping down one side. Her geraniums, along with the rest of her garden, appeared healthy and undisturbed.

Roxy hustled up the stairs and opened her apartment door. Before she entered, she checked that she was the only person inside, then dumped her purse on the kitchen table and opened her sliding glass door.

162

She walked onto her patio balcony and glanced around. No one was watching—at least no one she could see.

Alma wouldn't be off for another few hours. Roxy wasn't certain she could wait that long to retrieve the key.

Why had she told everyone where she had hidden the key? What a stupid mistake.

She went inside and opened a bottle of red wine; the nice one her niece had gifted her on her fiftieth birthday. Roxy had been saving the wine for a special occasion. What was more special than getting out of jail? She couldn't think of a thing.

The first glass coasted down her throat as though on skates. She'd never been a wine connoisseur, but she sure liked how this one tasted. She took a few more sips, then swirled the wine left in her glass and watched the liquid form "legs" down the sides. Roxy knew that quality wines had good legs. And that was the extent of her expertise. She wouldn't be adding *sommelier* to her resume any time soon.

Oaky notes, nuances of spice, smokiness. Wine lovers used these terms. All that seemed pretentious. The wine she normally consumed offered nuances of gym socks or the smoky notes of stale licorice candy. She couldn't taste the difference.

Well, until today.

She poured another glass, debating if she should go into Alma's home and nab the tiny key while Alma was still at work. She had already snuck in once using Alma's hidden key. She couldn't sneak in twice. Someone might be watching.

No, she'd wait until Alma came home.

That was, if Alma came straight home.

She'd been dating a new guy. The last time she'd seen her friend, Roxy would have sworn Cupid's arrow was sticking out of Alma's chest.

What was the guy's name? she wondered, halfway through her second glass.

Roxy let the wine relax her. In fact, she moved several degrees to the right of relaxed, headed directly to buzz country. She hadn't gotten drunk in so long it took only two glasses to get her woozy.

Can't get plastered tonight. Gotta keep my head on straight. Think. Think. Ricky, Randy. Something with an R. Ryan. No. Too common.

"Rudy!" she shouted into the air as the name appeared in her mind. "Yes. Rudy!" She lifted her wine glass. "Tell me, Alma, how are things going with Rudy?"

Roxy downed the remainder of her second glass, chugged some water, and curled up on her couch to sleep, maybe to dream. Maybe to subconsciously figure out what that dang key opened.

When Roxy's cell phone chimed, waking her up, she looked at her watch. She'd been asleep for three hours.

"Hello," she answered, before taking a drink of water to combat the cotton balls forming inside her mouth.

"Finally. I've been calling every five minutes for the last half hour. Where have you been?" Alma screeched in Roxy's ear.

"At my place. Guess I dozed off."

"Sorry I couldn't be there when you got out. Had to fill in for an early shift. Stacy said she'd take care of everything."

"How can I thank you for putting up my bail," Roxy said, gratitude swelling in her chest.

"Stop," Alma said. "Stacy and I figured it out. She said she'd ask Alex to pick you up. Did he?"

"Well yes," Roxy said, not ready to elaborate on her uneasiness about Alex. "Are you still at work?"

"No. I'm at Rudy's."

"Rudy. I knew it."

"Knew what? Rocks, are you okay?"

"Well, I have been better, but yes, I'm okay. Except that I'm a lousy friend. I haven't even asked how things are going with your new beau. How *are* things going with Rudy?"

"Beau? Are you messing with me right now? You're out on bail for a murder charge, and you want to have girl talk. Maybe I should pop over, and we can paint each other's toenails." Alma huffed at the end of her rant, emphasizing her frustration.

"Are you mad at me?"

"No. Well, maybe a little. You have to answer your freaking phone, so I don't have a heart attack. I thought something happened to you."

"I'm fine. Really. I'll probably have an enormous headache tomorrow, though," Roxy said, rubbing her temple.

"Now what are you talking about?"

"Doesn't matter. I had too much wine."

"*You* drank too much? Well, that's a first. But I guess being charged with murder is a first for you, too. You're getting to check a lot of boxes on your bucket list."

"Hangovers and murder are not on my bucket list." Roxy couldn't help giggling. "Seriously, when will you be home?"

"Well, I... maybe late tomorrow. Rudy and I have plans."

Roxy sighed. "Of course you do. And I'm glad. I can't wait to hear more about him and maybe meet him some day."

"You'll meet him, and soon. Can we talk over the phone for now? What do you need?"

"Wish I knew. There's something I'm missing. Some detail I should know. A clue I should have figured out by now. It's like I've walked through a spider web. I can feel it, but I can't see where it is to pull it off me. I'm going to get some more sleep and see if I feel better in the morning."

"That's a great idea. All your doors are locked?"

"Yes, Mother," Roxy answered. "Hey, since you're gone for a bit, need me to water your plants?"

"My plants?"

"Yeah, the ones on the patio," Roxy clarified, hoping to keep any emotion out of her voice.

"I know where my plants are. Actually, I haven't checked on them in a while. Sure. If you have time, I would appreciate that."

"On it!" Roxy said, too enthusiastically.

"You remember where I keep the spare key?"

"Yep." Roxy yawned, the effects of many sleepless nights catching up.

"I will call the minute I'm home. But Roxy, listen, if anything— and I mean *anything*—comes up that you need me for, you call. Rudy knows what's going on and what a bum rap you're working with here."

Alma paused, and Roxy thought she'd hung up. When she continued, her voice held a winsome softness that Alma reserved for her radio listeners. "Rocks, he is a good guy. Maybe I've finally met one."

"I hope so, Alma. I truly hope so." After they disconnected, Roxy thought about Alex and wished she had let him come home with her.

Was he one of the good guys?

165

Chapter Thirty-Eight

Roxy pushed herself up in bed to answer the ringing phone. "Alma. You got home earlier than I expected."

"Good morning, Roxy. It's Alex. Sorry to disappoint you. I didn't get a call from you last night and wanted to make sure everything was okay."

"Alex?" Roxy said groggily into the phone.

"Did I wake you?"

"Well, to be honest, yes. Guess I'm catching up on my beauty sleep. What time is it?"

"A little after eight. I'm headed to class and wanted to hear your voice first. Everything all right there?"

"Seems to be."

"Great. Is there anything you want me to tell Rita, like maybe when you'll be back?" Alex asked.

Roxy shook her head, hoping to clear her thoughts. "Back to class? I don't know. Guess I could ask my attorney. I'm not sure what I'm allowed to do."

"Check with your lawyer, but I'm guessing that as long as the police know where you are, you'll be fine. Want me to come over tonight?" Alex continued, and Roxy thought she sensed a neediness in his words.

"I'm supposed to catch up with Alma later today, so I'm not sure when I'll be available. Can I call you?"

"Absolutely. You know Roxy, you're special—and if I can help you in any way, just ask."

Roxy blew out a deep sigh. "Alex, we've known each other for such a short time. I don't understand why you would care. I doubt I would have been this caring if you'd been the one accused of murder."

"The length of time isn't the only way to measure how well you know a person," Alex said, his tone serious. "You didn't kill your ex. I wonder if you'd even step on a spider if you found one in your bathroom."

"But still," Roxy protested. "We hardly—"

"Yes, it's been a relatively short time." He paused. "And I like you. Not making any promises, but I have hopes. And you're in a difficult spot right now. I know everything will turn out, but in the meantime, your friends will get you through. Alma, Stacy, Cecile. I'm tossing my hat in, too."

"I appreciate that," Roxy said. "I'll call once I know how my day shakes out. Maybe we can get a quick dinner or something tonight."

"That would be great. I'll wait to hear from you," Alex said, sounding lighter. "Oh, by the way, did you retrieve the key from Alma's? Maybe you could show it to me tonight, and together we can figure out what it goes to."

"The key?" Roxy's skin turned cold, thinking this might be the real reason Alex had phoned.

"Yeah, the one you talked about yesterday. We all agreed it was key to your case. See what I did there?" A chuckle followed his play on words.

"Very funny," she stuttered, panic nesting in her stomach. *Why did I tell him where I hid the key?*

"Well, did you retrieve it?" Alex pressed.

"Uh, not yet. Didn't see a reason to move it. Seems safe for now."

"True. True. I'm intrigued about why Sam was hell-bent to get that key back. We'll talk more later. Anyway, get some rest," Alex said, changing the subject. "That is probably the best thing you can do. Let me know what your lawyer says about class."

"I will."

"Hope to see you later." Alex ended the call.

Roxy's mind spun, playing out different scenarios. Was Alex truly interested in her well-being, or did he have some covert reason for wanting access to the key? Was her overactive imagination causing her to behave like a fearful conspiracy theorist?

Roxy couldn't decide.

One thing for sure—she needed to find a new hiding spot for that key. And this time, she wouldn't tell a soul where.

Chapter Thirty-Nine

Roxy dressed quickly and headed toward Alma's apartment. Within seconds, she claimed the house key and let herself in. Mad at her recklessness in revealing the hiding spot, Roxy made a beeline for Alma's balcony. She hadn't wanted to believe Alex might be one of the bad guys, but she couldn't take the chance of putting her dear friend in danger by using her home as a hidey-hole.

Roxy eyed the geranium pot on the balcony, right where she had left it, and let out a relieved sigh. She stuck her hand in the dirt, her heart pounding so loudly she couldn't hear.

Terrifying seconds passed as her desperate probing couldn't locate the metal key.

Had someone taken it? She dug deeper.

Finally her fingers curled around a hard, elongated shape, and a grateful moan released from deep in her chest. Roxy nestled the key in her hand and brushed off the soil before tucking the treasure into her front pocket.

Roxy picked up a watering can, filled it, and within minutes, every living thing in Alma's patio garden enjoyed a healthy drink.

She turned at the sound of the front door lock clicking open.

Quickly, she searched for a weapon; something she could protect herself with if she needed to.

"Hey, Rocks!" Alma's voice rang out.

Roxy exhaled. "Out here, on the balcony," she responded. The pounding of her heart clogged her air passages, making speaking a challenge. "Watering your plants," she managed to choke out.

"Everyone will assume I have a green thumb, thanks to you," Alma said from the doorway before walking to Roxy and wrapping her in a hug. "You okay?"

"Yes. Peachy." Roxy set the watering can down and picked at the potting soil underneath her nails. "Are you home early, or am I running late?"

"I'm earlier than I expected. Rudy got called into work, so we had to postpone our plans." Alma looked around the balcony and returned her gaze to Roxy. "Girl, you sure get into greenery. How did you get so filthy?"

Roxy regarded her dirt-covered hands, turning them over to assess both sides. "I pulled some weeds and trimmed a few dead leaves," she replied, hoping Alma wouldn't search for evidence of the clippings. She plucked a dead petal off a geranium and ran her fingers along the top of the soil, smoothing over the hole she had just filled in. "Everything okay with you and Rudy?"

"Absolutely," Alma bragged in a way that broadcast exactly how *okay* things with Rudy had gone the night before. And probably again that morning.

"He pulls down a lot of bucks at his hoity-toity job, but once a month, he has to be on call in case of an emergency. And today, apparently, there was an emergency worthy of derailing our date." Alma pinched a dead frond from a fern and held it for Roxy to see. "You missed a few."

Roxy's teeth clenched. If her friend paid attention, it wouldn't be hard to see that minimal gardening, other than irrigation, had taken place. "Well, everything comes with a price tag, as I'm continuing to learn." Roxy wiped her hands on her jeans. "At least he's not always on call."

"That's true," Alma agreed.

Roxy shifted toward the sliding glass door. "You've never told me what Rudy does. Or, come to think of it, anything about the man," she said, hoping to move them inside and away from Alma asking about her plants. "Wanna come next door for some coffee or tea? We are overdue for a girl's chat."

"Yes, we are," Alma said. "Let me take a shower, and I'll be over in maybe thirty minutes. I'm not the only one with a juicy story this morning. I want to hear about being locked up, and how Alex came to your rescue."

Alex to the rescue.

Roxy nodded. "See you in a few."

Chapter Forty

Roxy scurried to her apartment, reassured at the feel of the key's scalloped edge digging into her thigh. With Alma no longer at risk, Roxy focused on finding a new place to conceal it. She paced her living room, searching for a spot, then finally pulled the darn thing out of her pocket.

Hefting the key as though its small shape weighed significantly more than a fraction of an ounce, Roxy acknowledged its true heaviness, an anchor tethering her to Sam, endless heartache, and danger. She traced her finger over the printing on the key head, as though touching each letter and number would provide divine insight.

FSR-444

Roxy reread the inscription, but no matter how many times she examined the printing, no hints or clues materialized. The figures only toyed with her memory, challenging her to recall something in her past.

I've seen keys like this one before. But where?
FSR must stand for something, but what?

With time running out to locate a new hiding spot before Alma arrived, Roxy put off solving the mystery, for now. Instead, she moved the end table near the couch away from the wall, pulled up a loose corner of the carpet and shoved the key deep underneath. As she pushed the carpet back into place and returned the end table to its original spot, a loud knock broke the silence.

Roxy raced to the door. "That wasn't a half hour," she said as she pulled it open, expecting Alma, hair still wet, to be standing on the other side.

"Hi, Roxanne."

"Sonya?" Roxy blinked at Chuck's wife, not trusting her eyes. "What are you doing here?"

"Checking in on an old friend," she said, hugging Roxy so loosely they barely touched. Sonya pushed past Roxy, set her designer handbag on the floor, and arranged herself on the sofa, crossing her long legs to their best advantage. "Do you have any coffee? We have a lot to catch up on."

"Well yeah, I have coffee—but really, Sonya, why are you here?"

"Like I said, I wanted to see how you are. I've been worried." Sonya shifted toward where Roxy stood.

"Worried?"

"Well, of course," Sonya said, recrossing her legs to give Roxy another view of her high heels. *They probably cost more than a car payment.*

"Ever since Sam abandoned you in such a cruel way," Sonya continued, "I've been frightened for you. I've wondered how you're getting along."

"Sam left awhile ago," Roxy said. "You're just now getting around to asking how I am?"

"Things have been busy, but I have been thinking about you, especially after the news of… well, Sam's death and your arrest."

Roxy remained standing, not interested in preparing coffee and settling down for Sonya's pity gabfest. "Now isn't a good time for us to play catch-up. I'm expecting company. Maybe another day." Roxy pointed to the still-open door.

"How *are* you getting along? Did you find another job?" Sonya continued, unmoving.

"You know I did," Roxy snapped. "I'm sure Chuck told you all about it." Leaving out the reason why she had to change jobs in the first place. "Why are you here, Sonya? We were never close, so you can stop this 'I'm worried about my dear friend' bull crap."

"Excuse me." Roxy turned to see Alma step inside. "Everything okay here? Rocks, we can reschedule our plans if something has come up." Alma jutted her chin toward Sonya. "Nice shoes by the way. Jimmy's?"

"No. McQueen," Sonya answered. "Aren't they slinky?"

"Slinky and pricey," Alma retorted. "I'm Roxy's neighbor, Alma Sanchez. And you are?"

"DJ Soul Sanchez. I've heard a lot about you. Well, Alma, you know your shoes. I got these beauties for under five. They're last season."

"Five hundred… dollars?" Roxy clarified, raising her eyebrows.

"Of course. They retail at double that. At the wrong stores, of course." Sonya sneered.

"Of course." Roxy swallowed. *Why won't this woman leave?*

"I'm Sonya Winston, but Roxy and my friends call me Sonnie. I'm sure she's told you about me."

Alma quirked an eyebrow at Roxy but kept quiet.

"It seems like you gals have plans, and I don't want to intrude. Just wanted to see for myself how my buddy is making out these days. You did say you have another job," Sonya added.

Not wanting to be drawn into any conversation with Chuck's wife, Roxy nodded but didn't speak.

Sonya stood, and Roxy allowed a gush of oxygen to return to her chest. "I'll call you, and we can come up with a time that works for both of us. I miss you and the fun the four of us used to have."

"Good times," Roxy said, dumbstruck that Sonya revised their history so easily.

"You have my number. Call if you need anything. Help with rent, attorney costs, a good bottle of bourbon. I'm here for you." Sonya ended with another air hug and disappeared.

"Who the flying fig was that?" Alma asked after Sonya was clearly out of earshot.

"A long and boring story. She's married to Chuck, the guy who owns the food truck and apparently has all along."

"Ohhhh," Alma drew out the word. "Guess I misspoke. You have talked about her, just not in the friendliest of ways."

"Sonya and I weren't bosom buddies. We hung out a few times because of the guys."

"Sounds like another juicy story. I'll start the coffee." Alma walked three steps to enter Roxy's kitchen and rummaged through her cupboards for coffee makings. "Continue."

"I remember the last time the four of us were together." A titter of amusement escaped Roxy. "I remember that night well."

Alma's eyes lit up. "So, go on and tell me."

"For some reason, Chuck got a bee up his butt for us to go ice-skating."

"Ice skating? Seriously, you could break a bone at your age," Alma chirped.

"At any age, dearie, even yours." Roxy chuckled.

Alma flashed an exasperated glare. "Stop dragging this out. You are the worst storyteller."

"I am not."

"Your stories are good, but you take too long setting things up. It's all in the delivery." Alma scooped grounds into a filter and clicked the basket in place. She turned on the coffee maker. "I can tell this is going to take awhile," she declared, pulling out a chair at Roxy's kitchen table. "Continue."

"Yes. Yes," Roxy said, fanning herself for effect. "I figured that skating would be worth a few laughs, a little exercise, right? Beats sitting around a steak house listening to Sonya rattle on about her nail polish. *Is it sunset orange or perky pink?* Dear God."

"True."

"So, we went to that rink not far from work. Do you know the one on Fountain Boulevard? Been there forever. Sam raved about their sausage pizza. Said we should find out who their vendor was and sell it on the truck. Just what we needed, another menu item."

"Sam was secret-shopping the competition?"

Roxy shrugged. "Nothing secret about it. He loved good pizza. And beer. Anyway, we had been skating for a few minutes, Sonya spending most of that time on her butt. Finally, she let out a yell. Something like *Mother Fudging Bastard.* I'm fudging on the F-word."

"Of course you are."

"Chuck skated over to her. Sam and I kept our distance, but from the way she punched him in the stomach, we figured out what was going down. Our skate session ended."

Alma beamed. "I can picture her flailing around the rink in designer togs and top-of-the-line skates."

"You got the picture. Never seen her so mad," Roxy said. "But she was dressed in her runway finest. If you have to look like a fool, no one was styled out better than Sonya."

"She seems like an uptight priss, always in control."

"You got her pegged," Roxy agreed with a nod. "The expression on her face when she ripped off her skates and threw them—blades out—at Chuck. Ha, definitely worth the price of admission. That was the most fun I ever had with her. Or him, for that matter."

"I'll bet."

Roxy grinned mischievously. "Do you skate?"

Alma frowned. "Well, I did as a kid. Why are you asking?"

"Could be a fun time. You, Rudy, Alex, and me. If nothing else, you can taste the famous sausage-topped pizza. Chase it down with an ice-cold beer."

"You're for real? Go ice-skating?"

Roxy nodded her head *yes*, feeling a bit juvenile, but heck, why not. "Could be fun."

Alma seemed to warm to the idea. "I'll check with Rudy, see if he's game."

"Fair enough. When I talk to Alex tonight, I'll do the same. I have lots of questions for that man. I'll add this to the list."

"Speaking of questions, I need to ask you a few. I'll pour, and we can get started on our hen session?"

"Hen session, hmmm," Roxy huffed. "Such antiquated vocabulary from a young chick."

Chapter Forty-One

Roxy phoned Malcolm Jump's office several hours later, after Alma had left, and listened as his paralegal explained the court process. Roxy could return to class but not until after her attorney notified the court system, and they acknowledged and approved the notice. The process might take as long as ten working days.

Roxy thanked the man before hanging up and dialed Rita, an overwhelming urge for normalcy engulfing her. More than anything, she wanted a day-to-day routine that didn't include bailiffs and jail cells or her apartment being ransacked. She didn't want to be the focus of legal terms she'd only heard on old episodes of *Perry Mason*.

"Hey, Rita, it's Roxy."

"Well, Roxy, I'm glad you called. I've been waiting to hear how you are and when you'll be back in class," she said, an exaggerated joy lacing her words. Her upbeat tone was a direct contrast to the businesslike, no-nonsense Rita she presented every day in class.

"You've got to know I'd rather be with you than where I've been the past several days."

Rita snorted. "No doubt."

"I spoke with my lawyer, and he said I could come back to school once the courts okay my request. Might be a full week or more, though, before I get the approval."

"Not a problem," Rita said. "You're on a different track than the rest of your class anyway, and you've already agreed to put in extra time to catch up. Or you can overlap with our next session. In either case, we'll make things work."

Roxy sighed. "Rita, you have no idea how much your support and flexibility have meant to me over these past few weeks. I'll be the student you'll never forget," she added, breaking the tension in her words.

"You were memorable before all this began," Rita said. "Needless to say, the entire class is invested in you. We want this to get straightened out, so you can resume your life."

"Exactly how I feel," Roxy said. "I don't know how I would have gotten this far without my friends, especially Alex. He's been at my side every step of the way. I'm glad he's been keeping you up to date."

"Not really," Rita said, sounding puzzled. "I talked to him the day after you got arrested. Jason learned about the incident on the police scanner and called me before the news broke. Obviously I couldn't reach you, so I called Alex. He had already heard. And, frankly, he seemed preoccupied when we spoke."

"Stacy must have told him. She and another friend put up my bail, but Alex picked me up. He said he'd been keeping you in the loop."

"Well, he did call Monday to say he wouldn't be at class for a little while. He didn't say anything about you being out on bail or when you'd be returning, though."

Roxy scratched her head. "You didn't see him today? When we spoke this morning, he said he was heading to class."

"Uh, no. Said he'd be gone for a few days. Something personal, he mentioned. I didn't pry," Rita said.

Roxy manufactured an excuse. "I probably misunderstood him," she said. "I can't thank you enough. You'll be among the first to know how things are going. Hope I'm back behind the wheel early next week."

"See ya then." Rita clicked off.

Roxy's spidey sense intensified.

Why had Alex told her he's in class when he's not?

***

Roxy had spent most of the afternoon rehearsing a non-accusatory way to ask Alex if he was a liar.

She genuinely liked the guy. Still, his odd behavior and so many unanswered questions left her fretting whether the Alex she knew was the Alex he claimed to be.

She didn't want to be taken for a chump—she'd recently left that role.

Roxy floundered her opening line, phrasing, and rephrasing what amounted to: *Why are you lying to me?* Within a few tries, she knew there wasn't a diplomatic way to ask someone about suspected dishonesty. So Roxy decided to take a different tack.

Alex was expecting a call from her, anyway. She curled on her couch, tucking her feet underneath her bottom, and punched in a text message:

How are you at ice skating?

A few minutes later, three dancing dots appeared on her screen as Alex typed. **Well, I'm no Scott Hamilton, but I can skate a mean figure 8. Why?**

Wanna go skating?

Now?

No. Tomorrow?

I guess so?

She sensed his reluctance but soldiered on. **Great. Meet you at 6 at the skate rink on Fountain. Do you know the one?**

I think so.

Alma and Rudy might join.

Roxy hoped they could. Having them in range would make the evening much easier.

A double date?

179

Maybe. Might be fun.

Instead of meeting there, I can pick you up, say 5:30? Alex asked.

Roxy texted back. **That would be wonderful. We can have a pizza dinner.**

And beer?

Yep.

What about dinner tonight?

Roxy paused and looked at her watch. *Six-thirty.* Not really late, but the day had mentally exhausted her, like a rollercoaster ride of highs and lows. She needed a night to refuel.

Learning she could resume school lifted her spirits. But that feel-good high crashed quickly after hearing Alex had lied to Rita about her. Sonya showing up unexpectedly like Roxy had been her long-lost BFF had drained her emotional reserve.

Being out on bail for murder might be the least of her worries.

And that frickin' key! Whatever it opened continued to needle her like a burr in her sock, poking her skin with every step. Getting into an argument with Alex could push her over the edge. What Roxy needed was extra time to frame her queries, so they didn't allege anything. *Just here asking innocent questions.* To pull that off, she'd need to talk to him in person. After a solid night's sleep that wasn't in a jail cell.

She tapped the keys: **I'm worn out. Think I'm heading to bed. Long day. We can talk tomorrow, OK?**

Of course. Sleep well.

He ended the text with a yawning emoji.

Roxy yawned at the image. Yawning was contagious; another one of life's mysteries she'd never solve. Looking at the clock, she quickly texted Alma.

**Skate date tomorrow at 6 with me and Alex?
Pleeeaaaasssseee** ☺

Forty minutes later, a thumbs-up appeared. **Rudy and I will see you there.**

Roxy couldn't help but giggle. The oceans of stress beating against her for the past several months receded temporarily.

She stood, determined to practice how to swizzle, ice skating's most basic step. Roxy put her feet in a V with her heels touching and then shifted them until her toes touched. The voice of her skate instructor rang in her head, sending Roxy back to when she was twelve. *The letter V. The letter A. And the letter V.*

For a moment, she savored victory. *I can still do this, although not as smoothly on loop pile carpet.*

Roxy continued making the movements faster and faster before toppling against her coffee table, eliciting another memory. Tenderly touching a black-and-blue bruise on her thigh the size of a grapefruit, she fell asleep wincing.

Sonya hadn't been the only one who hit the hard ice.

Chapter Forty-Two

Dressed in a pair of relaxed-fit jeans and a teal rib-knit sweater, Roxy looked ready for the evening. But even the additional day didn't render her the vaguest idea of how to question Alex without alleging dubious behavior.

No matter. At five-thirty on the dot, Alex's familiar *rap-a-rap-rap-rap-rap-a-rap-rap* played against her door. His signature knock blasted her from her thoughts, like a starter gun to begin a race.

She tugged down on the hem of her pullover and exhaled. *Here we go.*

Roxy opened the door and gulped at Alex, wearing a winter sweater with a pattern ugly enough to win a competition. His jeans fit nicely, though, balancing the horrifying effect.

"Hope we can rent skates," he said, by way of a greeting. "I've outgrown the pair my parents gave me for my tenth birthday."

Roxy accepted his hug. "You were an ice skater at some point in your life. No baloney."

He shrugged. "I wouldn't claim ice-skater status, but I have skated and lived to tell a tale or two." Roxy could hear the exaggerated danger in his voice.

"It's not like we're going skydiving or climbing Kilimanjaro," she joked. "Your biggest hazard will be avoiding the little kids skating circles around us."

"I'd forgotten about the munchkin set."

"Come on, Alex. A little danger spices up life."

"I'll take as little spice as possible, thank you," Alex answered. "I like my ice in a bucket glass topped with two fingers of bourbon. I'm strictly a *watch-the-other-fellow-take-the-thrills-and-spills* type of guy."

"Now I know you're playing with me," Roxy said.

"Finally, you understand. I just want to play." Alex winked. "Ready?"

"Yep." Roxy grabbed her purse and keys.

Alex stepped aside for her to pass, snatching her keyring from her hand. He locked the door behind them and returned her keys. "Adventure awaits, my lady." He swept his outstretched arm to the left.

Roxy curtsied. "Alas, a quest where all the ice isn't in a glass. How will we fare?"

"Let's find out." Alex wiggled his eyebrows up and down, reminding her of Groucho Marx.

Roxy chortled, holding on to her sides to keep them from aching. This man could bring happiness to her faster than anyone, even Sam during the early years when joy was all she saw when she looked at him.

Once inside his car and on their way to the rink, Alex changed the satellite station from the classic rock he always listened to.

"What in the world is this?" Roxy asked. "Elevator music?"

"You don't recognize this station? I'm shocked."

"Continue being shocked but tell me what the heck you're making us listen to," Roxy said, hesitating to break the light comical mood.

"There's a channel for every musical taste," Alex continued, obviously not willing to give up the answer quickly. "Yacht rock, ballet, low-rider oldies. Even St. Patrick's Day."

"And your point is?"

"You don't know."

"Nope, but I have to say, this song has a nice beat," Roxy confessed while swaying her body to the tune.

"This is ice-skating radio!"

Her mouth dropped open. "Seriously," she huffed. "Only you."

"I love your smile," Alex said, turning toward her while the light was red. "Your entire body beams, and that joy shows on your face."

Roxy blinked back a tear at what might have been the nicest compliment she'd ever received. Alex could muddle her thinking in ways she'd never imagined, with just a kind word and a gentle touch.

Still, she needed to stay focused. Now was her chance to ask, not confront, Alex about what he'd been telling Rita.

For a brief moment, she questioned her doubts. Perhaps she'd misunderstood and gotten what Rita had said about Alex wrong. There could be a reasonable explanation. The least she could do is give him a chance to tell his side; that is if he had a side.

"You're getting a bit of normalcy back," Alex said, with more caution to his voice than she thought necessary. "Some day-to-day average citizen. I'm glad to see that."

"Nothing more average-American than a visit to the skate rink," she replied.

"True. Don't get me wrong, I'm glad to have you back. Just saying how impressed I am that you're able to move forward with all the"—he paused, as if reaching for the right word—"misfortune invading your life. A lot of people couldn't cope."

"You've known me long enough to know that coping is my superpower. Gotta move forward. The alternative is too, I don't know... bleak."

Alex nodded.

"Better days are ahead, and why not start them now while all this craziness gets sorted out. My attorney says I'm good as long as I don't leave LA county. I know the cops will come to their senses and drop the charges."

"The police don't drop charges. They only gather the information. The district attorney decides if there's enough evidence to charge a suspect," Alex explained, with a heavy dose of criminology professor in his reply.

"Well, that makes everything worse. What evidence do they have? I couldn't have lifted a dead body. And I certainly have more brains than to hide my ex-boyfriend's corpse in the trunk of my employer's vehicle."

"Hey, hey... I'm on your side, all right? Everything you've said is true. But you still need to take this more seriously. A murder charge is a big deal."

Roxy twisted at the waist to face Alex. "I'm not taking this seriously?" Her voice raised in disbelief. "I think about nothing else. This has permeated every fiber of my life. Sometimes I can hardly breathe."

"Babe, I'm sorry I upset you. I didn't mean to."

"Since Sam took off, everything has gone to crap. Without you and Alma and Stacy, I don't know where I would be." Roxy swallowed, not allowing more tears to gather. "When he left me with nothing, I thought, man, things can't get any worse. Boy, was I wrong. I now look back on being abandoned with no money and lots of bills and think: Those were the good old days."

Alex chortled. "If we only knew then…"

Roxy turned to face the road. "It's like I'm stuck on a reality TV game show where each day chaos, confusion, and horror team up in some perverted contest that I can't win. I don't know how long I can stay afloat."

"Everything is going to be fine, I know it," Alex stated. "For all the reasons you've mentioned and probably more. But in the meantime, be a bit more cautious."

"Cautious? How?"

"What you talk about and to who. Don't do or say anything that can be misconstrued or spun into another allegation against you."

"Who am I talking to that I shouldn't be? And what could I possibly say that would get me in more trouble than I'm already in?" she spurted out, a decibel below a scream.

"That's what I'm getting at." Alex faced Roxy with a sympathetic grin. "What I mean is, you're too trusting. That's why you're in this mess."

"I'm the perfect patsy?"

"Might be. Don't trust anyone. For the time being, play your cards close to the vest." He turned back to the road and released an exaggerated burst of air.

Roxy eyed him, discerning a different person tucked behind the steering wheel; a façade he'd remained comfortably behind disappeared while he spoke.

Moments later, the disguise reappeared. The Alex warning her was not the same man she'd been casually dating. The man seated next to her worked hard to tell her something without exactly spelling it out.

"You're not making any sense, Alex. I don't have any cards to play."

"What I mean is, don't volunteer anything."

"To who?"

"Well, that Sonya lady, for one," Alex snapped.

"Sonya? How do you know about Sonya?"

"You talked about her," Alex answered too quickly.

"Did I?"

"She's Chuck's wife, right?"

"Why are you bringing her up today?" Roxy asked, reflecting on Sonya's surprise drop in the day before. She hadn't mentioned the visit to Alex.

He didn't answer.

Roxy kept going. "And while I'm asking, why did you say you'd kept Rita updated about what was going on with me?"

Alex stiffened. "You talked to Rita?"

"I called to tell her I would be coming back to class as soon as my attorney files the paperwork. She said you've been missing class, too." She let those last few words hang in the air between them.

Alex pulled into the skating rink lot and parked. He took a moment to turn off the ignition before he faced Roxy.

She waited for him to answer. When he didn't, she posed the question another way.

"What have you been telling Rita? According to her, you haven't attended class since I've been away."

Alex reached for Roxy's hand. "I've missed a few classes, that's true. Things are a little complicated for me right now. If I could tell you more, I would."

Before Roxy replied, the sound of fingernails tapping on the passenger side window startled her and ended their conversation.

"Hey, you guys going skating or what?" Alma boomed.

Roxy peered out to see her friend, a grin beaming from ear to ear. Next to her a tall, stocky man she supposed was Rudy, held Alma's hand.

"Guess we'll finish this later," Alex said, hustling to open his door. "I can't wait to meet your friends."

"A reprieve for now. But you can be sure we're picking up this topic as soon as we're done skating," Roxy hissed, but Alex had already closed his door and jogged around the car to open hers.

Chapter Forty-Three

Roxy stepped out of the car and flashed a glare at Alex before allowing herself to be swallowed in Alma's hug.

"I'm ready for some of that pizza you talked about and so is Rudy," Alma said by way of introduction.

"Happy to meet you," Roxy said.

Rudy opened his arms wide, swooping her in a friendly embrace. "I've heard so much about you, Roxy. If only half of the stories are true, you are one fascinating lady," he said, releasing his hold.

"Don't believe anything Alma says about me. She thinks every woman over fifty spent her youth shattering glass ceilings or some other lofty aspiration. Trust me, none of us pinned a suffragette banner on our high school lockers. I'm not *that* old."

Rudy laughed, but Alma rolled her eyes, not happy with the assessment.

"Just saying I'm no superwoman." Roxy hurried to change the subject. "Anyway, hope the pizza lives up to my hype." She quickly turned toward Alex. "Alma, you remember Alex."

Alma stepped forward and gathered Alex in a hug. "Sure do. Nice to see you again."

Roxy turned toward Rudy. "This is my friend Alex Montgomery."

Rudy extended his hand, and the two men shook. "You're more than a friend, considering all you've done for Roxy over the past few weeks."

Roxy blushed. She'd planned to keep Alex at arm's length, taking their relationship slowly. And here were Alma and Rudy, spilling all the beans like BFFs at a school dance. She didn't want Alex to get the wrong idea about her feelings for him.

Did she have feelings for him?

"Been a long time since I've gone on a double date," Rudy joked.

"I know what you mean," Alex agreed.

While her three companions exchanged small talk, Roxy stepped back and diverted her attention to the outside of the cement block building. A dated neon pink and green sign flashed *Fountain Skating Rink.* Near the lettering, a faded outline of a female skater flickered in animation. Reaching maybe thirty feet high, she glided across the building's façade, arms extended and back leg lifted in a perfect spiral.

"Memories?" Alex asked, snaking an arm around Roxy's waist.

"A few. Not much has changed since I skated here as a teen," Roxy said, "except for the graffiti and the smell of *carne asada* from Ernesto's taco shop across the street."

"Then, shall we?" Alex guided the group toward the entrance. "I know we're in a hurry to hurt ourselves."

Roxy shoved his shoulder playfully. "Alex thinks we're too old to go ice skating. Claims he wants his ice in a glass, surrounded with…" She faked a faulty memory. "Was it vodka or rye?"

"Bourbon if you don't mind," Alex retorted.

"Maybe you should have gotten a doctor's excuse or something?" Alma snarked.

"The man could have a point," Rudy defended. "Don't remember the last time I strapped on skates, but I'm certain the occasion didn't end well. Might explain this limp I have." He exaggerated a hobble.

Rudy held the door open for the ladies while Alex stood in line for tickets.

Inside, the rink hadn't changed since forever. The same dated posters of '80s rock bands, their paper corners curling, festooned the walls. The smell of pizza sauce mixed with stale beer assaulted Roxy's nostrils, and the music, still heavy on the bass, blasted through every speaker.

Alex paid for the foursome, and they reassembled at a bench inside after getting their skates.

"Should we eat first, then skate, or do some skating before?" Rudy asked.

"I'm hungry," Alma said. "And a beer or two might improve my skills."

"Agreed," Alex said.

"Looks like they have lockers in the back. Let's get a couple and dump some of this stuff," Rudy said.

The two men headed off to the bank of lockers against the back wall. Once they were out of earshot, Alma said, "Well, what do you think? He's a hunk, right?"

"He seems nice and willing to indulge us in this craziness."

"Yeah, but isn't he gorgeous?"

This wasn't a question, merely an affirmation of what Alma held true. "He is handsome," Roxy agreed. "What I'm interested in is how he treats you. How you feel when you're with him?"

"Like a kid on Christmas morning."

"That's good. But not sustainable."

"Who cares about sustainable? I'm not selling organic goat cheese to millennials. The man is hot as hell."

"You could get burned." Roxy hated the cautionary lecture spilling out of her mouth. Being in love with Sam had been the best part of her life—that is, until it wasn't.

Who was she to give relationship advice?

"Maybe, but getting scorched is better than cold, lonely nights," Alma shot back.

"Understood. Guess I'm looking at this from a different viewpoint."

"You're doing that pucker-y thing with your face," Alma complained.

Roxy quickly shook her head to clear the expression, as though her face was an Etch-a-Sketch.

"No, you're right. I don't know where our dating will lead. Maybe nowhere. So I'm enjoying the benefits being with a man like Rudy offers. Holding hands with an Adonis wearing tight jeans is one of them." Alma beamed.

"Don't elevate him to mythological levels," Roxy cautioned. "Having fun together while waiting to see if there's a future is smart. But if you ask me, it's already too late. You're all in on this guy."

Alma turned her head sideways and slid Roxy a bemused stare.

Roxy glared back. "I hate when you give me that look."

"This look?" Alma pointed a thumb toward herself. "The *I-can't-believe-you-said-that-to-me* look?"

Roxy kept an eye on where the guys stood. "Said what?"

"How can you be so self-unaware?"

"About what?"

"Who, you mean. About Alex. If anyone has pushed all her chips to the center of the table, it's *you*, Roxanne. Every other word out of your mouth—that is, when you're not talking about being arrested for murder—has been Alex," Alma hissed. "Alex. Alex. Alex. If there's one of us who's taken the L-O-V-E fall, honey child, it is you! Telling me to slow *my* roll is a joke."

Roxy considered this. Were her budding feelings for Alex that obvious? Wasn't he just a convenient guy at an inconvenient time?

Either way, Alma nailed her ass. Roxy's *do-as-I-say, not-as-I-do* motherly advice was stale and off-putting.

"Maybe in a different time and under different circumstances, Alex and I might have been an item."

"An item, like the milkshake you order to go along with your cheeseburger? Come on, girl. You light up like a firefly and glow every time I've seen you near the man. Stop pretending."

"Look, Alma. I want to like Alex. Perhaps I do. But right now, there is some weird stuff going on with him, and until I figure that out, I can't allow myself to fall any further."

"Aha. You admit it! You are falling for him."

"Guess so. Truth is, falling in love is a luxury I can't afford right now. I can't tamp down this niggling buzz in the pit of my stomach. Meeting Alex at the nadir of my life wasn't as happenstance as the powers-that-be want me to assume."

Alma's brown eyes rolled back in her head quickly, reminding Roxy of a slot machine right after the lever was pulled. When the reels stopped and the bells, cherries, and flags lined up, her payout would be Alma's wrath instead of cash.

Finally Alma regained her composure. "Geez, Roxy," she almost shouted, "you're talkin' some weird stuff. Happenstance? Powers that be? What the—"

"Sssh. Here come the guys. I'll explain later."

"Damn straight you will." Alma scowled, leaving no confusion about her position. She turned toward Rudy, her anger immediately melting into a smile rivaling a sunrise.

"Hey, babe." Rudy grabbed her hand. "Hungry?"

Alma nodded. "Famished." They strolled in the direction of the rink's eatery.

Alex approached Roxy and slid his arm around her waist. "How about you? Ready for some pizza before the punishment?"

A rush of love poured through her as she turned to face him.

His words were good-natured, and his touch was gentle. Everything about his behavior made her doubt her suspicions. Was she intentionally trying to mess things up?

She wished it were that simple. If she was overreacting, she could correct that. But she knew, as wonderful as this man appeared to be, he was concealing something.

"You betcha," Roxy said, holding back the ridiculous hope that had they met under different circumstances, they might have built a life together. She put her hand in his and ambled with him toward the café.

If only...

***

"Last dance," the DJ announced, and the notes of the final song of the night began.

Alex reached for Roxy, and the two glided to the far side of the rink. Roxy glanced over to see Alma and Rudy had paired off as well. Instead of Donna Summer's familiar closing anthem, the speakers blared with funky sounds of the Ohio Players.

Roxy threw her head back and laughed as Alex began singing, *"Your love is like a rollercoaster baby, baby..."*

Immediately Roxy's thoughts exploded in a joyful memory, a childhood filled with laughter, love, and great music.

She was maybe six or seven in the mid-seventies when the tune gained popularity. The upbeat record played on every radio station. Her mother sang along loudly, with passion and energy, as she washed dishes or drove Roxy to school.

Roxy blinked, recalling the bliss of those simpler times.

What would Mom think of her daughter now, a suspected murderer...

Shaking away the disquieting notion, Roxy sang along with Alex as the final few notes wound the evening to an end.

Much to Roxy's surprise, guzzling three pitchers of beer and eating too many slices of pie had benefited their skating. Floating on suds, pizza sauce, and pepperoni, the four had approached the rink quite relaxed, as though balancing over the ice on a blade was something they did every day.

Alma was right again, and for some odd reason, that bothered Roxy. She fought back being annoyed at having to acknowledge Alma's youthful wisdom once more.

Neither Alex nor Rudy had fallen during their session. She and Alma, while occasionally using their bums instead of their skates, managed to finish without a broken bone or a bloodied anything.

As they exited the ice, Roxy handed Alex a pair of yellow terry cloth skate guards that resembled elongated booties.

"These look like bananas," he quipped.

Roxy slipped them on. "Protects the blades and makes walking off the ice easier," she said as Alma and Rudy approached.

"I remember," Rudy said, reaching in the box to grab a pair for himself and Alma.

"Man, that was awesome," Alex said as they walked together toward the locker area. "I had such a good time."

"Me, too," Rudy added. "It's been too long since I got to act like a kid. Thanks, Roxy, for the idea and for including us."

Roxy caught his smile as they sat on the wooden benches. "Sometimes you have to not act your age."

"Amen to that," Alma said, yanking off a skate and toppling over.

"It's easier if you loosen the laces," Rudy instructed.

"Thanks, expert," Alma chided.

"Do you two have time for a nightcap?" Roxy asked. "That way, Alex can finally get some ice in his glass instead of under his feet."

"Ugh," Alma grunted, pulling off her other skate. "Wish I could, but I have an early call tomorrow. The station booked me at a supermarket opening at first light. Me, a small-town mayor, and some other guy in a suit will cut the ribbon at eight. And I gotta drive to Tarzana, all the way across town."

"Can we take a rain check?" Rudy suggested, before kissing Alma teasingly on her nose. "Let's get together when our celebrity here has more free time."

"Sounds great." Alex unlaced his skates. "Only next time, we'll plan something less extreme. Maybe parasailing over Marina del Rey or rock-climbing in Laurel Canyon."

Roxy looked at Alex. "Milquetoast," she chided, then nearly choked on the word.

On the bench next to him lay a small key, the dark yellow shank capturing her eye.

She swallowed hard, her attention abruptly switching from bourbon on the rocks to lockers. "Which one is ours?" she asked, holding up her skates.

"Across the way," Alex said. "Locker 303."

Roxy, every ounce of her shaken with realization and panic, opened her hand. "Mind if I get my shoes and purse?"

Alex placed the key in her palm.

Roxy let her fingers curl into a fist. She scurried toward the locker to study it, away from Alex's probing scrutiny.

Embossed on one side, **FSR-303**. On the other, an outline of an ice skate materialized before her eyes.

She recognized the shape clearly now and wanted to bang her head against the wall for not catching on sooner. Had she not suggested a skating double date, she might never have solved the mystery. A mystery Sam had set her up to untangle.

She hung her head in despair and relief. Whatever cost Sam his life, she would find stowed away inside a Fountain Skate Rink locker.

But she'd have to wait until tomorrow to learn exactly what was worth dying for.

Chapter Forty-Four

Roxy joined the group still sitting on the benches. She returned the locker key to Alex as everyone gathered their belongings and headed toward the exit. On her way out, Roxy paused to read the hours posted on the skating rink front door. *Saturdays: 12 p.m. – 9 p.m.*

"You coming?" Alma shouted. "Or are you planning to skate until you hurt yourself?"

Roxy hurried to catch up. "Very funny."

"What were you doing?" Alex probed.

"They have special skate hours on Sundays," Roxy lied.

"Thinking of perfecting your crossovers?"

"You never know," Roxy responded, annoyed she'd have to wait until tomorrow afternoon to open the locker and equally peeved that Alex had caught her planning her return.

After repeated hugs and numerous promises to get together soon, Roxy and Alex headed for his car, leaving Alma and Rudy to stroll to the far side of the parking lot.

Roxy settled in her seat, rolled down the window and took in the image of the couple, their backs to her, holding hands, heads tipped toward each other.

Alex pulled out of the lot and headed toward the freeway. Roxy craned her neck to wave goodbye as their car rolled past, surprised Alma didn't return the motion.

"You're not going to catch her attention," Alex interrupted. "Those two are far gone."

"You think?"

He snorted back a chuckle. "Use your eyes. And if that doesn't convince you, spend more than five minutes with Rudy. His every sentence begins with 'Alma says…'"

Roxy sighed, conceding the point. "Her conversation is pretty much the same. Rudy this, Rudy that. Must be love."

"Might be. Seems like early days, though. They're still in that infatuation period when everything your new heartthrob does is wonderful. Even leaving the toilet seat up."

"Not true. Even with her eyes glazed in crazed rapture, no woman is okay with the lid up. Put the dang thing down," Roxy said.

"Yes, ma'am. Hey, still want to have a nightcap? I know a great little neighborhood bar. Or, maybe your place?" Alex asked, sounding hopeful.

Anxious to pick up the threads of their earlier conversation, Roxy frowned at the idea of having drinks in a public place. She craved privacy. Privacy that her apartment would offer, but would that send the wrong message? Alex hadn't tried so much as a kiss yet.

In her mind, him making a move was long overdue. Would he assume she'd given him the green light by inviting him over late at night?

She ached for his kiss, a snuggle, any sign of physical affection. She'd spent many daydreamy minutes imagining how his touch would feel.

Still, as much as she would love to entertain Alex, the specter of what she imagined going on—what he was hiding—haunted her. She couldn't picture their future until he came clean with the truth.

Roxy slid a glance his way but remained quiet.

"Well? Where should I drive to?" Alex asked.

Roxy didn't respond, so he rephrased his question. "Roxy, should I take you home? Or would you like to have a drink with me at a bar?"

"It's just…" she stuttered.

"Just what? Am I coming on too fast? It's a cocktail, not an invitation to fly to Cabo for the weekend."

She shook her head side to side, bouncing her curls. "Wouldn't that be a nice escape?"

"Just the two of us," Alex added, "on a beach watching the waves."

Roxy turned. "But I'd be in violation of my bond."

"I was joking. I'd never ask you to do something like that. Well, maybe after this nonsense gets settled."

Roxy sighed. "I'd like to continue our earlier conversation. There are some things I need you to clarify for me. And I don't want to do that in a public place and, well, I'm a little reluctant to invite you over and risk—"

"Me attacking you?" He hooted. "I gave up hitting on grown women in their apartments for Lent. Anything we do will be mutually agreed to."

"I'm not worried that you'd assault me or anything. It's just…"

Alex turned into a lot, parked in front of a convenience store, and killed the engine. "Is this okay? We can talk here. We're under a street lamp and lots of people are coming in and out, should you need to holler for help."

"Wow. That was an overreaction. But yes, this will work."

"Ask your questions," Alex directed, keeping his focus out the front windshield.

"Why are you in my life?"

He turned and locked eyes. "Huh? What kind of esoteric question is that? Next you'll ask me what the meaning of life is."

"If you think leaving the toilet seat up makes me mad, keep discounting what I'm asking you," Roxy snapped. "I'm serious and you're not."

"Sorry, sorry." He put his hands in the air as a sign of surrender. "Shoot. I'm all ears."

"You are *not* going through a midlife career change. You are *not* the truck driving type."

"Now you're an expert on who I am and am not?"

Roxy took in the fire in his eyes and the way his nostrils flared. *Was he telling the truth or was he acting?*

She decided to push forward. If she was wrong about Alex, she'd chalk up her misgivings to rusty dating protocol. "What do you do for a living? What parachuted you into my life at this particular time?"

"Roxy, I don't know what answer you're looking for. I realize you're going through some tough stuff, and frankly, I don't know how you're keeping everything together. None of that has to do with why I want to spend time with you."

"Really?"

"Is that hard to believe? I like you. You're fun to be with. What's wrong with that?"

"A lot," Roxy said, irritated he continued to minimize her concerns. "Why did you lie about Rita? Why do you keep asking about Sam's key? Why do you turn up when I least expect you to— at Stacy's and at the jailhouse? How do you know Sonya? Who are you, Alex Montgomery? If that's your real name."

Alex released a deep breath.

She had worn rose-colored glasses where Sam was concerned— never challenging his version of events, trusting everything he said. He had taken advantage of her, misled her, and ultimately left her shattered. She'd be damned if she would let anyone do that to her again.

"You're watching too many suspense thrillers," Alex said, turning away.

"If you're not going to tell me what's going on, you might as well take me home," Roxy said, straightening in her seat.

Alex pushed the ignition button, bringing the engine to life. "Can't you just enjoy the time we share? Why do you have to ask so many questions?"

"Maybe because I'm out on bail for murder," Roxy shot back, feeling her eyes flame.

Was he kidding?

"The prospect of being sent to prison kinda changes your outlook." She crossed her arms as though adding an exclamation point to the sentence. In reality, she needed the strength of her own embrace to quell her shaking insides.

"Can't argue with that."

"We're not arguing. We're not debating."

"Then what are we doing, Roxy? Dissecting our relationship before we even get one?"

"Are you not listening, or are you purposefully being obtuse?"

"Now we're sinking to insults. Very nice," Alex said.

"You are intentionally not answering me. You're either dense, or you want to deflect from the topic. And I know for a fact that you are not dumb. So I have to wonder why you don't want to tell me the truth."

"Here's as simple a truth as I can manage. I like you. I'd like to get to know you better. You're in a tough spot, and I thought I could help. What else could you possibly want to know?"

"Why?"

"Because you're a nice, lovely woman who's had a few bad breaks."

Roxy nodded. "I want to believe that meeting you was a serendipitous moment in my otherwise trash-heap life. I keep trying to convince myself of that. But too many things don't add up. I can't pretend anymore. I need to know how you fit in all this."

"Fit in to all what? You think I had something to do with Sam's death?"

"No. But I know you're not being honest with me." She paused to lick her dry lips. "And if you can't or won't answer my questions, I'm not going to be able to see you anymore."

Alex nodded, put the car in reverse and pulled out of the parking spot. "If that's how you want things."

For the rest of the drive, they remained silent. Alex wasn't going to respond, leaving her more convinced than ever he was hiding something. She'd think about what that something could be later. Right now, there was a time-sensitive matter to take care of.

Roxy needed to open that locker, before anyone realized she had figured out what the key fit. Once she had turned over the contents to the police, she'd be in the clear.

Then she could approach Alex, perhaps renew their friendship. But she'd have to wait until after twelve tomorrow before finally getting the answers to her never-ending litany of questions.

She glanced at Alex, pushing down the urge to tell him about the key. Wishing she could trust him. That she could ask him to come with her tomorrow. She was being watched by Chuck and his loser friends. Maybe even by Sonya, although Roxy couldn't figure out how that vapid runway-model-wannabe figured into this.

She would feel safer with Alex in tow.

The words asking him to join her danced on the tip of her tongue.

He pulled up to the curb in front of her building and waited. She opened the door and exited. Alex pulled away, leaving her with a bland, "I'll call you."

Was he as hurt and insulted as he acted?

Roxy fumbled for her keys, walking toward her front door.

She'd call Alma in the morning and ask her to come along. Alma always knew the smart play. She'd be her wing-woman.

Chapter Forty-Five

Both mentally and physically exhausted, Roxy hoped she'd fall right to sleep, but instead, she tossed and turned, barely getting any meaningful rest. Adrenaline kept her eyes open and her mind racing. No doubt she'd drag through the next day, possibly the most important twenty-four hours for the rest of her life.

At barely eight-thirty, she dialed Alma, but the number rang and rang, unanswered. Just as Alma's phone flipped to voicemail, Roxy remembered why Alma had called it an early night. *She's at that frickin' ribbon cutting ceremony in Thousand Oaks or was it Topanga?*

"Alma, call me as soon as you get this message. I need you." Roxy clicked off and paced her tiny apartment. Without having any idea what could be inside the locker, and why its contents threatened her unknown assailants, asking Alma to get involved could be a harrowing blunder, one that put her best friend in peril.

Determined not to risk Alma's safety, Roxy redialed. "Hey Alma, me again."

She forced a giggle to infuse a calm she didn't possess. "Forget my earlier message. Actually, everything is fine. Better than fine. I'm a little jumpy. Didn't get enough sleep, I think. Gonna head to the mall and do some retail therapy to soothe my nerves. You know how much I love shopping for a new purse," she said, offering a fake laugh. "Anyway, hope your ribbon cutting went great and you get to spend the rest of today goofing off. Let's have lunch tomorrow, and I'll show you my shopping finds. And I'd love to hear what Rudy thought of our double date."

Roxy hung up, realizing that taking Alma off the hook did little to relieve the anxious worry invading her every fiber.

If I stay in this apartment another minute, I will lose my mind.

She placed her phone on the entry table near her car keys and headed to the bedroom. Once there, she shrugged into jeans and a pullover. Pulled on socks and sneakers. *Maybe going shopping until the skate rink opens isn't my worst idea.*

She quickly brushed her teeth, wondering if she'd be lucky enough to catch some employees showing up early. Even if they did come in before twelve, she still had nearly three hours to wait. She'd stop by the mall, get a chocolate croissant and a coffee. Maybe check out the new purses at her favorite boutique outlet, the one Sonya had told her about.

Purse shopping. That was the one thing—the *only* thing—the two women had in common. They both loved purses. Satchels and clutches for Sonya. Crossbodies for Roxy. Sonya's uncanny ability to spot the trendiest handbags at the best prices left Roxy green with envy. Chuck had some jingle, but still, Roxy was amazed at how Sonya could afford a new Gucci or Coach every other week, even if they were from the designer discount stores.

Roxy sprayed hair mist onto her tangle of curls and ran her fingers through, hoping to tame the mess. Shopping was the perfect way to kill time until the rink's day manager or whoever had the keys to the front door arrived.

She grabbed her purse from the hook on the back of her bedroom door and headed toward the living room, relaxed with her new plan and ready to retrieve the key hidden under the carpet.

Just as she wrapped her fingers around the end table's solid edges to yank it away from the wall, a hard knock vibrated against her front door. A biscuit-sized lump formed in her stomach.

"Roxy, it's me. Alex."

"What the heck?" she huffed, a mixture of relief and exasperation replacing anxiety. She looked at her watch. Not quite half past nine.

"Alex?"

"Yes. Here with donuts and hot coffee. My edible version of an apology," he yelled through the wooden door. "I feel terrible about how we ended last night."

When Roxy didn't respond, Alex continued, "Roxy, can you hear me? I'm sorry, and I'm saying it with glazed donuts."

"It's early. I'm not dressed," she said, looking at her jeans and light blue pullover. "Can you come back in a couple of hours?"

"Well, sure I can. Does that mean we're back to being friends?"

"We never stopped," Roxy said through the thick door. "Let's talk later."

"Okay. Can I hand you the donuts and the tote with the coffees? You could share with Alma."

"Still not dressed," Roxy snarked, swallowing hard. She couldn't let Alex see her ready for the day.

"I'll leave them on the mat. That is, after I sneak me a couple of cream filleds."

"That's fine. Alex, I'm going back to bed. I'm not feeling well. Lack of sleep. Let's connect later."

"Absolutely. Call me when you're up to it. And if you're not feeling better in a few hours, let me know what I can get you."

"Okay." Roxy slumped against the door and listened as Alex dropped something onto the mat. A few seconds later, the sound of his footsteps faded away.

With every retreating step, her heart rate decreased. After a minute or two, she peeked out of her window, craning her neck to check the corridor in both directions. No sign of Alex, but she couldn't be sure that he had left the premises. She stood straighter, taking a deep breath to regain her composure before dashing to the corner of the room.

Once again, she wrapped her fingers around the edge and dragged the end table several feet across the floor, clearing a space to peel back the carpet.

She crouched, reaching under the thin foam pad, frantically scouring the surface of the hardwood. Several long seconds passed as her fingers searched, eager to locate the metal object.

With a huff and a grunt, she lowered onto her hands and knees, barely fitting the tight space. "Good Lord, I am too old for this," Roxy hissed into the silence, ignoring the cracks, creaks, and pops releasing from her body like an aging symphony.

Roxy twisted into a sitting position. With both hands, she yanked a larger section of carpet, revealing more of the floor and allowing a better view of the area.

Two deep gulps later, right before her, about eight inches away from the wall, the tiny locker key lay undisturbed, apparently oblivious that its mere presence had caused a blizzard of chaos engulfing Roxy's quiet existence.

"Well, hello, FSR-444," Roxy purred, her gleeful tone resonating. She uncurled from the floor and stood, finally able to admire the key cradled in her palm before shoving it deep into her front pocket.

She patted the denim front of her jeans. "You'll be safe right there."

After kicking the carpet in place and shoving the end table back where it belonged, Roxy retrieved her handbag from where she had dropped it and looped her arm through her purse strap.

"Phone. Keys, both car and locker. Purse," she said aloud, verifying everything she needed. She released the deadbolt, turned the knob, and charged out of her apartment, slamming straight into Alex's chest, nearly toppling them both to the ground.

"Oh, Alex," she said, weakly concealing her flustered state.

"Roxy!" Alex regained his balance and opened his hand, revealing small packets. "Forgot the sugar and creamer in the car. I was about to tuck them into the coffee-carrier thingy."

Roxy nodded, flummoxed as to how to continue the conversation and more importantly, how to get him to leave.

Alex eyed her. "You're feeling better, I see. Dressed and ready to go."

"A little. Heading out to the drug store for some milk of magnesia," she supplied, hoping he'd grasp the urgent undercurrent of her message.

"I can get that for you," Alex insisted. "Get back in bed and rest. Be back in fifteen minutes."

"No, really. I'm okay to drive. I need to pick up a few things anyway, and I don't want to bother you."

"It's no bother. Is your stomach queasy? I can make you hot tea instead of coffee."

"No. And frankly, I don't want to discuss my health right now."

Alex took a step back.

"I don't mean anything," Roxy said, her voice softening. "I'm in a foul mood. When you call later, I'll be in a better place."

Alex nodded knowingly. "Oh. Lady stuff. I won't pry. My offer to make tea still stands. We could relax and watch a movie."

"Why do men always assume, if a woman isn't feeling well, it's girl problems?"

"I guess the way you worded it. You sounded private."

"Do you even know what milk of magnesia does? What people use it for?"

"Not really, I guess," he answered, looking down at his sneakers. "Cramps?"

Roxy shook her head in disbelief. If she wasn't in a hurry and in looming danger, she'd lecture this seemingly uninformed guy about *lady issues*, especially about women like herself, well past the age for monthly visits from Aunt Flo.

Could he be that naïve or uninformed? He was married for thirty-five years or something. Perhaps he wasn't as innocent as he appeared. She'd seen Alex play dumb in situations to serve his purpose, once with Stacy, and another time with Rita at the trucking school.

Today he seemed dead set on keeping her near and talking. Was that what this was really about?

"It's not for cramps. It's a laxative," she said, watching the dawn of understanding spread across Alex's face. "Look, I have to leave," Roxy said, purposely avoiding the word *go*. "Let's pick this up later when I'm, I'm not so... uncomfortable," she replied, playing on his uneasiness.

Alex stepped back, his body posture suggesting remorse. "Of course, Roxy. I thought... I mean, I figured our relationship was moving forward. My mistake. Enjoy the donuts when you're up to it."

"Alex, really—" she started to defend, a smidgen of guilt invading her being.

"Rocks? Alex?" Alma's voice rang out from behind them. "Just listened to your phone message. Is everything all right with you two?"

"Huh? Yeah. Alex brought donuts. I'm on my way to the drug store," Roxy replied, watching Alma fold a large envelope and shove it into her back pocket. "He was about to leave."

"Drug store? I thought you were heading out on a purse—"

Roxy interrupted, a curt finality to her words. "Plans changed. I'm not feeling great. I need to get some... medicine."

"She needs a laxative," Alex said, as though revealing a deep secret. "Won't let me pick it up for her."

"Okay. Well, if you want to go yourself, let me drive you," Alma suggested.

At the end of her patience, Roxy snapped, "Why is everyone worried about me?"

"Beats me. Maybe we care about you." Alma slid a glance to Alex.

"I'll take my leave. Roxy, I'll call tonight. Alma, there's a jelly-filled donut and a cruller that might have your name on them." He kissed the top of Roxy's head and walked away.

"Bye, Alex," Alma shouted to his back. "And thanks for the donuts."

When he was clearly out of earshot, Alma asked, "What in the hell is wrong with you? Don't you like him anymore?"

"I like him fine. Just not today."

"What's special about today? Girl, I swear you're making me crazy. You leave a message about needing me and then the next second, you call to say you're going purse-shopping. And now you're headed to the drug store? What the hell is going on?"

"We can't talk here. Someone might see us." Roxy looked around. She clutched the tote with two coffee containers. "Grab the donuts."

Alma secured the box. "You're scaring me," she added, glancing down the corridor, her face devoid of its usual bright glow.

"Exactly," Roxy finished, gesturing in the direction of Alma's apartment. "Let's go to your place."

"But I thought you had to go to the pharmacy or something."

"You're not exactly quick on the pickup," Roxy growled, shoving Alma in the desired direction. "Walk," she snapped, the last of her nerves fraying. "I'll tell you more once we're inside your place," she said, peering over her shoulder to confirm Alex was nowhere around.

Alma opened the donut box, selected a French cruller, and took a bite. "Whatever you say, crazy lady."

Chapter Forty-Six

"Crazy?" Roxy shouted once Alma had shut the front door. "I'll show you crazy!"

"Calm down. You know I didn't mean—"

"Mean what? Doesn't matter. Look Alma, we're into some serious shit. I don't know all the details, but Chuck and that food truck are at the bottom of everything that has gone to crap in my life."

"That's two poop references in two sentences," Alma said.

"Not the time to make me laugh," Roxy barked, turning away. "This is serious. Life-and-death serious. Sam's-death serious."

"Alex bought the variety pack. Want one?" Alma asked, proffering the opened donut box.

Roxy surveyed her choices and snagged a glazed twist. "He's soothing me with sweets. And you need to watch your mouth," she shot back, mouth full of pastry. "I'm not crazy, even though I feel like I'm going crazy."

Alma stepped closer and put her hand on Roxy's shoulder. "I know. Just wanted to give you a minute to breathe, gather some perspective."

"I have all the GD perspective I can handle," Roxy shouted, waving her donut like a baton.

"GD?"

"I went to Catholic school. Can't say goddamn without thinking I'm going to hell."

Alma snorted. "Me, too. Those nuns scared me something terrible."

Roxy dropped the remnants of her donut onto a napkin. "Can we discuss our common fear of parochial school later? I have to get to the skating rink."

"And that's the most important thing you need to do now because…?" Alma asked, a glint of disbelief poking out.

"Because the key Sam left in his baseball jacket is from there." Relief bolted through her at sharing the news. "It came to me last night when we were changing back into our street shoes. The answer to what's going on, the proof I didn't kill Sam, is inside a locker at the skating rink."

"Then let's go." Alma headed toward the door, licking traces of donut glaze from her fingers.

"Stop. They don't open until noon. That's why I was going purse-shopping. To kill time and to take my mind off all this craziness."

"Oh." Alma pulled a frown, her posture switching seamlessly from attack to defeat.

"How did the ribbon cutting go in Topanga… or was it Thousand Oaks?" Roxy asked, in an attempt to make peace.

"You mean Tarzana?" Alma asked.

"Tarzana. Hell, yes." Roxy slapped her forehead.

"Everything went fine, except for the actual ribbon cutting. The giant cardboard scissors broke in two right as the mayor and I posed for the staged photo. Some intern is getting his ass chewed as we speak."

Roxy nodded, sympathetic to the fate of a nameless subordinate. "Shit rolls downhill."

"A third poop reference. You got a hat trick!" Alma shouted.

"Stop counting," Roxy ordered. "This isn't a drinking game."

"Should be," Alma snarked.

"Listen, I'm gonna drive to the rink and wait in the parking lot until the manager or one of the workers shows up," Roxy said. "I'll call you once I have emptied the locker."

"You'll do what? You're not leaving without me. I want to know what's in there as much as you do. I'll drive. You're constipated, remember?"

"Dear God, in every way, today is turning to sh—"

Alma closed her eyes. "Don't. Don't say it. Otherwise, I'm going to award you a quadruple poo-poo trophy."

"Well, now you're on the scoreboard," Roxy announced.

"This is a competition?"

"Of sorts. I appreciate you wanting to keep me company, but I don't know what I'm walking into. I won't put you in danger," Roxy vowed. "I promised to call... what? Don't shake your head at me. Someone is threatened by what Sam stashed in that locker. Heck, they're threatened by me. You don't want to be in the middle of this."

"Do you hear yourself? Roxy, I *am* in the middle of this. Have been since the beginning when Sam left. And then turned up dead." Alma frowned. "We can debate all the reasons why you don't want me to go, but in the end, you know I'm going. You can't stop me. We can go separately or together. I'll let you choose."

"Some choice."

"Best I can do on short notice and little sleep." Alma stood, arms folded, head cocked, waiting. "Take it or leave it."

"Will you stay in the car?" Roxy asked, immediately receiving an icy stare. "Guess not."

"Tell you what I will do. I'll text Rudy and let him know where we are. He can track my phone. That way if we run into actual trouble, someone will know where to start looking."

Roxy huffed. She hated when Alma made sense. Sometimes she wondered which of them was the older, experienced one. "Nothing I say will make you change your mind?"

"Nope."

"You realize whoever these people are, they killed Sam or had him killed. I'm guessing they won't hesitate to kill again."

"Save your drama for your mama," Alma scolded. "You haven't been challenged to a duel at dawn. No one knows what that key opens or that you even have it, right?"

Roxy nodded.

"The smart thing to do is head over around noon, pay our fee to skate, empty the locker, then drive to some place safe, like the police station parking lot, and see what's what. Agreed?"

"Agreed," Roxy said, not convinced that any move they made would be safe or smart. Still, she had to admit Alma's plan made more sense than hers. And knowing Alma would come along lowered her stress level from unbearable to barely tolerable.

Alma looked around the room. "What time is it now?"

Roxy checked her smartwatch. "A little after ten."

"Okay, we'll leave in an hour."

"What do we do until then?" Roxy asked, her nerves tapping out the *William Tell Overture* inside her chest.

"We can talk about Rudy," Alma volunteered, a sexy smirk lingered at the corners of her lips. "And we have a dozen minus-a-few donuts to mow through."

Roxy pulled out a kitchen chair, plopped down and claimed one of the three coffees in the carrier. "Rudy, Rudy, Rudy," she chimed, removing the lid to dump sugar and creamer packets inside.

Once satisfied the powders combined adequately with the brew, Roxy lifted her paper cup in a mock toast and took a sip.

"Tell me everything I need to know about the man who has stolen your heart."

Chapter Forty-Seven

Roxy eyed Alma, still standing, pacing the room.

Does she want to spend the next two hours discussing Rudy? He's a nice-looking guy and all, but geez...

"Are you going to sit down or what?" Roxy finally snapped. "You're making me jumpier than I already am."

"Sit?" Alma said, as though this term was foreign to her. "Sit. Oh sure."

Alma stepped to the other side of the table, nabbed another donut, this time a jelly filled, but didn't take a seat. "I'll need a few extra napkins for this mess," she said, towering over Roxy. "Hand me one of those coffees. They're probably cold. Want yours warmed up?"

Roxy passed her paper cup and a second one to Alma, who quickly placed both inside her microwave. "I have real cream," she announced, "if you don't want to use that powdered junk."

"Too late," Roxy said.

Alma made her eyes big. "Alex thought he was going to have a little breakfast somethin'-somethin' with you, huh? Gotta give the man credit. He's a positive thinker."

The microwave beeped, signaling Alma to retrieve and distribute both drinks. She propped against the wall and took another bite of donut, strawberry jelly oozing from the sides.

"You like me looking up to you?" Roxy snarked.

"Very funny." Alma yanked out the chair across from Roxy and dropped her bottom down with an exaggerated thud. "Happy?"

"Overjoyed. Is there an apple fritter in the box?" Roxy asked.

"Don't think so. There is a cinnamon-topped jelly, though. Those usually have an apple filling. Will that do?"

"Guess so." Roxy accepted the donut. "Can't believe I'm eating two in one sitting. Why is sugar the perfect way to soothe your nerves?"

"I have no idea." Alma rearranged herself. "What the heck is poking me?" she muttered, tugging something from her rear pocket. "Man." She unfolded an envelope. "I forgot about this."

Roxy bent forward. "What is that?"

"Don't know. I opened my mailbox yesterday afternoon before we went skating. I sorted the piles last night but didn't bother looking through them until this morning before I left for the grand opening."

"Piles? Why do you have piles? Fan mail?"

"Hardly," Alma said. "Mostly credit card come-ons and grocery circulars, a lot of junk. I don't bother to check but maybe once a week. Just often enough to keep Ed the mailman from leaving me nasty sticky notes complaining that he can't fit any more into my box."

"Once a week?" Roxy declared in disbelief. "I collect my mail every day."

"You would. You like to hang out at the apartment's community mailboxes, like it's the company watercooler and catch up on gossip," Alma jokingly accused.

"Hardly," Roxy defended before taking a gulp of coffee. "Aren't you afraid you'll miss something important, like a check or a note from your mother? What about your bills?"

"I pay everything online. Haven't you heard of going paperless?" Alma admonished, wiping jelly goo from her chin.

Roxy tapped her glitter-tipped nails against the insulated cup barely keeping her coffee lukewarm. "I like a paper copy. And I want to know how much things are before they get deducted from my meager bank account."

Alma rolled her eyes. "Anyway, this must have been sandwiched in with the rest of my mail." She slapped the crumpled envelope onto the tabletop. "It came inside a manila envelope addressed to me and I nearly tossed it. No return address or anything. This is what was inside, with your name on it."

Roxy gazed at the envelope but left it where Alma dropped it, suddenly afraid of its contents. The only thing she knew for certain was the sender. The percussion section now residing inside her chest played double-time.

"That's the other reason I popped over, to give you this. But after all your wacko talk last night about Alex and conspiracies, when I saw him standing on your doorstep, I decided to wait until he was gone."

Roxy tilted in her chair, lost in thought. "Good going," she muttered.

"Well, will you open the envelope or what?"

"What?"

"Open the freaking letter," Alma demanded. A comic dot of jelly vibrated on her lower lip after each word.

"Wipe your mouth."

"Oh," Alma licked her lips, missing the jelly glob. Finally, she dabbed the napkin against her skin, waving the smear of strawberry jam at Roxy in victory. "Are you gonna keep staring until a crystal ball reveals the contents?"

Roxy forced a grin.

"I have an idea. Let's open the envelope and find out what's inside," Alma teased. "A novel approach, I agree, but one that is frequently successful."

"How can you be such a smart ass so early in the day?"

"I've been up for hours," Alma shot back, "and I'm tired. Lack of sleep makes me extra snarky."

"Heh," Roxy grunted. "Didn't think that was possible."

Alma took a quiet tone. "Rocks, to tell you the truth, I don't get the cloak-and-dagger. Like your life is a film noir, and not a good one. I get that things have been crazy since Sam left, him dying and all."

"And his dead body turning up inside the trunk of my limo. Along with MY kitchen knife covered with MY fingerprints."

"They call that circumstantial evidence," Alma argued.

"No, my dear friend, they call that tying me to the murder weapon." Roxy raked her hands down the side of her face. "He was stabbed with the same knife we used to cut up *carne asada* for tacos," she whispered, her mind swirling in an unlikely juxtaposition.

"I get that things look bad. You're being blamed, but we know they can't make those charges stick."

"Thanks for the vote of confidence," Roxy said.

"They'll find the real murderer."

Roxy nodded. "I'm praying for that, but I can't sit back and hope justice happens. I have to turn up something that proves my innocence. The DA is spending his time building a case against me. He certainly isn't looking for any other suspects. Definitely not searching for the real killer."

Alma waved her hands around in surrender. "True. True, and I support you with all that. The part I don't get is this conspiracy you've let mushroom in your brain. It's borderline psycho. You don't trust Alex. And now, a piece of mail drained your face of any color. What are you afraid is in there?"

"I have no idea. That's what scares me." Roxy dropped her head into her hands. "But what scares me more is knowing the envelope is from Sam."

"Sam!?"

Roxy lifted her head. "That's his handwriting."

Chapter Forty-Eight

Roxy tipped the paper cup, coaxing the last remaining drops of tepid coffee into her mouth. A stall tactic she and Alma wordlessly acknowledged. A reasonable way to delay the inevitable—reading what Sam had written. The unopened envelope rested on Alma's kitchen table, the proverbial elephant in the room.

"Do you wanna split that last cup?" she asked Alma, diverting attention from the expected action.

"Sure, but what I really want is for you to open this letter. Let's find out what the hell is going on."

Roxy placed the third cup inside the microwave, pushed a few buttons, and stood like a sentry waiting for the mechanical beep to indicate hot coffee.

She split the contents, pouring Alma a little more into her cup before sitting down to stir in real creamer.

"Damn, that's hot," Alma moaned. "How long did you heat it up for?"

"Two minutes, I think," Roxy replied, fingering the place where her name was scrawled on the outside of the envelope. She reluctantly lifted the long white rectangle, turning it in her hand for several moments as though a secret message might be revealed by her touch. She blinked back tears, then slowly tore open the flap and unfolded the contents.

Take a deep breath, Roxy thought, her will to stay in the dark melting away.

My dear Roxy,

I got myself into some crazy trouble. Thought I could straighten things out without involving you. I couldn't bear you getting caught up in this mess.

But if you're reading this, I guess I really screwed up, and I can't come to you in person.

"Out loud, for gosh sake. I meant for you to read out loud," Alma interrupted.

Roxy waved off Alma's complaint and continued reading silently.

I had to leave you. Please believe there was no other way. But my heart never left. Never. Rocks, everything I did was to keep you safe. Now this is the only way you can stay safe.

Remember that key? It's important. Call 213-555-0378. Ask for Heath. Tell him you have it, he knows the real story, probably knows everything. Anyway, he'll end this and protect you.

He tried to help me, but it was already too late. Maybe there's still time for him to fix everything. I'm so sorry, my beautiful muñeca.

Roxy struggled to make out the final few words, her tears landing on the page, mingling with teardrop stains from Sam.

Just wanted to make our life a little better. I now know that what we had was perfect. We had each other. We had everything. I love you very much, Roxy, and I always have.

Your Sam

Roxy's hand shook as she held the paper as though a priceless historical document rested there.

Alma lurched so far forward that Roxy pulled back. "Well?"

215

"He loved me." A warmness surrounded her. "He really loved me."

"He had to say more than that. Let me read it," Alma said, reaching.

Roxy handed her the paper.

"There's one thing to do," Alma declared a full minute later. "Call this Heath character."

Roxy reclaimed the letter from Alma's hand and set it on the table. She stared at Sam's handwriting, touching the places where he declared his undying love.

"I'll get my cell phone."

"You will not," Roxy shouted, slamming her palm onto the table.

"But Sam said—"

"I know. I read it, too," Roxy said, her heart pounding at this new revelation.

"Then why are you hesitating?"

"I'm not hesitating. Sam's dead, remember? You really want me to reach out to the guy who helped him?" Roxy asked, using air quotes around *helped*. "I can do without that kind of help."

"Could Heath be involved with Sam's murder?"

"I have no idea, but I'm not trusting anyone at this point. We're going to get whatever's in that locker and take the contents directly to the police."

Alma nodded, but Roxy could tell her friend wasn't fully convinced.

"Sam didn't tell you what the key opened. If we hadn't gone skating last night..."

"But we did," Roxy interrupted. "What's your point?"

"Sam didn't want you involved. He told you to take the key to Heath, not to go all rogue like you're some crime-fighting superhero. This was Sam's last-ditch effort to get whatever is in that locker to the authorities," Alma cautioned.

"And you think Heath is the authorities? I doubt it. He did a piss-poor job, and Sam ended up dead. He had something to do with Sam's death, or he failed miserably at protecting him. Either way, I don't want him involved." Roxy folded the letter into thirds and slid it inside the envelope.

Alma persisted. "Does this Heath guy already know what that key opens? Maybe Sam told him."

"Doesn't matter what Heath knows, whoever the hell Heath is. *I* know. And I'm going to do whatever I can to catch Sam's killer." *Maybe if I had helped sooner, he might still be alive.* "Do you still have the manila envelope this letter came in?" Roxy asked.

"What? Oh, yeah. I tossed it in the garbage. Why? There wasn't a return address."

"To check the postmark."

"I should have thought of that." Alma moved to her kitchen trash can, yanked out a mound of old mail and put the stack on the kitchen counter. "It's in here somewhere."

"You should check your mailbox more than once a month," Roxy scolded.

"I do. All this is just two weeks' worth of circulars and junk mail," Alma defended, sorting through the heap. "Maybe three."

Roxy stood, her patience thinning. "Let me help." Roxy methodically fingered each piece, making certain nothing was stuck in between. *How could one woman be on so many mailing lists?*

"Here it is!" Alma raised the manila envelope in the air.

Roxy snatched it. "Thanks," she said, immediately examining both sides, then flipping it onto the counter.

Alma retrieved the envelope and announced the postmark date. "That's two, maybe three weeks ago."

Roxy looked directly into Alma's eyes. "The same day I found him in the trunk, dead."

Chapter Forty-Nine

Roxy pushed the box containing the leftover donuts to the side, making room for her elbows to settle on the table. Haunted by the memory of her last words to Sam, she laid her chin on top of the triangle where her fists formed a sturdy platform and stared blindly into space.

Far as I'm concerned, you can crawl back to wherever you were and drop dead.

Her last words to him, cruel and damning.

Even worse, when Sam had called her the day of his death, she shot that message to her voicemail, convinced he had been the one who had ransacked her apartment. And she sure wasn't interested in listening to any lame-ass excuses he'd invent.

Roxy was mad, hurt, wounded by Sam's leaving. Hell hath no fury and all that. If only she could go back in time to give him the help he desperately needed and deserved. They were once a team. Had been for decades. How could she have believed he would dump her so suddenly and in such a heartless way? If she had truly loved him, been the partner she claimed to be, she would have recognized that something sinister controlled his actions.

But she was busy wallowing in her own pity party, blinded to anything else. And now Sam was dead, and she was out on bail for his murder.

"He doesn't give us any idea about what's really going on," Alma said, interrupting Roxy's regret.

Silence.

Alma returned the letter to the tabletop. "We've got no clue about what got him snuffed."

"Have a little respect," Roxy snapped, tears bubbling in her eyes. "You make his death sound like a mafia hit or something."

"Sorry," Alma apologized. "I didn't mean to offend. But Roxy, get real. For all we know, Sam could have crossed the mob or pissed off some gang, or—"

"Stop!" Roxy yelled, a mixture of pain and frustration exploding from inside.

Alma licked her lips in shame. "So what now?"

"Now I go to the skate rink, open that frickin' locker, and finally learn the reason why my life is being run through a tree shredder."

"One correction. *We* go."

Roxy sneered. "You think we should call Heath."

"I do, but that doesn't mean I don't respect your reasoning. Fact is, I'm not letting you go anywhere alone, but I reserve the right to call him after we know what we're dealing with."

"Reserve the right? You have no rights here, Alma. We don't even know who the hell Heath is."

"True. But we know Sam trusted him."

"And Sam is dead." Roxy spoke slowly, a deep ache coating each word. An ache she kept submerged in her soul, like a beach ball held underwater. Inevitably, the inflated ball burst from the depths through the surface, its path unpredictable. Devastating.

Her true feelings exploded in that moment. Roxy gulped at the realization that she no longer controlled her emotions. Grief snaked down her throat, compressing against her core, threatening to choke off her air.

"How could I have been so dumb," she yelled, tears finally escaping her eyes and falling onto her half-eaten donut.

Roxy pushed away from the table, shaking. She howled in agony, releasing a devastating pain buried deep inside, a misery that had festered in her soul for weeks. She buried her head in her hands and stayed that way, rocking back and forth, as though the movement would end the hurt.

After what seemed like an eternity, Roxy felt arms encircle her, embracing her where she sat. A quiet moment passed before Alma spoke. "I wondered how long you'd keep the truth from penetrating that force field you've created."

"What do you mean?" Roxy asked, wiping trails of tears from her cheeks.

"At a conscious level, you understand Sam is gone forever. But in your heart, in your being, every place that matters, you never let the reality enter. With so much else going on, you built a façade, a safe barricade to help you cope."

"What the hell are you talking about? I know Sam was killed and in the most horrible of ways. I've never pretended that hadn't happened."

Alma dragged her chair around and sat facing Roxy. "Yes, on the surface, you've accepted Sam's death. What else could you do? But on an emotional level… well, that's another thing."

"Alma, what is this Zen master stuff you're throwing at me? Conscious level. Emotional level. Next you're going to force me to drink organic green juice and enroll us in goat yoga."

"Sure, make jokes—but at the end of the day, when the charges against you are dropped, after you've passed your truck driving test and decide if Alex is friend or foe, when all the things you've been working toward are yours, Sam won't be here to celebrate or commiserate the outcome."

Roxy nodded, reality dawning. "I'm lucky you were here when my truth erupted."

"There's gonna be more eruptions." Alma handed Roxy a napkin printed with Donut Dynasty. "This is only the beginning."

Roxy wiped her face, blinking her eyes to loosen more tears. She turned the napkin over to engage a dry spot. "Oh, my gosh."

"What?"

"Alex bought these donuts at the Nasty." She put the pastry box lid down, but it was blank, as were the coffee cups.

"Huh?"

"The Nasty. Donut Da-nasty. And I ate two of them," she lamented, as though ready to gag.

"Pretty sure you had three. Maybe three and a half," Alma said, peeking inside the box for a tally. "What are you talking about?"

"Donut Dynasty proudly displays their B rating from the LA Health Department. I *never*—and I mean never—buy donuts there. No wonder they use generic boxes. I may barf."

"Mine were good," Alma insisted, more to convince herself.

"I better head to the skate rink before I do a tilt-a-hurl." Roxy got to her feet, fighting the urge to spit.

"Right behind you."

Roxy stopped. "You don't have to come. I prefer you don't. I will be fine. This is my mess to straighten out. I let Sam down, and I should have known better. So, I'm going with my gut. No Heath. No Alex. No you. If I get killed, that's on me. But I won't—"

"Just stop. There's no way in this world or the next that you're doing any of this by yourself. We have a plan. I'll contact Rudy, then we'll go."

Roxy glanced at her watch. "Still about an hour until they open."

"Hopefully, they'll let us in early. Tell them we lost your engagement ring the night before or some such crap. That the ring might have dropped on the floor by the lockers. Ask if someone found it," Alma said, spinning her story. "As your maid-of-honor, I'll put on a big show, crawl around searching the floor. In the meantime, you open the locker, grab what's in there and we vamoose."

"You're my maid-of-honor?"

"Yep."

"Wow, you cooked up that tale in a hurry."

"That's what straight As in Creative Writing will do for you."

"All right. We have a plan," Roxy agreed, optimism seeping into her veins for the first time in weeks. "But first I have to gargle with some serious oral antiseptic. The thought of Nasty donuts in my mouth makes me nauseous."

Chapter Fifty

For the second time that morning, Roxy slipped her crossbody bag over her shoulder, tapped the spot in her jeans where she had tucked the locker key, and sucked in a deep belly breath, a useless, vain attempt to calm the army of fireflies nesting in her stomach.

"Ready," she declared with more force than necessary.

Alma opened her front door and extended an arm outward. *"Aprés toi, s'il te plait?"*

"Merci," Roxy answered with a mini-curtsy. "Oooh, we're fancy."

"Guess I could have said *let's go*, but that doesn't have the same flair or sophistication." Alma locked the door behind them before looking around. "Things sound better in French."

"No argument there. You're acting weird, even for you. What, or who, are you looking for?" Roxy asked, her eyes tracking the space alongside Alma's. "Worried we're being watched?"

"Nah. Just cautious." Alma clomped down the staircase with her youthful bounce. "Weird is our new normal," she said over her shoulder.

Roxy followed but not at the same jaunty pace, steading herself against the handrail to avoid a spill. "Hey, wait up," she hollered to Alma's distant back. "That little bit of cardio isn't going to offset any calories from our donut sins."

"I know, I know," Alma said, heading toward Roxy.

"Were you scouting before I got down the steps?" Roxy asked, sucking in air. "You are worried."

"Not worried. Aware." Alma turned toward her parked car. "This way," she directed. "I'll drive."

"I'm too stressed to argue," Roxy said, meekly climbing into the passenger seat. "There's probably a tracker on my car anyway," she joked.

Roxy took in Alma's hard stare, telegraphing what they'd both thought, and the likelihood was not funny.

"It's a strong possibility," Alma said, pushing the ignition button. "I'm banking whoever is behind this doesn't know my car, but they could. I mean, if they've been stalking you, it wouldn't be hard to track me, too."

Roxy rested her palm on the door handle, considering her exit. "Exactly the reason I wanted you to stay here."

"We are way out of our depth," Alma said, the engine humming in the background. "Sure you won't reconsider calling Heath or the police? We could have them meet us there."

Roxy undid her seat belt and turned to Alma. "You know where I stand on Heath. And as for the police, that makes sense—*except* when you're a murder suspect. Then the police are your natural enemy." Roxy popped her door open and swung her legs around. "Once I have my hands on what's in that locker, I'll turn everything over to the proper authorities."

"Get back in this car," Alma ordered. "You're acting nuttier than I already knew you could. We'll go with your plan, but I want Rudy, maybe even Alex, to accompany us to the police station."

Roxy glanced at Alma, who gestured frantically for her to get back in the car. She relented.

"You make a good argument," Roxy said, settling in the passenger seat. "We'll get hold of Rudy once we have what Sam left behind. Okay?"

"That's fair," Alma said with exaggeration. "I'm texting him now to monitor me on Find Friends." She pushed Send, put down her phone and shifted the car into reverse.

Roxy was minutes away from the truth, however ugly or harsh.

From Sam's letter, she had a glimmer of why things ended up the way they had. All roads pointed to money. Soon she'd understand what quagmire Sam had immersed them in and how everything had turned so horribly wrong.

Chapter Fifty-One

Roxy gawked at the rows of cars filling Fountain Skate Rink's meager parking lot. "What the heck is going on?" Roxy questioned as Alma searched for a spot.

"You said the rink doesn't open for another forty-five minutes or so," Alma said, exasperated she had to squeeze her Beamer into a spot too small for the luxury SUV. "If my doors get dinged, you're paying to repaint them."

Roxy didn't argue. "Why are all these people here?"

"They must open earlier than you guessed," Alma said.

"I didn't guess," Roxy replied, annoyed not just at Alma's insinuation, but at the unexpected complication. She had hoped to get in and get out before any skaters showed up.

"Someone told you they open at noon?" Alma said, looking around.

"Well, not exactly. The hours were posted on the front door."

"No matter, now we can get in early."

Roxy joined Alma outside the car. "I wish there weren't so many people around. I wanted to do this without hoopla."

"Frankly, having people around is safer for us. John Q. Public is our best friend right now."

"I suppose. We can skip our dog-and-pony show pretending I lost my ring. Let's pay the fee, open the locker, and get out."

"That's my plan," Alma said, holding open the entrance door for Roxy to pass through.

The inside was dark, with magenta and chartreuse strobe lights flashing across the ice. Roxy blinked before approaching the ticket seller. "Two, please."

"Are you with the party?" a skinny teen with teeth covered in wire asked.

"Party?"

"Yes, Damien's birthday party."

"Well, no. We want to skate," Roxy said, toggling her thumb between Alma and herself. "Get a little exercise in, you know."

"Yeah. I know, but you're going to have to come back after twelve for open skate hours," the boy said, pointing to a handwritten warning taped to the glass window in front of his booth.

"What? People are skating right now," Alma protested.

"Yeah. I see that," he snarked, revealing a wider view of his braces. "Those are the guests."

Alma turned to Roxy, puzzled.

"There's a private party," Roxy said, defeated. "That's why they're open early."

Alma nodded, now comprehending. She shifted closer to read the teenager's name badge. "Look, Lonnie... May I call you Lonnie?"

The kid nodded.

"Great. Lonnie, I'm Alma Sanchez. This is my best friend, Roxy Adams. We were here last night. A big night for Roxy. She got engaged. Right over there, near those lockers." Alma pointed to the far side of the room.

"That's great, I guess, but I still can't let you guys crash Damien's birthday party."

"Lonnie, Lonnie, Lonnie. You're such a jokester." Alma leaned in. "We don't want to crash the party. No. No. No. We just need to get to the locker area and find Roxy's engagement ring."

Roxy shoved Alma aside. "What she's taking way too long to explain is that I lost my ring. Maybe it's in the locker we used last night. I want to check around. Can you let us do that, please? Please?"

"Don't you like the guy?" Lonnie asked.

"What does that have to do with anything?" Alma complained.

"I'm only seventeen, but I know if you give a girl a diamond ring, she doesn't take it off her finger. You must not have liked the guy or the ring."

Alma stomped, pretending to pull her hair out. "Listen, letters-to-the-lovelorn, she lost the ring, and we need to find it. We won't interrupt little Damien and his pals. They won't even know we're here."

"The party ends in about an hour. Can't you come back then?"

"You said it yourself, a diamond ring is a big deal," Roxy said, hoping her puppy eyes routine would find a soft spot with this young fellow. "I can't wait. I have to find my ring."

"She's meeting her fiancé for lunch. She can't show up without wearing that ring," Alma said, now using her velvety DJ Soul persona to plead their case.

"Hey, I recognize that voice. Are you on the radio?"

Roxy and Alma sighed simultaneously. Maybe they were getting somewhere with metal mouth.

"Why yes, I am. I'm—"

"You do those bladder control radio commercials. Wow, a celebrity in the house."

"You've got it wrong," Alma said, obviously insulted. "I've never done an incontinence commercial—"

Roxy stopped her. "Doesn't matter," she whispered. "Listen, Lonnie, can you let us in, not to skate, just to look in the locker?"

"I guess. What locker number was it? Someone else might be using it."

Roxy paled. "I'm not sure. It was three something. I'd know which one if I saw it. Can we take a look?"

A man wearing a Fountain Skate Rink polo shirt approached. "What's going on, Lonnie?"

"Oh, Paul, these folks lost a ring. She thinks it might be in the locker they used last night."

"A ring?"

"An engagement ring," Roxy clarified.

"I'm the day manager, Paul," he said with a slight at-your-service bow. "Let's find your ring."

They followed a few steps behind Paul to the locker area. "Thanks, Lonnie," Roxy said over her shoulder as an afterthought.

Alma raised her eyebrows up and down, ala Groucho Marx, making Roxy want to burst out laughing.

Roxy whispered, "Take him to the other side so I can open Sam's locker without prying eyes."

"The lockers without keys in the tumbler are being used," Paul said, apparently not noticing the women's conspiratorial chatter. "Which one did you have last night?"

"It was in the other bank of lockers," Alma said, skirting away from Roxy, whose gaze was trained on a different row of lockers.

"I'm going to check over here," Roxy said as the pair moved away. "Just in case."

Alma nodded, intent on keeping the manager occupied.

Roxy peeled off, waiting several seconds before ducking around the corner to find locker 444. She fished the key out of her pocket and crouched down to slide the shaft into the lock.

Glancing around the room, she assured herself of privacy before she turned the key. The tumblers released. Taking a deep breath, she opened the door, and peered in.

Propped against the gray metal side was the same-sized envelope that Sam had mailed to Alma. Roxy quickly removed the contents—a few photos hastily made on a color printer and a flash drive about the size of a key fob—prizes inside this quirky box of Cracker Jack.

With her heart pounding in her ears, Roxy thumbed through the photos, noting the odd angles and distance. She guessed Sam had taken them from an obscure location where he couldn't be detected.

Most featured what looked like a warehouse. Crowded against the walls were rows of pallets piled high with boxes, each with a designer brand logo stamped on the side.

The last picture, the only one with people, showed workers moving cartons in place. At first glance, Roxy spied a partially hidden woman near a pillar of cartons.

Sonya?

The quality of the prints was fuzzy, and Roxy didn't have time to look more closely. If she had guessed correctly, Sonya was directing laborers where to place the incoming inventory.

A deep sigh escaped Roxy's chest as she returned the empty envelope to the locker, closed the door, and locked it, dropping the key into her purse. Folding the short stack of photos into a small square, she tucked them, along with the flash drive, inside the front pocket of her running bra.

Guaranteed not to bulge, the ad had read. *No one will know where you've tucked your valuables.* She bought the bra months ago when she had committed to jogging three times a week. What a fortunate fashion choice she had made that morning. Her years-old Cross Your Heart bra couldn't have pulled off the same assurance.

Roxy walked to the far side of the room only to see Alma, on all fours, scouring the ground. After a beat or two, Paul extended a hand to help her rise.

She's really crawling around this filthy floor pretending to hunt for my imaginary ring.

Roxy approached, giving Alma a thumbs-up.

Alma scurried toward Roxy, her eagerness to escape Paul palpable.

"Did you find the ring?" Paul asked, following behind.

"I feel so stupid," Roxy said. "While I was looking around, I remembered that Alex—my fiancé—kept the ring. It was too big on my finger, and he insisted on taking it back to the jeweler to get it sized."

"You mean it wasn't here after all?" Paul said, a little perturbed at being dragged into a wild goose chase.

"Yes. I'm sorry. Thanks anyway for your help." Roxy flashed a toothy grin.

"Yeah, thanks, Paul."

Roxy grabbed Alma by the arm, and the two rushed toward the door.

"Hey, Lonnie, please wish Damien a happy birthday from DJ Soul Sanchez," Alma added in her sultriest voice as they passed, apparently not over his earlier slight.

Roxy shoved the door open and blinked, her eyes adjusting to the bright sunlight, her chest pounding with relief, her pace matching champion speed walkers.

"You got it?" Alma hustled to catch up.

Roxy patted the area near her decolletage.

Alma squinted a bewildered face but didn't stop for an explanation.

"Get your keys out," Roxy encouraged.

"Huh? I don't need to. Keyless entry, ever heard of it?"

Roxy shot back a scowl.

As they approached the SUV, the side mirrors moved into position, and the car beeped to life. "All the modern conveniences," Alma huffed.

Roxy yanked the door handle and then backed up a step. "What the hell?" she shouted. "Alma, you have a flat."

"Huh?" Alma rounded the car to where Roxy stood. "What the… I just had all four tires replaced. There's no freaking way I could have a flat unless I picked up a nail or something."

"Problem, ladies?"

Both Roxy and Alma spun to see a thirty-something brute of a man standing a few feet away. A stubbled beard and a T-shirt two sizes too small completed his look.

"No, we're fine," Alma said.

"Don't look fine to me. Looks like a flat. Want me to change it? Only take a few minutes."

"We don't want to bother you. I'll call the auto club. That's what they get paid to do." Roxy hoped her voice didn't betray her panic.

"I don't mind. You can tip me a twenty if it makes you feel better. Pop the trunk so I can get the spare and the jack."

"There is no spare or jack. Get in the car, Roxy," Alma directed. "Even flat, we can drive far enough to get the tire replaced. I have run-flat tires."

The man stepped back. "You're right. Didn't realize you had a—"

Before he could finish the sentence, a sweaty hand slapped across Roxy's mouth. "Stay quiet," the voice behind her directed.

She squirmed to find Alma immobilized by a third man. The thirty-something yanked Roxy's arms against her back and secured them at the wrists with a zip tie.

"Stay quiet," the first man repeated. "We don't want to hurt you, but we will." His solid grip anchored across her face caused Roxy to struggle for air and barred her from screaming for help.

A faded blue van approached, the side doors popping open long enough for Roxy and her male entourage to climb in.

"Sit," thirty-something bellowed.

She did.

He wrenched her purse from her grip, hurled it out of the van and slammed the door shut leaving Roxy with the haunting vision of a dazed Alma crumpled, battered, and shaking in the parking lot.

Chapter Fifty-Two

Roxy gaped at the inside of the van that caged her future. The repulsive blend of mold, rotten eggs, and never-washed gym socks assaulted her nostrils. She wouldn't be inhaling cleansing breaths to calm her nerves like her yoga instructor had taught her to do in times of crisis. Instead, she scrunched her nose and exhaled hard, her only weapon to combat the foul air residing inside the decades-old van walls from permeating her lungs.

The bumpy ride took maybe fifteen minutes but seemed longer to Roxy, who had been unceremoniously sandwiched between the two bruisers—one casually holding a gun as though a revolver was an accessory, the other staring into space. There were no windows to observe the scenery or recognize local landmarks as clues to where she was being taken. So she concentrated on clocking the drive time as if, by some slim chance, she'd escape from these fools and later could help the authorities track them down.

Beads of sweat gathered in the valley of her cleavage, a constant reminder of what was tucked between her boobs. She was certain this was what they were after; what they had tossed her apartment to find.

And equally certain that, for the moment, those photos and Sam's flash drive were the only reason she hadn't been killed.

She sent up a momentary prayer of thanks that the goons didn't abduct Alma, too. They must have thought she didn't know anything and, apparently, weren't worried about being identified.

To her surprise, she hadn't been blindfolded, and she wondered if that was a good or bad sign.

Probably a bad sign. A *very* bad sign.

Even with her limited knowledge of villains and their industry's best practices, Roxy knew leaving witnesses alive violated every crook's protocol. And these guys were card-carrying criminals and worse. Murderers.

She was grateful that Alma wasn't stuffed inside this suffocating van. Still, Roxy wished Alma's phone was. If only that phone was tucked inside Roxy's back pocket, Rudy could trace where these guys were taking her.

Relief rushed in momentarily when the driver finally pulled over and stopped. Fresh air was on the other side of the door. Goon number One, as she had mentally enumerated them, shoved her out of the van, grabbed her upper arm and escorted her inside a large industrial building. Goon Two, the one with the gun, trailed behind.

Roxy glanced around. Not a soul in sight. There was no one ready to save her. No handsome knight galloping in on a white charger to rescue her from these evil thirty-somethings.

Once again, the only person who could save Roxy would be Roxy.

Getting pretty used to that. Right when I've turned a corner; solved a mystery; untangled a quandary; the shit fan loads up like a bubble machine and spews more crap my way.

"Take her over there," Goon Three, the one who appeared to be in charge, directed. "Truss her to a chair."

Truss? The word choice alarmed Roxy. *Like a pig?*

"The boss will be here soon."

The boss? So these doofuses aren't running the show. No surprise there. They can barely...

Goon Two shoved Roxy hard onto the chair, her zip-tied wrists still bound at her back. Goon Three secured her torso and legs with a thin rope, the clothesline kind she remembered hanging in the backyard of her childhood home. Emerging against the lethal chaos came the vision of her mom's watchful eye as she shook one of Roxy's school jumpers out of the laundry basket and clipped the corners with wooden pins to the saggy cord. *Mom was always careful to space each garment, so they'd dry quicker.* The sweet smell of fresh laundry kissed by an outdoor breeze invaded her senses.

Roxy turned her head to use her sleeve to wipe a tear trailing down her cheek. *"Be your own hero,"* she remembered her mother telling her *weeks before she had died.*

Mom had been Roxy's hero. Now the daughter had to look inward for that same courage her mother seemed to easily tap into.

"Be your own hero."

How could those words infuse strength, determination, and courage?

Somehow Roxy would get herself out of this mess. She couldn't give up. Once they got the information they wanted, these guys would kill her, the same way they had killed Sam. Only she wouldn't be stuffed inside a limo trunk.

She had to stall as long as she could; give them a reason to keep her alive. But stalling would mean nothing if she didn't have an escape plan.

Roxy looked around the space, desperately searching for a way out. There were windows that she could reach if she climbed on top of some boxes.

Those boxes...

Roxy stared, recognizing the familiar designer names stamped on each carton; names that seemed out of place inside this run-down warehouse. Now that she was closer and not looking at a picture, the cardboard lettering printed on the box sides offered a pitiful imitation of the genuine designer logos.

She had seen this place before, if only in photographs. She cocked her head to replicate the view of the snapshot where she recognized Sonya.

This is the same place. Has to be. Some of those cartons are stacked exactly where they were several weeks ago when Sam snuck in for his covert photography session.

Were Chuck and Sonya fencing knock-off designer merchandise?

Worse, could it be stolen?

Chuck had to be behind this. But how... and why?

What was the connection to the food truck, and how did that link turn into a death sentence for Sam?

Roxy thought back to a year ago, forcing some of the pieces to fall into place in vague and eclectic ways.

One night, after one too many beers, Sam had confessed he didn't own the food truck anymore. Roxy had dismissed his words, thinking it was the booze talking. How she wished she had paid better attention.

And there were all those late-night, clandestine meetings Chuck would conduct at the tables outside the business. Unexplained cash inside their home safe, more than Sam would collect for a month of stellar receipts, and *Reyes of Sunshine* never had good, much less stellar, receipts in all the years she worked there.

And finally, the fact Sonya always wore the latest designer fashions, even to go ice skating. *What was a classy, society lady doing with the likes of Chuck the fat f…*

Roxy didn't bother to finish Alma's rhyme, even in her own mind.

Roxy's and Sam's money problems diminished weeks after Chuck started hanging around. Suddenly, there were funds to replace the fryer and the food truck's roof before the next Health Department inspection.

Sam expanded the menu, a step he said would double their business. Roxy couldn't see how fried zucchini and gelato could be the answer to their financial prayers, but the books always balanced with some extra cash in her pocket.

Apparently, Sam had prayed to a different god, the god of wheeling and dealing: St. Chuck. Sam had bought her a newer car and improved his wardrobe—if she could call throwing out his holey T-shirts and replacing them with polo shirts an improvement.

Roxy certainly had.

She questioned Sam about this newfound wealth. He dismissed her skepticism by saying he had leveraged investor capital in exchange for an equity stake. A lot of mumbo-jumbo banker words to Roxy, but she didn't pressure him for clearer answers. She was pleased they could replace the ancient, clogged sink and pre-1960s milkshake machine. Good on Sam if he figured a way for some hoity-toity Wall Street types to fork out the money.

She should have asked him what an equity stake was.

"Need to use the bathroom?" Goon Two asked, and Roxy almost blasted off the seat in surprise.

"Yes. I suppose so. It's going to be hard, though, with my arms stretched behind my back, you know, to do my business," Roxy complained, lifting her tethered hands as proof.

"Oh, honey, you'll figure something out." He untied the ropes, yanked her from the chair, and shoved her across the room. "In there." He pointed to a door labeled DOLLS. Right next to GUYS. "Don't take too long, I don't like waiting. Might come in there and help you along." He grinned.

"Reggie, knock that crap off. You're not intimidating her, and you're making a fool of yourself." Goon One shook his head. "Go to the bathroom. No one will bother you," he said, cutting the strap of Roxy's zip tie. "There is no other way out. I'll be waiting for you, so be quick about what you need to do."

Roxy rubbed her wrists and did a little nod-curtsy in appreciation of his pseudo-benevolence. She scurried to the restroom, her legs wobbly, the urge to pee mounting with each step.

As she turned the knob to open the door, from behind her came Goon One's voice, "Shut it, but don't lock it. That old slide lock wouldn't keep us out, anyway."

True to his word, there was no exit from this concrete square except for the one Roxy had used when she entered.

She finished. *No seat protectors.*

Washed her hands. *Cold water only.*

And dried them on her pant leg. *No paper towels.*

What had she expected? This wasn't the Ritz.

By now, Alma must have called the police. Someone has to be looking for me. Just don't get rattled. Find a way out; a ploy to delay them. Please, God, give me an answer.

Roxy raised her eyes to the heavens and blessed herself without realizing the ending to her prayer. She gulped down extra oxygen and exited the ladies' room.

"Hello, Roxy," a familiar voice rang out in an upbeat tone. "My, you look fetching today."

Roxy's blood froze. She halted, unable to move forward, blinking in disbelief.

Some six feet away, Chuck stood staring at her through ice-blue eyes, the goon triad at his side. The sight of him collapsed her heart like a beach ball punctured on a rock. A quiet *whoosh* slipped through her lips, confirmation of life exiting her chest. His motionless presence stripped away any thread of hope she had of escaping.

Roxy hadn't wanted to accept that Chuck was responsible for Sam's murder, although every sign pointed directly at him. Sure, over the years, she'd witnessed Chuck pull some cruel moves on dudes who paid late or hadn't come through like they'd agreed. He'd roughed up Sam once because of a discrepancy with the books. Or that's the story Sam told.

But murder?

Chuck was a putz and a jerk and a greedy SOB. But he was a show pony, not a killer.

Someone else had to be the mastermind. To her own demise, Roxy had ignored facts to convince herself that Chuck wasn't capable of organizing whatever this was, much less executing someone.

Perhaps that fabrication helped keep reality at bay. Made coping with unpleasant truths easier.

But no more. Chuck's face signaled there would be hell to pay.

And Roxy Adams held the bill marked *Overdue*.

No fairy-tale ending for this wannabe princess.

Chapter Fifty-Three

Before Roxy could gather her thoughts, Goon Two grabbed her upper arm and twisted, eager to zip tie her wrists behind her back again.

"No need for that," Chuck shouted, making a stop sign with the palm of his outstretched hand. "Roxy is an old and dear friend. I know she's ready to help us. Right, Rocks?"

Roxy wriggled away from Psycho Goon, formerly known as Goon Two, who looked deeply disappointed at the turn of events. She stepped forward to offer Chuck an insincere smile.

"Let's go over to the conference area and get reacquainted, shall we?" Chuck extended an arm directing her to a plastic, banquet-size table, the kind sold at a shopping club store and kept in the garage until someone threw a party.

"You still like iced tea?" Chuck asked, as though she had willingly stopped by his home for a visit. Maybe he'd offer her those rolled crispy wafer cookies with chocolate inside and bring out the nice china.

"Just some water," Roxy answered, before sitting on a metal folding chair at the end of the table.

Chuck waved at a minion. Seconds later, a water bottle appeared; an off-label brand chosen when shopping for quantity over quality. He unscrewed the plastic lid and slid the bottle in her direction before unbuttoning his suit jacket and dropping into a seat directly across from her.

"Didn't see you at the funeral, or should I say, the celebration of life for Sam." He moved closer as a concerned friend would. Notes of his woodsy cologne danced up her nose. "How have you been?" he asked, locking eyes.

Roxy didn't reply. Instead, she sipped her water, fighting the urge to gulp down the entire bottle. Who knew getting kidnapped could be so dehydrating?

She returned his stare, searching his face for a salient clue, a small sign that might reveal his motives, his end game. Would he kill her, or was this simply theater designed to scare Roxy into surrendering the only evidence that proved her innocence?

And Chuck's guilt.

She had been grateful to Chuck and Sonya for taking over the funeral details. The shock of Sam's death had left Roxy with neither the financial capacity nor emotional bandwidth to provide the final send-off Sam deserved.

The couple made the burial arrangements. And at the request of Lola, the wife Sam never managed to divorce, Chuck and Sonya had paid for Sam to be cremated, his ashes shipped to his family's plot in Tennessee.

Roxy had little input, not being Sam's legal next of kin.

Not to mention his accused murderer.

They also hosted Sam's friends at a local bar, a reception that happened on the heels of her arrest. Roxy's attorney thought it best Roxy did not attend. She complied. The jolting reality of Sam's death and the judgmental gawking of those who had once been her friends would prove too much to endure.

"Well, for my money, you look great," Chuck continued, snapping Roxy out of her daydream. "Leaving the food industry agrees with you."

Roxy placed her drink on the table, willing the mound of nerves, doubling as gelatin, to stop jiggling. She stared at Chuck for a moment. Same cool demeanor, slick talk, and gusts of endless bullshit.

Boy, how he loved to be in the spotlight. To be the front man, large and in charge.

Chuck, the perfect business partner to Sam, who worked hard, preferring to fade into the background. Everything seemed clear now. But none of her newfound insights would help her out of this trouble.

And as the minutes ticked past, the truth that she wouldn't escape alive became more a reality.

"All this 'old times' talk is lovely," Roxy said, not able to play the role of dear old friend any longer. "But for the love of God, will you tell me what's going on? Why am I here? What do you want from me?"

Roxy had gained a temporary victory over the wall of tears held tight behind her eyes. The tears swelled and receded as though they were a weakening wave not able to reach the shore. But she knew a tidal wave would be arriving at any moment.

Before she broke down, maybe she could learn what happened to Sam. And why.

"Why did you have Sam killed?"

Chuck bolted back in his seat, feigning shock at Roxy's directness. He regained his composure before responding.

"My dear, I know you're under a lot of strain. Losing Sam, changing careers, being on the verge of bankruptcy, being arrested for murder. And you're heading in the direction of Medicare, so I'm not going to be offended by any insults you lob in my direction. If I were in your shoes, at your age, I'd be looking for answers anywhere I might find them. I feel you," he finished, the cornflower blue of his eyes holding the smallest glimmer of moisture.

Roxy glared.

Chuck, the empath. *Your pain is my pain,* he would tell Sam.

Good Lord, this clown…

Chuck cared about Chuck. First. Last. Always. End of story.

If Roxy hadn't been scared for her life, she'd tell that asshole in a three-piece-suit where he could step off.

Oh, wait, she'd done that. And it was ugly.

After Sam's desertion, Chuck had such concern for his long-time friend that he asked *for a little extra on the side* as part of her restructured work arrangement. Recalling that night, Chuck's hubris at making the proposition as though he was doing her a favor had infuriated Roxy so much that she wanted to spit. Right in his face.

Maybe she would.

"We both need answers," Roxy finally said, mentally exhausted at trying to be in two brains at the same time. Although the deed shouldn't have been that overwhelming, Chuck only had half a brain on his best day.

"True. True." Chuck clapped his hands together and rubbed them back and forth. "Guess we're both tired of the pretense. Roxy, you know what I'm after. Sam's baseball jacket. The one he hid the key in. Tell me where it is, and you can go."

"I don't have any of Sam's clothes. He took them when he left."

Chuck sighed before standing. "I don't have scones today, Roxy. Also, your friend isn't here to interfere. You know I can be a patient man. I can also be a ruthless bastard. I don't want to go the ruthless-bastard route," Chuck said, gazing around at his minimal audience of three, who chortled their approval of his subdued bravado. "I especially don't want to do that to you. You know I like you. You're my Hot Rocks. My cougar."

Roxy swallowed hard, a bubble of vomit lurching up her throat. His statement was not the compliment Chuck thought it was.

"You know all this, but I'll repeat everything again, slowly. Sam has—well rather, *had*—something that belongs to me. He put it in his baseball jacket pocket for safekeeping. Are you staying with me so far?"

Roxy nodded.

"Good. Sam told me he left the jacket in the apartment. That he would return my property, but he needed you to let him in. Sadly before that happened, our dearest friend was killed. I'm heartbroken that Sam isn't with us any longer, but the world keeps turning. Might seem unfeeling, but these are the facts."

Roxy lowered her gaze, the prints and the flash drive poking her cleavage every time she shifted. If Chuck only knew. "What makes you sure I have this jacket?"

"Because Sam said you did. You found the key, and you were going to give it to him. Now you can give it to me."

Roxy blinked and turned her head away from Chuck's stare. He knew. Holding on to that key, even for an extra day, had cost Sam. That same choice would now cost Roxy her life.

"I wish I could help. I do, but I don't have any of Sam's clothes." Roxy faked calm. She kept her eyes focused on the boxes, away from Chuck. "He took everything when he left for Tennessee, if you recall. Took all the money from our bank account and the safe, too. All he left were bills."

Chuck slammed his palms onto the table, causing Roxy to jump. "Where is the goddamn jacket?"

Apparently Old Friends Week was rapidly coming to a close.

Roxy pushed down the mounting terror formulating in her chest. Time was running out, and she was in no better shape than when she first arrived. No incredible escape idea materialized, no cavalry breaking through the roll-up garage door, no thunderstorm to knock out the electricity.

The only storm coming was the one Chuck brewed. The man had the shortest fuse. Once Roxy had inadvertently witnessed the horrific results of his wrath outside the food truck. His anger ignited and burned powerfully. A young man who thought he could offer Chuck excuses instead of money now walked with a permanent limp.

She recalled closing her eyes, not wanting to watch the savageness of the beating. The young man's mother came by two days later, with full payment plus interest in a brown paper bag. Chuck had turned on the charm, accepting her offering as though she brought him a fresh batch of chocolate chip cookies as a neighborly gesture. The woman had left quickly without saying a word.

"There's some of Sam's old clothes in the trunk of my car," Roxy blurted out.

"Now we're getting somewhere. Why didn't you tell me?" Chuck asked, a wary frustration tinging his voice.

"I forgot they were there. He took almost everything. One day when I was feeling pissed off, I yanked down the few things he'd left behind, threw them in garbage bags. I planned to drop everything off at the donation box in the mall. Then he was gone, really gone. I never had the heart to do it."

"Where's your car now?"

"At my apartment."

Chuck walked away, Goon One followed. After whispered instructions, the Goon Squad left.

Chuck returned, and Roxy guessed that, within the next half hour, her car would be torn apart by the trio.

Chuck reclaimed his seat. "Let's relax until we see what the boys come back with. I hope you are telling me the truth," he said, sizing up Roxy. "Sam tried to play games, and we both know how that turned out."

Roxy knew too well. She could have helped Sam and perhaps prevented his murder. If only she had spoken to him. Listened to what he was trying to tell her. She wished she had, but right now, she didn't have time for what-ifs.

Right now, she had to figure out how to prevent her own murder. Stalling for time was her only hope.

That, and praying Chuck's team of losers wouldn't break into her apartment again—and find Sam's jacket hanging in her bedroom closet—empty pockets and all.

Chapter Fifty-Four

Roxy concentrated on creating diversions, delays, or how to execute some unlikely trick she'd seen work for the hero in hundreds of TV crime dramas. Even though the trio hadn't been gone for long, time dragged, the brilliant escape techniques of Houdini not materializing.

With no magic resolution in her future, Roxy turned her thoughts to alternative approaches. The garbage bags of discarded clothes were a quick diversion, the only one Roxy could invent at the time. And a stall tactic that might ultimately lead to her demise.

She needed another strategy. Being nice to Chuck? Could she suck that up... literally?

Mentally shivering in disgust, she filed that idea under Last Resort.

She could offer him the key now that she had emptied the locker.

Where had she put the key, anyway? Back in her purse? Come up with some cockamamie story that she found it in the back of the medicine chest, behind an empty cologne bottle. Would Chuck believe she didn't know what the key opened? Probably not, and then the torture would begin.

After pretending to not have any clue, she could suggest the skating rink. But Chuck would quickly realize she had claimed the locker's contents, and the torture would continue. Especially since that's where his goons had abducted her from.

There was no way out. No scenario where Roxy walked away unscathed. She might as well give him the items nestled in her bosom. Better to die quickly than to drag things out.

Chuck's phone chirped, and Roxy knew a goon was on the horn.

Chuck grunted. "I see. I know. Okay, get back here quick."

"Should I tell you, or do you want to guess?" Chuck said, disconnecting the call.

Roxy strained to hold a neutral expression. "They couldn't find my car?"

"Oh, they found the car, and they found Sam's old clothes in garbage bags. What they didn't find was his baseball jacket. Roxy, why did you send me on a wild goose chase? You know that's only going to anger me."

Roxy stared at the concrete floor, bracing herself for a wallop. When none came, she looked up. Where she thought she'd find frustration and rage, Chuck's disappointed stare met her eyes. She looked away.

"I can only protect you for so long," Chuck continued. "You've got to do your part. Please tell me where that key is."

Does he want to help me, or is this a slick variation on the good-guy bad-guy tactic?

Roxy wanted to trust that some bits of their friendship would sway Chuck not to kill her. But she'd seen this man in action. Most recent proof: her boyfriend's dead body.

"Oh, stare at the floor all you want. I know the truth. You know about the key in the jacket. Sam told you. He told me. At the end, he told me everything. We can play this game for a short time, and then the real bad asses show up, and I won't be able to help you."

Roxy lifted her head. "The same way you helped Sam? Frankly, with a friend like you, I don't need an enemy."

Chuck scrunched his face. "I am dead-balls serious here. I can save you, but you have to cut out this cat-and-mouse crap. Tell me where the key is, and we can all go back to business as usual."

"Really? Sam is dead." Roxy barely released the words before tears pricked her eyes. "Nothing will ever be business as usual again. How could you have let that happen? Sam trusted you. He believed in you, and I have to say, even though I thought you were a scum-sucking cockroach, Sam always defended you as a true friend would." She blinked, forcing the tears clouding her vision to drop. "That friendship got him killed."

"There's a lot you don't know," Chuck shot back, seemingly on the defensive. "A lot you don't understand, but all this can be fixed if you'd just give me the goddamn key."

"Help me to understand," Roxy said, her nervous core giving way to a peaceful inner strength. Unexpectedly, Chuck's earnestness caused her fears to recede and her confidence to expand.

"Where do I start? Well, Rocks, it's not all that complicated. Money. This is all about money. So, give me the key and you can go on living. Might even be able to talk the boss into a little finder's fee for you. Keep jerking me around and I won't be able to help you at all."

"Is that the same deal you offered Sam?" Roxy asked, hatred mounting.

"Pretty much." Sonya's voice, even and devoid of emotion, echoed from the far side of the warehouse.

Roxy and Chuck turned toward the sound of heels clattering against the concrete. An hourglass figure emerged from the shadows. Roxy watched Chuck stiffen at the sight of his wife.

Sonya approached, dressed as though she were on her way to a late lunch with society ladies. Her black and cream pencil skirt—cashmere, probably—and matching jacket cinched appealingly at her tiny waist, gave the illusion of added height. Her hair knotted in a fancy updo, the kind Roxy's tresses could never achieve, whispered understated elegance.

Even against a kidnapping-and-false-imprisonment backdrop, Sonya appeared as though she just walked off the runway at Paris Fashion Week.

Perched on three-inch stilettos and clutching an oversized leather tote under her arm, Sonya strode toward them, her every step reeking of imminent peril.

"And he was too stubborn to take the deal. Until the very end. Just like you." Sonya approached the table. Following behind her, the Goon triad. The crew took their places behind Sonya, eyes set forward, their posture assuming a military "attention" stance. No wasted movement from the men. These guys were no longer props for Chuck's performance.

Roxy sensed the energy shift. Even the air seemed to stand still.

They're intimidated by Sonya's presence. Power walked in, and she's wearing strappy platform heels.

Roxy slid her gaze to Chuck, who also stood at attention, accepting the role of foot soldier in Sonya's army. Clearly the boss was a Boss Lady.

"Do you have the key?" Sonya demanded more than asked.

Roxy remained silent.

"We were getting to that," Chuck said.

"Shut up!" Sonya yelled with a vocal cord strength never before put on display in front of Roxy. "You had your chance, now go sit down and don't say another word."

Sonya's strong backhand against Roxy's jaw came so violently and suddenly that she didn't register the impact for several seconds.

There's that wallop I was expecting.

Roxy reached her hand to the side of her face, blood dripping from where the diamonds of Sonya's wedding ring connected with her skin.

"Great. I've got your attention. You have the key. I want the key. And you know, Roxy, I always, always get what I want."

Roxy stared. How could this be the same woman who was so distressed at the thought of ice-skating but didn't blink an eye at the notion of killing a human being?

"Chuck is right. We don't want to hurt you, but we didn't want to hurt Sam, either. Sam was dumb. He was always a little slow." Sonya paused to take in Roxy's reaction. "Oh, don't look surprised or offended. You knew he wasn't the brightest guy in the room, but he was a hard worker." She stepped closer. "I digress. We're talking about *your* future now."

"I've already told Chuck…"

"Honey, I know the line you've been blowing up my husband's ass. He's partial to you, so he'll listen a lot longer than I will. I'm going to make this simple. Sam took something—*evidence*, he called it, didn't he, babe?" she said to Chuck, who nodded his agreement.

"Sam's dead, and you can join him if you don't play this smart." Sonya seemed to enjoy Roxy squirming at this not-so-veiled threat. "Give me the key he left in your apartment. Give us what we need and you can go, never to hear from Chuck or me again. Sound like an equitable deal?"

"Well, yes," Roxy said. "Especially the part about never having to see you or Chuck the …"

245

"Your girlfriend is a comedian," Sonya joked to Chuck. "Isn't that charming."

Roxy licked her suddenly parched lips. With Sonya's appearance, her options had narrowed. "Okay. I have the key, it's in my purse that one of your goons threw out the van door when they grabbed me."

Sonya turned to Chuck, her eyes afire.

"We didn't want her to have a phone. Prevent her from calling for help or being tracked here," he defended.

"Go get the purse," Sonya commanded.

"Her girlfriend probably took it," the head Goon said.

"You fools kidnapped Roxy, tossed her handbag, and left an eyewitness? What is this, amateur hour?"

All four men looked away.

This wasn't accidental amateur hour, though. Roxy suspected the actions the goons took were at the direction of Chuck, who she hoped still believed there was a way to keep her alive.

With Sonya now in the driver's seat, Roxy's anxiety had doubled, not just for her own well-being, but also for Chuck's. Sonya thrived on results, whether it be choosing the right hairstyle or the recovery of condemning evidence.

If Roxy wasn't willing to provide the goods, she'd be summarily swept aside, and a new plan would be implemented.

Both she and Chuck were about to be disposed of in the cruelest of manners. Roxy didn't imagine for a second that Sonya would let her go free.

This was it. The final chapter. She could surrender the information and die peacefully or jerk Sonya around a bit more, delaying the inevitable.

Fast death or slow death: what a choice.

Not the same as when the store clerk asks: paper or plastic.

Death was death, Roxy finally concluded. She might as well get it over with. She wasn't afraid of turning the page to her final chapter.

What prevented her from giving up too quickly was her pride.

She couldn't let Sonya win so easily; walk away from the horror she created.

Roxy had to stop that bitch from becoming the victor, standing atop the slain bodies of Sam, Chuck, and herself.

Chapter Fifty-Five

At Sonya's direction, a Goon retrieved folded paper towels from the restroom and handed them to Roxy. The rough pulpy paper, though abrasive to her skin, stemmed the blood dribbling down her chin. She moved the hinges of her jaw back and forth as though massaging the wound.

"I hated to do that," Sonya said, a half-hearted apology. "Didn't see any other way to get your attention."

Roxy reckoned Sonya had been waiting for this chance to hurt her. In addition to being attention-getting, as Sonya claimed, the slap she delivered was personal, the force behind the smack carrying a deeper message.

"Coulda taken off your two-carat diamond ring first," Roxy volunteered, no longer caring about Sonya's wrath. The brakes were off, and the full weight of Sonya's fury bore down fast and hard. All Roxy could do was shelter in place. "In fact, you coulda skipped the slap altogether. You already had my undivided attention."

"True. True. Perhaps that hit was for all the times I watched my husband hit on you," Sonya said reflectively, as though this thought just occurred to her. She turned to Chuck. "Should have slapped *you* a good one instead of Roxy."

Chuck took a step toward his wife.

"Stop. Not here. Not now," Sonya said. "We have a bigger problem and only about thirty minutes to solve it before my brother shows."

Chuck paled. "Anton is coming here? I... I mean, why's he in LA?"

"You know why. Because you screwed the pooch. He doesn't trust me to fix this. And hell, he never trusted you, so you know where that leaves us."

"I've got this, angel." Chuck's expression belied his words. "We know where the key is, we just have to get it from Roxy's friend. That should be easy."

"Easy. Sure. Assuming she hasn't gone to the cops yet," Sonya snapped.

"Looked like she'd already come back to the apartment complex," Goon One offered.

Sonya wrinkled her brow. "And you know this how?"

"We spotted her car in the carport when we went to get the clothes," the first Goon continued. "We let the air out of her tires instead of puncturing them. So she only needed to re-inflate them."

"Yes," Chuck said as though a gust of wind had filled his sails. "Me and the boys will head to Alma's, get the purse, and we're back in, say, twenty minutes. Thirty tops." Chuck stood a little straighter, the prospect of a solution seemingly within his grasp.

Sonya crossed her arms in front of her chest. "And what will you do with our deejay friend after she refuses to give you the purse?"

"Bring her back here? Should have never left her behind in the first place," Chuck said.

"I have a better idea," Sonya announced. "Give me one of those burner phones."

The three goons rushed to be first.

"One. I need one phone," she ordered, pushing the others away. She turned her glare to Roxy. "What's the number?"

Roxy furrowed her brow.

"Don't play dumb. Alma's cell number."

"Let me think," Roxy said, genuinely trying to recall. "I don't ever dial it. I just push the *Alma* button on my screen."

"Well, you better remember the number now. I don't want to have to say *or else*," Sonya bit back, her green eyes rimmed with red.

It occurred to Roxy that, amidst all her bluster and bravado, Sonya was terrified of her brother and what he might do to Chuck—and to her.

"Two-one-three," Roxy began. "Five-five-five, ten-seventeen."

"Are you certain?"

"Yeah. Especially the ten-seventeen part. That's Alma's birthday," Roxy said, rubbing her sore chin. "I never knew anyone who got their birth date as their phone number. Alma's lucky like that."

"Enough chatter." Sonya dialed. When the call was answered, Sonya simply said, "Be at the food truck in thirty minutes. Bring Roxy's purse. Come alone."

She tossed the phone to Chuck. "You guys better leave now to get there before she does. Make sure no one sees you. And make sure she has the key before you get rid of her."

Get rid of her. Roxy's heart froze. *They were going to kill Alma. Sweet Alma.*

"Get back here as fast as you can," Sonya continued. "I will stall Anton."

"Great. Great. We'll be back with the key in no time," he promised.

"You better not screw up, Chuck," she warned. "Anton doesn't like screwups."

Before Chuck and his goons left, Sonya had him zip tie Roxy's wrists again. She stopped short of binding her to the chair. For the next several minutes, Sonya paced nervously around the area, keeping a wary eye and a gun barrel trained on Roxy.

"They must be there by now," Roxy said, infusing an artificial helpfulness to her voice. "As long as Chuck comes back with the key, why do you need to get rid of Alma?"

"What?" Sonya replied, distracted by Roxy's interruption.

"Chuck will give you the key. When he does, I'll tell you what it goes to. You'll get whatever is in there, and all this goes away. Right? No reason to add another death to—"

"Just. Stop. Babbling," Sonya snapped, her demeanor shifting from the possibilities of a few moments ago to what Roxy perceived as hopeless desperation. There were no concrete solutions materializing. They hadn't heard from Chuck, and Anton would appear any moment, ready to take over her leadership role.

"Maybe you should call Chuck, you know, see how things are going. Tell him not to kill anyone else," Roxy suggested. "I'll give you what you want. I always planned to. Just please, for the love of all that is holy, don't kill Alma. She had nothing to do with any of this."

Sonya seemed to consider Roxy's plea. "You had nothing to do with any of this either," she finally said. "Sam dragged you in without any concern for you or your well-being. Aren't you the least pissed off by that?"

Roxy sighed. Sonya had a point.

"During the past few weeks, I've run the gamut of emotions about Sam. Anger, disgust, shame, guilt, contempt, horror, love," Roxy replied. "My biggest regret is he didn't trust me enough to tell me the truth. And then when he got the courage to do that, I wouldn't listen. If I had, we wouldn't be here today." Roxy swallowed hard. "You'd have your stupid key, and Sam would be alive."

"Woulda. Coulda." Sonya waved her hand dismissively.

"I realize there's a lot going on now that is out of your control, but uh, Sonya… We've known each other a long time. I've babysat your kids."

Sonya's lips formed a soft grin. "You taught them to put M&M's in the popcorn while it's hot so the chocolate will melt. They won't eat popcorn any other way since."

Roxy grinned at the memory. Sweet and savory. Always a winning combo.

She continued, knowing she was about to press her luck. "Would you mind filling me in? I mean, for old times' sake. I have a vague idea that something crooked was going on at *Reyes of Sunshine*. I always dismissed it as Chuck selling weed or maybe running numbers. I didn't ask any questions because for the first time, there was money in the bank. And I didn't want the details of how the cash got there."

Sonya nodded, keeping her eyes on the door as though Chuck or Anton would walk in at any second and reveal her fate.

"Not going to go into specifics. There are a lot of people involved. Many layers. Lots of big wheels. I'm a small cog. Chuck is even smaller. But basically, the food truck laundered money for the real business." Sonya pointed at the pallets crammed with boxes. "That's why your money problems disappeared once Sam let Chuck in as a partner. And then, well…"

"What? What happened that forced Sam to flee?"

"What usually happens. Sam wanted out. And when we told him there was no going back to his sleepy little life, he tried to force our hand."

Roxy attempted to stand.

"Nope. Don't move." Sonya wriggled her revolver back and forth. "I'm good with a gun. I won't miss."

Roxy reclaimed her seat. "I want to know why he died."

"You're not so good at connecting the dots," Sonya huffed. "Always thought you were the brains of the outfit, while Sam was the naïve and gullible one. Guess I was wrong."

"Sam was a good man," Roxy defended.

"No argument there. All I'm saying is he wasn't too bright."

"And that's what got him killed?" Roxy asked, worried she was running out of time to save Alma.

"In a sense. Sam didn't like being on the wrong side of the law. He wanted his business back, squeaky-clean. When Chuck told him that wasn't going to happen, Sam tried to blackmail us with some proof." Sonya made air quotes around the word *proof*.

"Sadly for Sam, he didn't realize this venture wasn't only Chuck and me. As I said earlier, there are a lot of factions. A lot of really ugly, mean, heartless people who don't give a rat's ass about your petty concerns. Not liking your role anymore? No problem. We'll recast someone else in your spot. And you, well... you are no more."

"Sam wanted out, and so they killed him."

"Eventually. Chuck tried to keep everything floating, but Sam wouldn't play along. His leaving you was a ploy, his way to keep you safe. He did everything he could to protect you from..." Sonya paused as though searching for a word. "From his new business associates. He wanted to keep you out of danger."

Roxy's throat tightened. Sam had shielded her from these treacherous men, sheltered her from what she guessed was an element of organized crime. This mafia-type kudzu invaded his life, choking him off from everything he cared about. Ultimately separating him from her.

"Sam threatened to go to the police," Sonya continued, as though finding her recap of the events helpful, therapeutic. "Spill the beans, if you will."

"But it was too late?" Roxy asked.

"Oh, most definitely. It was too late the first time Sam accepted money. No turning back, as they say."

"In the end, Sam saw things our way. Claimed he'd turn over his evidence to us, and we'd go back to how things were. Just one glitch. You wouldn't give him the jacket. My superiors got tired of waiting, and well, you know the rest."

"So, in a way, I did kill Sam." The realization invaded Roxy with the heaviness of a cement blanket, the mass enveloping her frame, burying her heart. *He died because of me.*

"You could say that. Still, Sam made choices, bad choices. None of that had to do with you."

Roxy gulped, attempting to absorb this new information and the part she played in Sam's demise. How had everything gone off the rails? She shook her head as though clearing the cobwebs laced through her brain.

Sonya tapped out a monotonous beat with the toe of her shoe. *Tick-tock. Tick-tock.*

Alma. I have to think of Alma.

Every second that passed kept her friend in danger. Roxy straightened her spine to sit taller, allowing her chest to expand. She needed oxygen, lots of it, to flow freely and keep her mind focused. "Maybe you should give Chuck a call," she asked again. "You know, and tell him Alma doesn't have to be killed. We can take care of this between us, right?"

"You're sure worried about that little powder-keg girlfriend. Why?"

"Alma is a nice and caring woman. She doesn't deserve any of this misery," Roxy explained.

"No one deserves this bullshit. Just sort of finds you, if you know what I mean."

Sonya retrieved her phone from the table and dialed. After waiting several rings, she hung up.

"Chuck's not answering. Not good," Sonya said.

"No, little sister, that definitely isn't good."

Roxy and Sonya turned abruptly to where the voice emanated, deep and threatening. Wearing an impeccably tailored suit and dark sunglasses stood a male version of Sonya. Two bodyguards flanked him.

Roxy swallowed hard and turned back to Sonya, now visibly pale. Her eyes shot back to the tall figure.

This is Anton.

Chapter Fifty-Six

With her arms still zip-tied, Roxy shifted her bottom on the hard metal chair hoping to catch bits and pieces of the argument between Sonya and Anton some five feet away. The evidence nestled inside her bra pressed heavy against her chest as though they were bricks, crushing both her airways and her spirit.

What would Anton do if he knew the information he sought—the proof he'd killed Sam for—was within his grasp?

Could Roxy exchange the flash drive and the photos for her life and Alma's?

Was Alma still alive? And where the hell was Chuck?

After seeing Chuck's shock at the news that Anton would be arriving soon, Roxy wouldn't be surprised if the man had put his own ass first and taken off, leaving Sonya to fend for herself. His anxiety was obvious, and Roxy suspected Sonya held the same angst, doubt, and worry about her brother's future actions.

Roxy craned her neck to capture the essence of their heated discussion, now sounding more like a set of orders from Anton than two siblings chatting.

"We're closing this operation because of you and that weak asshole husband of yours," Anton scolded, his ramrod-straight back and decisive manner underscoring his ruthless demeanor.

Just another day at the office for the real leader of this enterprise.

Roxy watched him tilt Sonya's chin to lift her gaze, seemingly a shift into big brother-little sister mode. When their eyes connected,

Anton said softly, "Why I let you talk me into hiring that buffoon, honestly, Sonnie, I'll never know." He kissed her cheek.

Roxy gulped, taken aback by what appeared to be a sweet moment; Anton calling his sister by a childhood nickname. Their exchange increased Roxy's dread of what was to happen next.

Sonya took a step as though setting a boundary. "What's happened to Chuck?" she asked. Her expression telegraphed her fear of the answer.

"We haven't killed him, if that's what you're asking," Anton shot back. "Where the hell is the bastard anyway?"

"Getting the key."

Anton snorted. "He's been getting that key for weeks. We're way past that now. When will he be back?"

"Soon, I hope. But as you heard when you walked in, he's not answering my calls or texts." Sonya raised her cell phone as proof.

"He'll be back with his tail between his legs, failing once again," Anton announced. "And I can't guarantee what will happen when he shows up."

Sonya bowed her head. "And me?"

"You, baby sister, are on a flight to Vienna. Leaving late tonight out of LAX. Mama and Papa will be happy to see you."

"And my children?"

"Of course. This is the perfect time for them to visit Opa and Oma. Our folks haven't been well, as you know. Grandchildren, I'm told, are the best medicine."

Roxy recognized the glistening tears filling Sonya's eyes.

"I... I'm sorry..." Sonya began with contrition.

"No time for apologies. We're on a tight schedule to pack up what we can. Four semis are arriving within the hour. I want us loaded up and gone in two."

The tinge of kindness Anton displayed moments ago evaporated. In its place, appeared a foreman of sorts, shouting orders. His new priority: maximum efficiency.

"Fritz! Milo!" Anton yelled. "Don't waste your time on those belts. Pull down as many pallets of purses that you can. That's where the real money is."

The two men discarded the cargo they had been preparing and shifted to the far side of the warehouse where larger boxes were stacked.

Purses. Belts. Roxy wondered what else those cartons held. *Was this stolen merchandise? Or fake designer goods? Either way, the entire operation was a scam.*

"Gather the documents, paperwork, you know the stuff I'm looking for. Put everything in a box. And Sonnie," Anton instructed his sister. "Make certain everything is loaded onto the first truck."

Sonya jerked her head in Roxy's direction. "And what about her?"

"Better if you don't know." Anton walked away.

Sonya lifted her gaze and locked eyes with Roxy. She offered a sympathetic glance, then seemed to dismiss her regret. Sonya turned her back and headed toward the office to gather the files Anton had requested.

Roxy watched her silhouette disappear through a doorway. The realization that Sonya had left her to suffer at the hands of Anton ignited deep uncontrollable sobs.

By now, Alma had been murdered. She was next.

Once Anton had arrived, Roxy knew no amount of negotiation would save her. The deal, as they say, was done.

Anton hadn't paid her any mind, as though he knew she was powerless. No threat here. *I won't be alive long enough for them to worry about me.*

Roxy attempted to wipe her tears on the shoulder of her blouse, but with her arms still secured behind her back, the action proved harder than expected. She blinked and swallowed, attempting to compose herself. For what purpose, she wasn't certain. These fools could shoot her while dear old Sonya would be winging her way to Vienna, so her children could enjoy a lovely visit with their grandparents.

Roxy prayed Anton didn't intend a long, painful death. If he planned to kill her, quick would be best. She saw proof of the callous suffering he was capable of inflicting when she discovered Sam's body crammed inside the limo's trunk. He had been tortured. Multiple stab wounds pierced his chest. They had used her carving knife to slice Sam's face, making him barely recognizable.

Roxy shook her head as though erasing the image of the last time she saw the man she loved. A visual indelibly stamped in her memory.

What is he waiting for? Why not kill me—or is his real priority getting the heck out of this warehouse? Is he waiting for Chuck to return so he could perform a package deal murder, sort of a two-for-one snuff-out?

A mountain of anxiety expanded inside Roxy. Her pulse raced, and her ragged, uneven gasps of air added to her terror. She had no way of knowing what Anton thought; what his true intentions were. Roxy wasn't even sure he would safely transfer his sister to Austria, not that she cared what happened to Sonya. This guy was desperate to save his empire, such as it was.

If Roxy couldn't be certain the man would save his own sister, what chance of survival did she have?

Roxy's heart pounded. *For whatever reason, Anton didn't have me bound to this chair. I can run. I can get up and run. He's in a hurry to leave. If I hide well enough, he won't have time to search for me.*

She turned her head at the noisy clanking of a metal roll-up door being raised. A large truck backed through the opening.

Everyone was busy. Make a break for it now and disappear.

But to where?

Roxy scanned the cavernous warehouse once again, pallet racking some ten feet high or higher surrounding her. Lots of hidey-holes appeared, but which one was the least likely to be discovered?

She glanced to the far side of the building where three men hurriedly moved pallets toward the open doorway, Anton frantically pointing out which cartons should be loaded first.

Eyeing the massive stacks of boxes on the near side of the building, the ones Anton told the men to skip, she wondered if that was the safest spot. She could wait there until they had cleared out, praying the entire time not to be found.

Maybe Anton's plan was to leave her behind, anyway. She could only hope.

To prevent her footfalls from being heard, Roxy took off her shoes using the ball of the opposite foot to slide them off. She inhaled deeply.

Before she could talk herself out of her escape plan, Roxy scooched to the end of the chair and used her tethered arms as balance, pushing up to stand.

Not daring to move, she surveyed the warehouse. She spotted a few workers hustling to load the cargo. Behind them, Anton yelled to move faster. There was no sign of Sonya who had gone to the office. Blessedly, everyone was too busy to pay her attention.

Roxy scampered to the deepest, most secluded part of the warehouse, edging her way against the cinderblock wall to find camouflage. Except for the loud drumbeat keeping time in her chest, the only noises she heard came from Anton still on the other side of the building.

Pleased with her hiding spot, Roxy crouched to make herself as small as possible and closed her eyes to pray.

Moments later when she opened them, Sonya stood in front of her, clutching a gun.

Chapter Fifty-Seven

Roxy took in Sonya's posture: anxious, trembling, and angry. The word *petrified* came to mind. Sonya's disheveled appearance evaporated any hope Roxy held of escape, like water drops on a hot skillet.

Stooped, Roxy embraced a wave of anger and contempt rising inside her chest. She'd had enough of this bitch and her arrogant, snobbish attitude. Hell, the woman couldn't even keep her balance on ice skates. A gun wouldn't help her now.

"You're not going to shoot me," Roxy said, fed up with Sonya's power plays.

"You're making me look bad," Sonya snapped.

"To Anton?" Roxy questioned. "You're worried about your brother?"

"You should be worried, too. Stand up and walk," she ordered, using the gun barrel as a pointer. "That way. And don't do anything stupid, or I *will* shoot you."

Roxy rolled to her side and used the edge of a large carton to gain purchase, her balance compromised because of her bound hands. In her stocking feet, she straightened her back to stand taller, as though wanting to look her best for this death march.

"Get moving," Sonya directed.

The hard gun barrel pressed against Roxy's back, forcing her to arch. They hadn't cleared the row of boxes when gunshots rang out. Roxy ducked, thinking they were being fired at.

Would Anton gun down his own sister?

258

"This is the FBI!" a deep voice boomed. "Drop your weapons and put your hands in the air!"

The crack of more bullets followed. Then everything quieted.

"Anton Huber, you are under arrest for…"

I know that voice, Roxy thought. But before she could place it, Sonya grabbed her upper arm and shoved her in the opposite direction. "This way," she snarled, now at Roxy's side.

"I don't think so." Roxy swung her hips and the entire right side of her body into Sonya's ribcage, knocking the woman off her spike heels. Roxy ran, but Sonya caught her by the arm and twisted.

"Yeoooooow!" Roxy shrieked in pain and frustration. She'd blown her chance to escape.

"Like I said, this way." Sonya wrenched Roxy's arm harder this time, digging the rigid plastic bindings into her skin.

With a gun at her back, Roxy staggered through a maze of shipping boxes, Sonya's firm grip and jabbing gun barrel directing her every turn.

Just as the women approached a doorway, a man appeared, an assault rifle trained on them. FBI was emblazoned on his baseball cap; a badge dangled from a chain around his neck. Under his dark blue jacket, Roxy could make out the bulk of a bulletproof vest, both items silk-screened with the initials FBI in yellow.

A second agent approached. From a distance, Roxy thought he could have been an older version of the first officer. "I'm FBI Special Agent Heath Erickson. Put down your weapon."

That familiar voice attached to an unfamiliar name rang out again.

Sonya moved her revolver from Roxy's back and placed the barrel against Roxy's temple. "Let me pass. Otherwise, I shoot her."

In normal circumstances, Roxy would have frozen in place at the prospect of being in between two gun-toting FBI agents and a suspect. But that's not what rooted her to the spot.

The man she knew as Alex faced her, gun in hand, eyes focused on Sonya.

"Alex?" she asked weakly, but before Roxy could rectify the discrepancy, a shot rang out. Sonya fell to the ground. Stunned, Roxy stepped back only to see blood blossoming from Sonya's shoulder, ruining that beautiful jacket and the silk blouse underneath.

She thought the shot had killed Sonya until a piercing scream rang out, and Roxy watched as Sonya writhed on the floor in pain.

A swarm of officers poured into the space, surrounding the fallen woman and immobilizing her. "Sonya Huber Winston, you are under arrest for trademark counterfeiting. You have the right to…"

Roxy looked at the agent who was speaking.

An older agent. A man she knew. A man she might even love. Once he finished, she asked again, "Alex?"

"It's me." He stepped toward her with open arms.

Roxy fell against his chest, dropping her cheek against his FBI raid jacket. A moment later, her hands were freed, and she hugged him properly, as though never wanting to let go.

"Are you all right?"

"Alex?" she asked tentatively.

"Same person. Different name."

Roxy pulled back. "You're Heath? The same Heath that Sam—"

"You can call me Alex."

"I don't understand."

"I don't expect you to. There is plenty of time to explain," he said. "For now, what I want you to know is your nightmare is over. Your murder charges will be dropped, and you have the bureau's eternal gratitude for helping us to bring down one of the biggest counterfeit luxury merchandise rings in the world."

Roxy shook her head. "Counterfeit? All this stuff is fake?"

"Every last stitch. And thanks to you, we have the proof to nail them on dozens of charges, including Sam's murder," he said.

Roxy exhaled deeply. "And Alma? Chuck and his loser thugs were meeting her a while ago."

Heath hugged Roxy again. "Alma is perfectly fine, except for being frantic about you."

"Special Agent Erickson," the younger man interrupted. "When you're done here, we need you."

"Roxy, I have to go book these assholes. Can I call you? Then I can fill you in on all the details."

"Of course," she said. "But Alex… or Heath… before you go, will you tell me what this is all about? Were you undercover? Play-acting to get next to me?"

"I wouldn't say it's all been play-acting, but yes, I've been undercover, working to get a line on these guys. You helped in immeasurable ways."

Roxy shook her head. "I could have helped more." She reached inside her bra and removed the items tucked inside. "Here," she said, handing over the flash drive and the photos.

"What's this?" he asked, sorting through the snapshots.

"Everything Sam died for. Proof of what Sonya and Chuck were doing. He had stashed this evidence in a locker at the ice rink. I figured out what that key opened the night we went skating. Alma and I retrieved this stuff, and that's when they kidnapped me." Roxy looked down at the hole in her sock and wriggled her toes.

Finally she muttered, still looking at her feet, "I should have trusted you, but…"

"You're a tough lady to keep safe, I will say that. But if I were in your shoes, I'm not sure I'd have trusted me either. Thanks for this," he said, raising his hand holding the evidence. "I have to go. I'll see you later, and we'll talk. Not everything I've done these past several weeks has been pretend." Alex kissed her on the cheek and left.

A moment later, a female agent approached. "I've been instructed to take you home," she said and ushered her into a waiting vehicle.

Roxy slid into the back seat and buckled up.

Home. I can go home. I can finally go home.

Chapter Fifty-Eight

Roxy exited the black sedan parked in front of her apartment building. Before she stepped onto the sidewalk, Alma was there, enveloping her in a deep hug. "Oh, my God, I've never been so scared."

Roxy squeezed Alma tightly and stepped back, searching her friend's eyes. "I was scared to death about what might be happening to you. Frantic that I put you in danger, once again. When Sonya called to arrange that meeting between you and Chuck, well, I didn't know… I'm sorry. Sorry about so much."

"Don't apologize. I was never in danger. I called the cops after they grabbed you. Then Alex showed up at the skate rink. He flashed his FBI identification. I'm all 'what the hell?' He grinned and said he and his team were handling everything. They knew where you were and that you were going to be fine. He told me to wait until I heard from him. He texted a couple of minutes ago. That's how I knew you were on your way here."

Roxy listened, wide-eyed. *Alex knew I was in that warehouse?*

"Did you know? I mean, that he was a Fed?" Alma asked.

"Not until a few minutes ago. He told me his real name is Heath. Heath Erickson."

"The Heath that Sam wanted you to contact!"

"Seems so." Roxy waved goodbye to the agent who drove her home.

"Hmmm." Alma put her arm around Roxy's shoulder. "Let's go inside and have some tea."

"Tea with a shot of bourbon, please."

"Coming right up," Alma said. "You know, things could have been much easier... safer, even, if you hadn't gotten weird about Alex. Or Heath. Whoever."

"I know that now," Roxy said half seriously. "Short of you and Stacy, I didn't trust anyone, even Sam. My doubts got him killed."

"Sam's actions got Sam killed. You were an innocent bystander, as they say. Collateral damage. The decisions he made nearly got *you* killed." Alma opened the door to her apartment. "I'll put the kettle on and make a few sandwiches. You find the Four Roses."

"Happy to oblige." Roxy headed toward Alma's liquor cabinet.

Minutes later, the women met at the kitchen table, much the same way they had started the day. But instead of a donut box between them, a bottle of small batch bourbon and two teacups took its place.

Roxy consumed the last of the brown liquid and handed Alma the empty cup. "Refill, please. And I could use less tea and more whiskey this time."

Alma headed to the kitchen, and Roxy heard the flame of the gas stove ignite. Hot tea was forthcoming. She looked at the clock on her phone. Nearly midnight.

Hours had passed since the FBI raided that warehouse and rescued her. Long hours since a gun was held to her head. Liberating hours since learning she was no longer under the dark veil of a murder charge. Since she last saw Alex, now known as Heath.

She hoped he would have called by now, if only to check in.

How long did FBI paperwork take to complete, anyway?

Having another round of drinks with Alma, even disguised as a tea party, probably wasn't a good idea. She needed sleep. Hours and hours of uninterrupted, dream-filled sleep.

Alma returned and added a splash of English Breakfast into Roxy's cup, allowing ample space for a shot, maybe two.

Roxy lifted her cup close to her lips. "This will be the last one. You know how I can't hold my liquor," Roxy said. "Besides, I need to go home and get some rest. And you? Shouldn't you be on the air right now?"

"I phoned the station manager. Told him an abbreviated version of what happened today and that I arranged for Mighty Milton to fill in for me."

"The sports announcer?"

"Yeah, he's a pal. After I told him what had happened, Milt was happy to help." Alma snickered. "Station manager said I had the most original excuse for calling out he'd ever heard. And even if only half of the story was true, he'd be happy to give me the night off, on creativity alone."

Roxy grinned. "Our lives have been unbelievable recently. What's Rudy have to say about any of this?"

"A lot. He checked in every few minutes by phone or text, keeping me sane while waiting to hear from Alex."

Roxy took a sip and whimpered at the burning sensation on her tongue.

Alma wrinkled her nose. "Too hot?"

"A little."

"Take the cup back with you and put it on your nightstand. Such a lovely nightcap. A relaxing equalizer to a viciously horrific day."

Roxy put her palms out face up, as though they were the scales of justice. "Whiskey-laced tea," she lifted one hand. "Gun to my head," she lifted the other. "Yeah, you're right. Keep all things in balance."

Roxy rose and hugged Alma before purloining her teacup. "I'll check with you in the morning. Not early morning, though."

"Understood."

Alma took the cup from Roxy. "Find your house key."

Roxy fished the key out of her purse, reclaimed her tea, and tipped in for a short, armless hug. "Thank you."

"You would have done the same for me," Alma joked.

"Let's pray I never have to," Roxy said.

Seconds later, Roxy unlocked her door and looked back. Alma stood on the landing watching her, a ribbon of moonlight illuminating her beautiful skin. Roxy smiled, pushed the door open, and went inside.

Home at last.

Chapter Fifty-Nine

The incessant chirping of Roxy's cell phone startled her out of a sound sleep. She rolled over and covered her ears with her pillow to dim the noise. No help. If anything, the blaring sound seemed to get louder.

She blinked rapidly, attempting to clear her vision, and read the clock on her nightstand. *Nearly noon.* She'd been nestled under her comforter, asleep for some nine hours and still craved more.

The pounding grogginess of a hangover invaded her skull. The result of a whiskey-induced helmet in the making. The steady thump of a jackhammer beating against her brain worked overtime, a souvenir of the night before. While waiting to see if she would be racing to the toilet, she quickly remembered why she avoided too much alcohol.

Her phone rang again, and she rolled to her side, afraid to lift her head, certain the action would cause the room to spin and the contents of her stomach to spew before she could hug the porcelain god.

She tapped the screen, and it illuminated. Alex. *Alex.*

"Hello," she managed to croak, overcoming the fuzzy cotton balls coating her tongue.

Where was her water bottle?

"Good morning?" he responded a little too enthusiastically for her mind to process. "Are you all right? You sound funny."

She licked her parched lips before answering. "I guess so. Alma and I had a few cups of tea last night before turning in."

"Tea, huh? Anything other than sugar in that tea?"

In spite of herself, Roxy laughed. And it hurt. "You're on to me, special agent."

"That I am. Hey, can I head over in a bit? I'll bring donuts."

Roxy gagged, the thought of food an insult to her roiling stomach. She *would* be throwing up. And soon. "I'll make coffee," she managed to say. "I want you to fill me in on everything. But I'll need some time to, ah, clean up."

"How's one o'clock?"

"Make it two," she countered.

"Works for me."

"Ugh, do I still call you Alex?"

"You can until you get used to calling me Heath."

"One more thing, *Heath*," she forced the name.

"What's that?"

"My favorite donut is an apple fritter, not jelly filled."

"Noted," he said, before disconnecting.

Roxy carefully pulled herself to the edge of the bed and slowly flung her legs over the side.

So far, so good.

She managed to keep everything in place as she crawled to the bathroom. Once there, Roxy shoved two fingers down her throat, forcing her body to empty her belly. She flushed the toilet and crept on all fours into the shower where she sat on the cool tile, allowing the warm water to pour over her, rejuvenating her body and mind.

She slid on a pair of capris and added a hot-pink scoop-necked top that accentuated her waist. Within thirty minutes with her hair styled, fresh makeup applied, and a spritz of perfume, she was ready to receive her guest. If she didn't know better, she'd think she was dressing to impress Heath.

Roxy brewed a pot of coffee, smelling the rich aroma of the French roast. She glanced at her watch.

Would it ever be two o'clock?

Chapter Sixty

Relief and anxiety vied for Roxy's attention, neither willing to take a back seat in her thoughts. She wanted to soak her heart in the deep relief that the mystery of Sam's murder had been solved. She was no longer a suspect. Sam had never stopped loving her.

But anxiety invaded what little serenity Roxy cobbled together, trumpeting the fact that Alex was not the man she believed him to be. A fresh reminder that nothing is as it seems, even something as innocent as a new friendship.

At exactly two o'clock, a loud knock sounded.

That man was punctual.

She opened the door, his emerald eyes immediately capturing her attention. She couldn't turn away. In contrast to last night's raid uniform, his tight-fitting blue jeans, polo shirt, and sneakers humanized him, turning him into the Alex she once knew.

In one hand, the familiar bakery box—not Dynasty, thank God. In his other, he held a newspaper.

"Here you go." Heath handed her the paper. "It's the early morning edition. Some of the answers you're looking for are in there." He moved toward the coffee table where he set down the donuts. "I smell coffee."

"Help yourself." Roxy pointed to the cupboard where she kept the mugs. "Creamer and sugar are by the pot."

"Thanks," Heath said.

Roxy shifted toward the sofa and sat, curling her feet underneath her bottom as though preparing to enjoy a juicy mystery.

"I had a late night, too," he said, walking into the room. "Talking to reporters. A little caffeine is just the thing."

"Mind if I start reading this?"

"Not at all. I'll fill in the blanks after you're done."

Heath positioned himself across from Roxy and sipped his coffee, his gaze a constant as she read:

FBI Agents Seize $2 Million in Counterfeit Fashion Merchandise at Local Warehouse

Anton Huber, 45, and his sister Sonya Huber-Winston, 40, were arrested last night on trademark counterfeiting charges.

The siblings, both citizens of Austria, are accused of illegally manufacturing and selling items that displayed copyrighted logos from several high-end fashion brands, including purses, wallets, shoes, and belts. Chuck Winston,42, husband of Huber-Winston, is also being held.

An ongoing investigation is underway to determine a connection to money-laundering activities and the murder of Sam Reyes, owner of the "Reyes of Sunshine" food truck.

FBI special agents from the Counterfeiting and Piracy Task Force began surveilling Huber and Huber-Winston early last year, with several undercover agents making luxury fashion purchases from the pair. After receiving a search warrant, the agents found more than 500 cartons of merchandise stored in a Cudahy warehouse.

More on page A13

Roxy folded the paper and placed it on the coffee table next to the donut box, unable to absorb what she'd just read. Sonya and Chuck had taken advantage of Sam.

And when he tried to end their partnership, they killed him.

She struggled to regain her composure before asking, "You have been investigating them, this counterfeiting ring, for over a year?"

Heath nodded.

"You watched what happened to Sam? You did nothing?" Fiery tears found Roxy's eyes. She didn't bother to combat them. They were a release, and she allowed them to cascade down her cheeks.

"That's partly true but not the full picture. After reading the article, you get a better idea of the scope of the investigation. What was at stake. Why things played out the way they did."

"You watched Sam die. You watched me get blamed. You pretended to have romantic feelings for me. What kind of person does that?"

"Roxy, I can—"

"Explain everything." She stood, finishing his sentence. "I've heard that line in every movie I've ever watched. I'm certain you are excellent at what you do, whatever that is. And the collateral damage discarded along the way is the price for good triumphing over evil."

Heath remained still, as though he recognized Roxy's need for anger and understanding to erupt.

"You watched from the sidelines as my life was shattered into a million pieces. You lied to me about everything. *Everything.* I'm sure there's some legal mumbo-jumbo about upholding the law and whatever the hell else. You got your man or, in this case, woman. Congratulations, Agent Erickson. Now will you leave?"

"No," Heath said, a heaviness to his reply.

Roxy stood. "No? NO! This is my home, and I'm telling you to go."

"I will leave, but not until you understand the whole story, about everything that went down and why things were done the way they were."

"By the book? Isn't that what they call it? But where was your compassion, your humanity for the people involved? I was expendable in your mission to crack a case. A case where my boyfriend, my life partner, ended up dead." Roxy reclaimed her seat and crossed her arms. "Go ahead, Special Agent Erickson, explain. I'm all ears."

"You're not expendable, Roxy. Not to me as Alex, and not to me as a sworn federal agent. I realize this is a lot to absorb, but we got to know each other well. You know me better than to believe I'm some heartless—"

"Stop right there. If you want to go on believing you're a good guy, then I validate that. You are a good guy. You saved my life. You took care of Alma. A gold star for you. But spare me the act that I meant anything to you or what sprouted between us was important. It was staged just the way you planned. I was a lead, and you worked me. Although in the nicest possible ways. Dinners, movies, donuts."

Furious, Roxy flung the donut box, pastries flying across the room. A cruller barely missed Heath's head.

"Now that was a waste." He bent down to retrieve nearby donuts and put them back in the box. "Three-second rule," he announced, lifting a glazed in the air. "Your apple fritter is smashed against the wall over there. It will probably taste fine, though. Put it in the microwave for a few seconds."

Her mouth dropped open in shock. "What are you, some kind of psycho? Take your damn donuts and leave me alone."

"You're overreacting," Heath said from a safe distance across the room. "Yes, some of what I told you isn't the entire truth."

"Like your name, your career. Who you really are," Roxy screeched.

"Yes, but many of the things I told you were true, as true as I could manage and keep within the confines of my assignment. And, most importantly, keep you safe. If you're done throwing a fit and ready to listen, I'll explain. Then I'll go, but not before you understand I care for you, well beyond my official capacity with the FBI. Things didn't start out that way, but damn, woman, you grow on a person."

Roxy sat down, a scowl on her lips and remained silent. The sooner Alex/Heath said what he had to say, the sooner she'd get him out of her apartment and her life.

Heath blew out a deep breath. "Here goes. Yes, we've been tracking the Huber counterfeit ring for close to two years. When we got a lead about eighteen months ago that Chuck was the new owner of a local food truck, we started surveillance. The pieces were beginning to fit. I met Sam, talked to him a few times and gave him my contact info. He was a great guy, and your truck made the best sloppy joe dog in LA."

"Continue," Roxy said, not touched by his attempt at a compliment.

"I watched you a time or two, working in the back, but you were always busy, kept your head down, your back to customers. It was obvious to me, even then, that you were someone who got stuff done. When Sam disappeared, I started tracking you."

Her mouth dropped open for a second time. "You've been following me since Sam left?"

"In a manner of speaking, yes."

Roxy huffed her exasperation. "You picked up where you left off. Next informant, please."

"Will you let me finish?"

Roxy glared and crossed her arms.

"You quit working for Chuck. Good on you, by the way. That guy is a lecher. That's when I signed up for truck-driving school—which, by the way, might be my second career when I retire. Anyway, yes, you were a lead, but as time passed, you became more than a connection to these criminals. The dinners out, ice skating, whatever we did, that was on my personal time. I knew I was getting close to crossing the line, but I didn't care. You became important to me. You *are* important to me."

Roxy huffed again. "And then…"

"You didn't make things easy, but I did my best to keep you out of harm's way. We had this apartment under surveillance when Sam lived here. When those goons ransacked it, I knew I was on to something." He gulped some coffee.

"Here's a part you probably won't want to hear. When Sam disappeared, we lost track of him, but several weeks later, he reached out to me, said he had an insurance policy of sorts, evidence against Chuck and Sonya. If I could guarantee his safety and yours, he'd bring me the proof. I agreed. We planned a meeting, but he kept delaying it, and a few days later, he was killed. He was never able to access the insurance policy he'd put into place. So I was surprised when you turned everything over to me yesterday. We couldn't find the key Sam talked about, and even if we had, he left no clue as to what the key opened."

Roxy pursed her lips, tears finding their way to her eyes once again. "I'm the reason he couldn't give you what was in that locker. I had the key and dismissed his cries for help. In my own way, I killed Sam."

Heath crossed the room, knelt at Roxy's feet and reached for her hands. "You must never feel responsible for Sam's death. He wouldn't blame you. No one would. Sam got himself into a bad situation and, by the time he realized how bad, the walls closed in. I want you to know he tried to do the right thing. He was a hero."

"A dead hero," Roxy replied, surprised at the pain that surged through her. She had once loved Sam. Truth is, she still did, even though her feelings for Heath were growing.

"You can remember him that way. I'll remember Sam as a man of principles and values. He strayed from the path for a short time, but being a criminal wasn't in his genes. He couldn't live in the underbelly, even though the money made that lifestyle appealing. He wanted to do the right thing. He wanted to keep you safe. And most of all, Roxy, he loved you."

"Too much. All of this is too much. I can't. I can't."

Roxy closed her eyes, hoping when she opened them this nightmare would magically be over. That Heath would be gone. That none of the horrors she'd endured actually happened.

She took in air to calm her ascending pulse and allowed a silence to stretch between them. She finally opened her eyes, dragged her gaze to Heath and locked on. "I just can't," she croaked.

"Can't what? Bear the truth? Sam made mistakes, big mistakes. He worked to correct them. Most important of all, he never stopped loving you. That's the short version of a convoluted and heart-wrenching tale of being involved with organized crime."

All this talk of Sam's selfless love suffocated Roxy. The way she had doubted him, stopped trusting him, paralyzed her and overwhelmed her with regret. She couldn't process this truth. This guilt. Not today. Possibly never.

Roxy changed the topic. "How did you know where they had taken me?"

"Well, you made that hard. When I stopped by, I knew something was up. You weren't yourself. When you wouldn't let me hang out, I slipped a tracker into your purse and attached another one to your car. I left a couple of agents behind to keep an eye on comings and goings. I couldn't run the risk that the Hubers were coming after you."

"Why would they come after me?"

"Because you were the last link to Sam. Anton was putting big-time pressure on Chuck to locate whatever evidence Sam had threatened him with. But you and your sidekick Alma decided to take her car on whatever adventure you had in mind. And then after grabbing you, your abductors tossed your bag into the parking lot. That left me no way to track you down.

"When Alma phoned the police, they patched me in. I showed up at the skating rink, and she told me what you two had done. Some of Chuck's crew came back later to search your trunk. We followed them back to the warehouse and watched them leave again. Alma called, told me what Sonya had demanded. Instead of Alma making the meet, we went instead and arrested them on the spot."

Roxy nodded her head in sudden understanding. "That's why Chuck never returned. I thought the coward ran off, leaving Sonya to face Anton."

"Chuck is in custody, spilling his guts as fast as he can. Doesn't want to take any blame for Sam's murder. Put all the responsibility at the feet of his wife."

"Sonya had Sam killed?"

"That's how it's looking. She had to have something concrete to offer her brother who was growing impatient. In the end, you and Sam provided all the proof we needed to raid the joint, arrest Anton, Sonya, Chuck, and the others. You are brave, Roxy Adams. And I am proud of you."

"I don't feel brave. I feel sick, heartbroken, numb," she said. "Is there anything else you can tell me?"

"Well, not at the moment, not until the case is filed and more details are uncovered. I guess there is one more thing," Heath said.

"And that's?"

"I like you. A lot. No, I'm not retraining to become a trucker, well at least not right now. I was married to Becky, but she passed away almost two years ago. I miss her every day. I'm ready to move my life forward, and I'd like to do that with you. Of course, only if you're interested and when you're ready."

Roxy stood and moved toward her front door.

"Guess it's time to leave. You have my personal number, Roxy. I hope you'll call me."

Heath stood, swiped a glazed donut out of the box, took a bite and left.

Epilogue
Two months later

Roxy stood in front of the full-length mirror inside Sleek's Ladies Only Changing Chamber and took in the tailored effect of her black wool suit.

Decker did it again. Even my butt looks good in these pants.

Instead of donning a traditional man's tie, Roxy reached for the beaded necktie Alma gave her the day she passed the commercial driving test. The hot pink rhinestone crystals glimmered against the crisp white shirt as Roxy straightened the glitzy ends.

Tonight was the first time she'd be driving a Sprinter limo party bus, taking twelve ladies to celebrate a friend's fiftieth birthday at a nearby speakeasy.

"Kismet," Cecile had said when she offered her the gig. "You're a perfect match for this group."

Roxy marveled at how her life had gone full circle. Tonight, she would attend to her peers, commemorating their milestones. Still, Roxy had her own milestones to celebrate. *There will be time for that later*, she thought, taking one last look in the mirror before heading out the door. Right now, she was glad to be earning a steady paycheck.

When she had arrived an hour earlier, Roxy wondered why the depot was empty. No one was in the office, and no *chauffeuses* were in the changing chamber getting ready. She made one more swing through the building, looking around for a friendly face, before signing for the vehicle. Roxy pinched imaginary lint from her trousers and headed toward the Hollywood Hills. According to Cecile, the partyers were pregaming at the birthday girl's home.

Would mature clients be less rowdy than the bachelorettes on Hank and Herb's Scottish-themed bus? Probably worse.

Roxy wasn't excited about driving the bigger vehicle and even less happy about doing this job solo. Cecile had explained the other drivers were booked or unavailable.

On a Wednesday? Roxy had wanted to ask.

"Stacy and I know you'll rock this," Cecile had added. "After all, it's just a few tipsy fifty-somethings."

Women and whiskey, sure, no problem.

Driving a nice stretch limo with a max of ten guests, that was Roxy's comfort zone. Still, she was grateful for everything Stacy had done for her the past few months. If she needed to flex into becoming a party bus driver occasionally, she was cool with it.

Some twenty minutes later, she pulled the disco-lit party ride to the curb in front of a mid-century modern home and waited. Through Sleek's automated notification system, the client received a text when she arrived.

After several minutes, Roxy opened the bus door, exited, and stepped around to the side, eager to assist the guests. However, no one responded to the text or appeared to greet her and provide details for the evening.

Roxy checked her watch. Five-fifteen.

Cecile had clearly said five o'clock pickup for a five-thirty reservation. Roxy scowled.

Something must have gone wrong with their communications.

She trekked the long walkway to the front entrance. Before she could ring the bell, the door flew open.

"Hello," she said to no one standing there. "Hello," she repeated. "Your party bus from Sleek Limo is here." When there was still no reply, Roxy took a tentative step inside to look around.

Gleeful shouts of "SURPRISE! SURPRISE!" rang out, leaving her with a pounding heart and a confused mind. She stepped back to gain her balance, blinking in shock.

Stacy's was the first face she recognized. Standing immediately next to her, beaming as though she could light up the world was Alma, holding hands with Rudy.

"SURPRISE!!" everyone shouted again.

Cecile pulled her inside the entryway, where everyone vied for a hug. Roxy accepted embraces and kisses from her coworkers Jade, Margo, Simona. *This is why no one was at the depot today.* Even Decker the tailor was there, and she thanked him for how she looked in her uniform.

Hank and Herb waved from where they stood, too many people to swim through for their chance to greet her. Overwhelmed, Roxy placed her hand over her chest, her heart pounding as though it might explode.

At first, she didn't recognize a group clustered in the corner. Until her instructor Rita Penn turned and blew her a kiss. Jason and the rest of Roxy's Rowdies waved. Behind them stood Detective Scavino and Lieutenant Reynolds, the two cops who had arrested her.

Seeing them, Roxy frowned until she saw who they were speaking to.

Heath is here.

He appeared to be absorbed in conversation with his fellow law-enforcement pals, beer can in hand. She hadn't seen him in person since the day he told her about his role as an FBI agent.

They'd spoken a few times on the phone, mostly when Heath had news to report about Sonya, Chuck, and Anton. Trial dates, new charges, when they would need her to testify.

His handsome profile caught her off guard and familiar emotions rose; buried feelings flew to the surface. Turning in her direction just as she was about to look away but couldn't, he mouthed, "Hi."

Roxy smiled, hoping he would approach, but before she could move, Malcolm Jump wrapped his arms around her. "Honey," he said, releasing his hold, "this is the infamous Roxanne Adams. Roxanne, my wife, Peggy."

"Lovely to meet you." Roxy accepted Peggy's extended hand. "I don't know where I'd be without your husband." She turned. "Malcolm, wonderful to see you," she said to her public defender with deep sincerity. "Thank you again for everything you've done. Getting the charges dismissed as quickly as possible, and... well, just everything."

Roxy turned back to Peggy. "Your husband does amazing work."

"He tells me that you are an extraordinary client." Her smile was genuine, glowing among the many guests apparently gathered in her honor. Roxy glanced around the house and spied Stacy's twins as well as Cecile's kids, mingling among the guests, offering drinks and appetizers.

This was their home—Stacy and Cecile's home.

Stacy clapped her hands. "All right, everyone take your seats, and we can get started."

"Started with what?" Roxy asked, but no one answered. She took in the massive living room arranged with chairs placed haphazardly. Rita stood at the front, directing Roxy to join her.

What in the world?

Roxy approached and hissed, "What is going on, Rita?"

"Nice to see you, too," she snapped. "This is your graduation ceremony."

"My what?"

Stacy joined them. "We are celebrating your accomplishments, too many to list, but mostly how you've turned your life around under the most sinister and dangerous conditions I can imagine. We are proud of you, so take your place, Roxanne, and we can begin."

Roxy stood awestruck, staring at the sea of faces gathered for her. Everything softened like a Monet painting, with vivid colors blending into a majestic scene. She listened as Stacy welcomed everyone before introducing Rita.

"Many people of all walks of life, circumstances, and desires show up at Friendly Roads Driving Academy," Rita began, "thinking they'll achieve their dream goal. Most are looking for a reliable paycheck. Security for their future. When I met Roxy Adams, she wanted those things, too. But more than that, Roxy wanted to make her own way.

"In class, she showed us that no matter what obstacles life throws at you—and we all know the bad breaks that landed on Roxy's path—you still have choices," Rita said to a room full of nodding heads.

"Daily, Roxy made good choices. She had the courage to take on hard decisions, no matter how frightening. Those decisions ultimately led to this moment."

Rita turned to face Roxy. "We don't usually do this. You know, have a graduation ceremony from our trucking school. But there's nothing usual about you. You have more than completed our program. If it was up to me, I'd award you a master's degree in Navigating Life. But since I'm not able to grant college degrees, this certificate will have to do."

Rita displayed a gold-framed document to the crowd and then read:

> For successful completion of the requisite
> course of study with aptitude,
> excellence, and determination,
> **Roxanne Adams**
> is certified as a commercial driver with the
> rights, honors, and privileges thereunto.
> Friendly Roads Driving Academy

Everyone clapped and clapped and clapped. Roxy accepted the certificate with one hand and wiped tears from her cheek with the other.

Rita extended her arm for Roxy to speak. "Say a few words."

"Are you kidding me?" She madly swiped at her cascading tears. Among the faces, she glimpsed Alma, whose tear flow matched her own. "What do I say to everyone here? Everyone who, in one way or another, helped me through the hardest, bleakest, scariest time of my life. Thank you from the bottom of my heart."

Roxy lifted her certificate over her head with both hands.

"This piece of paper signifies more than knowledge gained," she said, looking at Rita and Stacy. "This represents a trust that God and friends can only bestow. Thank you for loving me," Roxy finished and stepped to the side, wanting to exit center stage.

"Oh, you can't leave yet," Stacy said, pulling Roxy to a stop and slipping the certificate from her. "I'll hold on to this for you."

Frozen to the spot, Roxy nodded, staring at her empty hands.

What else could this woman have in mind?

Stacy turned to face the group. "Special Agent Heath Erickson, if you please."

Before Roxy could react, Heath stood next to her at the front of the room, thanking everyone for coming. He prattled on about a leadership award. As much as Roxy wanted to focus on what he said, her ears seemed to clog with background noise, thoughts of how things might have bloomed.

The *what-ifs* of a life with Heath invaded her mind relentlessly.

Alex/Heath. Did she have feelings for him? Or did the trauma of her circumstances confuse the issue? Situational bonding? Stockholm syndrome?

Whatever the psychological term, this couldn't be true love.

"It is with great pride and personal pleasure that I award Roxanne Adams with the FBI Director's Community Leadership Award for her unrelenting efforts in combating the many injustices that organized crime inflicts on our community."

Heath read aloud:

Federal Bureau of Investigation
In recognition of outstanding service to the local
community and of enduring
contributions to the advancement of justice, the
Director's Community Leadership Award
is presented to
Roxanne Adams

"Congratulations," Heath said, handing Roxy the plaque. "Next year, Ms. Adams will be honored along with other recipients of this award at FBI headquarters in Washington, DC."

Roxy accepted the plaque, worried the thing might slip through her sweaty hands and crash to the floor. If only she could wipe them on her pant leg first.

She stared at Heath in disbelief. *An award. I don't deserve an award.*

"Speech, speech," a female voice broke the momentary pause.

Heath stepped aside, clapping.

"I... I... don't know what to say. To be honest, everything I did was to save my own neck. I don't deserve—"

"Knock that off!" Cecile shouted. "You are a hero. *Our* hero."

"Well, I'm not sure about that, but I'm sure Alma Sanchez is. She went along with me on this crazy ride. I could have gotten us both killed, but she stayed by my side," Roxy said, staring at her friend.

"Alma, you have been there since the beginning, all those long nights after Sam left, when I was frightened and confused. And then when I was arrested. I wanted to stay in my lane, but you seemed to know better. You pushed me to change my life. To change lanes, and I guess I've been changing lanes ever since."

The crowd laughed.

"Stacy and Cecile, there are no words to adequately thank you for giving me my life back. For helping me to reclaim my world."

"We know, we know," Stacy said as Cecile blew Roxy a kiss. "Just keep being our hero."

"If you all will indulge me for a second, I have one more thank-you. Special Agent Erickson. Alex, who we now know is Heath, kept me safe in spite of my poor choices and misguided suspicions. Thank you for staying focused. You are the real hero. Oh, and thanks for all the donuts."

Heath grinned and an awkward silence hung in the room.

"Okay, everyone," Stacy broke the quiet, "that concludes our official program. Now let's party. Bar's open. There's a taco guy in the backyard ready to serve. Eat, drink, and most of all… congratulate Roxy!" Stacy lifted her glass in a toast.

"To Roxy!"

Every voice repeated, "To Roxy!"

She gathered her awards and turned to thank Stacy and Cecile. However, Cecile had disappeared, and Stacy had moved toward Heath. The two had their heads together.

"This was a great idea," Roxy overheard Stacy say.

"But you're the one who made things happen," Heath said. "Combining the two accomplishments into a party."

Stacy shook her head. "I provided the venue, but you, sir, had the brilliant idea of having a ceremony. That made all the difference."

"If you say so," Heath replied with a shrug, not wanting to belabor the point.

Stacy turned. "There you are. Were you surprised?" she asked, herding Roxy into their circle.

Roxy set her awards on a nearby chair. "Surprised is an understatement. I'm flabbergasted. When no one was at the depot, I should have figured something was up."

"We tried to keep everything simple, so you wouldn't catch on." Heath nodded.

"Hey, you two, I have to check on things." Stacy scooped Roxy into a massive hug and hurried off.

Roxy was tongue-tied, not knowing what to say, so she remained silent.

"Do you want a drink?" Heath asked. "Stacy has a nice selection of wines."

"Maybe in a minute." Roxy grimaced. "You're really the mastermind behind all this pomp and circumstance?" Roxy asked, scanning the room, soaking in all the wonderful people there for her.

"It took real courage to do what you did. I wanted you to know how important you were to our investigation," he said.

"Al... I mean, Heath. I'm not courageous. Stubborn, maybe, but not courageous. I wanted my life back. If I was convicted of murder, everything would—"

Heath smirked. "Courageous or stubborn—either way, you played a huge part in our Task Force taking down Anton and his gang. I'd pick stubborn over courageous any day."

"Thank you again for saving me. And Alma." Roxy initiated a hug, hanging on a beat longer than necessary. Heath didn't seem in a hurry to end the embrace, though.

"You could have ran away. Left LA. Tried to forget about everything that had happened. But you stayed and fought. You're a fighter, Roxy. Not a runner."

"That's a nice thing to say."

"Well, you should be talking to all your admirers." Heath tipped his beer can toward the folks gathered around the house. "Everyone turned up."

"They did, didn't they?" Roxy giggled. "Even those two detectives who arrested me. Can I call them dicks now?"

"They've earned the moniker." Heath stepped closer. "Ah, Roxy. I know this might not be the right time. You have a lot going on, but I'm wondering if in the future maybe, we could talk. I mean in person, not over the phone. I have things I want to say to you. To straighten out."

"Me too, Heath. If that's your real name." Roxy raised her eyebrows.

"Oh, it's real all right." He kissed her cheek. "And that's not all that's real."

"What do you mean?"

"We have something extraordinary," Heath whispered.

"Something bigger than cracking a two-million-dollar counterfeit operation?" Roxy quipped.

"Much bigger."

"Well then, Special Agent Erickson," Roxy said, jangling the party bus keys at eye level. "Let's get out of here and take a drive down Sunset. Maybe we'll find out how big."

Heath grinned. "It's like you're reading my mind." He kissed the back of Roxy's hand before entwining his fingers with hers.

Roxy followed him to the door where Alma stood, as though she were a bouncer at a nightclub, keeping the riffraff out. "You two going somewhere?" she asked, eyes aglow. "Oh don't bother making up excuses. Just go. I'll cover for you."

Roxy and Heath scurried through the open door.

"Where to?" Heath asked once they were safely out of earshot.

"Surprise me," Roxy said, before kissing him.

The End

Author's Note

Changing Lanes is my fifth women's fiction novel and my seventh book. This wonderful adventure would be empty without friends and family who support me and often ask about my writing. Mostly, I'm grateful for those of you who listen when I reply.

One of those great listeners continues to be author Sharon C. Cooper. It wasn't that many months ago when I lamented, actually complained to Sharon, about my frustration at finding a literary agent. My work-in-progress didn't include a trendy topic or the perfect trope agents were looking for. Sharon, being Sharon, said, "Okay, what do you have?" And that is how Roxy Adams was born. I'm forever indebted to her for not letting me quit!

Sending my endless gratitude to my ultimate reader, Donna Greeley, who has the first and the last word. And a huge thank you to author Heather Webb for her encouragement, critical eye, challenging questions, and spot-on insight that always enhances my words.

A huge thank you to Rachel Escobedo Fadden and Lisa Nawrocki Fadden for their creative insight, design expertise and genuine encouragement.

A tip of a chauffeur's cap to Debra Magedman, who brings joy and inspiration wherever she goes.

Elaine Payne, I'm still signing books with the Waterman you gave me last century. Laura Moore Vickery, because of you I'm an ardent reader, and that idea of a book club you planted so many years ago still blooms.

This novel is dedicated to the Cousin Crew, aka the Quad Squad: Winnie, Gracie, Maxie, and Miles, my grandchildren. The four of you make everything brighter, funnier, deeper, lovelier, and kinder. I'm in awe of the lessons you teach me and grateful to be your student.

Lastly, this novel is a work of fiction. Any errors, mistakes, or missteps are my own.

About the Author

Pennsylvania-native Claire Yezbak Fadden lives in Orange County, California with her husband and two spoiled dogs. She spends her spare time playing with her four grandchildren and immersing herself in the words of other authors.

Follow her @claireflaire, email her at claire@clairefadden.com or visit her at clairefadden.com.

Other Titles by Claire Yezbak Fadden

Wishes, Lies, & Fireflies
Woman@Heart
A Ribbon of Light
Promises To Keep
A Corner of Her Heart
Maybe This Time